Yellow Snow

Yellow Snow

A. Forester Jones

iUniverse, Inc.
New York Lincoln Shanghai

Yellow Snow

iUniverse, Inc.

For information address:
iUniverse, Inc.
2021 Pine Lake Road, Suite 100
Lincoln, NE 68512
www.iuniverse.com

ISBN: 0-595-27992-9

Printed in the United States of America

Acknowledgments

I have been an avid reader all my life. I enjoyed so many books and authors I concluded that it must be easy to write a book. I was wrong! It takes a frequently unheralded army to produce a book. The army must encourage, threaten, nit pick and cajole for the work to proceed. The army must protect and correct the dim-witted author from his constant production of poorly defined and punctuated drivel. I have been blessed to find such an army. Not to acknowledge their manifest contributions would be petty, selfish, and contemptible. Those attributes are inconsistent with the Midwestern culture to which I subscribe.

The desire to acknowledge the army's contributions is tempered by one fact. The army consists of hard working, God fearing, talented, honest citizens who would prefer no formal recognition that they are even remotely acquainted with this author. Those members of the army who did not automatically intuit this survival instinct were advised by their attorneys or parole officers to stay well clear of this particular literary effort.

As a solution to this dilemma, I would like to acknowledge some members of the army by first name only. I hope they take comfort in the fact, that of this writing, the Feds have yet to locate Ossama Bin Ladin or the individual responsible for hiring Craig Livingston, the former head of White House Security. Your support and talent may remain a secret.

To David whose effervescent Southside Irish personality remains intact, despite his professional training as an accountant. His command to stop talking shop during lunch inadvertently started the ball rolling many years ago.

To Pat and Bob who were involved from the onset with encouragement, technical research and cover design. Bob earned the title of "Heathen Nitpicker in Chief." Without Bob and Pat's enormous contributions, this book would not exist.

To Jackie in far away Louisiana and Leonard in nearby Villa Park who offered numerous solid improvements in the story as well as grammatical and spelling expertise. Both of these stalwarts endured real pain in an attempt to make my manuscript readable.

To Bob, the articulate civil servant and Mike, Paul and Elsie you have my heart felt thanks. I wish I could tell the world your full identities because you are great stories as well as being great people.

In particular, I am grateful to my wife and family who had to endure more than you can imagine during the writing and constant rewriting phases. In ways that I am totally incapable of putting into words, I owe a great deal to a very special Golden Retriever.

To one and all—THANK YOU!

CHAPTER 1

A quick glance at the diamond-encrusted Rolex confirmed what he had already sensed—the plane had taken off exactly on time this Sunday morning. That fact was immensely reassuring to the senior bank executive, a man of precision who demanded precise execution of plans and schedules.

The tropical shoreline of Belize soon faded away as the plane gained altitude on its journey north. The warm weather and the vibrant colors of Belize had proven themselves a delightful surprise. Although this trip had been extremely short, it was a pleasant break from the brutal winters of Chicago. Now that his financial concerns were eliminated, he had impulsively decided to purchase a second home in this newly discovered paradise. The house buying transaction would be completed within the next two months. In the short term, it would be an excellent place to vacation and in the not too distant future, it would become the perfect retirement location. The fact that his financial windfall would come at the expense of thousands trapped by drug abuse was of no concern.

A flight attendant arrived next to his soft leather seat with a polite smile and a complimentary glass of champagne. Although it was certain to be a less satisfactory vintage than he normally imbibed, he was looking forward to it. The banker was in an ebullient mood, which would ensure enjoyment of the beverage despite its quality.

The mood was entirely justified. This trip marked the conclusion of a business arrangement with the head of the Chicago syndicate. The deal had taken more than three years to put together. The elegant yet simple plan to launder drug money was developed while commuting to his home in the affluent suburb of Winnetka.

Conceiving the plan and implementing it were two entirely different tasks. The first step was to volunteer for, or become associated with, every committee involved in security at the big Chicago bank. Informally they soon referred to him as "Mr. Security" within the executive ranks. It was a perfect cover for the scheme. Arranging to meet with the syndicate to present the proposition was a difficult and delicate operation. Shady characters searched him on countless occasions for "FBI wires." Eventually the syndicate recognized the beauty of the plan and his unique position to administer the operation. It would be so lucrative for the "mob" that they did not begrudge their new partner the small "handling fee" that would enrich him. All parties involved deemed the plan foolproof.

The syndicate's "chief executive," Mr. La Morte, agreed to the concept in its entirety and they finalized their relationship last evening. A string quartet played classical music as the new partners enjoyed a gourmet dinner and some excellent wine. It was apparent that Mr. La Morte had impeccable taste, an attribute the banker held in high esteem. The fact that La Morte was totally ruthless was insignificant. All men of power were ruthless.

Belize was selected as the final meeting place because the syndicate considered the area to be devoid of FBI surveillance. The discovery of this tropical paradise as a location for a future home was a bonus to a delightful and profitable trip.

He raised a toast to the sun rising from the Atlantic and to himself for a job well done. The acquisition of the bonds would start first thing on Monday upon return to his Chicago office.

* * * *

The sun that arose from the Atlantic and illuminated the tropical shores of Belize never appeared in the Chicago sky this same Sunday morning. Although both Chicago and Belize are positioned to receive the dawn at about the same time, the sun frequently hid behind clouds in Chicago during February. The sun did manage to turn the dark sky a tone or two lighter gray. The sky assumed the same shade of haze gray that adorned virtually every square inch of U.S. Navy ships. The extra light in the bedroom at first startled Adam, who thought he had overslept and would be late for work. Then came the realization that it was Sunday, the one day of the week where it was possible to catch an extra hour of rest. His wife was up and he could smell the coffee brewing. How Alice could get up from bed and make the coffee without awakening her husband was always a mystery. It was a mystery that would remain unsolved, but not unappreciated.

As he sought that first singularly important cup of coffee, Adam noticed Dave, their eldest, eating breakfast. The younger of the two boys, Mark, was comfortably ensconced in front of the TV. Scotty, the family's golden retriever met him in the kitchen. As usual, Scotty was demanding, not requesting, attention. The undisguised glee in the dog's eyes rewarded Adam as he reached out to pet and scratch behind Scotty's ears.

One look out the window proved to Adam that it was a typical, late February day in Chicago. The low slate-gray clouds that hung over partially melted snow-cover produced a variegated look that was neither winter nor spring.

Alice was in full "I'm running late" mode as she pointed out the clothes that she had pressed for the boys to wear to church. As usual, Alice would leave early in their second car to participate in the choir warm up and practice. The Sunday morning routine was well established and rehearsed to the point that the boys had given up protesting their active participation. The "Nobody goes to church" excuse offered frequently in the past had not produced the desired result.

While enjoying the first sip of coffee, Adam viewed the stack of bills whose preparation had consumed the majority of his Saturday evening. Stacked neatly on the kitchen table, each with a self-adhesive stamp and return address label, they appeared fairly attractive. Adam thought perversely that if someone did a still life drawing of the stack, the title of "Cash Flow" would be appropriate. The problem was that the cash flowing out always exceeded the cash trickling in. Every time it appeared he was getting ahead, a need for a new expenditure would arise. Sometimes it was a major expense like Mark's braces. More commonly, it was a new sump pump, oil change or water heater.

"O.K., boys, let's get rolling! I want to stop by the post office on the way to church." There was a Sunday evening pick-up of mail at the post office. Based on experience, the time in the postal system added to the creditors processing time, plus the time to clear checks would be longer than he needed to make a deposit. He was confident that none of the checks would bounce. Technically this was called "check kiting" and was against the law, but he needed to do it in an attempt to close the gap between income and expense. Hell, everybody did it.

The entire male contingent of the family piled into the car, slipped past the post office, and got to church in time to claim their favorite seats in the balcony. The habit of securing the balcony seats started during a Christmas Eve Candlelight service several years before. From the higher vantage point, the candles being passed between members on the main floor while "Silent Night" was sung would have converted any heathen or atheist. The boys simply loved it. Thus, the habit of "taking the high ground" became firmly established.

Adam did a quick review of the bulletin to see what was in store for today's service. He was delighted to see an excellent assortment of good hymns. Adam couldn't carry a tune if forced at gunpoint, but despite that handicap, adored familiar hymns with meaningful lyrics and tunes. They provided a significant share of the responsibility for a good service. It wasn't that the scripture lessons and sermon were unimportant. If he found himself humming a hymn an hour after the service, it was a great service.

Today's service featured "Eternal Father," perhaps better known as the Navy hymn. It was sung every Sunday while attending boot camp. The Navy drilled that in as much as "Right Face!" and "Left Face!" The purpose of that drilling, like most of the meaning of boot camp, was unclear at that time. It was later, while serving on a large heavy cruiser that he became unable to stand unaided in a passageway. The ship was in the middle of a major typhoon in the Pacific. It listed so violently that more than once he thought it would capsize. That's when the tune and lyrics of "Eternal Father" appeared automatically.

The lyrics and music for "Eternal Father" were carefully reprinted in the bulletin, as this great hymn along with many others no longer resided in the denomination's new, official hymnal. Many of the older classics were deemed politically incorrect by some authoritative group of zealots and thus eliminated.

The pastor and members of his congregation adjusted by changing the rules. The expunged hymns found their way into the bulletin as reprints. People in the congregation kept singing the old lyrics, instead of those in the new approved hymnal.

The pastor introduced the New Testament reading, which was the basis for his sermon. "The scripture lesson for today is John 5 verses 2-9."

> ***Now there is in Jerusalem by the Sheep gate a pool, in Hebrew called Bethzatha, which has five porticoes. In these lay a multitude of invalids, blind, lame, paralyzed. One man was there, who had been ill for thirty-eight years. When Jesus saw him and knew that he had been lying there for a long time, he said to him, "Do you want to be healed?" The sick man answered him, "Sir, I have no man to put me into the pool when the water is troubled, and while I am going another steps down before me." Jesus said to him, "Rise, take up your pallet and walk."***

The sanctuary fell completely silent. The words of the lesson reverberated in the members' minds and hearts. The pastor slowly moved from the pulpit, and started to walk down the center aisle. Looking directly into the eyes of the parishioners and speaking extemporaneously, he began the sermon:

"The pool described in today's lesson was well known to all of the inhabitants of Jerusalem. It was known as having the power to cure. The cures would take place when an angel would descend from heaven and trouble the waters. Please note that the individuals surrounding the pool apparently suffered from a wide variety of physical problems. There is no mention of emotional or mentally crippled people being present. Either those afflictions were not present or they were undiscovered in biblical times. The definition of 'sick' that we use today covers a much wider variety of ailments. Apparently, only the first person to be immersed in the pool when the waters were troubled was cured. The unnamed man in the lesson had seen the angel descend and trouble the waters; however, it was evident that he had a 38-year problem with timing.

"Jesus commanded the man to 'pick up his bed and walk,' which he did. To all present it was considered a miracle. The miracle was performed on a Sabbath, which was against the rules. The ensuing conflict that the miracle created will be the subject of another sermon.

"As always, the words of the New Testament have meaning and pertinence to us today, as they have had throughout recorded history. Let me assure you that everyone in the congregation has problems, or a 'sickness' of one kind or another. That may be news to those of you who feel they are exclusively afflicted. You are not carrying the burdens of the world on your individual shoulders. You are not alone.

"Some individuals within our congregation need a cure for a medical problem. For them, the assistance of highly skilled medical professionals will appear as angels descending from heaven. My heart and prayers are with those truly in such a need.

"Many of the problems faced by our members are more prosaic, but nonetheless real. Many are having troubles paying bills. "Amen," thought Adam. Others have relationship woes, or a wide variety of family issues. In many instances, like the man by the pool, these problems will require outside intervention to resolve.

"My question to you today, however, is: From that great list of concerns and worries that preoccupy your every waking moment, how many could you solve **WITHOUT** outside help? How many from your lengthy list can you, by yourself, through your own imagination, faith, and creativity resolve?"

Adam thought for a minute that he was alone in the service. The words spoke directly to his soul. It's not that he hadn't listened intently to other sermons before. They just seemed to be more applicable to other members. The pastor is hitting close to home today.

"Let's go to the specific question posed by Jesus—'Do you want to be healed?' How many, when they first heard this lesson thought—'What a dumb question?' Obviously, any invalid who waited 38 years by a pool of water wants to be cured! Is it that obvious? I think not! In fact, the corollary question that may better fit the flavor of our modern time is: 'Do you want to be sick?'

"I have been dismayed at how many in our congregation, and society at large, would answer that question with a resounding: YES! It seems that many are constantly searching for a reason to be annoyed, insulted, or sick! The key phrase of the day is—'it's not my fault.'

"The justification for this situation seems to be driven in part by our inability to take responsibility for our lives, actions or decisions.

"'I don't drive the car I want because I was served too many Twinkies when I was young!' Optionally, it can be, 'I wasn't served enough Twinkies!' Whatever reason you can invent will work providing you can convince yourself, or someone else, that it isn't your fault.

"Perhaps wanting to be sick serves to get us the attention we all need. When greeting a spouse returning from work, who doesn't complain about a busy day or that they are beat? It always gets you a hug and some attention.

"I propose, as a partial remedy for our current situation, that we provide hugs and attention as a reward to the spouse that proclaims: 'I had a great day today!' If we individually emphasized the positive, we could eliminate a ton of fatigue and associated ailments. I would also urge each of you to count your blessings. Review your talents and capabilities. Find reasons to do things instead of excuses for inaction.

"That is the purpose of my words today. We cannot eliminate all of our concerns by ourselves, but by critically examining our personal list and asking: 'Do I really want to be healed?' You may in actuality, significantly reduce the number of afflictions distracting your life. Secondly, stop looking for a reason to be sick, different, or special just to garner attention. You have the power to 'Pick up your bed and walk!' So do it, and do it today!"

It is never considered correct or appropriate to applaud after a sermon, but Adam was about to break precedent. The organist started the introduction to "Eternal Father." That melody was the only thing that stopped the impulse. As Adam rose to sing, he wondered if other members had been similarly moved. It was politically incorrect to think this way, but he had experienced one hell of a service. It was a clear call to take charge of your life, to be less passive and defensive.

CHAPTER 2

After returning from church and grabbing a light lunch, Adam knew what routine was expected. Scotty was impatiently pacing the floor with that patented golden retriever plaintive question in his eyes, "Have you forgotten me?" Adam was convinced that he owned the only dog in the world that could tell time.

The minute Adam got up from the table to retrieve a winter coat and heavy gloves, Scotty became visibly excited. "Time for a walk is it, Scotty?" Adam bundled up, attached the leash, and headed out the front door.

Within 50 feet, Scotty found a small pile of snow and immediately mounted and anointed it. "Don't eat the yellow snow!" Adam remembered his mother's impassioned command while growing up in the Midwest. All mothers throughout time must have issued the same command in snow country. When Adam was young, his immediate family and most of the neighbors did not have dogs, so it was impossible to recognize the exact meaning of the command; however, the tone used to communicate the edict was unmistakable. It was the ultimate, non-negotiable, authoritative mother's tone that you never questioned. As with so many things in life, as he matured, the meaning of the "why" behind the authoritative tone became evident. Reviewing Scotty's work, it was possible to see how a child, without parental guidance, could easily mistake the soiled snow for a lemon flavored Italian Ice.

"Don't eat the yellow snow" was damned good advice. Adam wondered if this was the basis for the term "yellow journalism." If so, his mother's wise words still pertained. Today there seemed to be so much yellow or biased journalism that the only way to avoid eating some is to abandon the media entirely. That's a difficult goal to achieve since spin and disingenuous commentary can be found in every facet of society.

Scotty turned the street corner without guidance. The golden knew the routine by heart. Adam became convinced that the dog had a complete memory map of every thing and person in the neighborhood. His superior powers of sight, hearing, and smell humbled Adam daily. Scotty was inordinately skittish to anything new or different in his world. A neighbor once erected a sign proclaiming, "It's a girl" replete with balloons and flags. Adam feared the poor dog was going to die of heart failure when he first spied it. Not only was it new, it made noise! This bizarre behavior at first bothered Adam, but over time, he learned to trust and respect the dog's sensitivity. Something was getting Scotty's attention even now. His head was up, a little stiff, almost, but not quite, on point. What was bugging him?

"Hi, Adam, do you mind if I join you?" It was Frank, a trusted neighbor and friend, who emerged from behind a car. Scotty somehow knew Frank was about to join them. How the dog could determine that so quickly was a question that Adam had long ago stopped asking.

"By all means, Frank. You could obviously use some exercise." Frank would occasionally join Adam and Scotty on their walks and the two men enjoyed engaging in irreverent banter.

"Don't humor yourself with the thought that it's you I want to walk with, Adam! Scotty is the one I want to be with. After all, your dog has more brain power than everyone in your household combined." With that rejoinder, Frank reached down to pet Scotty.

"Same old Frank, quick with the barb, and slow with the brain. How are they hanging, neighbor?"

"Well, now that you asked, I'm starting to feel the aches and pains of old age creeping in."

"I don't want to hear about that, Frank. In fact, I was warned this very morning about people like you!" Adam's tone was purposely arrogant intimating he possessed knowledge that Frank couldn't possibly have. Frank looked puzzled for a moment as the trio walked to the lake, Scotty lunging ahead to get to a favorite tree.

"So, tell me more, learned one!" Frank replied.

Adam then summarized the church service, which was still very much in his mind. From Adam's passionate description, Frank knew the service had moved his young neighbor.

"Very interesting! I don't think I can quibble with any of the thoughts of your pastor, especially with the admonition to take control of your life. If I were to criticize anything, it might be that his advice wasn't fulsome enough. The pastor left something of great importance from the sermon. Considering his position in society, I can understand why."

Now it was Adam's turn to look confused, as they turned north into a fairly brisk breeze. "What do you mean left something out?"

"Based on my extensive and varied experience I have concluded that the only way to win in life is to change the rules!"

"That sounds profound. Are you quoting Madison, Adams, Jefferson or perhaps Milton Friedman?"

"Actually, Adam, I first heard that philosophy proclaimed in a *Star Trek* movie. I think it was *The Wrath of Kahn*, if I recall correctly."

Adam couldn't resist laughing aloud. If people were watching, they would have concluded that the two men were swapping bawdy jokes instead of debating philosophy. "I'm trying to inform you of a deeply moving and inspiring service based on Holy Scripture and you counter with a thought from a movie? You are completely nuts, Frank!"

"I'll grant that you have an infinitely more credible source, but disregard that fact for a moment and consider just the thought. I prefaced my comment with the sentiment that based on my experience, changing the rules made sense; where I first heard that expression is irrelevant. Please recall that Jesus performed the miracle as described in scripture on the Sabbath, which was against the rules. You pride yourself on being a senior systems analyst and project manager. You have frequently remarked that such status is unattainable without a pure, undiluted logical mind. Thus, may I ask if you are open to a logical argument that will buttress my contention?"

Frank was a professional salesman and Adam could see the skills at work. How could he refuse to engage in a logical argument after being lauded as a systems analyst? "Don't give me the junk about a senior systems analyst. I'm a stereotypical average guy with two kids, a very common name, and a lot of bills. I am unique in that I have no uniqueness. Other than that minor clarification: take your best shot."

"All right. Let us first review the rule makers: your employer, the government, your church, and society in general. Many individuals and organizations want to, and do, make rules in an attempt to govern your life. How much input or clout do you have over their agendas? As a mere junior middle manager, you have never been invited to a Board of Directors meeting. It's not likely that you have ever enjoyed a lousy lunch in the executive dining room. However, you are totally responsible for all of the work and the complete accuracy of forecasts. It's the manager's job to meet goals and objectives the executives set each fiscal year, perhaps during the soup course at the country club. Last year instead of a monetary raise, which you clearly need, you received a new title, a plaque and more responsibility."

"Frank, your verbal shots are hitting very close to the truth, but you forgot to include that I've had to carry my idiot boss, whose only achievement to date is that he's connected. He is the nephew of a member of the Board. In addition, for your information, last year was bad for plaque awards at First Continental. Nobody received one."

"I know what you are going through, Adam. Based on a lifetime of gathering data, I have concluded that nothing succeeds in business better than nepotism or inheritance. Look beyond the workplace for a moment. You don't think of yourself as rich, but the Democrats do and thus ignore you. The irony is that the Republicans don't think you're rich enough, which is their justification for ignoring you. You're not old enough to be attractive to AARP. You aren't the right color for the NAACP. You aren't the right gender for NOW. As a manager, you are poison to any part of the AFL-CIO. You aren't a doctor, dentist or lawyer and thus don't have one professional organization on your side. You work at a bank, but the American Banking Association only supports member banks, not individuals. You weren't eligible for the VFW, and since you don't own a gun, the NRA could care less about you. Your heavy workload, exaggerated no doubt because you have no managerial support, kept you from joining the LIONS or KIWANIS. I have noticed, however, that you have done laudatory volunteer work with the Cub Scouts and Little League in support of your two boys. I don't know how you were able to squeeze that effort in, but you can take all the power, image, and prestige from those two organizations and it would amount to nothing. Aside from your family, Scotty and on some rare days me, nobody gives a damn about you, Adam! You could even qualify to be the unnamed man beside the pool cited in your Pastor's service. You have been sitting quietly, playing by the rules for 38 years and waiting for a miracle."

"Tell me something I don't know." Adam had long ago mentally visited the same ground as explored by Frank with the identical result. "Given that I have little or no impact on rule-setting, what's the answer?"

"Crime," Frank calmly replied.

"Crime?" Adam responded angrily. "You want me to become a crook in order to get ahead in the rat race?"

"What do you mean become a crook?" Frank laughed. "You already are!"

"Who the hell are you calling a crook?" Adam shouted. Scotty froze. The faithful dog had never heard his master yell like that, unless he had done something really bad. Scotty was sure that nothing had been done to justify the shout. Adam immediately sensed what was wrong with the dog and stopped to give a reassuring pet. It calmed Scotty down, but left the dog a little confused, much like his master.

"Well, Adam, I believe I saw you conduct a wiener roast for the Cub Scouts in your back yard a couple of months ago. It was charming, with all the kids grouped around the bonfire."

"Yes, I did, but what on earth does that have to do with our discussion?"

"It's against EPA regulations to start such a bonfire! So, don't tell me you're not a crook! I even thought about turning you in. The EPA provides a bounty of $10,000 for reporting big, evil polluters like you. I didn't, however, because the kids seemed to be enjoying themselves and it reminded me of when I was in scouting."

"Were you in the scouts before or just after the Civil War, Frank? I had no bloody idea I was breaking any law or regulation, much less inducing a bunch of young men to do the wrong thing."

"Do you need more evidence that you are a crook? O.K., can you admit to me that you've never kited a check?" Adam groaned inwardly knowing he had just that morning mailed over a half dozen kited checks. Frank, looking closely at Adam's expression didn't wait for a response. "I also assume that you obey the posted speed limits and have never taken an incorrect or exaggerated deduction from your income taxes?"

"I'm not sure on your last point, Frank. The tax code is so arbitrary and convoluted we have all probably screwed up without knowing it."

"That's exactly my point! Frequently you don't even know you are breaking the law. None of us does. Need I remind you that ignorance of the law is no excuse? I maintain that the tax code and innumerable additional regulations have made every citizen a wrongdoer, or if you prefer, a crook. My logical extension to this fact is: If you are in for a penny, why not a pound?"

"I'm starting to see why you proclaimed that my pastor left this portion of advice out of the sermon. It was not, however, because of his position. I am certain my pastor left it out because he is a moral man. He is also practical enough to recognize that unpleasant changes in lifestyle frequently occur when you get caught committing a crime."

"That's the other justification for my new thinking, Adam. Very few crooks appear to get caught. The few that do get arrested don't seem to get convicted. Furthermore, in today's world if you are one of the handfuls caught and convicted it's highly possible you will receive a presidential pardon. 'Crime and Punishment' isn't a principle of law in American society; it's the name of a Russian novel. We have a former president who was such a liar that he had to have the Secret Service call in his own dog. I was extremely offended when the apologists in the media said: 'Everybody lies!' Hell, I for one didn't lie at that time, but I'm beginning to think about doing it more and more. What a great legacy he left for the country! Of all the scandals that you have read or heard about, I'll bet you that you can't name three people that have actually gone to jail." Adam didn't respond. Frank didn't push him on this point. Frank knew Adam couldn't answer because he couldn't think of three, either.

"Adam, I want you to consider one final argument to my break the rules pitch." Adam simply nodded, knowing Frank would make the pitch regardless of what he said.

"This is another point your pastor left out. You don't have to do anything wrong or anything that can be perceived as wrong to get punished in society today. You can be going along as if you were a brontosaurus eons ago munching on a fern, obeying the rules, when whack, an asteroid hits the other side of the planet and you are exterminated. If you haven't experienced this situation yet in your life, you soon will. It's becoming a standard feature of modern American culture."

"Are you saying the risks for receiving punishment are as great or greater than if you actually did something wrong?"

"Adam, you are starting to show signs that you are becoming as smart as your dog."

They had completed walking the trail around the lake. Scotty was slowing down, having smelled every tree, fence post, and light pole on the route. Adam was having difficulty trying to assimilate Frank's entire message. The last possible event that he could have foreseen happening on a Sunday afternoon would be for a neighbor to champion the desirability of adopting a life of crime. Yet, Adam couldn't logically disagree with Frank's arguments. He too was disappointed and distressed at the declining moral climate and spectacular fall from grace of a variety of celebrities, including politicians at all levels.

"Well, Frank, I'm almost home. It has been one of our most memorable walks. I'm not sure I can accept your reasoning in total, but your statements are thought provoking. Is there any additional perspective I should entertain before I consider changing the rules or accepting crime?"

"Actually, yes. Don't think of changing the current situation as crime per se. Think of it as a system or business problem. Your objective is to regain what is yours. Write a business plan on how to accomplish that. What is your ultimate goal? Who are your competitors? What resources are required? You have great talents in this arena. Even if you don't follow through, the exercise will expand your mental acumen. The key, as always, is people. With the right people, you can accomplish anything! Thanks, Scotty. You too, Adam! Have a nice day!"

Adam could smell a roast beef and fresh bread baking when they returned to the house. Alice was an outstanding cook and Adam was looking forward to their big Sunday meal. First, he had to check on how the kids were doing with their homework and then maybe slip by Home Depot for a new faucet. Working long hours during the week meant a lot of tasks had to be accomplished over the weekend. There was always something that needed tending, replacing, or fixing.

As Adam quickly went about trying to organize what was left of the weekend, the words heard during the day from both the pastor and neighbor would flash in and out of his consciousness. They were two unique points of view that were passionately articulated. The two views at this juncture did not appear as mutually incompatible. They were not necessarily linked either. As was his custom, he would continue to ponder both thoughts. Perhaps a connection existed beyond the fact that both were heard for the first time today.

CHAPTER 3

With a swift, well-calibrated swipe of his left hand, Adam silenced the annoying alarm. It was pitch black in the room, providing the first clue that it was Monday morning. With great reluctance, he initiated the morning ritual. It was important to keep moving. The 6:32 METRA train out of Bartlett waited for no one.

Adam had assembled everything needed for work and placed it in his briefcase the previous evening. The clothes he would wear had also been laid out to minimize the inevitable early morning confusion. This preparation saved approximately eight minutes of precious morning time. A total of 20 minutes was required, in good weather, to drive the beat up "commuter car" to the station and find a place to park. The rest of the morning ritual was a well-programmed blur.

Technically, it was possible to wait for the 7:09 train and still make it to work on time. Although it cost a half-hour of sleep, Adam preferred having the backup of the later train. Like most systems analysts, he revered backups. In addition, as if by magic, the boss, Jim Post (who the staff universally referred to as *Snake*), would appear and hover by Adam's office door when he was later than the normal routine had established. Snake had never been observed when Adam or his staff worked after hours or on a weekend to meet a deadline.

This morning everything worked as planned. Adam had acquired the morning paper and coffee at a convenience store near the station. These additional items were almost more important than having a monthly train pass. He then joined the small crowd of regulars huddled against the cold at a seemingly invisible marker on the platform.

The big silver double-decked behemoth rolled into the station right on time. The train hissed to a stop exactly at the spot on the platform where the crowd thought it would. That allowed Adam to get on the usual car and climb the stairs to claim his favorite seat on the upper deck. A quick glance showed that all the regulars from earlier stops were where they were supposed to be. The same train, the same car, the same seats were selected every day. The other passengers were total strangers, who over the course of time had become familiar as family. In one respect they were better than family...they remained silent. Rather than being annoyed by the rigidity of this cultural ritual, Adam was strangely comforted by it. It was one of the few constants in a world of continuous change.

After placing his heavy winter coat and briefcase on the rack, Adam took a good long swig of coffee in celebration of another successful, wild dash to the train. Now it was time to examine the paper. Like every guy on the train, Adam started with the sports section. The Blackhawks were trying once again to reach the playoffs. The Bulls, without Jordan, were going nowhere and were as exciting as watching CSPAN. To be a true sports fan in Chicago was, with few exceptions, a painful existence. It was comparable to having perpetual heartburn and no medication. Nonetheless, all guys on the train started with the sports section. It was a dim, but persistent hope of living vicariously through the success of one of their teams. It wasn't a cure, but it did serve as a partial antidote to the sameness of their lives.

The bulk of the paper read the way it always read. Allegations and evidence of official corruption, ineptitude, and malfeasance, trouble in the Middle East, all interspersed with the gory details of local street crimes. The staples were always represented. A special interest group was protesting some affront either real or imagined. There was the usual editorial support for some new regulation and a feature story illustrating the growing dangers of global warming. Adam rarely reviewed the business section. It was never topical and seemed to be written by reporters who had never worked for a real company or held a real job. Thank God for the comics and weather!

At 7:07 the train pulled into Franklin Park, which was about the halfway point in Adam's morning commute. By this point in the commute, the paper was read and the coffee was long gone. Frequently, he thought about just skipping the habit of acquiring the paper. Considering its overall value, most of us would be better off without it. The concern was that without a paper, how would it be possible to fill the 24 minutes he spent reviewing it? Besides, the conductor might not allow him to board the train without a paper. Since every passenger had one, it was obviously part of the uniform.

The remainder of the trip was Adam's favorite time of the day. Other than the one perfunctory stop at Western Avenue, the train became an express to Chicago's Union Station. It was quiet, with only the sound of rustling papers and the occasional cough from the familiar strangers during flu season to interrupt the serenity.

As Adam sat looking out the window at the passing scenery, he would note the progress of home improvements, road construction, and the annual installation of holiday decorations. He could correctly predict the time of year, within a week, by observing the variety of wild flowers in bloom beside the tracks. This was the reality of Chicago, as opposed to what was reported daily in the newspapers; real people, doing real work, struggling to keep their heads above water.

The high-speed run into the city produced a gentle rocking motion that reminded Adam of his days at sea. It produced a trancelike state that inevitably helped him formulate good ideas. It was the perfect time to think, reflect, review, and plan. The interlude had helped produce a number of innovative solutions to a wide variety of system problems in the past.

His reverie was interrupted by the realization of their arrival at Union Station. It was 7:34 and the train was precisely on time. There was no need to rush, since the lower deck commuters would have to exit before the riders on the upper deck could move. He unconsciously put on the winter coat, grabbed the all-important monthly pass, and followed the crowd down the platform and into the station proper. A cool, overcast morning greeted him as he emerged from the station. If that didn't wake him up, viewing the ice floes in the Chicago River beneath the Jackson Street Bridge surely would!

Adam glanced north while crossing the river to witness the huge crowd of pedestrians crossing the Madison Street cantilevered bridge a short distance away. They were flowing out of the Northwestern train station and from this distance looked like a herd of Caribou. The city vibrated with energy. Hustlers had founded the city and their offspring were still present. Just as in the past, today's pedestrians had to keep hustling or they would be run over by the crowds. All generations knew to keep moving to prevent being frozen where they stood!

The heart of the loop was four blocks away and the distinctive sound of the traffic cop's whistles echoed off the massive buildings. The sound was profoundly unique to Chicago. It was a significant part of the city's DNA.

Adam soon arrived at First Continental's edifice. It had been his home away from home for the last eight years. He showed the obligatory security badge to a guard whom Adam had known for at least four of those years. The guard presented a knowing smile and "Good Morning" which Adam returned. After a short wait for an elevator, he sped to the 24th floor. Instinctively, he headed to the canteen for a cup of coffee before proceeding to the office. Adam had been awake for almost three hours and traveled some 40 miles. It was now 8:12 and time to start the day.

"Good morning, Adam! How was the weekend?" asked Stan Wilkowski as he walked into the office. Stan was Adam's trusted right hand man and senior programmer. The two had worked together for over four years. It was enough time, enough late-night sessions, and enough crises, for them to develop a deep personal bond based on mutual respect.

"Not bad, about usual." "How was yours?"

"The same, no big surprises," laughed Stan.

Stan and Adam were currently leading a project team of six people. It was their goal to build a system to trade, record, transfer, convert, and value "Euros"—the new monetary medium for Europe. The entire effort was considered "Top Secret" at First Continental, their employer. This was a market niche the bank had historically avoided, resulting in its New York competitors having free reign in the international money markets. The First had hoped to secretly use this new system to expand its market share, principally among large Midwest corporations with European offices, factories, and subsidiaries.

Adam and Stan's total combined knowledge and experience in this area was non-existent at the onset of the project. They were rewarded with the assignment to develop the new system because no one else at the bank would touch it. There were simply too many variables contained within the proposal to entice the bank's senior project managers to compete for the assignment. How would England participate, or would they participate? The list of unknowns and political uncertainty was endless. No project leader at FIRST CON who could spell "career track" wanted to be in the same room with anybody working on "Trade Master," as the embryonic system was dubbed. The entire project had death written all over it to most of the seasoned bank managers.

Adam and Stan, being contrary by nature and perhaps entrepreneurs at heart, took a different view. Since everything would be a new game, the experience and knowledge of their hated rivals in New York would be to no avail. In addition, they had gained insight and some experience with commodity trading systems. That knowledge base was centered in Chicago. If their team could incorporate some Chicago based experience; they might achieve an edge over any rival—especially those that were headquartered in states touched by salt water.

Snake, their department head went totally ballistic when Adam and Stan volunteered to take on the project without his permission two years ago. Snake was the living personification of the phrase "risk adverse." He illustrated his intense displeasure of their action by distancing himself from the team and the project.

Snake had barely spoken to them or inquired about their progress for months. This form of punishment suited everyone on the project team perfectly. Their collective definition of management support was non-interference.

Adam and Stan had done their homework. Both knew the importance of the requirements definition stage of system development. Before writing one line of code or selecting an operating system, they asked hundreds of questions of potential customers, regulators, lawyers, and accountants. This first phase of the project, always the most difficult and time consuming, was made more so with "Trade Master." Thousands of pieces of preliminary information had to be gathered in total secrecy. The clandestine operation was more like planning a bank robbery than building a new system!

Once the definitions were complete, the technical aspects were dealt with expeditiously by these two seasoned pros. Both men thought they had finally produced an outstanding system. Both envisioned a significant increase in their personal income as a result of their efforts. Adam could actually visualize never having to kite another check. Financial security, a goal they both sought, would finally become a reality. All that remained was to test and document their baby.

"How's the testing going?" Adam asked Stan. That simple question was the full extent of the formal reporting requirements that seasoned, knowledgeable, trusting professionals needed.

"All the standard testing has been successfully completed. Somehow, I'm not too happy or comfortable, as you say it. Something just don't feel right!"

Adam noticed the slight shift in language that indicated Stan was retreating into his second-generation Polish heritage. Stan, a proud member of a large population of Polish immigrants in Chicago, was hard working and under normal conditions very articulate, however, when flustered Stan would lose confidence in his ability to find the exact words in English to express his concerns. Many within the bank had noted this intermittent loss of confidence. Stan had been known to go through entire department meetings without saying a phrase other than "pass the coffee."

Adam could care less about Stan's struggle for the right word or sentence structure. He was acquainted with many people at FIRST CON who spoke eloquent English and had nothing of value to say, but said it anyway. Stan's skills and prodigious work ethic were legendary in the bank and the only thing of importance to Adam. One of Adam's strengths as a leader was that he was sensitive to Stan's lack of self-confidence. Adam also knew that anything troubling Stan would be factual and highly significant.

Adam slowly got up and started walking around the office. "Are you suggesting, Stan, that beyond a certain point it's impossible to fully test an on-line, real-time, operator dependent system with traditional methodologies?"

"Yes, that is exactly what I'm trying to say!"

Adam was aware of the problem in a generic sense. It was frequently characterized as the "man-machine" interface. It had dogged the information industry for decades. In "Trade Master," it was more critical than in most applications. Fortunes could be made or lost in tenths of a second. If traders felt encumbered by system constraints to the extent that they were slow in executing trades, they would never adopt the program. That would leave FIRST CON and the team with an expensive "white elephant." In all probability, that outcome would create the opportunity for the entire team to hit the streets in search of new employment. A chill went down Adam's spine as he contemplated the consequences.

"Stan, I think I understand what you're saying. When I coached my son in little league, we had kids concentrating exclusively on their stance, distance from the plate and how they were holding the bat. In the process of worrying about how they looked, they forgot that the objective was to hit the crap out of the ball!"

"How did you solve such a big problem?"

"To be honest, some kids never learned, but most improved greatly. The key to their improvement was the amount of time they spent in batting cages."

Stan looked confused for a brief moment, then blurted out: "Adam, is a batting cage the same type of thing as a simulator?" Both men realized at that instant that they had somehow stumbled into something. "Adam, I can make such a simulator from the existing system with such little effort. A rookie trader can practice making trades without hurting position too much financially, until their confidence is like rock."

"Let's do it!" Adam exclaimed. "No, wait! Let me think for a second." He continued pacing around the room stopping only for a sip of coffee. Stan was familiar with this behavior and knew to wait patiently. "Stan, perhaps we should take this concept one step further. Simulators exist now for the training of airline pilots. They really task the hell out of pilots by throwing emergencies at them like simulating the loss of an engine. They are designed to test the pilot's thinking under duress. What if we took the knowledge and data we gathered at the beginning of this project to similarly test new traders?"

"I'm not sure I understand. Can you give for me please an example?"

"Well, let's say you are employed trading 'Euros' and the French Ministry of Agriculture releases a report saying the grape harvest in France is going to be a disaster. What does a trader do with that information? I'm not sure what I would do and I'm willing to bet they don't know what to do either. However, I know that during the initial stages of our project, we collected a timetable showing when all of the official government reports were issued. Furthermore, we collected much, if not all of the history of monetary movements in the market after the release of those reports. We could correlate the effects of the issuance of the reports to historical market movements. Stan, I think you have all the raw material you need to test the hell out of our existing system and as a by-product, produce a world-class simulator to assist user acceptance. That capability could give us a distinct competitive advantage when we start marketing the system."

Stan was visibly shaking with excitement from the new idea. He had come to Adam's office with a real problem, which now appeared to be solved. Additionally, there was now an opportunity to produce something truly unique. Programmers, like all creative types, dream of such an opportunity.

"I'll get right on it. Thanks, boss!" Stan virtually flew from the office, his face red with emotion. Stan almost physically knocked Snake into the next zip code just outside Adam's office, but never paused. Snake took note of the enthusiasm in Stan's motions, but as usual said nothing.

Adam continued pacing around the office, genuinely happy that they had stumbled into an apparent conceptual answer to a major problem. There was also a feeling of guilt. As a manager, he wouldn't be allowed to do the real work. All he did was produce a lame analogy to get Stan's mind in gear. Perhaps, in the final analysis, this is what managing is all about. You don't do the real work, you support the people who do and then get the hell out of their way.

He then remembered that one of his primary managerial duties was to attend boring meetings. The monthly staff meeting was about to start and he was the designated goat from operations required to attend. Snake had once again slithered out of that particular responsibility. The staff's nickname for Mr. Post was highly accurate. So Adam had to go despite the fact that he was commanded, for security reasons, not to report on anything.

Adam entered the main conference room on the fourth floor and looked for the most comfortable seat, furthest from the podium. He had stopped feeling guilty about Stan. He now felt both envy and disdain for Stan simultaneously. Stan would be doing real substantive work while Adam had to come up with ways to stay awake during the landscaping and similar useless reports. One trick that usually helped was to observe and count the use of "Frank's Law." Frank had once advised him to "be careful of corporate communication that contained four tenses."

"I only know the three traditional English verb tenses: past, present and future," Adam responded.

"To that list, add 'pre' tense," Frank quipped.

"How do I know when 'pre' tense is included?"

"Generally, it follows a pattern of: in the past we had a problem, now we found and fixed it. As a result of our hard work, the future looks great! When you see that pattern you can be assured that 'pre' tense is in use!"

Adam ruefully had to admit that Frank was right. Each month he would count the use of four tenses in each staff meeting. It seemed every department head identified that they had a problem only when it could be described in the past tense. In four years of attending these FIRST CON sessions Adam never once heard an executive say: "Hey, fellow workers, colleagues, friends, whatever; we have a big hairy-legged problem plaguing my department that we don't have a clue how to solve. Can anyone out there in this huge concentrated pool of managerial talent help?"

Adam knew why the question was never asked. To admit that you had a problem would indicate that you, as a manager, were not in control. That in turn would be interpreted as an indelible sign of weakness within the corporate culture. "Image" was the God, the one and only God, revered by all in attendance. "Image" was measured in "Style Points." To ask for help from fellow workers would generate negative "Style Points" in such abundance you would need to visit the "field of Astronomy" to obtain units of measure large enough to total them.

Adam stopped his daydreaming when Phil, from the security department, slipped into the chair beside him. Adam knew Phil in the typical corporate sense. They frequently sat in the same meetings, nodded to each other in the cafeteria and each knew the other's departments. Beyond that limited acquaintance, there was nothing. Adam impulsively decided to do something about that before the meeting started.

"Say, Phil, there is something I've been meaning to ask you, but it's none of my business."

"Fire away, Adam."

"When we devised security procedures for the data center, we were forced to adopt irregular and staggered intervals for all of our activities. The consultants wanted to keep us from being typecast by some real or imagined enemy. Yet, I see a Brinks truck come to our facility at the same time every day. Only my METRA train is more precise in its movements. How did you get out of the staggered timing requirement?"

Phil smiled and responded: "Actually it's a good tactic not to be too regular and I recommend that you keep your staggered schedules. In the case of the Brinks truck, operational needs for check clearing and inter-bank transfers negated the security concerns."

"Doesn't that pose a risk that the truck could be robbed based on its rigid schedule?"

"In theory it does enhance the risk. In reality, it's a very small risk under any scheduling routine. The trucks themselves are virtual battleships on wheels. You would need a nuclear powered can opener to crack one. Furthermore, if some bad guys did obtain such a can opener, how are they going to get away from downtown? The traffic alone would stop them, plus the Loop is covered with cops. Last but not least, thanks to the electronic transfers that you guys do in your fancy digs on the 24th floor, there is almost no real money left for the trucks to carry. I'll bet the average truck is carrying less than 10-15 million."

"Well excuse me, Phil, but to us hermits on the 24th floor, that sounds like a lot of money!"

"It is to me also, Adam. Whatever the reason, nobody has tried to knock off a Brinks truck for over 20 years in Chicago, or any other major city that I'm aware of. The few robberies that occurred in the past were all 'inside' jobs and quickly solved by the police. Nevertheless, thanks for your question. This has been the most interesting staff meeting I've attended in years." Both men smiled knowingly and settled down for two hours of drivel.

One speaker after another droned on with all four verb tenses in copious use. Adam realized that the significant work and information exchange within the bank frequently occurred exactly like his discussion with Phil. There were chance encounters before and after scheduled meetings or random conferences in the hall or around the water cooler. In total, these exchanges were referred to as the grapevine. The existence, speed, and accuracy of the grapevine always mystified top management. The employees, however, knew to heed the grapevine as their principal news network. You ignored it at your peril.

When the meeting mercifully ended, Adam left the building for lunch. The normal routine was to have lunch with Stan, or some of the team members. Today, because of the extended length of the staff meeting, he decided to run over to Berghoff's for a corned beef on rye.

Adam felt refreshed upon returning to the bank. On the way back to the office, he noticed that the conference room door was closed. Conspicuously posted on the door, was a hand-lettered sign saying, "KEEP OUT!" It would appear that Stan, along with the rest of the team, was in fact getting right on it.

Returning to his desk, Adam decided to attack the never-ending requests for project updates, budget requests, and forecasts. In addition, there were personnel issues on overtime, vacation schedules, and reviews. Between the pile of paper, phone calls and e-mails, there wasn't a dull moment until 5:00. If he left immediately, it would be possible to catch the 5:26 p.m. train to Bartlett and for a rare treat, enjoy dinner with the family.

His departure took him past the conference room door, which had remained closed all afternoon. From inside he could hear shouts, laughter, squeals, and some cussing in Polish. The sounds of creative productivity, thought Adam. He recalled similar sessions with fondness before joining the ranks of management. It was a great temptation to open the door. He didn't. Adam knew that in his presence, everyone inside would assume the serious mien that was the preferred corporate professional image. The magic of creativity would disappear. Reluctantly, he turned and left to catch the early train.

Adam arrived home to a surprised and happy family. It wasn't often that he got home early on a Monday, and they seemed sincerely pleased. Alice reminded him after her greeting that the day's mail was on the dining room table. He ambled over to do a quick review of the mail certain that over 90% would be discarded without opening. One unusual letter looked official. Adam opened it and felt his knees buckle. For a moment, Adam thought he was going to pass out, throw up or both!

Alice, immediately sensing something was terribly wrong, approached him, and asked, "Are you O.K., Dear?"

"No, as a matter of fact, I'm not!"

CHAPTER 4

Alice desperately wanted Adam to reveal the source of his emotional reaction to the mail. The husband and wife exchanged a quick glance that silently communicated a great deal. "This can't be discussed in front of the kids. Wait until later and we will go through the whole deal."

The kids went to bed shortly after completing their homework. Scotty had enjoyed his walk and was now resting comfortably. The food was put away and the supper dishes cleaned. With the daily chores completed, Alice approached Adam at the kitchen table to finally get the complete explanation for her husband's reaction earlier that evening. This topic might be postponed, but not ignored.

"All right, Adam. What the dickens was in that letter? You scared the hell out of me!"

"It was a 1099, dear." Adam replied as calmly as possible. Staying calm and in control was extremely difficult at the moment.

"What is a 1099 and why did it upset you?"

"A 1099 is one of 649 standard IRS forms and schedules. It's the form used to report income paid to individuals with no taxes withheld. FIRST CON sends them to everybody they paid interest to. Illinois sends them to anyone who received a tax refund from the State. In effect, it alerts the IRS that a firm paid someone who is not a normal employee for something done that year. That individual had better report the income when filing his 1040 return on April 15. In other words, this guy owes you money, we didn't withhold a dime, you better get your share of it!"

"I thought money was withheld from your checks to cover all taxes."

"That would be true for regular employee paychecks. Those sums are reported on a W-2 form, which has to be included with your April 15th filing."

"You received income from someone other than First Continental or the State of Illinois?"

"Yes, I did, Alice. The 1099 was issued from Second Republic Bank of Chicago."

"They are your biggest competitors. Why would you get money from them? I'm sorry, Adam, this is quite confusing!"

"Don't feel alone, dear. It's a bit confusing for me as well. Let me try to simplify the situation."

Adam tried to start from the beginning. "Almost five years ago I was assigned by FIRST CON to join a committee exploring ways to improve Internet security. The bank was scared to death, with good reason, that a 'hacker' would enter the bank's files through the Internet and do all kinds of mischief. Banks have a moral and fiduciary responsibility to protect their clients' money and data. The committee I was assigned to, like most large committees, had made no progress in achieving that important goal. They were hopelessly deadlocked over which approach to take. On one hand, they had discovered two vendor packages that appeared to be capable of providing security. Vendor 'A' had one third of the committee votes and Vendor 'B' had garnered the support of another third of the group. The remaining third of the committee was holding out for an in-house development plan. No amount of discussion, arm-twisting, or cajoling had changed votes. Therefore, they did nothing."

"I remember some of this vaguely, but I don't see how it relates to the receipt of a 1099," Alice complained.

"It will, trust me.

"When I joined the committee, I had no idea what to do either. As I normally do, I did an extensive amount of homework. In the process, I learned a great deal about the Internet and security, however, there was nothing in the literature that gave a clear indication of what to do about security. Management by this time was getting nervous. We had to do something because the risk to our customers' security was too great.

"Actually, you are responsible for the breakthrough in this story, Alice, my dear."

"Me! What did I do?"

"One weekend during that time frame you got all over me to replace the front door lock. I took measurements and went to *Home Depot* in search of a replacement. Once there, I stood bewildered in front of hundreds of different locks on display. A good salesman took pity on me and helped me get what I needed. I remember telling the salesman that there should be only one lock of one type to help keep homeowners like me from going crazy. It was meant as a joke, but the salesman took it seriously and proceeded to prove to me that multiple locks were almost exponentially better than one lock. In other words, if you take a normal lock and add a dead bolt to it you get four times the protection instead of just doubling the protection. I then realized if what he said was true for my front door, why not for the bank's computers?

"I proposed the concept of improved security through multiple locks to the committee the following Monday. I recommended that we purchase both Vendor A and Vendor B's products. Secondly, we form an in-house development team to find a way of streaming both vendor packages together without slowing down the system or violating the integrity of either vendor's product. In essence, I broke the either/or deadlock by suggesting all of the above.

"The committee bought the idea. I was a hero! In lieu of a raise, I was given the title 'project manager' and told to install the new system by no later than yesterday. That's when I first started working with Stan. There are a lot of details about data packets and firewalls that I won't bore you with. Let's just say that the concept wasn't as easy to install, as it was to visualize. Thanks in no small measure to Stan's talent and the hard work of our team, we were successful."

"I thought we were going to talk about 1099's," Alice was becoming testy.

"I know! I know! I'm just trying to put this whole mess in context." Adam knew he had to move faster.

"Shortly after we installed the new system, FIRST CON started realizing the value. We were intercepting hackers and providing valuable information on the culprits to the FBI, while our competitors were getting whacked. That's when my idiot boss, Jim Post, better known as Snake, got involved. Snake didn't ask, he demanded, that I write a paper on the system we had developed and installed. Furthermore, he wanted me to present the paper to the American Banking Association at their annual convention last summer. Snake obviously wanted to receive 'Style Points.' What better way to impress an industry that is dedicated to and almost paranoid about security than to brag about having the latest and greatest Internet security system in existence? Snake wanted to rub our peers' noses in that realization. The fact that this system was sponsored and designed in part by First Continental greatly enhanced our image.

"Well, in this instance, Snake seems to make sense to me, Adam."

"At one level, namely image building, he was. My concern was that if we bragged about our security in an open public forum, such as the ABA, we would be waving a red flag in front of a world full of depraved geniuses who wanted to gain the prestige of cracking into the impregnable."

"Now I understand your argument. My God, what a dilemma—build up the prestige of First Continental to keep your job versus inviting attacks that would threaten the bank's very existence. I'm so sorry, Adam. I've often wondered why you frequently arrive home with a scowl on your face. I had no idea what you were going through. How did you solve the dilemma?"

"In a very real sense I didn't, I'm sorry to say. I tried. I called a friend at the ABA and scheduled my presentation for late in the afternoon of the last day. My thought was if I couldn't stop the presentation, I would expose it to the smallest possible audience. The convention was in Palm Springs last year and both my friend and I were convinced everyone at the convention would be playing golf on the last day."

"That's brilliant! Why didn't it work?"

"As luck would have it there were big thunderstorms that day. They are virtually unheard of at that time of year. The conference room was full. My friend said later that they set a new attendance record for a business meeting on the last day."

Alice just sat quietly, absolutely stunned.

"The paper was very well received. That was surprising, since I had eliminated virtually all technical references to how it actually worked. A lot of people came up to me after the speech wanting to know more. I deferred or provided vague answers to their questions. Many wanted to buy the product. I had to tell them that to the best of my knowledge, it was not for sale. In particular, a Mr. Alister Lewis came onto me like I was a liver treat and Mr. Lewis was Scotty."

"Who is Mr. Lewis?"

"It turned out that Mr. Lewis was a senior VP at Second Republic of Chicago. I had heard of him before, but we never met until that day in Palm Springs. That's not too surprising, now that I think about it. I was never permitted to go to the ABA convention in the past. Mr. Lewis was desperately looking for Internet security. He confided in me that their committee at Second Republic was as bogged down as ours had been. Lewis wanted to buy the system, and he wanted to buy it then, that instant, in the hotel lobby. I repeatedly announced that the system was not for sale and even if it were, I wasn't a salesman. I knew Second Republic was our major cross-town competitor. I didn't want to be seen talking to Alister Lewis. That's when he invited me to dinner."

"You went to dinner with Lewis?"

"Yes, I certainly did. I had already shot the measly per diem expense that FIRST CON provided me for lunch. I had to eat something and the cost of a

Palm Springs dinner was destined to come from our budget. So, if a competitor wanted to buy dinner, why not? It turned out Mr. Lewis was a gracious host. We enjoyed a great meal and some excellent wine. He really is a great guy and a true Chicago Bears fan. Lewis also pointed out to me that if a hacker hurt one bank, all banks would suffer from the public's mistrust. My product would not help enhance Second Republic's financial performance. It would only help preserve their security. That in turn helped the entire industry's image of trust and security. I had to admit that I had not thought of industry security interest in that way. Mr. Lewis said that I wasn't alone. Too many people looked at the world in 'us' versus 'them' terms instead of 'we.' For example, he noted that we could never enjoy a meal like this in Chicago because we were competitors. Here in Palm Springs, we could meet, have dinner, and enter into serious discussions of industry issues. That is why he urged that we reach an agreement that night, before we returned to Chicago."

Alice watched her husband closely as he related the story. She was way ahead of Adam now. She could see what was coming. In many areas of life, she deferred to her husband's intellect and experience. She also knew he had a big weakness. Adam was probably the oldest Boy Scout in America. She heard a lot of phony lines during her dating days, and she instinctively recognized the one offered by Lewis. 'Industry concerns,' my butt. If Lewis walked into her kitchen at that moment, she wasn't sure what she would have done with her knives. She wanted to scream at Adam: "Watch out, this guy didn't make senior VP because of noble concerns for the industry. He had not achieved a senior position at the bank because he was known for putting gold coins into the 'Salvation Army' kettles at Christmas. If anything, experienced bell ringers would have grabbed their kettles and run at the banker's approach. All were trained to do this maneuver at the sight of a national political figure. Lewis made VP because he was a smooth talking, back stabbing, politically motivated, con man!" She couldn't say it. Nor could she express, without the use of vulgar language, her sentiments for Snake. The arrogant idiot had forced her husband to buy a new suit for this presentation and then didn't provide adequate funding for Adam's meals. Additionally, probably to reduce costs, they did not think to send a seasoned executive along to protect Adam from the sharks that constantly roam industry conferences looking to steal ideas.

Adam, with a slightly vacant look in his eyes continued. "About the time we got to dessert, Lewis persuasively suggested that during my vacation last summer I install the security system at the Second Republic Bank. After all, I was allowed to use my vacation time any way I pleased. The goal was to help all of the big banks in Chicago protect their customers from the low-life scoundrels that lurked a modem away. Of course, Alister felt an obligation to compensate me for my time and effort. Mr. Lewis had calculated that the amount would be $5,250, for two days of work. It would, of course, be tax free, as he did not see the need to report this transaction to anyone!"

"Isn't that illegal?"

"Technically, yes, but everybody does it."

"Well I'm glad that point is cleared up," she replied sarcastically. "I'm also not surprised that Mr. Lewis did not keep his word, judging from your reaction when you determined that there was a 1099 in the mail. Let's cut to the chase. You went over and installed the product during your vacation. Were there any problems?"

"Actually, yes. I never saw Lewis during the entire process. I dealt with Nelson Powers, his close assistant. The two of us just didn't hit it off. The security project was Powers' responsibility before I came onto the scene. Since he didn't deliver, he scored many negative 'Style Points.' The fact that Lewis rescued Powers by contracting with a competitor could not have helped his image one bit. I believe Powers wanted to take out his frustration and anger on me. Looking back, it was a very bad deal and one I'm totally ashamed of."

"What did you use the money for?"

"If you remember, that was the time we became aware that Mark needed braces. Frankly, that was one reason I agreed to the deal. Before the offer from Mr. Lewis, I had no idea where to find the money for Mark's braces. So $1,500 went to the orthodontist, $1000 into savings, and the rest to pay off some small credit cards and the loan on my commuter car."

"Nothing for the sweet young thing you keep on the side?" Alice asked with a smile.

"Not yet, but the way things are going, I may need a backup plan when you dump me because I made such a bone-headed play."

"You should be so lucky, Mr. Easy." She knew Adam's motivations were honorable; however, his tactics were unbelievably naive. "How do you plan to get us out of this mess?"

"I'm not really sure. If it were just the 1099, I would have to pay state and federal taxes on the income. That's a real problem. It would be about $2,000, which we don't have. The significant problem is that the 1099 is for the wrong amount—namely $55,250."

"What did you say?" Alice screamed. "They overstated the amount on the 1099 by $50,000!"

"Now you're starting to understand why I almost threw up when I opened the mail. I have no idea how to fix this issue. I have never been in this situation. Probably, we will need an amended 1099 from Second, if they will agree to provide one. Even if they do, that almost guarantees us of an audit by the IRS, because their records won't match my return. If they agree that the first 1099 was in error by $50,000, they will still poke around in my returns for the last eight years looking for something else that might be incorrect. Remember, under administrative law we have the burden of proof."

"Those bastards!" Alice was using language that Adam only heard when she was extremely upset.

"Which bastards are you talking about, my dear, those at the Second, or the crew at the IRS?"

Alice didn't respond. She was on the verge of crying. She simply rose from the table and started getting ready for bed. Adam wondered if she would be able to sleep. He was certain he wouldn't. He felt trapped by the system.

Adam started laying out appropriate clothes and his briefcase for tomorrow's run for the 6:32. He could not shake the concern over how to fix the 1099. Sleep under these circumstances would be impossible. Perhaps some night air would reduce the anxiety.

Scotty looked at his master quizzically. This wasn't part of the normal routine. The dog adjusted quickly when Adam approached with the leash. A walk is to be savored, whether it was part of the usual routine or not.

The night air was cool and refreshing as they ambled down the street. Scotty once again performed the "I'm nervous" dance. It was then that Adam noticed a figure approaching from the left. Scotty recognized Frank before Adam did and his tail started wagging in anticipation.

"What are you doing out so late at night, Frank?"

"I've been working on my taxes, and I had to take a sanity break." Frank replied while warmly greeting Scotty.

Adam could not stop the muffled scream of pain when Frank mentioned taxes. "I see I have company with the anguish of tax preparation. Well, it's that time of year."

"It's more than the pain generated in an average year, Frank. Just out of curiosity, what do you know about 1099's?"

"As an independent businessman, I've dealt with scores of 1099's over the years, and I know enough about them to know that you should not have received one."

Adam confided to the good neighbor the whole story of "how" and "why" he got a 1099. Adam concluded the story with a plea for help.

"Well, Adam, of all the 1099's I have received over the years, none were for the wrong amount. I suspect that your Mr. Powers at the Second is guilty of a little 'pay-back' for making him look bad. That is beside the point. You will need an amended 1099 from the Second for the correct amount sent to you and the IRS. When you get audited, and you undoubtedly will, you will have to pray that the idiots at IRS don't look at the two 1099's as additive. By that, I mean, they could believe you received $57,500 that you neglected to pay any taxes on. The penalties alone on that amount could be breathtaking under the new rules."

"Ah, shit! I didn't think of that." Adam was now close to tears, as the full dimension of the entrapment became clearer.

"Remember the mindset of the IRS, Adam. They are protecting the sovereign nation of the United States of America from rich tax cheats like you. They are compelled to find something wrong to justify their existence. I suggest you obtain a good lawyer."

"I guess I'll have to, but I have no idea how I'll be able to pay him."

"It's considerably cheaper than the alternative, Adam!" Frank stopped and looked closely at his neighbor. This really wasn't a good time to bring up this subject, but perhaps he had to overlook that thought. "One additional question, if I may, Adam?"

"Certainly, Frank, I appreciate your help."

"The last time we talked, I suggested that to succeed, you had to break the rules. Breaking the rules in our society is characterized as a crime—at least by those in authority who make and promulgate the rules. Little did I know that you were way ahead of me in the crime department. My only question is why did you expose yourself and your family's financial security for a measly $5,250? In our current culture of repeated wrongdoing at the highest levels, that barely counts as a misdemeanor! If you are going to follow my instructions, do something worthwhile. You live in Chicago, home of Dan Burnham, who once said: 'Make no little plans!' You have a rich heritage to live up to. Quit acting and thinking like a measly 'Cheese-head.' Think big! I used to think that you were smart. Hell, I know your dog is!

With that rejoinder, Frank turned and entered his house. Adam was momentarily stunned by Frank's remarks. Frank's analysis was correct. That was a mistake he vowed would never happen again. "Come, Scotty, its time to go home. The 6:32 will arrive at its usual time."

CHAPTER 5

Adam had barely managed to catch the train on this Tuesday morning. He was too sleepy to bother with the paper and coffee. Thanks to the late-night discussions with Alice on the implications of the 1099 and the accidental rendezvous with Frank, many precious hours of sleep were lost. Both he and Alice tossed fitfully through the night. Uncharacteristically, Adam slept on the swaying train all the way to Union Station.

The walk through the bustling streets of the Loop started to revive him, as it always did. The ice floes on the Chicago River had disappeared. A sure sign of spring, Adam thought. Of course, it was a sign of spring—this was the last week of March. An involuntary shudder took over his body with the realization of how little time was left before their taxes had to be filed. Resolving the 1099 fiasco had to be his number one priority. Adam was semi-alert when he entered the office area on the 24th floor. Then he saw the conference room.

The room looked like it had been attacked by a large group of rodents on steroids. Chairs were askew. Empty pizza boxes from Uno's littered the entire area. A residue of tomato sauce and assorted pieces of cheese, onions, and green pepper were everywhere. The empty Dunkin Donut boxes provided concrete evidence that breakfast had been consumed in the room, in addition to dinner. Cups and glasses, some filled with cigarette butts, littered the table. Using the cups as ashtrays was logical, thought Adam. The official ashtrays were removed when the entire area was ruled a no smoking zone years before. Large sheets of paper from easel pads were taped on walls throughout the room. Each one was covered with flow charts, notes, and system diagrams in different colors. It was obvious that at some point, the rodents had run out of easel paper. They continued by writing on the conference room walls and the walls along the hallways leading to the conference room. The floor was covered in ripped, wadded, and crumpled paper.

Adam could easily read the signs. Stan and the team had pulled an all-nighter. Yesterday, while poised outside the conference room door, he heard the sounds of creative productivity. Today he saw the sights and smelled the aromas associated with that activity. All but one member of the "Trade Master" team was married. It was evident that the team needed to make difficult arrangements to accomplish an all-nighter. It was a certain bet that they had not made those sacrifices for good old FIRST CON or out of loyalty to him. They did it because active participation in a spontaneous creative process, when everybody is clicking, when the magic is present, is almost as good as sex. Adam could not wait to see what they had accomplished. Based on experience, it would be either very good or very bad. He also surmised that he would view no results for at least 24 hours. The experienced Trade Master team would want to do some testing in the cold light of day before any announcements or demonstrations were rendered.

The delay in seeing the results was fine with Adam. As their manager, he was absolutely confident that he was going to catch unmitigated hell no matter what they had accomplished. Just at that moment, Jim, the head of maintenance, entered the conference room. Jim's face was red and his body shook from anger.

"Just look at this dump, Adam! How the hell can I keep this place within specifications when the juvenile delinquents that you supposedly manage are running around? If I get dinged on my salary review because of this, I'll kill somebody! Who the hell did this?"

"I'm not sure Jim, but I'll find out," Adam lied.

"Don't give me that bull, Adam! This is your area and undoubtedly your people are responsible! I sense Stan's involvement with this!" Jim was livid. He kept better care of the bank than his own home. Historically, Jim viewed Stan as a troublemaker. Stan didn't obey the rules.

Stan was not the most popular employee within the bank's corporate culture. Stan, among other things, was claustrophobic about transportation vehicles. Thus, he was the only employee in the bank's history who commuted to work on a Harley motorcycle. Stan would do this in any weather. Adam had never seen Stan on the cycle, as he arrived for work from the west. Stan generally blew in from the near north side, and parked at the underground truck entrance on the east side of the bank. Employees who witnessed Stan's arrival claimed he looked like the "Red Baron," complete with leather jacket and scarf. The same characteristics that many at FIRST CON found so objectionable were exactly the ones that Adam coveted.

"As I said, Jim, I'll look into this. Is there any chance we can get this cleaned up before Snake sees this mess? I don't want my boss to have a heart attack or get sick to his stomach and create a bigger mess."

Even though Jim was really unhappy, he had to smile at Adam's remarks. "I've got a crew on the way, Adam. You know, in the old days, we used to have conference rooms trashed like this quite often. I haven't seen one this bad in years!"

"Nor have I, Jim." Adam thought that he might have just discovered an insight on how to measure corporate health and creativity. Adam dismissed the thought when he observed Phil from security waiting in his office.

"Good morning, Phil! How can I be of assistance to you today?" Adam knew exactly why Phil was there. Being upbeat and helpful was a classic bank strategy and perhaps the best defense to what he was certain was coming.

"It's not a good morning, Adam! My sleep was interrupted all night long with calls from my security guards requesting direction on what to do with your band of zealots in the conference room." Phil was genuinely upset, and added: "Don't your people know what the work hours are at this bank?" Phil was on a roll. The security manager didn't wait for Adam to respond and continued with: "The worst part of this situation was I didn't know what to tell the guards. There is absolutely nothing in our procedure manuals to cover this situation. If you had provided me with a 'heads-up' that a late hour session was scheduled, I would have been better prepared."

Well, now I know the real problem affecting Phil, Adam thought. Phil had lost image points. The night supervisor didn't have an answer for the guards. In Asian cultures, it's referred to as "loss of face." Adam thought for a moment before responding, knowing that the words had the potential to affect his career status at the bank.

Phil was a good man, a good soldier, who always followed the rules. It would be impossible to describe to a man whose most creative task was to fill in a weekly duty roster that creative brainstorming sessions simply did not adhere to schedules. You might as well attempt to schedule the arrival of spring in Chicago. Spring arrived when spring arrived. When the creative "muse" spoke, you took advantage of it. You couldn't predict its arrival. The Phil's of the world wouldn't or couldn't understand that truth.

Adam realized that at this moment he didn't possess anything close to a finished product from the team. There was no documentation to reference that could illustrate how productive the session had been. A traditional defense would not work. It was time to take a different approach. Adam would tell Phil exactly what he wanted to hear. Just like a senior manager or national politician would do.

"Phil, I am truly dismayed that your sleep was interrupted!" Adam wanted to add that a loss of sleep had been true for him as well, but could not. "There is simply no excuse for it. I apologize personally and on behalf of my staff for their infantile behavior. There may be fines and letters of censure issued when I complete my thorough investigation into the entire situation. As you know, those disciplinary measures, in accordance with Chapter III, Title 2, paragraph 10, of our Policy and Procedure Manual, are very stiff. That should ensure that there would be no repeats of this incident. Furthermore, I personally guarantee that I will notify you and your department, a minimum of 48 hours, in advance when we schedule the next brainstorming session." Adam lied and bit his lower lip for maximum effect. His face reflected genuine sadness, helped in part by his own loss of sleep.

Phil was astonished at Adam's comments. Adam earned a considerable reputation within FIRST CON for going to the wall to protect his staff. He was known for arguing vociferously with accounting, personnel, and others for vacation schedules, comp time, raises, etc. Thus, Phil expected a vigorous defense by Adam of his staff for their late-night shenanigans. Instead, Adam talked about reprisals! He even quoted from the appropriate chapter of the Policy and Procedure manual. Perhaps Adam was a better bank manager than Phil had been led to believe.

"Well, thank you, Adam. I'm glad you understand the problem from the security viewpoint. I believe your apology was heartfelt and I accept it. I guess I'd better get back to my area and count noses. Let me know if I can help with your investigation."

"I will, Phil. Thank you for bringing this to my attention." With that, Phil left Adam's office. Adam figured correctly that Phil would now report to his boss. Phil would brag to his superior about the apology and future reprisals that he forced from a reluctant project manager.

Adam realized that more trouble lurked on the horizon. Predictably, there would be one additional challenge emerging from last night's activities. The signs that Adam so quickly perceived from the condition of the conference room could be easily read and interpreted by others. The "Trade Master" team achieved a major breakthrough. There was no other explanation possible for an all-nighter. The "Trade Master" team was hot, and everybody loves a winner! People within the operations department and others who avoided any previous contact with the team would now want a piece of the action. Creative types in any department, assuming there were still any working at the bank, would want to be part of the project. There was one simple reason for this—they just wanted to be close in case the "muse" spoke again.

Sure enough, Adam's first e-mail was from a graphic designer in marketing. She was requesting a transfer to his group for the purpose of creating a brochure. "A brochure on what?" Adam wondered. How could the grapevine correctly determine from gossip about pizza cartons that there was a big deal coming? The fact that this news extended 14 floors in less than 15 minutes astounded him. While composing a polite "thank you" response to the graphic designer's request, Adam started to wonder how secret the project was. He was beginning to feel that the entire bank, with the exception of his immediate boss, knew what was going on.

Once the e-mail was sent, Adam took time to follow up on the number one priority. Carefully, he slipped out of the office and went down to the lobby. Once there, he produced the cell phone that he brought from home today to contact Mr. Alister Lewis. Using the office phone didn't seem prudent. It could prove to be embarrassing trying to explain a call traced to Second Republic's phone number, or explain the conversation if someone barged into his office. In Palm Springs, Mr. Lewis provided Adam with a business card with a personal direct number penciled on the back. Adam's first attempt at calling was unsuccessful. The line was busy. For some unknown reason, that made him angry. He continued to walk around the marble clad-lobby for a few minutes and tried again. Still busy, now he was really getting hot! He left the bank and scurried down the street to a *Starbucks*, ordered a tall Mocha, and tried again.

The unmistakable, sophisticated, urbane voice of Alister Lewis answered. "Hello, this is Lewis."

"Yes, Mr. Lewis, this is Adam Jones, your Internet security system provider."

"Adam, how are you?"

"Actually, not well," Adam replied from a quiet corner of *Starbucks*. "I thought we had an agreement that I would be paid in tax-free dollars. Yesterday I received a 1099, almost a full month later than the law allows, and for the wrong amount. If you wanted me to pay taxes on an extra 50 thousand, why didn't you provide the cash in the first place?"

"Yes, Adam, I'm truly sorry about the 1099. We have new auditors. They forced me to send them out even if they were late. I didn't know anything about the incorrect amount. I had Mr. Powers deal with the entire matter."

So, Frank was right about Powers. "How do you propose to remedy this situation, Mr. Lewis?"

"I don't know if there is anything to fix Adam. The auditors were very explicit in their instructions on this point."

More than the words, which were bad enough, the arrogant "let them eat cake" tone that Lewis adopted really set Adam off. From deep inside his inner being came a voice that was so cold and ruthless, Adam didn't recognize it himself. "Mr. Lewis, please be aware that I personally installed your Internet security system. It is an outstanding system, but not perfect. As its principle architect and designer, I know what it can and cannot do. If you don't believe me, I would be happy to provide you with a demonstration of the system's strengths and weaknesses."

"Are you threatening me?" Lewis demanded.

"No, I'm simply stating facts. Continuing with the facts, your agreement was for tax-free income. I don't care about your auditors or their instructions. The 1099 has been issued. You are correct in assuming we can't do anything about that fact. The IRS has received their copy electronically. Therefore, you will provide me with an amended 1099 and a check for $6,000. I want the check drawn from your personal account, not Second Republic's corporate account. I trust that will cover my tax liability, penalties and the cost for an attorney during the inevitable audit that will result from your error. That is how we fix the situation, Mr. Lewis. None of this turmoil would be necessary if you had not reneged on our agreement. The amended 1099 and accompanying check will be sent, by express mail, to my home by no later than Friday afternoon!"

There was a long pause before Lewis responded. "I'll see what I can do, Adam."

"Just do it, Mr. Lewis!" Adam hung up totally angry and frustrated, but in a strange way exhilarated. All of his life he had been pushed around by those in authority. This was the first time he ever pushed back. It bothered him a little that he enjoyed the feeling.

Lewis, upon hearing the dial tone, hung up and stared at the phone for a minute. The senior banker was simultaneously confused and upset. "What gotten into Adam? He must be nuts if he thinks he can blackmail me." Lewis was far more comfortable with the role of conning someone than being the target of a con. Obviously, the kid was bluffing, thought Lewis. Adam was too honorable to do otherwise. If Adam were less honorable, he would have been in a higher position at First Continental. However, Adam may have had a valid complaint about the incorrect amount on the 1099. "What did Powers do with that assignment?" Lewis picked up the phone to find out directly from Powers. "Yes, Nelson, this is Alister, I need to talk with you about something, quite urgently!"

Powers replied that he was unavailable at the moment as the entire staff was scrambling to restore power to the data center. "You mean everything is down?" Lewis asked. Nelson Powers replied that everything, the data center, all cashiers; ATM's and networks had all crashed. Lewis concluded the conversation with Powers and called his broker. The bank executive instructed his broker to transfer funds to his personal account. He then went to accounting to obtain an amended 1099.

Second Republic's center was down but a mere 30 minutes. The fault was later traced to a transformer failure in an underground vault owned by Commonwealth Edison. That failure coupled with a faulty circuit breaker in the bank's UPS system led to the outage. Lewis never believed the technical report for the outage. He knew the real reason for the crash, but could say nothing. Lewis was surprised that he had miscalculated Adam's sense of integrity. The banker just knew that if the situation had been reversed, "the shot across the bow" of shutting down the data center was the precise action that he, as a senior executive, would have taken.

Adam, while departing *Starbucks*, was totally unaware of the mass confusion and chaos taking place at his competitor's shop. Adam felt that he had been successful in intimidating Lewis to do the right thing. Time would tell. He still felt uneasy about the overall predicament. How could he have been so naive? The efforts at Second Republic could lead to instant termination. All could be lost for a lousy $5,250.

When Adam returned to the office, he noticed that the conference room was now sparkling clean. Jim complained incessantly, but did good work. Maybe things were starting to return to normal. It was exceptionally quiet in the office and Adam realized that not one of his staff had arrived at work today. Even Snake, normally oblivious to the world, would take note of this egregious assault on bank etiquette. There would be more explaining to do before normality returned. Stan, he thought to himself, this better be good! I'm taking a lot of spears in the back for your little indiscretion. I certainly hope it's worth it!

Adam started checking his voice and e-mail messages and concluded there were now eight new volunteers for the "Trade Master" team. If someone from the group didn't show up soon with some answers, he just might start recruiting. As he began answering messages, Snake walked into the office with a stranger.

"Excuse me, Adam. I want you to meet Mr. Twilliger." Snake had apparently not lost his voice or forgotten where Adam's office was. The unexpected visit by Snake with a stranger in tow had occurred before. Adam knew from those historical events this was likely a large problem about to be dumped on him.

Adam approached the stranger warily and shook his hand. There was something about the man that instantly bothered Adam, but he couldn't quite place it. Twilliger's weak, fishlike handshake further concerned and alerted him.

"Mr. Twilliger is an inspector with the Occupational Safety and Health Administration," Snake announced proudly.

Adam was now on full alert. Snake continued: "OSHA has received a complaint that we are operating an unsafe workplace. Mr. Twilliger will conduct an inspection to determine if we are in compliance with all worker safety regulations. I am quite confident that we are in compliance. I am also confident that you can demonstrate our compliance with the law to Mr. Twilliger's satisfaction."

"You have to be shitting me!" Adam responded, truly bewildered. He noticed Snake wince at his impulsive use of vulgar language. Vulgarity was not in keeping with the image the bank wanted to project. Adam continued: "We don't operate any overhead cranes, blast furnaces or forklift trucks here. We are just an office and data center. Our last 'on the job' accident was a paper cut which occurred over three years ago."

"Nonetheless, Adam, Mr. Twilliger has a complaint to investigate. You will accompany the inspector wherever he wishes to go and extend to him all courtesies of the bank. You will provide to Mr. Twilliger all due respect as a representative of the Federal government." Snake delivered his speech with passion in a blatant attempt to curry favor with the inspector. Snake then turned and walked, in Adam's view slithered, out of the office leaving the two men alone.

"I suppose you can't tell me who filed the complaint or what the nature of it was?" Adam asked.

"You suppose correctly. That information is confidential," Twilliger responded haughtily.

"Where do you want to start?" Adam wearily asked. Adam surmised in general what might have led up to this inspection. The latest way to seek revenge on an employer for a real or imagined affront was to file a grievance with a government agency. Generally, the complaint was filed with EEOC. Less frequently, it was filed with OSHA. The truly creative and informed used the EPA for revenge. The agencies involved inevitably believed the complaint to be credible. The targeted companies were always viewed as the devil incarnate. The companies named in the complaint had the legal burden of proving their innocence. As a revenge tactic, filing a complaint was highly effective. It was interesting to speculate on who had initiated the original complaint. Snake had lost a secretary not too long ago under strange circumstances. The grapevine said that Snake had been hitting on her and she left in disgust when management ignored her complaints.

Twilliger never answered the question of where to begin. He just started walking through the offices and hallways. Adam followed a short distance behind. It's just like walking Scotty, he thought. Both Scotty and Mr. Twilliger sniffed at everything. Occasionally, Adam would have to produce a key to open a storage locker or closet. Thank God Jim had the conference room cleaned before this jerk showed up.

They continued their tour through four floors of offices and the main data center. Adam noticed a pattern emerging from Twilliger's sniffing. At every fire extinguisher, and there were many across four floors, the inspector produced a tape measure. Twilliger also seemed very interested in two maintenance closets. Adam could see no reason for such activity, as Twilliger never seemed interested in determining if the fire extinguishers were filled or inspected, which Adam knew was mandated by law. Throughout the tour, Twilliger never asked a single question.

Halfway through the walk Adam experienced a strong feeling of "déjà vu." When he first reported for duty on a new ship in the Navy, he and some other new shipmates were assigned the duty of preparing the ship's office for Captain's inspection. In an effort to create a good first impression, they worked all night to transform the office to a surgical room level of cleanliness. The next morning their Chief Petty Officer looked disappointed at their effort, which totally bewildered Adam and his shipmates. The reason for the Chief's reaction became obvious when the Captain arrived for the inspection. He could find nothing wrong! The more time the Captain spent looking for a mistake, the more agitated he became. Adam and his new shipmates were unaware that the Captain played golf after completing the inspection. Their hard work meant a delayed "tee" time. It was beyond the Captain's ability to say "Good job." He was compelled to find something wrong. My God, Adam thought, Frank made the identical comment about the IRS last night. A shiver went down Adam's spine. Twilliger's attitude could be the same as the Navy and IRS; after all, he is a representative of the federal government. Perhaps there was a defective gene in the DNA of all federal employees.

They concluded the inspection at about 3:15 in the afternoon and retired to the conference room that mere hours before had been used for productive work. "Well," Adam asked, "did we pass?"

Twilliger was busy writing something and brusquely responded: "Better than I thought, but there are a couple of minor things that I am compelled to cite."

Adam's previous assumption was confirmed. Twilliger had found something wrong. Finding something wrong was ridiculously easy for Twilliger. OSHA regulations exceed 4,300 pages at 60 lines to the page. Twilliger would justify his time at the bank and sanctify the complainant by issuing a violation report. Adam wondered what the minor things consisted of.

Twilliger finished writing, looked over the report, and handed it to Adam. "I'm officially notifying you that all of your fire extinguishers are mounted incorrectly. They are mounted 5/8 of an inch too high on the walls. Additionally, there are no MSDS sheets posted in the maintenance closets that describe the chemicals stored within. You have 30 days to reach compliance. I will return in 30 days to review the action you have taken. Failure to reach full compliance will initiate penalties from $7,000 to $70,000 and/or potential court action. Have a nice day!"

Adam felt like he had been kicked in the solar plexus. "Wait a minute, Mr. Twilliger! How is worker safety compromised if my extinguishers are mounted 5/8" too high on a wall?"

"Worker safety is not my concern! Compliance with the regulations is all that I'm interested in. You are not in compliance with 29 CFR 1910.132, Title 3, Section 6, Paragraph 14 as amended."

Adam recognized the same legal "mumbo-jumbo" language that he used with Phil earlier that morning. Nobody in his or her right mind would challenge or attempt to verify the legal specificity of that language. "All right," said Adam. "What's an MSDS sheet?"

Twilliger looked at Adam with unconcealed contempt. "That is a Material Safety Data Sheet. It must be posted in areas where there is chemical storage."

"The only chemicals I saw in the closets were floor wax and ammonia."

"That's correct."

Adam was clearly confused, and asked: "Both items are clearly labeled as to their contents. Are you saying I need to post an additional sheet of paper, hanging on the wall, stating there is floor wax and ammonia stored in here?"

"That's what the regulations require and you are clearly not in compliance." Twilliger answered smugly.

"If I post additional pieces of paper in the closets, wouldn't I be creating a fire hazard and be subject to fines from the City of Chicago fire inspectors?" Adam sincerely wanted to know.

Twilliger never answered the question. The inspector just leaned forward as if to grab his report from Adam, and asked: "Do you want me to add to my report that you, as the duly authorized representative of the bank, were uncooperative and intransigent?"

"All I'm doing is asking questions for clarification. Is that considered intransigent?"

"It can be so interpreted!" Twilliger smiled.

"Never mind." Adam knew when he was licked. "Have a nice day!" With no further acknowledgment, Twilliger left the office confident in his accomplishments. Twilliger knew that Federal inspectors last year raised $82,074,814 in fines or approximately $70,150 per inspector. He was always ranked in the top 10% of agents nationwide. He was certain that First Continental would help improve his ranking, although no fines had been levied yet. That would come on the next visit. Twilliger was confident that the bank would not be in compliance in 30 days.

Adam's first call upon Twilliger's departure was to the bank's legal department. Adam had never worked with anyone in that department in the past and hoped he never would. This was a radically different situation. He needed help desperately. After much effort, he finally talked to a real lawyer, who sounded and acted as if he could care less about Adam's problem.

"Just do what OSHA tells you to do and accomplish the action items within the time constraints so indicated. The legal department will spend no time or even open a file on a potential case where the bank's liability is less than $100,000. You should be able to meet the OSHA requirements listed in the report for less than that amount. If it leaks out that we were contesting this OSHA action, and it will, the *Tribune* will run a headline that states: "First Continental violates OSHA ruling!" That type of media attention is inconsistent with the image we at First Continental wish to convey."

Once again, it comes down to image, Adam thought. "One last question, counselor. Why isn't this action by OSHA considered extortion by you or anyone in the legal department?"

"We feel that technically there is a distinction between legally sanctioned, official extortion and your common, garden variety extortion perpetrated by civilians."

"I'm glad you can see that distinction. From where I'm sitting, none exists." Adam replied with the resignation that was fueled by extreme frustration. What was it that Frank said? "You don't have to do anything wrong to get into trouble. You can be like the average brontosaurus eating a tropical plant, when an asteroid hits the opposite side of the planet!" Adam felt a new empathy for the gentle giants of long ago.

Adam composed an e-mail message to Jim in maintenance requesting his assistance in meeting the OSHA mandate. How could Snake be so successful in dodging his responsibilities? Snake's boss must have assigned the OSHA inspector to him and he immediately dumped the problem on Adam. It was probably a part of Adam and Stan's punishment for attempting to create "Trade Master," and Snake dumped the assignment because he could. There was an outside chance that Snake dumped it because he caused the original complaint to be filed. That might be difficult to prove. To hell with everything—I'm going home, Adam thought. He was anxious to give Alice a report on the conversation with Lewis.

CHAPTER 6

The train ride to Union Station this Wednesday morning was accompanied by a late winter snow, which had not been predicted. Winter never retreated gracefully in Chicago. Forecasters had never learned that essential fact.

Alice was delighted with the news that there was a possible solution to the 1099 problem. She was proud of Adam for pushing their case with Lewis. Adam wasn't the only individual in the metropolitan area performing intimidation games on Tuesday. Mr. Twilliger appeared to be a master player. Adam wondered if the inspector rehearsed the move for the report, while saying: "Do you want me to add to my report that you were uncooperative, perhaps intransigent?" The SOB probably had a side job coaching rookie members of the Mafia on how to extort money. That thought raised an interesting question. Did the Mafia send 1099's to their independent consultants? It was amusing to speculate on the confusion that would result within the IRS if they did.

Adam wasn't surprised to see Stan waiting for him in his office. Stan rarely went too long without checking in.

"Good Morning, Adam." Stan seemed tired but cheerful, which Adam felt was a good sign.

"Good Morning. Have you recovered from your wild fling by now?"

"Just barely. We need now to talk."

"Indeed we do! Fire away."

Stan started the discussion with an apology. From his long tenure at the bank, he was aware that his late-night session would create a host of problems for his boss. Adam simply shrugged, as if it was not a big concern. Stan knew better, but respected Adam for trying to minimize the impact. Stan continued: "I'm also sorry for being AWOL yesterday. Some of my good friends in the neighborhood work at Board of Trade. I had to show them our new simulator to get from them their reaction."

"Stan, you know we're supposed to keep this project under wraps. How could you do that?"

"No problem, boss. I didn't tell them it was system. I told them it was a big new video game that I was fooling around with to develop."

Very clever, thought Adam, and somehow completely appropriate. "What happened, Stan?"

"They all wanted to buy it now!"

"I'm sorry, Stan. That's encouraging, but what I meant to ask was what happened Monday evening and Tuesday morning?"

Stan inserted a compact disc into Adam's PC. "Let me show for you," he said with a broad smile. "You can see how we added a pull-down menu for the calendar. It lists the date and time for all future official reports."

"What happens if a trader forgets to check the calendar?"

"We display a warning message 24 hours before the issuance of report. The message is bold red script and flashes like crazy. The only way to kill it is to tell to the system that you know about the report with your secret password."

"Very good, Stan! How did you phase in and incorporate the historical data we had collected?"

Stan started shaking his head. "That's where we ran into big headaches! At first nothing made sense!" Adam just sat quietly and let Stan roll on. "Let's take your example of the French grape harvest being a disaster. We all know what a big deal wine is to French government. You would think a bad harvest would have to hurt French economy big time. The historical data showed that a bad harvest made better the economy! It driving us nuts! We couldn't predict direction, much less degree, of market reaction to release date, and content of reports." Stan and the group were personally annoyed when the numbers didn't add up correctly. No wonder the team stayed up so late.

Stan continued with the account. "We digging deep into your grape harvest example and someone in group, I forgot who, found that French government spends big tax bucks to subsidize grape production. What's crazy is if you have a bad harvest, government shells out less money for the subsidies. Also, the huge pile of wine in the government's warehouses, from the past harvests of old, increases dramatically in value. It is now easy to see with the 20/20 hindsight, that if you applied common sense only to these official reports you will get burned big. 'Good' reports can be bad for the economy and 'Bad' reports could be good for the overall economy. Government messing in the market skews the interpretation and validity of the reports. It's all 'yellow snow' as you keep always saying. Everything today is so much interconnected it is very hard to forecast events."

"How stupid can the French be? What am I thinking? That's the same nation that gave us the 'Maginot Line' as I remember!"

"Remember that thinking, Adam, on your next trip to Wisconsin. The state is covered with the government warehouses filled with the surplus cheese paid for with your tax dollars! That is one of our big findings. All governments in world are messing with the market on all kinds of commodities. They seem to have their fingers on just about everything. The free market isn't much so free anymore. We used the brute force of statistical analysis and we were generally able to understand correctly impact of a given report."

"If I understand you correctly, Stan, when the Swiss government issues a report saying unemployment is down, you could predict that this would be 'good' or 'bad' for the future of the Swiss economy, based exclusively on historical interpretation."

"Exactly!"

"This is outstanding work, Stan!"

"There's a big deal more, Adam. Bear with me a little please." Stan took a deep breath and continued.

"Once we think we got a handle on direction of market reaction, we simply could not get good correlation on the degree or the rate of the change. In other way of saying, if we thought the market would go up 100 points, it would go up, but only by the 50 points. It was weird. There was a fairly consistent pattern of 95% accuracy on direction, but only 50% accuracy on the degree. We were about to give it up when someone, once again I forgot who, realized that late-night hours in Chicago are morning hours in Europe. So, we started calling our friends in the correspondent banks all over Europe. I'm sorry, Adam, we probably shoot the big hole in your telephone budget."

Adam winced. It was bad enough to take spears in the back from security and maintenance. Now he would take big spears from the pointy-headed bean counters in accounting that he loathed. "Why did you call our friends all over Europe?"

"Two big reasons. First, we asked from correspondent banks, that they push on our behalf to have their governments transmit their reports on-line to our data center. Time is really so important in the system. If we can show the entire official report on our system within minutes instead of days, we win big time!"

"Stan, you know we are not supposed to initiate requests like that without going through the bank's chain-of-command!"

"It seemed like really good idea early Tuesday morning. We didn't want to wait to fill in the stupid paperwork. We were on large roll!"

Adam's earlier concerns about the bean counters paled into insignificance. Snake and the entire upper echelon of FIRST CON's management were going to have a collective hissy fit. They would scream, like football purists do when the Bears score a winning touchdown against the Packers on a broken play. To Adam's way of thinking, the objective was to beat the accursed Packers. To the image crowd, the objective was to eliminate broken plays regardless of the results. The difference in these two perspectives was irreconcilable.

"What was the second reason for calling, Stan?"

Stan continued, apparently oblivious to Adam's increasing discomfort with his explanation of the all-nighter. "We could not understand our inability to forecast degree of the market reaction. From many places in Europe, we learned something huge. The big, serious players in the 'Euro' market don't trust on government reports. They know politicians produce the reports. Politicians or their buddies will 'spin' the reports to protect their political interests."

"It would seem the European mind-set isn't too different from ours," Adam contributed. "I have personally discounted the value of the unemployment statistics issued by the U.S. Labor department. The disillusionment began when I became aware of how they were using 'fudge factors' in determining their reported numbers."

"A very good story, Adam. Once the trust is gone, the game is lost. It turns out that the big guys, who are about 50% of the total market, spend their own money to gather the independent data. It's no wonder many call them the 'smart' money!"

"That would help explain the discrepancy in the degree of the market reaction, but how on earth can anyone solve the believability issue?" Adam was bewildered at what Stan had already discovered, but doubted that an independent source of data could be located.

That was the cue Stan was waiting for. He stood, smiled broadly, and announced: "The problem is most obvious, Adam. For the market to perform efficient it must need data; not just any kind of data, but stuff nobody can screw with. It must be an objective source of facts that everyone could share at any time."

"O.K. Stan, I understand that, but where did you find such a source? Was it in the pizza cartons or the donut box?"

"Perhaps was both, Adam! At some time during our discussions, someone, once again I forget who, brought up Landsat satellite images."

"Landsat satellite photo images from outer space? Are you crazy? What the hell were you guys drinking?"

"Listen closely please! We logged onto the Internet and found them just lying there, hundreds of photographs in amazing detail, for all Europe. Many were taken with the special infrared or ultra-violet cameras and the filters. Based on the energy frequency bounced back to the bird it is possible to determine crop health, acreage under cultivation and effects of weather. Basically, they contain all of things you need to figure out the crop yield. They are updated every 24 hours and they are impossible to be screwed up by the politicians.

"We still had a major problem. There is much more to economic measurement than just the forecasting the farmers. Imagine our joy and the surprise to find an answer residing on same satellite images. We knew that much of European economy is based on the sea borne trade. So, we looked for the merchant ships in select harbors, waiting patiently at anchor for the unloading berth to free up. It's like overflow parking for cars at Soldier Field. The more ships waiting at the anchor, the more and bigger the economic activity and the trade. When we totaled the ship count from just a couple of the key ports, we got the close correlation with the overall economic activity."

Adam sat stunned, completely shocked by Stan's report. He was convinced that he was privileged to manage the most creative, innovative, reckless team in the industry's history. This was a truly groundbreaking discovery. The economic benefit to First Continental from sales of this product would be astronomical. The bank's image and prestige boost would be beyond measure. Then Adam saw Jim from maintenance, pacing impatiently outside the office door.

"Don't go anywhere, Stan. Give me a minute to attend to something. I have many more questions."

"Take your time, Adam. I need the coffee!"

"Yes, Jim, how can I help you?" Adam asked as he met Jim just outside the office.

"It's your e-mail message, Adam. I don't have the staff to remount all the fire extinguishers. There must be over a 100 of them. This is a really big deal!" Re-calibrating his brain from the truly creative to the truly mundane was almost more than Adam could take. He had been swept up to the heavens with the potential inherent in Stan's discussion. Jim's comments brought Adam back to reality.

"According to legal, we have no choice but to get the job done, Jim. We have to find a way to get it done, and within 30 days!"

"I'll have to go outside and try to find an independent contractor to do the work, Adam. That means involving purchasing and obtaining at least three bids. You know the bank's procedures for this! I also have to check with the property owner and the architect. In all probability, I'll need to obtain a building permit from the City of Chicago." Adam took a deep breath and slowly said: "Do whatever it takes, Jim!"

"O.K., Adam, I just wanted to check in with you and make you aware of the complexity. I see you are talking with Stan. Are you giving him hell for trashing the conference room?"

"You guessed right, Jim."

"Good! I don't want to tell you how to manage, but if it were up to me I'd dock Stan's pay!"

With that comment Jim went to purchasing, which historically couldn't issue a Purchase Order in 30 days under any set of circumstances. The bank would need those 30 days to complete the construction work or be fined for being out of compliance.

"What was that all about, Adam?"

"Believe me, you don't want to know. However, before I forget, if anybody asks, I just chewed you out!" Stan nodded and winked. He fully understood the game.

"If I follow you correctly, Stan, you have integrated into our base system a new calendar of future events, namely the official report release schedule. Those governmental reports may soon be transmitted to us on-line. Furthermore, you have characterized the historical record in a new way that provides greater meaning. Lastly, through commercially available satellite technology, you are providing prospective users of our system with an independent, incorruptible source of data for their own analysis. That would allow them to determine how badly official reports have been 'spun.' Is there more, or did I miss anything?"

Stan was amazed how quickly Adam could grasp concepts. "One minor point. All aspects of the system you have talked about are in a simulator. I have provided to you with such a copy. I just stuck into your PC."

"What's the current status?"

"Counting ships in satellite photos is a pain in the butt! I have Liz working on a subroutine to have ships optically scanned and allow computer to count. First tests look pretty good, but it needs the more work. When we get that working very good, we will be able to test more and possibly better ocean ports, which should make our correlation the better. If we can get subroutine to work smooth, we could maybe to monitor the back and forth of rail cars from the sidings over all of the Europe. We think that will help make our numbers on economic activity better. The Swiss transmitted their first official reports to us yesterday. That information has been received and is now on your prototype simulator. We hope to get the first report from Germans tomorrow. If this gets rolling big, we may need more disc storage, modems, and bandwidth, but for the short time we are O.K."

"Stan, as a retired Navy man, I'm wondering what happens to your ship count when the Sixth Fleet pulls into port and you count men-of-war instead of merchant ships?"

"We checked that out. The exact same picture you talked about we saw in Naples. Please recall that our objective is to track economic activity. We could find no big change in our data. It would look that all the swabbies spend a lot of the money on booze when in port."

"Stan, I can personally verify your data!" They both enjoyed a laugh while Stan spent the next 10 minutes training Adam on the nuances of the new system. Before Stan left to check in with the team, Adam shook his hand and sincerely expressed personal thanks for a job well done.

Adam rejoiced in the moment. The detailed, color photos from space displayed on the computer monitor were breathtaking. Reluctantly, his mind returned to the OSHA problem. The more Adam thought about it, the more concerned he became. Having Jim go to purchasing was equivalent to sending the problem to a black hole in space. When the bids came in, they would all be characterized as "too high!" Vendors would be accused of "holding up the bank." Why that thought would be entertained and the question of the bank being "held up" by OSHA would be ignored, was beyond Adam's understanding.

Adam suddenly became aware of a change in the department's environment. My God, he thought; I've walked Scotty so much, I'm becoming a Golden Retriever. He noticed that the background noise was less intense. There was a hush, an almost calm before the storm kind of sensation. Adam went to the door of the office to ascertain what was going on. Then he saw the source of the disturbance. Two "suits" were wandering aimlessly through the work area. Adam recognized one of the two men from a photograph in the annual report. It was Mr. Winfred Palmer, Executive Vice President, and Head of Marketing. Adam had never met the VP or even attended a meeting with him. To the best of his knowledge, Mr. Palmer had never set foot on the 24th floor. It was possible that the elevator Mr. Palmer took to his personal office didn't even stop on the floor where Adam worked.

Mr. Palmer and his companion appeared to be lost. The stranger wore a European cut, lightweight suit. The visitor is either stupid, European or from the West Coast, Adam thought. Nobody wears a lightweight suit in Chicago at this time of year. Based on working with Snake over the years, Adam was having increasing difficulty distinguishing between the truly stupid and residents of California.

I wonder if the stranger is from Europe, Adam thought. What if it is someone that showed up because of Stan's phone calls and he is inquiring about "Trade Master?" Mr. Palmer was a logical first choice to talk to about the system; however, Palmer didn't know beans about it or who was working on it. The VP couldn't admit that to the stranger without appearing to be out of control. I'd better help the executive out before he digs too deep a hole in his image. How can I introduce myself to Mr. Palmer in front of the visitor? This could be tricky. The stranger probably thinks Palmer knows all about "Trade Master" and therefore knows me.

"Mr. Palmer, I'm Adam. You may not have recognized me as I recently removed my beard. Can I help you?"

"Ha, Adam, there you are. You look like a different man. No wonder I had difficulty locating you." Mr. Palmer shook Adam's hand warmly, as if it were a daily occurrence. Adam had guessed right about Palmer needing assistance to protect his well-crafted image. "I'd like you to meet an old friend, Mr. Renee Schugart of Swiss National, our correspondent bank in Switzerland."

Adam observed something in Renee's eyes that indicated that the Swiss banker hadn't bought the phony story about the beard for a second. He was just too polite or perhaps shrewd enough not to make it an issue. Adam extended his hand: "Mr. Schugart, my name is Adam Jones. It is a pleasure to meet you!" Adam received a warm greeting and a strong, confident handshake from Renee.

Mr. Palmer went on to explain that Renee had showed up unexpectedly this morning. He was requesting information on a new system under development. "It would appear, Adam, that Swiss National received some strange, unauthorized communications from some of your people late Monday night Chicago time. Renee is here to follow up on those calls. We can chat about those unauthorized communications at a later time. At the moment, I wish you to assist Renee with whatever information he requires. Mr. Schugart has received official clearance by the Board of Directors to be briefed on 'Trade Master.' Can you help Renee?"

"Of course, Mr. Palmer." Adam recognized that Palmer's question wasn't a routine request. He was also concerned about Palmer's reference to future conversations about unauthorized communications.

"Very good," Palmer acknowledged. "I'm afraid I must attend another meeting. It was good to see you again, Renee. I'm leaving you in the best of hands. Thank you for taking time to visit." Winfred was a man that always adhered to schedules. Renee's visit was an unauthorized modification to the VP's itinerary. Palmer had an uncontrollable urge to get back on schedule, even if it meant assigning a middle manager, he had never met to accommodate Renee's needs.

As Renee and Adam returned to Adam's office, Adam began to wonder: "How could Renee get here so fast?" The time lapse from the last phone conversation until now hardly allowed room for the actual flight. The European undoubtedly had to face bureaucratic delays in arranging for tickets. In Addition, he had to allow for the gain of eight hours in time zone differential. "Renee, it looks like you don't believe in letting the grass grow!" Adam stated, truly amazed.

"I'm sorry, Adam, I do not understand your comment." "Well, I just found out that Renee might speak English, but he is not familiar with American idioms. Fair enough, at least he asks a question when he doesn't understand. How refreshing!"

"I used a bad illustration, Renee. I meant to comment on the speed of your decision to come all the way to Chicago."

"Actually, Adam, I wish I had spent 10 extra minutes for research before my departure. If I had, I believe I'd be a great deal warmer now." Renee was apparently self-conscious of his lightweight suit. Adam had to laugh. He was beginning to really like Renee. Self-deprecating humor, asking questions, and admitting you don't know something were character traits that were seldom observed at First Continental.

"Don't feel bad, Renee. If I knew that I was going to meet a Swiss banker today, I would have obtained one of your famous secret accounts. However, I must admit that I don't have one. It makes me feel naked and unqualified to talk to you without one." Adam made the statement to put Renee at ease, but it was a statement based on fact. By the time both men were seated in Adam's office, they had become quite comfortable with each other.

Renee started the discussion by explaining Swiss National's extreme interest in "Euro" trading. In particular, they were interested in "Euro" trading by American multi-nationals. When Stan and his people started calling early Tuesday morning, his time, they began to suspect that FIRST CON might have an answer. Renee was immediately dispatched to Chicago to check it out.

Adam picked up the phone and reached Stan. "Stan, could you please return to my office? I have someone here that you should meet in person, although you may have talked to him earlier this week on the phone." Within minutes Stan arrived, formal introductions were made, and the demonstration of "Trade Master" began.

Adam realized that he would gain two additional benefits by sharing the spotlight with Stan. First, he would learn more about the actual system through direct observation of Stan's demonstration. Secondly, he would be better able to observe Renee's reaction. Frank once advised Adam to concentrate on the "eyes" of a prospect. If someone were truly excited, the eyes gave it away by becoming wider. It was an involuntary human reaction. Nobody could fake it.

Renee played the role of a reluctant and skeptical buyer perfectly. He raised numerous questions, objections, and problems. Most of the issues, but not all, Stan could easily rebut. To an untrained observer it looked like a draw, however, Renee's eyes throughout the presentation had grown as wide as the "*Good-Year*" blimp. Adam was now confident there was something of great value in this system. He would have to thank Frank for his unwitting sales consulting.

By late afternoon, over two hours into the presentation, Renee finally gave up. "Gentlemen, this is a revolutionary breakthrough. It was certainly worth a Trans-Atlantic flight, which I must admit I was reluctant to take at first. Please excuse me for a minute." From inside his suit coat Renee produced a cell phone and hit a speed dial number. Renee talked excitedly for 15 minutes in French while Adam and Stan sat impassively. He only paused once in the conversation to ask Adam for his personal e-mail address.

Renee finally finished the conversation. He looked at both men from First Continental. "Gentlemen, thank you for allowing me time to place my call and for showing me a truly innovative system. I will be departing from O'Hare late tonight for what you call a red-eye back to Europe. I want to keep this dialog moving, so I instructed my bank with this call to forward a letter to your management. The correspondence should arrive by this time tomorrow. The letter will strongly request that Swiss National be granted first right of refusal to purchase and install 'Trade Master.' Additionally, if it is determined that additional capital or manpower is required to complete and test the product, we would like the opportunity to invest in that development."

Adam and Stan were dumbfounded. They had anticipated that their system would sell, but they had no idea that a commercial firm could move, make decisions, and commit as quickly as Swiss National had just illustrated. If Adam only had access to their Purchasing Department, he could solve the OSHA debacle overnight. Stan left the group momentarily to spread the word within the team that they had secured their first sale, and it was a coveted international account. It was a most fitting reward for their hard work and creativity. A "sale" is the ultimate acknowledgment of good work.

"Adam," Renee continued, "You will no longer need to feel embarrassed when talking to a Swiss banker. I've taken the liberty of obtaining a secret numbered Swiss account for you at Swiss National. All fees have been waived as a professional courtesy. You will receive activation information and instructions on establishing a password by e-mail no later than Friday. What you do with that account is, of course, your concern. I suggest you deposit the large bonus from First Continental that you will undoubtedly receive for 'Trade Master' in that account. We pay a better interest rate than First Continental does. However, I will deny having ever said that!"

When Stan returned, he found both men enjoying a hearty laugh and a slightly conspiratorial look. "One last question." Renee asked. "Do you guys ever eat? I'm famished!"

When the two Chicago residents determined that Renee had never been to their fair city before, the answer became obvious. "Pizza? Yes, I had some in Italy!"

"Doesn't compare!" both men said simultaneously.

Adam then realized that he had committed to his son that he would attend a Little League organizing meeting that evening without fail. One such meeting had been missed last year for business purposes, and he had to live with a sulking boy for weeks. Adam wanted desperately to continue the meeting with Renee; however, he wouldn't be able to explain the situation to David or Alice.

With great reluctance, he left Renee in Stan's creative hands. Stan's mission was to acquaint Renee with deep-dish pizza and show the Swiss executive as much of the city as possible before his departure from O'Hare. It would be an evening that Renee would never forget.

CHAPTER 7

As the train departed Franklin Park and began its high-speed run into town, Adam fell into the trance of deep thought. Many things had occurred this week to fuel his reflective state of mind. The amended 1099 from Second Republic had not yet arrived, but it wasn't expected before Friday. Once it did, all of the information necessary to file his taxes would be available; hopefully, before the April 15 deadline. The OSHA problem was still a bother. Adam also had to thank members of the project team for their effort. It was interesting to note that in Stan's verbal report he could not recall who had specifically contributed any one idea. How typical of a brainstorming session, Adam thought. If the FBI administered truth serum to every member present, each would have provided the same response as rendered by Stan. Nobody in the crew knew or cared about authorship during those sessions. The ideas just rapidly evolve. Adam would have given anything to be an active participant of the now infamous Monday/Tuesday bell ringer.

It became obvious to Adam, during Stan's presentation to Renee, that the team had achieved a major philosophical objective in the design of "Trade Master." Many people who use systems are unaware of any philosophical foundation of the systems they are using. The foundations are subtle, but present nonetheless. Throughout the history of information processing, the goal of virtually all system designers was "control." The designers assumed there was but "one way" to accomplish any given task. Thus, they designed a system to control, force and mandate users to follow the "one best way." It was comparable to driving a herd of cattle through a narrow chute.

The designers utilized the control approach because it reflected the prevailing management philosophy. Since management funded and approved system development, it was natural for them to approve only those systems that strengthened and supported their worldview. That worldview was widespread in the private sector. It was the only philosophy permitted to exist within governmental agencies. Scholars believed that this philosophy first originated with the Roman Legions. Adam felt it probably could be traced back to the Pharaohs of ancient Egypt or beyond.

Adam and Stan rejected that ancient philosophical concept at the onset of the project. They did so out of respect for the intelligence and creative approach of market traders everywhere. They believed in the old adage, "In the Land of the Blind a one-eyed man is King." They were resolved to create a system that liberated and enabled traders to choose their own course. Scanning ship hulls was a neat feature within "Trade Master," however; the most substantive advantage was that the system didn't mandate a specific course of action. "Trade Master's" design philosophy permitted and even encouraged traders to think and act independently.

The disconcerting irony of all of this was that Renee, from a bank thousands of miles away, understood and applauded the product and its inherent philosophy. Adam's own boss and members of FIRST CON's management were either unaware or hostile to the project. A phrase started to emerge from the back recesses of his memory. "A prophet is without honor in his own land" or something like that. Where had he heard or read that? Was it in a sermon, the newspaper, or a bumper sticker? Adam wasn't sure. It probably was in church, but it could have been on a bumper sticker, as they were getting better. He saw one last evening that stated, "Don't Steal, the government doesn't like competition." Normally, he would have found that amusing; however this week he had to work on taxes and deal with OSHA.

Stan met Adam at the coffeepot this morning. "I trust there were no accidents or arrests last night, Stan?"

"Oh no, Adam. We had the greatest of times." Stan went on to explain how he obtained a set of heavy coveralls for Renee. This allowed for a quick, fairly encompassing tour of Chicago without literally freezing the Swiss banker. It turned out that Renee had never ridden on the back of a Harley. They had some excellent pizza at Malnati's, covered downtown, and zipped out to the Alder Planetarium to view the skyline before heading to O'Hare. Adam slowly closed his eyes. He could picture Renee clutching to Stan while heading northbound on

Lake Shore Drive. Thank God Renee had phoned Swiss National and placed the order prior to his adventure.

"Just out of curiosity, Stan, what, if anything, did Renee like best?"

"He loved almost everything, Adam!" Stan looked somewhat offended. He thought that riding a Harley in the winter was as natural as brushing your teeth. "Now that you question, I was surprised at his amazement about Lake Michigan. Like many Europeans, Renee had no clue for the bigness of Lake Michigan. He kept insisting it was an ocean. In addition, he could hardly believe that the city had reversed the flow of the Chicago River. I showed to him the locks between the lake and river. The lake is now almost running six feet bigger than the river. The whole lakefront scene, Grant Park, McCormick Place as well as the locks just blew the guy away. We almost missed the flight. I was proud to be doing 75 mph outbound on the Kennedy expressway to the airport." Adam shuddered and walked to the office wondering if he would ever hear from Renee again.

Adam began the day by checking his voice mail. There was a strange message with no name mentioned. He couldn't mistake the urbane, sophisticated voice of Mr. Alister Lewis, so there was no need to leave the name. The message said: "Your package is being sent today by express mail. Please do not schedule another demonstration!" What the hell was Lewis talking about? Adam wasn't sure, but the news about the package being shipped relieved him greatly.

He had to do something about the OSHA problem. It would be nice to forget about it, but that was irresponsible. Adam decided to go down to the 13th floor and plead the case in person to purchasing rather than rely on e-mail or an in-house memo.

When Adam arrived on 13, he found Joe Weber, the Head of Purchasing, screaming obscenities into the speakerphone. Adam secretly hoped that Joe was talking with Snake, but realized it had to be a vendor. Joe hung up the phone and with no discernible difference in tone or attitude asked: "Who the hell are you? What the hell do you want? Why would you think I give a shit?"

Adam had never worked with Joe before on a specific project. He had the same corporate acquaintance level of relationship with Joe as he had with Phil in security. Adam identified himself and started to explain why expedited service was required to a manager whose face reflected many battles.

"Golly Gee, Adam, I'm so glad you're here! I was just thinking that it's been a whole hour since some overpaid Harvard trained manager requested that we drop everything and save their lousy bacon! I was starting to think the bank failed and no one bothered to tell us! We are generally the last to know anything."

Adam could see the frustration in Joe. He realized for the first time that purchasing was at the end of a bullwhip. Management moved the thick end one-inch and Joe and his people had to move three yards. "Joe, I'm sorry. You're right. I don't believe there is anything you can do. Please excuse my interruption. I'll see you around."

"Oh, sit down, Adam! If you had the guts to come and see me, the least I can do is listen." Joe snarled. "There is a wide assortment of crying towels stacked in the corner. Select the one you want and fire away."

Adam went on to explain the OSHA inspection and Legal's advice. Joe's invitation to use the crying towels was ignored; he simply summarized the dilemma.

"Do you have any recommendations for a prospective vendor to do the work?" Joe asked.

"I don't have a clue as to who could do this. I was hoping you would."

"Well, Adam, you just proved to me that you're an honest man. It's amazing how many 'Drop everything and do this' requests we get that are accompanied with a vendor recommendation. By sheer coincidence, the vendor will turn out to be some shirt-tail relative of the requisitioner." Adam sat bewildered as Joe continued. "Actually, in this instance, it would be helpful to have a vendor lined up, especially if it was a women owned or minority enterprise. That I could push through, at any cost to the bank, in a heartbeat!"

"I'm sorry, Joe, you lost me on that one."

"Don't feel bad. Everybody is lost on that one. The City of Chicago recently set a target to award 20% of their purchase orders to minorities and 10% to women owned and directed firms. First Continental, in an attempt to enhance their image and avoid being called 'racist', increased it to 25% and 15% respectively. Of course, nobody checked with us in purchasing. I have no personal problem with the goal, but I just can't find minority vendors for the commodities we buy. I'm tired of getting body slammed as a 'bigot' at every staff meeting for something I can't control. It's going to be slow going on your request unless we strike gold by finding a minority supplier."

"Joe, let me see if I understand this. I may be in serious risk of being in non-compliance with an OSHA violation report. I can't readily resolve the situation because of an indirect EEOC requirement initiated in part by the City of Chicago."

"For a FIRST CON manager you catch on pretty quick!" Joe, despite himself, smiled.

"Which agency has preference, or takes priority?"

"That's easy—they both are number one!" Joe smirked. "I'm serious, Adam. Every individual I've worked with over the years from any agency has a religious zeal that would make an actual cleric turn green with envy. They honestly think they are God or at the least an archangel. Any delay in meeting their demands is heresy, even if the delay turns out to be caused by another agency. Thus the more I think about it, the more I feel compelled to help you. I don't doubt that some empty suit dumped this hot potato in your lap and you had nothing to do with the original installation. I appreciate the fact that you didn't whine about it. You are about to receive your MBA from the school of hard knocks, Adam. No guarantees, but I'll see what I can do."

"Thanks, Joe. That's all I can ask. I appreciate the insights rendered about minority vendors. I had no idea." With that comment, Adam left to return to the 24th floor with a new sense of appreciation for how difficult it is to get anything done in a large organization. He could visualize the headline in the *Chicago Tribune*: "First Continental Abandons Worker Safety to Enhance Diversity Image!"

Adam noticed another stranger waiting impatiently for his return to the office. Now what? He thought.

"Hi, you must be Adam. My name is Bob Nelson. I work in marketing and I desperately need to speak to you."

"What's on your mind, Bob?" Adam wondered what this was about. He rarely talked with marketing and now it was twice in the last two days. Nelson looked like marketing—well attired and groomed. He was also young and appeared gracious and energetic.

"Well, Adam, I need your help. The bank has assigned me to start a business relationship with Universal Paper in Appleton, Wisconsin. Marketing chose them as one of the targeted prospects for 'Trade Master'." Adam just shook his head. Everybody in the bank, other than Snake, must know about 'Trade Master.' "Universal has been very skeptical about our capabilities in this application area. I have kept them on a string for some time because I didn't have anything to show them. Universal finally told me to 'put up or shut up.' I need you to visit with them and illustrate our knowledge, or we could lose the account forever."

"Whoa, Bob! What makes you think I have anything to show them?"

"Come on, Adam, the grapevine is buzzing about you and Stan knocking the socks off Swiss National this week!"

"Never believe the grapevine, Bob!"

"I will always believe the grapevine if it's the last, best chance I have to save an account!" Adam was starting to like Bob. The kid's got guts.

"O.K. Assuming we could show them something, why me? The last time I looked, sales and marketing were not mentioned in my job description. Furthermore, as a devoted Bears fan, I have developed an extreme disdain for "cheese-heads!" Bob reacted strangely to Adam's comment. The salesman squirmed in his chair and looked very uncomfortable.

"They asked for you by name, Adam."

"Quit the BS, Bob! Nobody at Universal knows me by name or reputation, and I don't know a soul up there either!"

"They do now." Bob answered sheepishly. He then got up and closed the door to Adam's office. "Bear with me, Adam. I wasn't supposed to say anything about this. Universal got your name by reviewing some old documentation on your security system. We supplied them with unedited system documentation by mistake when we installed your security system last year."

"What? They got my name from the security system documentation! How in the hell did they get the system in the first place?" Adam was becoming furious.

"We sold it to them 18 months ago. You should be proud of that system—they love it. So do all the other accounts!" Adam was literally without words. Bob continued. "We started using your security system as a crowbar to get into accounts who in the past wouldn't even return telephone calls to us. In some instances, we installed it for free in return for investment banking transactions or opening new accounts. When it was obvious that it was a hot product, we demanded dollars plus transactions. Our highest billing to date is $50,000 for the product. In total, we have secured 28 new accounts and rewarded 18 existing customers with the system. On behalf of the sales department, I would like to thank you and tell you how much we look forward to the release of 'Trade Master' as a new product."

The same cold voice that Adam first heard while talking with Alister Lewis at Second Republic returned. "Why was I kept in the dark on this?"

"Your boss did not want this mentioned to you. He stated that he did not want any interruptions on the 'Trade Master' effort. Potentially that could happen if you became involved with the selling of the security system."

"Did you buy that reasoning, Bob?"

"Officially, I had to accept it. Personally, I think your boss didn't want to face any requests for raises or bonuses. Now you see why I'm in a pickle, Adam. Universal Paper has always felt we couldn't do anything because we are from Chicago and thus Bear fans. The security system really altered their perspective. When they found out that you personally were the common link between the two, they demanded a demo or presentation from you and nobody else but you. I couldn't figure out how to get your personal involvement without leaking information on previous sales. On the one hand, I lose an account. On the other, I could lose my job."

Adam felt that he could literally kill Snake. He felt empathy for Bob, who was just trying to do his job. Maybe the best idea would be to cool down for a second and think. Bob's information could be very helpful when he was confronted with the budget overruns on "Trade Master." Perhaps it's time to play politics with the politicians, Adam thought.

"O.K., Bob, I won't say anything about the security system. You are also in luck. As of yesterday, I have something to show Universal that just might impress the dull, lifeless mind of a Packer fan. That's assuming they are bright enough to get it."

"Just because they are Packer fans doesn't mean they are totally stupid." Bob replied.

"One condition, Bob. I'm not a very good corporate politician; however, I am good enough to recognize that Snake must be invited to attend this demonstration."

"No way, Adam! I don't want that empty suit within miles of an actual customer," Bob pleaded.

"If he doesn't go, I don't go. That's final!"

"O.K. You win."

"When do we go on this trip, Bob?"

"It's set up for tomorrow at their corporate headquarters. Be at Meigs Field by 10:00 AM. Universal is sending their corporate jet for us. You should be back to Meigs by about 5:00."

"You don't believe in letting the grass grow, do you Bob?"

"No sir, and I promise we will have Mr. Post aboard, but I have a bad feeling about inviting him."

By the time they had concluded, Adam had just enough time to catch the 5:26.

CHAPTER 8

Once again, the familiar routine engulfed Adam as the METRA train proceeded east from Franklin Park. As always, there were a number of issues to rehash. Alice was pleased to hear of Lewis's intention to amend the 1099 and deliver a much-needed check. That meant Adam would have everything needed to spend the weekend preparing taxes. Alice, for a number of years, had bundled up the kids and gone to her mother's during the tax preparation ritual. Her stated reason was to ensure that Adam would have no interruptions. The real reason had more to do with Adam's inevitable loss of control as he totaled various state and federal levies. Involuntarily, vulgar phrases uttered at extreme volume frequently accompanied the preparation process. Although Alice supported "learning experiences" for the boys, she felt they should be sheltered from this particular remnant of Adam's Navy life.

The enhanced vocabulary inevitably surfaced during fruitless searches for tax deductions. With 2.8 million words in 9722 sections of federal tax code, there were ample opportunities for emotional outbursts. Adam often wondered how the tax code could have become so convoluted and complicated. Moreover, why did the citizens of a free society put up with it, he pondered? This was a mystery he was sure couldn't be solved within his lifetime.

Renee had been faithful to his promise. The provisional purchase order from Swiss National arrived yesterday. Adam was somewhat perplexed that no one at FIRST CON had asked him to explain it. He knew the inquisition was inevitable. Going to Wisconsin to visit Universal Paper today was probably a good thing. If he could obtain a purchase order from a key domestic account to add to the international order, he would be armed to take on the bean counters when the "Trade Master" cost issues came up.

Adam stopped at the office long enough to secure the compact disc that contained the version of "Trade Master" with Stan's simulator. For no reason in particular, he printed a copy of the Swiss National purchase order and put it in the brief case. Stan was notified of his travels by e-mail. Noticing no urgent e-mail or voice messages, Adam left the bank and secured a cab for the short ride to Meigs.

Adam arrived at Meigs at 9:00 AM, a full hour before flight time. A vending machine provided a comforting cup of coffee as he looked to the west from the front door of the terminal. It was a cool, bright, beautiful, sunny day in early April, perfect for flying. The brilliant sunlight made the lake sparkle, providing the first clue that spring would finally triumph over winter.

This would be Adam's first flight from Meigs. All of his previous flights were via commercial airlines from either Midway or O'Hare. From Meigs you could see McCormick Place to the south, Navy Pier to the north and the entire skyline of Chicago to the west. All the points of interest along the lake seemed connected by Lake Shore Drive. The Drive, although not classified as an interstate, carried the bulk of north-south traffic along the western edge of Lake Michigan.

As Adam toured the tiny airport terminal, he found a commemorative inscription proclaiming that Meigs Field was constructed on reclaimed land using debris from the great Chicago fire. Its official name was Northerly Island. The 1909 Plan of Chicago by Daniel J. Burnham called for four man-made islands to be placed along the lakeshore. Only Northerly was built.

Continuing his tour, Adam discovered more interesting tidbits displayed on plaques and colorful posters. Although the airport featured a runway that was only 3900 feet in length, it remained very popular with general aviation. The proximity to Chicago's business district was of vast importance. It also provided an excellent location to view the city's numerous skyscrapers, which rose up behind Grant Park like the Rocky Mountains. Natives of Chicago like Adam tended to forget how truly beautiful the city could be. It frequently took an out-of-town visitor like Renee to reacquaint them with the city they all too often took for granted.

Completing his tour, Adam returned to the lobby to find a man in a pilot's uniform with a nametag from Universal Paper. The pilot notified Adam that they would be flying a Cessna Citation Bravo jet today. Depending on traffic enroute, the entire journey to Appleton would take less than 45 minutes.

Bob Nelson arrived at Meigs with Snake in tow. "Nuts!" Adam thought. Although he insisted that Nelson invite Snake, there was always the hope that he would decline.

Two executives from Universal Paper, who were returning home after conducting business meetings in Chicago, joined the three First Continental men. They quickly boarded the fueled and inspected plane. After receiving clearance from the tower, they rolled from the parking ramp to the taxiway.

Adam secured a seat on the port side of the aircraft. Flying in a private jet was a new experience and he was surprised at the breathtaking visibility from the large window. Snake took the starboard seat adjacent to him. There was barely enough room to walk between the seats within the narrow cabin. As they rolled south down the taxiway, Adam had a clear view of the lake to the east. A water in-take crib about three miles out in the lake was easily visible. The Michigan shore with its magnificent sand dunes was also due East. It could not be seen as it lay over the horizon some 50 miles away. "It is an enormous lake," Adam reminded himself. At the base of the taxiway, the pilot turned left and sat at the absolute end of the runway awaiting clearance for a take-off directly north. Adam could clearly see the city to the west. Then he observed a fairly unusual sight. A large merchant vessel was departing the lock that provided passage from the lake to the Chicago River. It appeared to be carrying large rolls of newsprint, probably for the *Chicago Sun-Times*, whose production facilities abutted the river. In route to the newspaper's production facility, the ship would pass under the Lake Shore Drive Bridge.

Adam began to recall some of Chicago's unique history. Chicago once served as a major seaport. Although inland shipping on the Great Lakes had diminished in recent years, it still had an important part to play in the economy of the Midwest. For that reason, all of the bridges constructed over the river, a total of 55, were cantilevered. They were designed to swing up and allow large ships to pass beneath the bridge. Adam could clearly see the great bridge on Lake Shore Drive opening. The traffic on the thoroughfare came to a complete halt in both directions. Thank God we got here early, Adam thought.

A great surge of power pushed the passengers back into their seats as the plane roared north on the short runway screaming to lift off. The Cessna was an excellent choice for Meigs as it rotated and was airborne with room to spare. The pilot banked left and flew directly over the open bridge. Adam could see traffic backed up for miles to the north and south. The plane continued northwest as it gained altitude. Adam could now see heavy traffic on the Kennedy and Dan Ryan expressways as well. Phil, from security, was right when he mentioned that nobody would attempt to knock off a Brinks truck in the city proper. There was no easy, fast, police-free route out of town.

The plane turned due north and passed over rich farmland and the fast growing suburbs to the north of the city. Shortly thereafter, the pilot announced that they had crossed the "Cheddar Curtain" and were over Wisconsin. Adam started visually searching the land below for large warehouses stuffed with surplus cheese, purchased with his tax dollars.

In short order, the plane began its descent into Appleton. Adam observed a very large body of water emerge from below the wing. Snake, who up to now had said nothing, asked Adam if they were now flying over Lake Michigan. "No," said Adam, "I believe that is Lake Winnebago." Winnebago at 28 miles in length and 10.5 miles wide is a large lake; however, it is small compared to Lake Michigan at 300 miles in length and 60 miles in width.

"Does it freeze in the winter?" Snake inquired. Adam still had difficulty grasping Snake's total lack of comprehension of geography. He wanted to scream, "You know how cold it gets in Chicago—and we've been flying north at a high rate of speed for some time!" Nevertheless, Adam resisted the temptation. He simply said: "Yes, it surely does."

Snake still looked confused and Adam could see the manager was wrestling with the concept of a body of water that large freezing. Adam decided to help him out. "As a matter of fact, Lake Winnebago is renowned for its ice fishing." Snake was now truly bewildered. He looked panicky and Adam could almost see a question forming in Snake's tiny brain. My God, Adam thought, he's going to ask me what the fishermen do with the ice once they catch it. Fortunately, the question was never posed, as the pilot announced it was time to fasten seat belts.

Upon arrival at Appleton, they were met by a Universal Paper limo for the short ride to the plant. The production facility also housed their International Headquarters. Adam started to think that the "sales game" wasn't a bad deal. He could really warm up to private jets and limos. That thought was amplified as the group was ushered into a private room adjacent to the executive dining room. Bob Nelson formally introduced Adam and Snake to a half dozen Universal executives, including the Chief Financial Officer and the Head of International Operations. Nelson has done a hell of a job setting this up, thought Adam. The right people for the presentation were in attendance.

After an outstanding gourmet lunch, the entire group sat around a large table enjoying a cup of Kona coffee. Adam was now convinced that he had missed his calling. A bond was starting to form with the Universal guys despite the fact that they had to be Packer fans. He silently wondered if they wore yellow and green underwear beneath their expensive suits.

Adam was struck by the irony that he was enjoying lunch in an executive dining room of a prospective customer. A middle manager wouldn't be allowed to use the executive dining room at FIRST CON. He was meeting with "brass" at a level never accorded any project manager at First Continental.

Bob Nelson had briefed Adam and Snake concerning this portion of the sales call. They were not yet in "official presentation mode." Having just enjoyed a great meal, they would be relaxed and mellow. Their guard would be down. This is the exact time, Nelson warned, that the Universal team would probe, using small talk, to determine the type of people at First Continental and the depth of their character.

"Whatever you do, DON'T talk football, politics, religion or sex!" Nelson was emphatic. This bothered Snake enormously because on the few occasions where he did talk, those were the only subjects he was comfortable with. "Then act like a deaf/mute!" Nelson strongly advised him.

Snake never could take direction, especially from an employee who he considered inferior in rank. In an attempt to be relevant, he said to the group: "Adam advised me that Lake Winnebago freezes in winter and people up here like to ice fish." The Universal crowd looked at Snake with disbelief. It was as though he said: "I've observed that most wheels are round." Adam inwardly groaned: "He didn't believe me. Snake won't turn loose of it! We're in trouble!" The Chief Financial Officer of Universal was the first to recover. In an act of civility rarely observed with "Cheese-heads" the CFO stated: "Adam was correct, Mr. Post. It's the principal way to fish for Sturgeon, which inhabits Lake Winnebago in goodly numbers. Actually, you don't fish for sturgeon in a conventional sense; you must spear them. If you spear one less than six feet in length, the state DNR will fine you."

"Are you telling me there are fish in that lake that are greater than six feet in length?" Snake asked incredulously. When everyone simply nodded yes, Snake looked totally bewildered. Nelson was getting so concerned that his coffee cup was rattling. "That's right!" Snake exclaimed. "All large fish come from salt water!"

That did it! No Midwesterner wants to be connected with salt water or the people who live near it. They take pride in being hundreds of miles from salt water. Snake had just branded himself as a blithering idiot. There was undisguised contempt showing from every one of the Universal executives. Nelson, to his credit, took immediate action. Seeing this great sales prospect evaporating before his eyes, he whispered something into the ear of the CFO. Snake was as oblivious to the reaction as most things in life. Snake sat with his coffee and beamed, proud that he had not talked about anything from Nelson's forbidden list of topics.

"Mr. Post, Bob Nelson informs me that you are a native of Southern California and may not have had an opportunity to visit our plant. Would you like a tour?"

"That would be great!"

In short order, a beautiful young secretary arrived to give Snake a guided tour of the plant. She was stunning with long blond hair, blue eyes and a big bosom, confirming her Scandinavian heritage. Snake was instantly smitten. He left the lunch crowd, following her closely. Snake would have followed her anywhere, including into Lake Winnebago. These guys at Universal are efficient, thought Adam.

"O.K., Adam, let's get down to business!" The CFO led the group to a conference room with a PC and large monitor. Adam felt that Snake might have inadvertently helped him. All citizens of Wisconsin disdain anything or anyone from Illinois in general. They specifically disliked Chicagoans. It was more than the football rivalry. It was based on the fact that most of the best shorelines of their many lakes were owned by the "flat-landers" from Chicago. They also resented the reach of Chicago-based media, which minimized locally produced output. The divisions were real and deep, regardless of the justifications.

Despite the real divisions, there was one great unifying force between natives of adjoining states in the middle of the country. The "great equalizer" wasn't the famous "Colt 45," it was the Midwestern Winter. The winter showed no respect for status or station in life. Your ears could be frost bitten regardless of the educational degrees or assets you had accumulated. The ugly sounds of an engine trying to start in 20 below temperatures were the same for a Chevy or a Cadillac. The winter scraped layers of artificiality and phoniness off a person easier and faster than you could scrape off old wallpaper. You soon learn to set priorities in life when your physical safety is threatened two or three times a season. The single greatest threat to physical security in Snake's life occurred when he ran out of avocado dip at a party he once hosted in LA.

The Universal executives knew this intuitively. Perhaps Adam was a Bear fan from Illinois, but he also endured the winter. That fact trumped everything else. Adam was a kindred spirit despite the surface differences. Additionally, it was obvious that Adam was working under duress, with an "empty suit" from California as his boss. All of the Universal executives had experienced that predicament at one point in their careers, but the "empty suits" rarely lasted long in a manufacturing environment.

Once the group assembled, Adam sensed he was among friends. Adam began by simply citing the design philosophy used to develop "Trade Master." He also stressed the simulator approach to training and some of the facts about the official reports uncovered by the project team. Then Adam booted up the system, invited the members to try it, and got out of the way. Adam walked to the back of the room as Nelson gave him a "thumb's up" signal.

For over an hour, the group took turns working with the system. It reminded Adam of his kids on Christmas morning. The reaction in total was virtually identical to Renee's. Finally, the CFO said: "This looks very good, Adam. In particular, I want to say how pleased I am with the emphasis on training. We know from experience the importance of confronting people's fears. Have you shown the system to anyone else?"

"Only one, sir. Actually, we haven't started marketing the system. We are still smoothing some rough edges and completing documentation. In something of an accident, the system was shown to Swiss National."

"What was their reaction?"

"Rather than try to describe it, let me show you what they wrote." Adam took the copy of the Swiss P.O. and gave it to the CFO.

"This document is from Renee Schugart! I have met him. Renee is a good man."

After reading the document, the CFO stated: "It looks like our positive reaction to your system was more than endorsed and verified by Renee. If I may keep this copy, I would like Universal to respond in a very similar manner, hopefully by Monday. Would that be satisfactory to you, Adam?"

"It would indeed, Sir. Here is my card with my current e-mail address."

Everybody was standing and shaking hands when Snake returned from the tour. "What happened?" He asked. Nelson grabbed Snake by the arm and said: "Everything is just fine, Mr. Post. We must hurry to catch our plane!"

The return to the Appleton airport and then on to Meigs was uneventful. The notable exception was Bob Nelson, who was almost doubled over in glee. Bob was counting commission dollars in his head and complementing Adam repeatedly on Adam's natural sales aptitude. Neither Bob nor Adam saw Snake wince with every compliment.

Adam chose not to go the office when they arrived at Meigs. It was 5:15. He went directly to Union Station and caught the 6:08. He was dead tired. It had been one hell of a week.

After the train arrived in Bartlett, he remembered that this was his designated bachelor weekend. This realization mandated a stop at the store to pick up some frozen entrees. Since the bachelor status was for tax preparation, a bottle of gin was added to his grocery cart.

Alice greeted Adam with a big smile and hug. "It's here!" she said, jumping up and down with excitement. Adam could see the "Priority" mail envelope on the dining room table. Inside was the amended 1099 and a check for $6,000 drawn on Lewis's personal account.

Alice had prepared his dinner, packed the kids gear, and was ready to go.

"How was your trip to Wisconsin?" she inquired.

"It went very well, dear. I think we got the order."

"That's great! Does that mean a big bonus or a raise?"

"I sincerely hope so, but you never know."

"Well I should think you would! You've earned it!"

"I don't know if that makes any difference anymore. I don't think creating something tangible means much in today's culture. I don't know if playing by the rules means anything either." Adam was tired and his frustration at style overruling substance was bothering him. "I'm sorry, Alice. I'm just rambling. You and the kids have a great time at your mother's. I'll see you Sunday night."

With that, Alice and the kids left him with dinner, tax forms, and a bottle of gin. Adam wisely consumed the dinner first. He then filled a glass with some gin and took out the tax forms. Scotty came into the room and gave Adam "the look." "O.K., big fella, let's go for a walk!"

Adam was hoping to run into Frank this evening. He couldn't wait to inform Frank of his newfound sales prowess. This evening he would not be disappointed.

"Good evening, Scotty. You too, Adam." Despite the warm greeting, Adam sensed that Frank was feeling low. Adam ignored Frank's depression, and regaled the neighbor with the details of his first actual sales call, concluding with the statement: "I'm now two for two. This sales game is a piece of cake!"

By now, they were halfway around the lake. Frank said nothing during Adam's boastful description of his conquest of Universal Paper. Finally, Frank asked: "Mr. Sales Pro, have you received payment in any form for your sterling achievements?"

"Well of course not, Frank. The conquest just occurred today. I'm sure I will be compensated for my achievements in due course. Why did you ask?"

"The sale is not completed until you are paid. I'm tempted to characterize your achievements thus far as a 'gift' to First Continental. You are right to note that selling can be fairly easy. If you prepare yourself, know your customer and his needs, and have the right product, it can be easy. The hard part is getting paid what you earned. Just today for example, I found out that one of my principles is attempting to avoid paying me $32,000 in commissions. We call it a commission-dectomy!"

Adam was starting to understand Frank's mood. "What's a commission-dectomy?"

"That's salesman parlance for getting screwed out of commission dollars earned." Frank replied.

"It must be a fairly common occurrence if there is a phrase in the vernacular to describe it."

"Hell, yes. Everybody does it!" Frank was unhappy and the tone of voice clearly reflected it.

"Is it greed?" Adam really wanted to know.

"Short answer is yes. I think there might be more to it. After any sale, bean counters generally bring to management's attention the enormity of the commission check, relative to time spent by the rep to secure the account. They forget that our contract was not denominated in dollars per hour. Sometimes other individuals, like engineers, say they designed such an outstanding product that it sold itself. It's the old: 'A poorly dressed chimpanzee could sell this product' excuse. They conveniently forget they couldn't sell one unit on their own without sales intervention. It's the old image game dressed a little differently. The best sales presentation in the world is the one you never saw. Thus, it's difficult to defend the value added by the salesman. It's comparable to proving a negative."

"Frank, that's terrible! How do you avoid this?"

"You can't entirely, Adam. As I said, everybody does it. The only defense is to only sell small jobs infrequently. You must train yourself to ignore the big opportunities. That's where I screwed up. I ignored my own advice and sold a big deal. The income from that one deal made my annual compensation appear to be the same as the CEO of the company. That raised a big red flag. The commission-dectomy was virtually assured, much like your future IRS audit." Adam turned pale.

Frank continued: "Don't feel sorry for me, Adam. I have my lawyer working on it. Based on previous experiences I'll get something, but not everything I earned. You should worry more about your situation. If I heard your story correctly, you are perfectly positioned for a commission-dectomy. First Continental must know this is a big deal. Big deals can produce big glory, which management will not want to share. If you, with no sales training or support, sold two deals out of two, they will think of the poorly trained chimp analogy. If I were you I would spend time this week-end updating my resume."

"Frank, they wouldn't dare! Alice thinks I'm getting a raise and a bonus, not sacked because I was successful!"

"Life is full of surprises, Adam. I suggested last week that the only answer was to change the rules, or commit crime in the eyes of authority. I believe you thought I was joking. Nobody makes jokes about the subject after they have been commission-dectomied. Believe me, Adam; it is a life-altering event. Well, I'm home. Good night."

Frank's abrupt departure left Adam alone with his thoughts and his faithful dog. Upon returning home, he began to work on the taxes. While on the computer he decided to pull up his resume and noticed it was hopelessly out of date. Frank was undoubtedly wrong, but it wouldn't hurt to spend some time this weekend working on a new resume. It would be a break from the tax routine and it never hurt to be prepared, "Just in case."

CHAPTER 9

Monday mornings are generally ranked as depressing by most workers. For Adam, this Monday had to be the worst of all time. Through the mental fog and anguish, he vaguely remembered a movie entitled "*The Lost Weekend*." It was as though he starred and personally performed all of the physical stunts in the movie. Alice was correct once again in her decision to take the kids to her mother's. When he calculated the penalty for not filing estimated taxes on the $5,250 from Second Republic, the self-employment tax and the added State income tax, he flew into a screaming rage. While Adam worked on the computer, Scotty normally slept by his feet. It was readily apparent he had lost control when he found Scotty cowering in the basement. Fortunately, the $6,000 from Lewis covered the shortfall. However, there was very little left for an attorney to assist with the inevitable audit. At least I accomplished something positive this weekend. The resume revisions suggested by Frank were completed, the taxes were finished, and so was the bottle of gin.

Adam started to recover from his deep funk while crossing the cantilevered Jackson Street Bridge. This bridge is designed to be raised just like its counterpart on Lake Shore Drive. Without a pillar for center support, these bridges would bounce each time a bus or truck crossed over them. The resulting sensation always spooked tourists who did not understand the design. Each bridge had a tender's cubicle located in a little tower at the foot of the bridge. Now that's a great job, Adam thought. It was manned 24 hours a day. One just had to sit there, wait for a ship that was big enough, and raise the bridge. Of course, one had to stay alert for "jumpers." These individuals occasionally wanted to commit suicide by going into the river. Adam wondered what the correlation was between the number of jumpers and the date of April 15. The principal appeal of the job lay in the fact that as a tender, he would not have to put up with Snake or his ilk.

Stan was waiting for him in the office with a strangely somber look. There were no pleasantries today as Stan motioned to Adam to sit down while he closed the door. That was a clear sign of big trouble.

"Adam, what I am about to say is very hard for me, so please just listen." Adam nodded consent as his concern mounted.

"I have now been at bank 11 years. I was ready to quit many times for years until I started working with you. You are good manager. You know when to get involved and when to go away. You have always backed me up and fought for my battles. You never were the complaining by my poor English. You always just judged me on my results. Now I must go. I couldn't do that without saying special 'Thank You.' I am wishing for you and your family the best big luck possible."

Adam immediately knew how difficult the speech had been for Stan. He probably spent hours rehearsing it in front of a mirror. Adam was deeply touched and alarmed at the same time. "Stan, you can't possibly do this now! I strongly believe we will receive a purchase order from Universal Paper today. 'Trade Master' is going to be a huge commercial success. There will be large raises and huge bonuses for everybody on the team. How on earth could you consider leaving at this time?"

"I also am believing that 'Trade Master' will be a success. I'm less certain FIRST CON will be knowing that fact, much less be agreeing rewarding the people doing real work. I am surely certain that the work that remains to be done on the system is the house cleaning and documentation. I hate that stuff. My work here is already done. Also, I know that I will never get big important job at bank. FIRST CON wants good image from polished people, not Polish people! I bet you not one of the big bosses at bank ever eating Kielbasa or the tuna casserole. I loving both which is already proof I don't fit in this place!"

Adam could not think of an argument to attack Stan's assessment of the oppressive culture that was prevalent at the bank. Stan, unfortunately, was dead on in his assessment. "What do you want me to do?"

"There is nothing you can do to make my mind change. I have made all other arrangements. Since I have had more experience with bank procedure than you have, I will ask you now to make call to the Human Resources. Everything is like automatic from that point. You have never done this before, Adam. It is not so pretty. I do not wish for you to worry. Everything is fine. Have please the faith. Please remember the deep personal respect I have for you. Now please make call!"

Adam recalled reading the Policy and Procedure manual one time shortly after he was designated a project manager. The bank's policy was that if an employee desired to leave, they were to be escorted out of the bank immediately. FIRST CON didn't want someone hanging around badmouthing the firm or boasting about great opportunities that might exist with some other employer. Adam could see the logic in the policy, but Stan was right, he never had the occasion to execute it. Adam also knew that management was particularly concerned with departing programmers who had access to the mainframe computers. The phrase in the department was: "A pissed-off programmer is a greater threat than a terrorist." Adam thought that sentiment was ludicrous, as a good programmer could leave a "time bomb" in the system where it could never be found. It would be set prior to an employee announcing his departure and may not go off for years.

Adam reluctantly complied with Stan's request and notified Human Resources.

Within 10 minutes, Phil arrived from security with Stan's last check. The check included two weeks severance pay. Phil then asked Stan to return to his work place and demanded that Adam accompany them as a witness to the proceedings. The three rode the elevator in complete silence to Stan's floor.

Adam noticed immediately that Stan's desk was completely devoid of personal effects. Adam realized that Stan had a productive day while he was in Wisconsin. There was a possibility that Stan had accomplished other pre-planning activities, but Adam decided not to question that possibility. Phil stood perplexed at Stan's clean desk. Phil didn't seem to understand that he, at best, was a checkers player and Stan was a chess master.

"O.K., Stan, if you have no personal effects to remove, I need your keys, employee badge, insurance card, and a list of all passwords to any systems." Phil had extensive experience with this particular procedure and his delivery was flawless.

"You forgot to read Stan his Miranda rights, Phil!" Adam snorted.

"This isn't funny, Adam!"

"I couldn't agree more," Adam rebutted. Executing the policy, which looked good on paper, was demeaning in actuality. If there was ever an employee who deserved recognition or perhaps a gold watch for his service and contributions, it was Stan. Instead, they were recreating the "French Foreign Legion" practice of drumming someone out of the Corps. Stan was being treated like a disloyal crook. It was humiliating and spiteful. Adam could hear a female programmer crying softly just down the hall. The atmosphere throughout the office was heavy with emotion.

Stan seemed completely relaxed and totally under control. He was familiar with the procedure and was prepared. Adam wasn't prepared, and the whole exercise made him want to throw up. Phil was just doing his job, oblivious to the emotion, taking inventory, going though the checklist, until was satisfied that all was in order. "O.K., Adam. Please escort Stan from the premises."

Adam and Stan slowly walked to the underground truck garage to retrieve Stan's Harley. They met some employees along the way, who shook Stan's hand and wished him well. The damned grapevine worked faster than the speed of light.

As they approached the garage, they were asked to wait at the door by the guard on duty. The Brinks truck was being loaded and no one was allowed to enter the garage during the procedure. Right on time, thought Adam. Both men watched as the three-man crew from Brinks executed the transfer with precision. One man always stayed with the truck, a big International diesel. The side of the door was emblazoned with the Brinks shield and the logo "Security since 1859." Finally, the Brinks men departed and the bank guard left the garage door open to facilitate Stan's departure.

As Stan started the big bike, he turned to face Adam. "Please remembering my words. Everything will be really good. Have the big faith!"

"That's not easy for me to believe, Stan, but I appreciate your sentiments and all of your hard work. I will always miss you. What are your future plans?"

Stan just smiled and gunned the engine, which responded as only a Harley can. The bank guard was getting impatient. "Adam, I'm not totally for sure. Maybe I go to Europe!" Stan then shook Adam's hand and roared out of the garage. Stan stopped momentarily in front of the bank, gave the whole edifice the finger, and roared off with his scarf blowing out at a right angle from a breeze off the lake.

After the large door squeaked shut, Adam stood silently, physically unable to move. His standing there made the guard uncomfortable. Reluctantly, Adam turned and left the vacant garage. The thunderbolt didn't hit until he was on the elevator. "What did Stan say? He was going to Europe. Renee, you SOB! You just robbed me of my key employee! What the hell does that mean? Why did Renee do it? Where do I go from here?" There were dozens of questions swirling in Adam's head, which was now splitting.

In an attempt to escape the nagging questions, Adam started checking the e-mail. The Universal Purchase Order was there! They had plagiarized the Swiss National letter shamelessly. It had been forwarded directly to him. Neither Snake nor Bob Nelson had received a copy. That's strange, Adam thought.

The next message floored him. It was from Joe Weber in purchasing. Joe had found some vendors who could remount the fire extinguishers, but he had yet to issue a P.O. As a courtesy, Joe was providing Adam with a heads-up that the project cost would be around $30,000. Adam was not only upset with the projected cost, but with the fact that Snake had been copied on the message.

Adam turned from the monitor in time to see Snake storm into his office with a printed copy of Joe's e-mail. "What in God's name, did YOU do? What did YOU say to the OSHA guy that made him angry? This is ridiculous! We don't have budget dollars allocated for this work! Where is this huge amount of money going to come from?" The words poured out of Snake's mouth in an unrelenting torrent.

Adam took a deep breath before replying. "I didn't do or say anything to upset Mr. Twilliger. The inspector seems able to project an obnoxious attitude quite naturally. Secondly, no company, including ours, would budget for a future OSHA expenditure; there is no precedent to do so. Even if you had a precedent, how could you determine in advance the amount you would be fined? That's why we have prudently placed contingency funds in the budget. That is where I suggest you get the money.

"By the way, Stan resigned this morning."

"Well, at least that's one piece of good news. I never liked Stan's attitude or his complete disregard for proper procedure. I'm tired of living in fear that senior management would some day find out that Stan rode a Harley to work. Don't try to throw me off the track with your good news. The bad news is, there is nothing left in the contingency account. I'm also not pleased with the way you characterized an official of the Federal Government. No wonder Mr. Twilliger flew off the handle! The question remains, how do you plan to cover the cost for your screw-up in handling the OSHA issue?"

Adam could actually feel his blood starting to boil and surge through his veins. He would ignore the inane comment about Stan. It was fruitless to argue with an idiot. Adam suddenly thought of a way to answer Snake on the budget issue. "Why don't we funnel some of the substantial income that the bank has received from selling the security product that my team developed? The license fee from just one of the 28 sales will more than cover the OSHA costs. We could distribute some of the remaining funds as bonuses for the entire team."

"You are not supposed to know about those sales! Who told you about them? I'll have the informer fired this instant!"

"The question remains, Mr. Post, why not do the right thing?"

"It's not the right thing. If it were the right thing, we would have established an internal accounting procedure for intra-departmental crediting. That procedure doesn't exist within the bank's accounting system, therefore it's not right by definition. We have anticipated every correct occurrence within our system!"

"What does it take to establish a proper accounting procedure at FIRST CON for a new situation that wasn't anticipated?" Adam inquired as gently as possible.

"I don't know and I don't care! I know how to solve this particular problem, and I knew you didn't have a clue as to the proper course of action. You will cut your staff by two employees and you will do it today!"

"You want me to cut two people from a project team that may have developed the best profit generator this bank has seen in decades? Do you have any idea of the chilling effect that may have on anyone else in this bank who may have a creative bent?"

"Don't talk to me about future sales or profits. The problem is now! We have a large expenditure forthcoming and no budget dollars available. We must reduce costs immediately. Certainly, you must understand that. Didn't you have any business training?"

"There is no way I'm going to sack two people who worked through the night just last week to produce a meaningful product for this damned bank! That's not the reward I had in mind for creative, productive work."

"I knew you were soft. You identify with your employees more than the needs of FIRST CON. That's O.K., Mr. Adam Goody Boy. I will take care of this myself. I enjoy reducing overhead." Snake's face bore an unmistakable, sadistic grin. Adam thought for a minute. He wouldn't give Snake the satisfaction. It was obvious that the Snake was not bluffing. The SOB was actually looking forward to it.

"No, it's my job." Adam said remorsefully. "I'll deal with it."

"Very well. Do it today! Any two people, I don't care who. Make sure security is involved and the correct procedure is followed precisely."

Snake stormed out of the office leaving Adam slumped in the chair as if he had been run over by Stan's Harley. Emotionally, he had. With Stan's departure, the team was down to five people. Which two do you pick from the five remaining souls? It was like playing God. Adam could pick the two that would have the best chance of getting a new job. Another option was to do the traditional thing and pick the two souls with the least seniority. Two members of the team were not married. If he picked them, there would theoretically be less trauma and hardship for those chosen.

Under normal conditions, Adam would feel compelled to pick the two who had contributed the least to the team in the past. It would be important to keep the best people to help launch "Trade Master." That logical option no longer had merit. He had made the decision to leave the bank. How the bank treated "Trade Master" in the future was no longer a concern. It was during Snake's presentation of the budget issue and his derogatory comments about Stan that Adam finalized his decision. Although the decision to leave was made quickly, it was irrevocable. The only questions remaining were "how" and "when" to do it.

It was time for lunch. He could resolve which choice to make between the five remaining employees over a solitary sandwich and a couple of stiff drinks. It did help a little. After the third drink, he decided that Liz and Howard would have no trouble in finding new employment. They were significantly underpaid and each possessed the talent that would cost FIRST CON the most to replace.

With great reluctance, Adam returned to the office and placed a call to both Liz and Howard asking them to join him. They arrived together and sat awkwardly in front of the small desk. There was a long, silent pause. Adam literally didn't know where or how to begin. Surprisingly, it was Liz who started the meeting.

"It's O.K., Adam. We know why we're here and we know what you have to do."

"The grapevine is working well today, I see." Adam still was in awe of its speed and effectiveness.

"Let's just say that Snake's voice carries well. We know the box you're in and we respect the fact that you would not permit the Snake to do the dirty work." Howard explained.

"Don't worry about us, Adam. We're in pretty good shape. We had a hunch some time ago that this would happen. Both Howard and I are close to securing new jobs and we cleaned out our desks during the lunch break." Liz announced.

"How did you know who I would pick?" Adam asked.

"It was the logical choice. Over the years, you have always been logical. That was your great strength as a manager. You are the only thing I'll miss from this bank." Liz was close to crying.

Adam was feeling like a complete ass. These two fine, hard working, talented, and loyal employees had the misfortune of being at the wrong place at the wrong time. Trying to control himself, he asked: "Is there anything I can do to help—perhaps provide a reference?"

"No, I believe we're past that stage with our job search. We appreciate your offer. We may have to come back to it. May we have your home phone number and personal e-mail address?" Howard asked.

Adam quickly complied, giving each the information requested. "If it were up to me you both would have received several raises by now. Don't sell yourselves short with any new employer. You're both A1 in my book."

"Thanks, Adam. We feel the same about you. If you would, please make your call before we all start crying." Liz was close to losing control. Adam called Human Resources for the second time today. Phil arrived in 15 minutes.

The procedure of "Drumming out of the Corps" was repeated. It wasn't any easier the second time. If anything, it was harder. The grapevine had alerted more people. From all over the bank individuals came forth to embrace and console Liz and Howard. Many strangers from other departments couldn't understand the emotion surrounding the event. They failed to grasp the fact that when you work closely with people to solve real problems, a kinship similar to men in combat emerges. When one of your comrades falls through no fault of his own, it produces the rawest of emotion. If Adam hadn't made the decision to leave FIRST CON earlier today, he would have made it now.

The artificiality and callousness of Snake's decision appalled Adam. He couldn't help but wonder if the individual who had filed the OSHA complaint had any idea of where it could lead or who would have to pay the price.

Adam completed the escort to the door. They wished each other well and vowed to keep in contact. Once they left, Adam returned to the small office that had served him for years. He carefully and systematically started removing all personal effects and placed them into his brief case. Physically and emotionally, he felt like a dishrag that had been wrung out.

"To Hell with it!" Adam left the building, and for the first time in his tenure at the bank, caught the 4:50 to Bartlett.

CHAPTER 10

An overwhelming premonition of finality engulfed Adam as he settled into his usual upper deck seat. This was quite possibly the last train ride he would take for some time. Between the gut wrenching events of yesterday and Frank's pithy remarks, Adam's shield of naiveté was rapidly being replaced by cynicism. The reality of just how ruthless people could be when their status or power appeared threatened was at best unsettling.

Adam couldn't enjoy the early spring scenery of Flowering Crabapples and Forsythia speeding past the window. It was imperative that he reviewed his strategy for the confrontation that would surely greet his arrival at First Continental. The best he could hope for was a temporary reprieve or postponement of his inevitable termination. That might provide adequate time to search for a new job. It's much easier to negotiate for a new position if you're currently employed. If that didn't work, the only route left would be to create enough fear and distrust in upper management to insure a larger severance package. Anything more than the normal two weeks would be a victory, and in today's economy perhaps a necessity for survival.

In preparation for that strategy, Adam had "logged on" to the bank's computer last night and explored in depth some highly sensitive files. Normally, the security system would have stopped anyone cold. Since he designed the security system, it was a snap to by-pass it. There was a sub-routine in the system that would attempt to identify unauthorized hackers who broke past the first secure layer. Adam left that sub-routine intact. He had logged on using Snake's password. Any attempt to determine who the hacker was would lead directly to

Snake, who was too dumb or lazy to change the password Adam had issued to him months before.

If Adam were dealing with honorable people, none of this preparation would be necessary. With his newly acquired understanding of management behavior, he had to be prepared. It was fruitless to argue his case on the merits. The bank's management was just like a government agency and couldn't understand the principles of merit. They only understood intimidation. "When in Rome, do as the Romans do," Adam thought. The preparation effort left a sour taste in his mouth, regardless of the justification.

Not surprisingly, Snake was waiting impatiently in Adam's office. "We've received a request to attend a special meeting upstairs." Adam didn't bother to reply. He just quietly followed Snake up the elevator to the executive suite thinking that in all his years at the bank he'd never set foot on this floor. How ironic that the first opportunity to visit the inner sanctum would occur today, he thought. Snake led Adam to a small conference room adjacent to the CFO's palatial office. The Chief Financial Officer himself, Mr. Randal Parks, was present as well as Mr. Winfred Palmer of marketing. Adam had first met Palmer about a week ago during Renee Schugart's surprise visit. This would be his first and probably last meeting with Mr. Parks.

The Kangaroo Court is now assembled, Adam perceived. The amount of brass in place for this meeting conclusively proved that a reprieve option would not be available. The entire exercise was window dressing for a decision that had already been reached. The trial was designed to maintain the bank's illusion of "fairness" for the remaining employees.

There could be another, more substantive, reason for this high-level charade. Undoubtedly the Human Resources and Legal departments reviewed his file. Under EEOC definitions, Adam could contest his eminent dismissal as a minority. This high-level review before dismissal was probably designed to eliminate or mitigate such an appeal. The entire meeting was a classic corporate CYA exercise. Adam, as a law-abiding taxpayer, felt his status as minority was earned, so perhaps HR and Legal were correct.

Adam recalled another of Frank's comments made while walking Scotty. "We, as supposedly civilized people, have not advanced much from the Incas of old. We still require human sacrifices to maintain the fantasy of order. The only difference is that the Incas did them in public. We do it now behind conference room walls." Frank was right. The establishment called FIRST CON needed a human sacrifice to the great God, "Image." Adam would be that sacrifice. His only option was to do whatever it took to secure a reasonable severance package. "Let the Games Begin!"

Mr. Parks, as the senior man present, started the meeting, which was consistent with FIRST CON's customs and procedures. "Adam, as you know, we hold the managers of First Continental, such as yourself, to high standards. Principally, we demand that they be in total control of their areas of assigned responsibility. Our managers should at all times be able to accurately forecast future events. There are no surprises or unforeseen expenditures in a well-managed enterprise. First Continental is first and foremost a well-managed enterprise. We abhor uncertainty and ambiguity as they lead to a loss of control. Several items have come to my attention that indicate, on the surface at least, that you have failed to manage to that basic, fundamental standard. I felt we should have a little chat about those items and straighten them out." Parks had spoken the words flawlessly. His voice was smooth, urbane, and full of confidence, much like a news anchor at a major network. Mr. Parks' expensive well-tailored suit reflected the perfection, elocution, diction, and professionalism of the voice.

"By all means, Mr. Parks! I am extremely grateful for the time you have afforded from your hectic schedule to discuss these items. Can you give me an example of my alleged mismanagement?"

Snake, who had been straining in anticipation like a dog on a leash, jumped in. "Just yesterday, Stan Wilkowski left our employ. He was without a doubt the best man in the entire department with a sterling list of accomplishments that spanned 11 years. You apparently were completely unaware of Mr. Wilkowski's impending departure. By any definition, you were surprised at his action. You did nothing to reverse Stan's decision when it was announced. You obviously created an extreme and inhumane working environment that precipitated his decision to leave. I believe that he and your entire staff were recently forced to work all night to meet a deadline."

"Aha," thought Adam. Snake, through his words, had announced the choice of weapons for this duel. The choice of weapons would be the "Big Lie." Snake could have used the truth if the idiot had known about Adam's involvement with Second Republic. He could have used the little lie, the white lie, lying by omission or simple misrepresentation. Instead, Snake chose the technique of the "Big Lie" right out of the KGB, and Clinton War Room playbook. Adam knew that the principal advantage of using the "Big Lie" was that it reduced your opponent to incoherent sputtering. Adam elected not to play to those cards.

"Well, in general, I must agree with Mr. Post." Adam paused for a long time to let the statement sink in. In the ensuing silence, he noticed nervous glances exchanged among the three FIRST CON executives. "Stan was a gifted and talented employee as Mr. Post just eloquently testified. I see you have Stan's personnel record in front of you, Mr. Parks. If you review it, you will see that I requested significant raises for Stan over the last eight consecutive quarters. Mr. Post approved none of them. Additionally, Mr. Parks, your records will indicate that no member of my staff, who do work long hours, requested overtime." Adam's voice never wavered or rose to a high pitch during the delivery. He was totally calm, his voice almost serene.

"You mean your people worked all night and didn't request overtime? I've never heard of such a thing!" Parks, the chief bean counter, was incredulous and starting to fidget.

"It may in fact be unusual, Mr. Parks, however, that doesn't mean it should be characterized as mismanagement. Just to set the record straight, Mr. Post was probably within his rights to deny Mr. Wilkowski the raises. Stan would never allow Mr. Post to ride on his Harley motorcycle despite Mr. Post's numerous requests. I believe all present in this room can understand the motivation of payback! Stan did confess to me that he had grossly underestimated Mr. Post's lust for what Stan thought was just a mode of transportation."

"This man, Wilkowski, rode a motorcycle to the bank? Our bank?" Parks was mortified.

"Every single day, Mr. Parks, regardless of weather." With that statement, Adam realized the issue of Stan, or his mismanagement of people, would never be brought up again.

Now it was Palmer's turn. "Adam, I am dismayed with this Swiss National purchase order. You aren't authorized to conduct marketing, much less international marketing. How could you possibly pursue such ambition? You didn't follow procedure or honor the chain-of-command!"

"Mr. Palmer, I didn't pursue any ambition. If you recall, you brought Mr. Renee Schugart, of Swiss National, to my office and told me to answer all of his questions. You assured me that the Board of Directors had cleared him for all information pertaining to 'Trade Master'. I respected the chain-of-command to such a large extent that I did exactly what I was told to do by you."

"Is that true, Winnie?" Parks snapped.

"Yes, but Adam has sold something I know nothing about. It didn't proceed correctly through the proper channels." Palmer was truly embarrassed. As the head of Marketing, he should have stayed with Renee and witnessed the demo instead of running to some insignificant, but scheduled meeting. Palmer wouldn't or couldn't accept responsibility for that. Someone had to pay for his personal embarrassment and discomfort.

"Speaking of unauthorized marketing…" Snake simply would not give up; he would now take a different tact. "Adam intentionally kept me from participating in a key meeting with Universal Paper. If I had been permitted to attend the presentation, we would have received a purchase order by now. Making a fool out of a FIRST CON manager by a fellow manager does not support our image or the concept of team play!"

"Well, Adam?' Parks asked warily.

"I did nothing or said nothing to make a fool out of Mr. Post. He seems able to do that quite naturally on his own. Some have called it a gift." Adam thought Snake was going to jump over the table and attempt to choke him. Snake didn't, as the wimp simply didn't have the courage. That one was for you Stan, Adam thought. "The complaint of my lack of marketing experience and authorization is acknowledged as true. However, I was asked by Bob Nelson to personally intervene at Universal. I honored that request as a team player. Out of my respect for the chain-of-command, I insisted that Mr. Post be invited to attend. It's true that Mr. Post did not participate in the business meeting, as he was preoccupied with a comely young lady. I guess I did all right without his presence and invaluable support." With that statement, Adam slid a printed copy of the Universal P.O. to Mr. Parks.

"What?" Palmer interjected. "You sold another major account? I'm the head of Marketing and the order was sent to YOU? I don't even know what the damned product is supposed to do! This is totally out of control!"

"Would you like me to send the orders back, Mr. Palmer?" Adam asked calmly.

Palmer never answered. He had now completely lost his composure. The VP of Marketing's face was flushed. He was sputtering incoherently and constantly wringing his hands.

"Let's talk about this OSHA fiasco, Adam." Parks jumped into allow Palmer time to recover. "How do you plan to pay for this unexpected cost?" Leave it to the bean counters to ask about money and not people or progress, Adam thought.

"As a matter of fact sir, Mr. Post and I discussed this very topic yesterday. I believe my team should be rewarded and the OSHA costs recovered from the substantial and unexpected income generated from the sale of the security product we developed. Mr. Post informed me that this was impossible because of inadequacies in your accounting systems, Mr. Parks. Could you, and your system, possibly be that inadequate?"

Parks answered defensively. Nobody had ever challenged him on a real or perceived inadequacy in the accounting system, including the members on the Board of Directors. Parks literally had difficulty in formulating a response. "Technically, that may be true, but of no importance. There is a larger, more fundamental issue at stake. If the bank extended or encouraged monetary rewards for every little achievement, we would have lines several blocks long at my door every morning. I personally would be at the head of that line in an attempt to cash in on my manifest accomplishments."

"But you already have gone to the front of the line, Mr. Parks! It's true, you don't receive mere monetary rewards, as I've suggested for my team. You refer to them as 'stock options', or in some cases, they are in the form of 'interest free' loans. It depends on what your definition of money is. My team is adaptable and resilient. We can accept the same reward that you routinely receive—no problem!" Adam's research, completed the previous night, indicated that the bank's Board had just provided Mr. Parks with a $250,000 "interest free" loan. The Board wanted to reward the CFO's performance in cost control by helping him to acquire a second home.

Parks and Palmer exchanged horrified glances. Adam sounded so confident, but how could the middle manager know? Surely, Adam was bluffing, but could they be sure? This was not going according to the established plan. They had seriously underestimated Adam's capabilities. Snake had forecast that Adam was a mere disrespectful, dumb, middle manager. The two senior executives now knew better. Adam was articulate, prepared, and knowledgeable. That made the scapegoat very dangerous. Dangerous men who could play "hardball" with flair had to be treated with respect. Snake was still oblivious to the threat as he walked to the easel pad in the front of the conference room and wrote $30,000 and a large question mark.

"Let's get to the real source of our OSHA problem." Adam continued. "An apparently anonymous complaint was filed with OSHA against the bank. Through some diligent research on my part, the complainant is no longer anonymous. It appears that a Miss Virginia Sommers filed the complaint. Until recently, Ms. Sommers was in the bank's employ as Mr. Post's secretary." Adam didn't know that for certain. He just threw it out as a verbal harpoon for the sheer hell of it. Judging from the Snake's physical reaction, he had scored a direct hit.

Time to take it home, Adam thought. "Apparently, Ms. Sommers was less outraged at Mr. Post's pathetic, infantile advances than she was with management's indifference to her request for help or a remedy. I found that odd, considering the bank's unrelenting concern for its 'Image.' Then I established, through careful research, how many sexual harassment complaints flow from the confines of the executive offices."

Adam paused for a moment for dramatic effect. His probing of the sensitive files last night revealed that Mr. Parks had four complaints on file. Mr. Palmer had two complaints pending review. All of the bank's executives had complaints on file as well. Adam had no way of knowing who would serve on today's Kangaroo court. It turned out that it made no difference. Adam had memorized every FIRST CON executive's record. He had incriminating data on anybody who might have showed up at this hearing.

Adam decided it was time to go for the throat: "In the absence of a proper accounting procedure to settle the OSHA cost, I recommend the horny old codgers in the executive suite tap their 'stock options' or their 'interest free' loans to pay for the OSHA expenditure. In that way, they help pay for their mistakes and total lack of ethics!"

The room exploded into total chaos. The FIRST CON men reacted as if a live grenade had landed in their midst. All three jumped from their chairs as one. Parks was actually hopping up and down uncontrollably, his face purple with rage. Post was foaming from the side of the mouth while turning rapidly in tight circles. Palmer reacted the least to the grenade, in part because he had expended so much emotion earlier. The marketing chief was the first to gain some control and asked Adam to leave the room at the first pause in the bedlam, which Adam readily did.

From the hallway, Adam could hear the trio screaming and cursing. A loud crashing sound hinted at the possibility that someone had thrown a chair against the wall. Much of the abuse was directed at Snake. Adam was certain that his objective was reached, but took no great sense of pleasure in that. The whole episode was stupid beyond belief.

After waiting about 45 minutes, Winfred Palmer emerged from the conference room and walked up to Adam. "Let's go to your office, Adam." Palmer had calmed down a great deal. On the elevator going down to 24, he exclaimed: "Damn, Adam, you can really light a fire!" Adam sensed a little respect in that statement, but said nothing.

They reached Adam's office and Palmer quickly surmised that all of the personal effects had been removed. "You knew?" Adam nodded yes.

"Grapevine?" Palmer asked.

"No, simple deductive reasoning."

"I should have known." Palmer was distressed. "I fear we are in the process of making a stupid mistake, Adam. When I slowly regained my senses in the meeting I realized I should be happy with any order, no matter who obtained it. I got caught up in my own emotional underwear. I sincerely apologize."

"Is it true that you never had a beard?"

"My wife would kill me if I ever attempted to grow a beard."

Palmer was struck with the thought that the man who he had just accused of not respecting the chain-of-command had used extraordinary creativity to rescue him from his attempt to spin a Swiss banker. Palmer longed to help a man like Adam, but could not. Like every executive at FIRST CON, the flypaper of lies and deceit trapped him. Any attempt to formally do the right thing would jeopardize the rule of: "Look out for #1."

"Adam, you're 'hell on wheels' in a meeting. I would rather have you on my side than have you sitting across the table; however, it's too little and too late for me or the bank, to regain some sanity. You made a very powerful adversary today in Mr. Parks."

"It wasn't done today, Mr. Palmer. I've been fighting Parks and his army of mental midget paper pushers for years!"

"Adam, I may use that descriptive phrase myself in the near future. We in marketing are continuously fighting with accounting over expense reports and sales forecasts; however, the sad fact remains that a decision has been reached to terminate you immediately. For all it's worth, I think that is wrongheaded. The best I can do under the circumstances is to record your departure as a resignation rather than a termination. Additionally, we will grant you an eight-week severance package. I will permit no one to bad-mouth you or your work. If you need a reference, use me. Here is my card. My home phone number is penciled on the back."

Palmer seemed sincere in his belated realization of the truth. "Thank you, Mr. Palmer. When will Phil be here?"

"Altogether too soon, I fear. Adam, I sincerely wish you the best of luck. I would ask that you consider a word of advice from one of the horny old men. Think about a career in sales and marketing. You conduct memorable meetings!"

Palmer excused himself as Phil, the grim reaper, appeared. Phil didn't have to say a word to Adam as he entered the office. Adam had already compiled a complete list of what was required and laid it out on the desk. Without a word, Phil inventoried the pile and handed Adam an envelope containing the eight-week severance. There was total silence in the work area surrounding Adam's office. It normally hummed with activity. Once in the elevator, Phil coughed and mumbled: "I'm truly sorry, Adam. We may have had some differences in the past, but I'm certain they nailed the wrong guy."

"Thanks, Phil." That's all Adam could say. The last six workdays had been very tough.

The word of Adam's dismissal spread through the bank like wildfire. The remainder of the project team greeted Adam by the front door. There were hugs, tears, thanks, and wishes for the best. Adam appreciated their efforts and kindness, but all parties recognized that nothing could be done.

Once outside, the full enormity of the day's activities swamped his emotions. Surprisingly, it was the emotion of complete loneliness that prevailed over all else. Adam simply could not control the flood of emotion. He wanted to cry. He wanted to scream. Neither seemed appropriate, or adequate.

As Adam stood alone outside the huge bank edifice, he remembered Stan's parting gesture. It seemed at the time to be a vulgar, stupid, and worthless demonstration. Now he couldn't restrain the urge. Adam turned, faced the bank, and gave it the finger.

He started the journey to Union Station, knowing the gesture had accomplished nothing—but it sure felt good!

CHAPTER 11

Eight weeks had elapsed since Adam's involuntary departure from First Continental. On his last train ride to Union Station, he noticed the Flowering Crabapples, Daffodils, and Magnolias of early spring. They were soon replaced by Iris and Columbine, which were in turn replaced by Lilacs and Peonies. The inevitable natural cycle played out while he continued the fruitless search for new employment.

This was Adam's first experience with unemployment. As all newly corporately challenged individuals, he made mistakes in his approach to the problem. Initially he tried to hide the predicament from friends and family. That approach was the direct result of shame. He soon discovered how common the plight was; and that there was little stigma associated with it. Chicago, by any conventional definition is a large city; however, its citizens frequently behave as if they lived in a small town. Everybody knew somebody through a myriad of connections. Adam failed to take advantage of the networking possibilities presented within the community. That was finally rectified and, hopefully, some leads from friends and associates would begin to emerge. Nonetheless, exposing his predicament for all to see left him feeling vulnerable.

One of the few bright spots in this most dismal of trials was the realization that the Midwestern heritage of "neighbor helping neighbor" was alive and well. Adam's church offered modest financial help. He graciously declined the offer, but the way things were progressing, he might have to accept it. Frank thought he would get a limited settlement from his commission-dectomy lawsuit and promised support. Individual neighbors and members of the congregation dropped off meals. They were always kind enough to say: "This recipe makes so much we just couldn't eat it ourselves. It would be a shame to waste it. Please help us out. Take the food." It was a lie, but unlike the many other lies at FIRST CON and in the press, he was grateful for it.

Adam had no idea how important the bank job had been to his mental and emotional status. The train rides in the morning and evening served as bookends to frame the day. The familiar routine supported his existence in a profound way. When it vanished, he felt rudderless and adrift. Frequently, Adam forgot what day of the week it was. Once he even found himself missing the profoundly stupid monthly staff meeting.

Alice was unbelievably supportive during the crisis. She found a part-time job, which helped ease the monetary obligations. That was of particular importance now that the severance pay was consumed. Adam in turn helped support her by assuming the majority of the household chores. It was nearly a complete role reversal, with a dark and unexpected consequence. Adam was reared with the belief that as the "head of the household," he should be the sole breadwinner. Now he felt somewhat less like a man. Frequently he talked out loud while doing chores. "Should the formerly, highly skilled and respected project manager add the soap before the clothes or after? Shall we now clean the commodes or boil some potatoes?" These verbalized self-debates proved unsettling for Scotty, who watched his master intently for a recognizable command.

While working at the bank, Adam dreamed about having big blocks of free time to invest in home improvement projects. Painting the house or replacing the sod in the yard were but two examples of the many projects he wanted to accomplish. Now he had unlimited time, but not the money. It was impossible to justify spending money for paint or sod that might be required to feed the family. The depression produced by this paradox alone was overwhelming.

One of the most painful parts of being unemployed was not knowing who would, or would not, respond to the many resumes he sent out. The vast majority of the 200 some odd resumes mailed to prospective employers produced no response whatsoever. The handful that did produce a response was less than impressive. Sensing his situation, many prospective employers low-balled their initial offer, sometimes as low as 50% of the salary Adam made at the bank, which was below the prevailing market to start with. Employers call this practice "bottom feeding" and for a surprising number of firms it was a way of life.

One prospective employer would only hire him if he would agree to work in the Middle East. Adam assured that firm that he would never work for a concern where it wasn't possible to obtain deep-dish pizza or an Italian beef sandwich for lunch.

He was particularly intrigued as to why there had been no interest on resumes sent to the banking industry. Despite the assurances from Palmer, Adam was confident that he was being blackballed within the banking community. He considered filing suit against the bank's executives, but concluded that his case would be impossible to prove.

One of the least pleasant experiences occurred during a meeting with a headhunter who had ruthlessly criticized Adam's resume. "You haven't listed the accomplishments that you personally achieved!" Adam responded that as a manager, most of his accomplishments where achieved through and with members of his team. The recruiter, with no obvious successful managerial experience of his own, was askance. Adam felt that the headhunter must be a devotee of LBJ and the religion of micro managing. Having a President make decisions on what outhouses to bomb in Vietnam was the headhunter's standard for leadership. Adam startled him by saying: "A good manager knows when to get out of the way of his people."

"Then lie!" The recruiter responded. "Hell, everybody does it!"

The sum total of Adam's jobless experience to date was acute depression. He started snarling at Alice and the kids, the very people who were most in his camp. The growing depression prevented a good night's sleep. The knowledge that he had been wronged led him to start feeling sorry for himself.

The absolute low point of this journey occurred when he finally visited the State of Illinois unemployment office in Elgin. Adam was a member in good standing of a generation that firmly believed in strong, but unwritten rules. One never asked for help. If you disobeyed that rule, you would be branded as a welfare recipient or a beggar. It would be impossible to locate the author or authors of these societal rules, but all in his generation obeyed them. The effect on one's personality was more powerful than any rule written by Congress. They were written into his code of conduct in indelible ink. As much as Adam tried to heed Frank's advice to break the rules, he could not. It was an immense, crushing personal defeat to face reality and decide to go to Elgin.

The multiple lines in the Elgin office were long and filled with men and women of every race and nationality. Many of those in line had brought their children with them. Most of the children were crying or sobbing. It was impossible to discern if the children were crying from boredom or hunger. It was possible that someone could harvest human misery and despair by the gallon within the office. The atmosphere actually reeked with the emotion, which was reflected in the vacant stares of the adults in the lines.

The clerks employed by the State were uniformly rude, distant, and mechanical. The paperwork was endless and mundane. To use the restroom, you had to have someone behind you "save" your place in line. Then you had to secure permission and the actual key to the restroom from an uncaring clerk. Adam felt that he was being treated as a child in a reform school. That impression plus the cumulative effects of unemployment was convincing evidence that he had slipped from adult status to that of a misbehaving adolescent. Adam desperately wanted to leave the stupid office until he remembered that his employer had contributed money for every day he worked to the unemployment fund. "He had earned the right to be here! Why should they make it so miserable for the previously employed to make a simple withdrawal? What difference did it make how they treated him?" In the final analysis, there would be no dramatic or heroic exit from this hellhole. He needed the money.

After waiting in various lines in the proper sequence for five hours, Adam was finally seated at the desk of a middle-aged woman who looked and acted almost human. She greeted him with a genuine smile and Adam could detect some warmth in her eyes. She must be a new hire, Adam thought.

"Mr. Jones, I'm afraid we can't offer much assistance to you with a job search from our listings. Frankly, we never considered that executives like you would need our help. We have very little information for your job classification, it simply wasn't in our forecast."

"I understand that comment completely. I didn't think I would ever be here either, but sometimes it happens. I don't expect nor need the State's help in finding a new job. I just need some short-term financial assistance. I can personally guarantee that the need will be as short as possible, returning here is certainly not on my list of priorities!"

"Have you explored all the openings that are listed in the banking industry?"

"Most of them. I have the feeling I'm being black-balled, but I can't prove it."

"Mr. Jones—that is against the law!"

"Do you really think that makes any difference?"

The clerk looked furtively from side to side in an attempt to see if she was being watched before she responded. "No, I don't think it does make a difference, but I can't acknowledge it. I'm approving your request for the maximum benefit for someone with three dependents and I personally wish you the best of luck."

Adam sincerely thanked her and finally left the office. He wondered how long she would last. The rudeness and distance exhibited by the other clerks had to be a defense mechanism. How could anyone survive emotionally if you took each sad commentary from all those in line to heart? It had to rub off if you didn't erect an impenetrable shield of indifference. Even though he was desperate for a job, he wouldn't agree to work at that office under any circumstance.

As Adam returned home, Scotty greeted him warmly. The dog looked into his eyes with the unmistakable message: "I still love you even if you are on welfare."

"Thanks Scotty, I love you, too. Let me get a load of wash started and we'll go for a walk." Scotty picked the word "walk" from the long sentence and started dancing in anticipation.

The walks had been a major source of help over the last few weeks; they provided time to think. Adam had analyzed the situation at the bank numerous times. No matter how he looked at it, the results were always the same, the conclusion inevitable. There were forces at work that he could not control or even remotely influence. Twilliger hadn't acted immorally or unethically. The inspector was just doing his job. Twilliger logically was trying to avoid the problem of unemployment that now plagued Adam. "How dumb was that?" The same could be said for all of the people Adam met and worked with. The one possible exception was Snake whom Adam felt was truly evil. The executives at FIRST CON whom Adam had found to have EEOC complaints lodged against them were probably no guiltier than he was with OSHA. It's dammed difficult to prove your innocence. All Parks was trying to do was get some tax and/or interest free income. "That wasn't dumb either." What was dumb was the convoluted Byzantine tax code that was the driving force for the majority of "white collar" crime across the country.

Scotty and Adam were halfway around the lake when they spotted a boy crying by the edge of the water. The boy had been sailing a model boat in the lake when a gust of wind capsized it and left it out of the boy's reach. Scotty quickly retrieved the boat and gently laid it at the boy's feet. The boy's tears were quickly replaced with a big grin.

"You've got a nice dog, Mister!"

"Thank you. I think he's nice as well."

As they continued their walk, Adam remembered when the time he was about to capsize in the Pacific. That memory brought the haunting tune of "Eternal Father" to mind. The hymn resurrected his memory of the pastor's sermon last February. Adam felt that he had been blessed, or cursed, with an excellent memory. The pastor's sermon soon replayed itself in his thoughts.

"Well, Lord, I'm by a lake in Bartlett, not a pool in Bethzatha; but I sure want to be cured!" Adam said aloud. "Come, Scotty, let's sit down and think." They both rested in the shade of a maple tree. Adam realized that if he wanted to "pick up his bed and walk," it would be necessary to forego the rehashing of past events. It served no purpose. He was reacting to the symptoms of the situation and was not trying to cure the underlying disease.

"What was his disease?" The system analyst voice in Adam's mind resurrected itself. "You know how to get out of this mess. You start by defining the problem. It's called the requirement definition phase in case you forgot. The ugly fact that you had trouble articulating before now was that you are nothing more than a slave."

Adam had lost or perhaps never possessed economic freedom. If there were a way to achieve economic freedom, he would gain independence. Gaining economic freedom would permit him to choose the right thing to do. That simple, but profound thought started the thinking. The systems analyst voice took over his mind again.

"When Lewis had approached you in Palm Springs, you deluded yourself that you were helping friends and neighbors gain protection against hackers. It was a sincere and true sentiment, but not a complete answer. The real reason was that you needed the money for Mark's braces. The unvarnished truth is that you are vulnerable to a bribe.

"When you decided to leave First Continental, concurrent with Snake's diatribe on Stan's character, you didn't leave instantaneously as a man of true character would have done. You rationalized that you couldn't afford to. You didn't even leave when ordered to fire two innocent, outstanding employees. You claimed that you didn't want to give Snake the sadistic satisfaction. That was a true statement, but the real reason was that you needed to buy time to improve your position. It wasn't that you were physically shackled to an oar in some ancient galley with Snake beating a drum shouting ramming speed. It might as well have been because the economic shackles are just as strong, perhaps stronger than the iron ones of long ago. In truth, you are susceptible to being extorted.

"No wonder you feel so miserable. Intellectually and morally, you know the right thing to do, and then you wimp out because of your concern for the economic well-being of the family. You chickened out and still succeeded in jeopardizing the family's welfare as well as your own emotional well-being. Playing 'prevent defense' and being dishonest with yourself cost you a job and your self-confidence. You should never do that again! Frank was right, 'If you are in for a penny, why not a pound?' Reflect on those thoughts," the little voice commanded.

Adam took a moment to watch the boy play with his sailboat. The inner voice raised a good point. He didn't achieve financial freedom and independence for

$5,250, as he once naively believed. The realization of this fact brought his thoughts to a tip point. Mentally he had crossed an imaginary line in his reasoning.

"If the goal was to gain economic freedom, how does one do that?" Adam understood statistics well enough to disregard the option of the state lottery. Doing the best possible work within a salaried environment wouldn't cut it either. The tax preparation effort this year proved conclusively that at least 50% and perhaps 60% of a normal salary was scraped off the top by various governmental agencies. The number of hidden taxes made it impossible to refine the actual percentage. It was like the Russian treatment of prisoners in the "Gulag," just enough food to survive and work, but not enough food to break out and gain independence. The employers were willing co-conspirators in this situation. Independent, free workers didn't foster corporate discipline. For the first time in his life, Adam recognized the interdependence, interconnection and inter-twining of economic, religious, and political freedom. If you lose one, you lose them all.

Adam considered the American dream of starting your own company as a means of gaining economic freedom. He had enjoyed attending the MIT Enterprise Forum meetings where start-up companies presented their ideas in an attempt to garner venture capital. As a systems analyst, he knew how the game was played. He also recognized that at this time there wasn't a worthwhile idea to pursue or present. Renee and Stan would probably bring "Trade Master" to fruition. The Internet security system was not his to develop or sell. Even if he could duplicate the product, it had already been provided to many accounts. It was now a small market. However, the "model" of a start-up company appealed to Adam with its emphasis on "Risk-Reward" ratio.

No, he thought, if I want to be cured in less than the 38 years the man in the scriptures endured, "I will have to steal it." That realization totally alarmed Adam. He always considered himself an honest man despite the arguments advanced by Frank. Adam was convinced that he maintained an excellent moral compass. What good is a moral compass if you don't have a course charted? You can't chart a course until you establish a destination. As of now, a firm destination was established. Its name was economic freedom. The next logical task was to compute the compass heading and speed to the final goal.

Adam, like most Americans, was willing to be led, but despised being pushed, bribed and extorted. It was time to push back. The only success he had obtained in recent months was when he pushed back against Lewis and the trio at FIRST CON. The analysis was now complete. Adam was going to gain economic freedom by pushing back, by selecting his destination and ignoring the destination chosen for him by self-appointed controllers.

"O.K. Scotty, let's go. I have to transfer the clothes from the washer to the dryer." As the two resumed their walk home, Adam spied a large flock of Canada geese strolling through the grass adjacent to the lake. He slipped the leash off Scotty, which was strictly against the rules of the village. Scotty took off on a dead run, gleefully chasing and routing the flock of more than 150 birds. "Endangered species, my butt," snorted Adam, while dodging droppings. Chasing the geese made Scotty's day. Maybe changing or ignoring the rules does make sense, Adam thought. Some of his worries seemed to take flight with the geese.

CHAPTER 12

Two weeks had elapsed since Adam made the irrevocable decision to gain economic freedom. Making that decision had not significantly reduced the acute depression as he had hoped it would at that time. Nothing positive had developed on the job front. However, now there was a purpose, a destination, and a plan of attack. In the short term, any kind of job to help pay bills was paramount. Long term, he was totally committed to obtaining economic freedom even if it involved crime. To Adam, this approach was the same routine as designing a system. You started with the requirements definition phase. You gathered the facts, selected a philosophy, and created a strategy. Adam was well trained in this procedure, but never thought he would use the acumen polished at First Continental for the result that was now contemplated. The mental exercise provided meaning and was fulfilling in a strange way.

The Internet proved to be an invaluable tool in gathering the basic information. Adam had access to an inexhaustible supply of data that he could peruse anonymously from his home office. The need to be discreet had been honed to a fault during the creative phase of "Trade Master."

Adam was somewhat chagrined to find that Frank was right, once again. The FBI web site was awash with facts, figures and tables, but little in the way of meaning. As with most government agency web pages, it was filled with public relations spin. The formulation of "yellow snow" was now high-tech and federally funded. For the most part agencies were advertising through their web pages to Congress for increased funding. Patterns did emerge, however, that substantiated Frank's assertion that first time offenders rarely got caught, much less convicted. Crimes were most often solved because the perpetrators were dumb, lazy or more frequently, repetitive. They stuck to one playbook with religious fervor. The police studied the *modus operandi* to solve the vast majority of crimes. The other major crime solving procedure involved obtaining leads from "snitches" or from insiders turning in their associates for immunity or sentence reductions.

Utilizing the insights garnered from the data, Adam formulated the strategy of staging a one-time event. Committing one, and only one, crime would greatly minimize risk as the data suggested. Repeating the M.O. was a certain ticket to arrest. Furthermore, he concluded that risk could be greatly reduced through the careful screening of personnel recruited to help him. If help were needed, he would recruit individuals who had no previous records, mug shots, or fingerprints on file. It was imperative to keep the number of helpers to an absolute minimum. That reduced the possibility of leaks before and after the event. A small group had the added benefit of reducing the number of members requiring a share of the proceeds. The strategy stood conventional wisdom on its head. You couldn't test your methods on small jobs and work up to the grand climax. The data suggested that the "walk before you run" approach was doomed to failure. This had to be an all or nothing exercise without the benefit of a rehearsal.

The phrase, "The price of freedom is always high," took on a new meaning. He could achieve personal financial independence with a tax-free gain of two million dollars. That amount would be enough to cover college costs for both boys as well. Hypothetically, if he needed a crew of five to pull it off, it would be necessary to liberate $10 million. That was a large challenge, but he lived in "make no small plans" Chicago. A one-time raid on the local White Hen convenience store would not satisfy the criteria. Considering the prices charged; a "*Starbucks*" might be a possibility.

Adam forced his mind to take a break from the "Financial Freedom" project. That was rare, because once Adam started on a project plan, he was relentless, almost obsessive in the pursuit of solutions. He was feeling increasingly uncomfortable on his first train trip downtown in months. It felt as though the other passengers were looking at him as an interloper, a stranger in their midst, someone who didn't belong.

Adam wasn't riding the train by choice. He had received a command invitation from the IRS to discuss his recent tax filing. Frank's forecast of a certain audit had come to pass. The filing was only 12 weeks old. It amazed Adam how fast an agency could move when they wanted your money. With great reluctance, he decided to fight this audit without legal assistance. There was simply no money remaining from Mr. Lewis's check for an attorney. In preparation for the appointment, he carried two briefcases stuffed with records and receipts. It wasn't going to be enough, he feared. "How much blood can they get from a turnip?"

He arrived for the appointment 15 minutes early. The receptionist merely grunted when he announced his name, and motioned with a wave of her hand to take a seat in a straight-backed metal chair. The office was pure federal government: cold, gray, impersonal, and totally utilitarian. Adam thought the Navy had employed better interior decorators. It looked like a prison, probably by design, once he thought about it. Everybody waiting to be called looked nervous and downcast. One elderly couple looked as though they were in a doctor's office awaiting a biopsy result. Pure intimidation, Adam thought, but highly effective. The fear and anxiety spread through the reception area like an airborne virus. It oozed into his pores and nostrils despite his attempts to ignore it.

They called Adam 30 minutes late and ushered him into the office of Ms. Myers, an IRS senior auditor.

"May I see some ID, Mr. Jones? A valid State of Illinois driver license, passport, and Social Security Card will do." Adam provided everything but the passport. He had never obtained one because there was never enough money for travel of any kind, much less international trips.

"Are you represented by counsel today, Mr. Jones? If not, I would strongly suggest you obtain an attorney. I will postpone our meeting 48 hours to allow you time to obtain one."

Adam carefully looked at Ms. Meyers, a middle age, no nonsense, career bureaucrat totally lacking in humor or humanity. "Thank you for your consideration, Ms. Meyers. It's not likely that I'll have more funds to pay an attorney in 48 hours than I do at present."

"That may prove to be a very expensive decision on your part. I'm obliged to inform you that we see some serious deficiencies in your tax filing. Are you certain that you want me to continue?"

"I have no alternative." Adam ruefully replied.

"Very well." Meyers sat down at her clutter filled desk and searched for the JONES file. This was the part of the job she loved. She had seen her share of tax cheats, frauds, and phonies over the years. She personally despised every one of them. They tried to withhold, or avoid, "their fair share" of taxes. That revenue was needed for countless programs that she supported. The cheats always proclaimed they were innocent or had lost their records. "Not on my Watch" was her official motto.

"Let's see. Yes, our computer has noted that you failed to report $55,250 in taxable income, which I view as a potential felony. Your filing and the 1099's don't match. What can you say to explain that very serious omission on your part, Mr. Jones?"

Adam took a deep breath, and showed Ms. Meyers the original and the amended 1099. He recounted the entire story, noting that he had claimed and paid taxes on the correct amount of $5,250.

"How can you prove that you didn't receive the larger amount as indicated on the 1099?" Adam recoiled wondering how anybody could prove that money wasn't accepted. He produced the bank deposit record for last year in an attempt to illustrate actual income. The record showed the deposits for his regular salary checks and the $5,250, but no more. Showing these sensitive, personal documents and records to a complete stranger was very unnerving. It felt as though he was totally naked in public.

"That doesn't prove spit," she screamed. "You could have deposited the larger amount in another account. For all I know, you have a secret Swiss bank account." For just an instant, a shadow crossed Adam's face. He instantly remembered one of Frank's sales lessons: "If the truth sounds like a lie, you are better off saying nothing." He didn't have a chance to respond. Meyers had been at this interrogation game for a long time. She had seen the shadow briefly cross Adam's face.

"You DO have a Swiss account! Don't try lying to me! Not only did you avoid paying taxes; you tried to avoid the law by going offshore! You will rue the day you decided not to get an attorney." She was furious. She hated international accounts and her inability to subpoena them.

Adam, desperately trying to retain composure explained the whole situation, and concluded with: "All I have received is authorization to activate the Swiss account that was provided as a courtesy. I've never used the account!"

"You mean to tell me that you have a high interest bearing Swiss account that you've never used? How stupid do you think I am? Why on earth wouldn't you use it?"

Adam was now close to panic. His response reflected primal fear and frustration. "I didn't use the damn thing because I don't have any GOD DAMN MONEY! In fact, the way things are going; I may never have any GOD DAMN MONEY." Adam was close to tears. The emotion was raw and unmistakable.

Even the dour and unflappable Ms. Meyers sensed it. She had been an interrogator for ages and she could recognize true sentiment. Her fellow agents fervently believed she was a human lie detector. "Do you want a cup of coffee?" She asked. Adam could only nod in the affirmative.

The rest of the audit went fairly well. Adam knew he had caught a break, even though he hadn't done anything wrong. It could be perceived that he had done something wrong, and in today's age, perception was everything. Ms. Meyers regained her stature as a federal worker and disallowed some deductions for used clothing. Most had been donated to the VFW. She was compelled to find something wrong. She concluded that he owed an additional $214.76. Adam had used Lewis's entire original $6,000, save $300. He wrote a check to the US Treasury for $214.76 and considered himself lucky. It was difficult to explain why he felt lucky. If an official from a foreign country had conducted this audit, Adam, as an American citizen, believed we would now be at war. You couldn't go to war with your own government. Hell, you couldn't even sue them.

He stumbled out of the IRS office and headed back to Union Station. The route took him past First Continental. For a split second, he thought about going in, but rejected the idea. Leaving an institution is never as clean as many people think. Adam had heard that Liz and Howard had secured new employment. That made him happy on one hand, and yet dismayed at his personal lack of achievement. Subsequently, two other members of the team split, leaving Edward in charge. Edward was a good man, nearing retirement, and the new workload was overwhelming. "Trade Master" was acting peculiar on occasion. It would be impossible to tell if Stan had left a going away present or if the system was inadequately supported.

Adam finally reached Union Station and dumped the two overflowing briefcases on the floor of the Iron Horse Bar and Grille. He had very little money, but the exchange with Ms. Meyers earned him a drink.

"Hey, Adam! Let me buy you one!" That was possibly the nicest thing anybody said to him in months. It was Joe Weber from the bank's purchasing department, who was obviously taking an early afternoon break or a very long lunch.

"Joe, I can't tell you how much that means to me."

Actually, Joe bought several drinks as he, with numerous foul adjectives, informed Adam how Post screwed up the OSHA deal. Snake couldn't decide which vendor to choose in a timely manner. Twilliger came in, gave FIRST CON another 30 days and a $10,000 fine for non-compliance." That's interesting, Adam thought. The price for ineptitude is being quantified. Adam thanked Joe profusely for his generosity and hurried to catch a train. Joe seemed totally relaxed and not particularly anxious to return to the bank.

Adam arrived home at 3:00, slightly ahead of Alice and the boys. He noticed a big black limo parked down the street. It stuck out like a sore thumb in the middle class subdivision. The limo pulled into his driveway as he was unloading the precious tax records. Mr. Winfred Palmer emerged from the back seat.

"Hi, Adam! May I talk with you for a second?"

What could this possibly mean? "Certainly, Mr. Palmer. What can I do for you?"

"Please excuse this informal setting and the fact that I did not secure an appointment. You can do a lot for me, Adam. We would like to cordially extend an invitation for you to rejoin the bank's staff."

Adam was absolutely stunned. Through the grapevine and Joe's recent statements, he knew the bank was in serious trouble, but not to the extent that they would hire him back. The bank never did that. It was totally against policy. Adam knew that Palmer had to be aware that the severance had expired and that he would be desperate. The question was who was the most desperate, the bank, or he? Let's see if we can determine who is in first place, he thought.

"I'm sorry, Mr. Palmer. Would you please repeat your comment? I'm not sure I heard you correctly."

"Yes, you heard me correctly! We want you back at the bank, not at the same salary, of course! We plan to increase it significantly and provide you with a new title. You may recall that I thought we were making a big mistake when we last talked. When Swiss National and Universal canceled their orders upon learning of your departure, I was convinced."

So, it's the bank that's in deep yogurt, Adam thought. However, his situation was identical. Here was a chance to put all the misery and despair aside, an opportunity to regain his routine and confidence. It was the opportunity to forego household chores and manage adult people, doing significant work. The offer was consistent with his newly established short-term goal.

As Adam contemplated the end of his 40 years in the desert, Winfred added: "You will report directly to me. Mr. Post has been transferred. Mr. Parks is no longer with the bank. I still don't know how you found out about his EEOC problems, and I never want to. One of those complaints was apparently valid. Parks resigned yesterday."

Palmer, who was no slouch at selling, had correctly read Adam. No amount of salary increase or change in duties could offset the grim reality of Post and Parks. The news shocked him. It would mean an entirely different working environment. The change was long overdue.

"That's very interesting news, Mr. Palmer, and very encouraging. A phrase keeps popping up in my mind: 'You can never go home.' I can't for the life of me recall the author, but the sentiment is true and applicable to my situation. I must decline your kind offer. I recognize that it wasn't easy for you to come all the way out to Bartlett and say the words you said. This is a truly unfortunate situation that did not have to occur. I've lost a great deal during this ordeal, including my self-respect. I'm starting the process of rebuilding it and my confidence. Both exist today, but in a tattered form. I have dedicated myself to their complete recovery. Although the atmosphere and culture at the bank may have improved, it's still not sufficient, in my opinion, for the growth of self-respect. Thank you, and I wish you personally the best of luck."

Palmer noted the finality in Adam's tone. It wasn't a negotiating ploy for a signing bonus, which Palmer had been prepared to offer. Adam was a man of character, he finally realized. Palmer was an astute businessman and he desperately wanted Adam back at work. Palmer had also been informed that Adam was very close to bankruptcy. He questioned Adam's intellect in turning down the offer, but the bank VP stood in awe of Adam's courage and resolve.

"Thank you for listening and entertaining my offer, Adam. I wish you the best of luck in the future." With that, Palmer returned to the limo and left the drive just as Alice arrived.

"Who was that?" Alice inquired.

Adam told Alice about Mr. Palmer, the changes at the bank and the offer to return. He also informed her that he turned Mr. Palmer down.

"Adam how could you? We're broke!" Alice was shocked and dismayed.

"It didn't seem to be the right thing to do. The reality is that the offer was pure yellow snow. I have been raised to ignore it." Alice looked closely at her husband. She could not understand his thinking or the analogy. She also knew that her husband would be unable to explain it completely either. This was an intuitive choice on his part. She trusted Adam's "gut" instincts, perhaps even more than he did. There would be no more discussion or criticism of the decision. It was obvious that her husband was in extreme pain. As Adam often said: "piling on is a 15-yard penalty." It was time to change the subject.

"How was your trip downtown, dear?"

CHAPTER 13

Adam was a great believer in the use of high-tech tools. The Internet was used extensively in all of his previous endeavors. There was no reason to abandon the custom of using the tools in his current line of work. Now his searches of the Internet were of great help in finding household cleaning tips and nutritious, easy to prepare meals. Adam was particularly pleased with the discovery of a new recipe after an extensive search. It illustrated how to slow roast a corned beef. He loved corned beef, but sometimes felt it was too salty. By slow roasting more than seven hours with water and a variety of vegetables, you were supposed to produce a subtly flavored, tender, not too salty end product. It should prove to be healthier for the family as an added benefit. Preparation for the new recipe had started early this morning with cleaning and chopping onions, celery, and carrots. He would have to adequately allow for the seven hours of cooking time. It was extremely important to have the meal ready to serve and the house cleaned as the family arrived home.

Adam was proud of his achievements as a newly minted "house husband." He quickly finished with the carrots and ran downstairs to start a load of clothes. My "whites" always turn out brighter than Alice's, he thought, but it is unlikely that she would ever admit to it. She and the boys take my efforts for granted. The only chore he literally could not master was folding a fitted sheet. You would think that anybody who knew the details of Abstract Syntax Notation One (ASN.1) could fold a fitted sheet. It must be a male DNA thing. How did the Army train troopers to fold parachutes, he wondered? It was a great mystery.

Scotty was growing impatient. With his long lead-time chores completed, Adam attached the leash and took Scotty outside.

A week had gone by since Adam turned down Palmer's offer to rejoin the bank. The luxury of second-guessing his decision was not permitted. It was a hard rule to keep with Alice constantly giving him "the look" that said, "I told you so!" There was really no choice but to ride it out.

The Yucca and Tiger Lilies were now in bloom throughout the neighborhood. As the duo started down the road to the lake, "Project Freedom" took control of Adam's thinking. Adam was critical of himself for not thinking clearly at the onset of the project. Willie Sutton, the infamous thief, was once asked why he robbed banks. The criminal mastermind replied: "That's where the money is." That phrase had been repeated in many training sessions at FIRST CON as an example of "Pure Logic." Each time Adam thought about where to find $10 million, the phrase automatically appeared and stopped him cold. Having worked for a bank, Adam knew it was no longer possible to rob them. The guards, motion detectors, Closed-Circuit TV, and hi-tech safes made the modern bank impregnable.

It wasn't until three days ago that Adam recalled Phil's innocent statement that the Brinks truck "only" carried about $10 million. Adam silently cursed the memory of Willie Sutton's statement for blocking his thinking.

Adam's persistent perusal of the Internet located a number of closed circuit cameras monitoring traffic in the Loop. After watching hours of coverage, he identified a Brinks truck, probably the same one he saw at First Continental, take the same route at the same time every day. It always stayed in the right-hand lane adjacent to the lake before exiting Lake Shore Drive at Illinois Street. The Brinks truck was the only depository with the required amount that was mobile and relatively vulnerable.

Adam skipped right past the problem of how you cracked an armored car open to the problem of how you escaped from the scene. Just yesterday, while walking Scotty, he observed Canada geese landing on the lake in Bartlett. "The lake, of course!" He shouted to himself. Lake Michigan had 35 miles of open shorelines within the city proper. It would provide an immediate, available expressway devoid of traffic and police. He then recalled the Lake Shore Drive Bridge swinging up and blocking traffic. That was the way to bring the Brinks truck to a safe, natural, stop mere yards from the lake. A myriad of details still remained, but conceptually, on a broad sketch basis, the project appeared feasible.

Another benefit of the Lake Michigan escape route, which occurred to him, was the possibility of sealing the proceeds into watertight containers and depositing them in 40-50 feet of water adjacent to the Michigan shoreline. If the team were intercepted after the deposit, the authorities would have no physical evidence to tie them to the crime. If the team could wait until the Statute of Limitations ran out, they could get away Scot-free. That concept might work, but it would require more research. The plot was starting to resemble a new venture start-up. Instead of investors, it required helpers who were patient. A new requirement for personnel just emerged in his mind.

At the far end of the lake, a middle-aged woman with a Golden Retriever pulled into the south parking lot. "Be patient, Dot. I know Mr. Jones walks near the lake, but I'm not sure when. Ah, there is a gentleman coming up the path with a beautiful dog just like you! That must be Adam—let's go, girl."

Adam was so caught up in planning that he failed to notice the woman and her dog walking toward them. Scotty, as usual, had not missed a thing. The dog was on full alert. The strangers approached slowly and the two dogs entered into the involved ritual greeting that dogs inevitably do. Within seconds, Scotty bowed down with both front legs extended. It was the universal dog language for "Let's play!"

"It would appear that our dogs are very compatible," remarked the neatly attired woman in a pleasant yet competent voice.

"Scotty gets along with everybody! I haven't run into you or your dog out here before. What's your dog's name?"

"Dot, short for Dottie, a female who just turned five. My name is Ann, and you haven't seen me because I've never walked Dot here before."

"Welcome to our lake. My name is Adam and I'll make sure that Scotty doesn't chase all the geese away. We'll save some for Dot to go after."

"Dot would appreciate that greatly. I don't think she would know what to do if she caught one, but she sure enjoys trying. Do you come here often, Adam?"

"Scotty won't let me do anything else. It's his favorite place to walk. Actually, it's mine too, and it gives me an opportunity to think. What brings you to our beloved lake on this beautiful day?"

"I am planning to do an interview."

"You are going to conduct an interview while walking your dog? I thought I came up with unusual ideas. Who are you interviewing in such an unusual location, if I may ask?"

"Why, you, of course. Do you see anyone else out here? Scotty looks like an excellent worker, but I don't think he would qualify for our insurance plan. Dot and I were beginning to think you would never come out!" Ann lit up with a warm smile as she observed the shock on Adam's face. She took great delight in catching people unaware and off guard. Adam was totally speechless.

"I'm sorry to shock you, Adam. I found out years ago that you can determine a great deal about someone's character, or lack thereof, by the way they treat their pet. It's certainly more insightful than a resume, which is most often filled with boasts, exaggerations, and outright lies. Secondly, I feel calling someone into the office for a formal interview is like telling Dot to 'heel.' I'm not looking for subservient, well-trained people who are locked to a set of outdated rules. My firm is desperately searching for a manager who is capable of making quick, independent decisions based on the situation at hand. I believe you could be the man we are looking for. Why not meet on neutral ground, and as a bonus, see how you and Scotty interface."

"About the time you think you've seen and heard everything!" Adam was completely nonplused, but began to see the logic in her unorthodox approach. "I will agree with your comment on the dogs. One of these days a smart politician will say: 'Vote for me. I'll treat you like a dog!' Non-pet owners will be greatly offended. The dog owners, cognizant of the time, money and attention we give our companions, will enthusiastically vote for the guy."

"I believe your phrase 'smart politician' is an oxymoron, Adam." She was laughing now—a genuine, sincere laugh.

"I stand corrected. I also stand confused. What on earth do you know about me? Why would you even think I could be of assistance to your firm?"

"In today's high-tech world there is precious little we can't find out about an individual. If you thought you had a 'right to privacy,' think again. The volume of information available to me is unbelievable. It's very helpful and concurrently, extremely frightening. In addition to the high-tech and conventional tools at my disposal, I caught a lucky break when I had a discussion with Howard, who used to be on your staff at First Continental. Howard couldn't say enough good things about you. In my book, an unsolicited testimonial from someone you managed is worth a hundred resumes."

"So you came to my lake to verify Howard's comments?'

"Well yes, in part. I represent a small firm with unusual problems. You might have rejected an offer for an interview out of hand if I had proceeded in a conventional manner. The way Dot and Scotty are playing, you'll have to stay long enough to hear my story." Adam was deeply impressed. This is a gal who plays hardball with an iron fist disguised within a velvet glove. She would be a formidable opponent in a game of chess!

Ann continued. "I represent Allied Manufacturing, a small supplier of metal parts to the automobile industry. Our plant is on the southwest side, but our administration is housed in the Loop, one block from your former employer. We are marginally profitable with 200 people employed."

"Hold on, Ann. I'm deeply impressed by the effort you have made, but I honestly don't think I'm your man. I don't know diddly squat about manufacturing."

Ann thought, an honest statement in an interview, how refreshing. She was now convinced that she had the right man and was determined to pursue him. "Adam, what did you know about 'Internet Security' or 'Euro' trading before you designed systems for those applications at FIRST CON?"

"Absolutely nothing!" The depth of her research awed Adam.

"I rest my case. Systems are more than an eclectic mixture of hardware and software. People have to be sold on their importance. They have to be trained and supported. Although we are nominally going to call your position VP of Information Technology, it is your internal sales ability and general problem solving that we need. By the way, we don't put much stock in titles; I'm the VP of Administration. That title allows me to make coffee and take out the mail." Adam had never heard self-deprecating humor in use by VP's at FIRST CON.

"The firm was started by Adolph Tollinger, who came to the States from Germany at the tender age of 19. Adolph was an excellent machinist and a natural leader. He started the company three years after his arrival and incorporated it as Germania Production. The name was legally changed at the onset of World War II to Allied Mfg. Mr. Tollinger is very much alive and still legally in control of the company.

"I'm going to give this to you straight, Adam, with all the bark on. Mr. Tollinger hired me 15 years ago when nobody else would. It was shortly after my husband died in a car crash. I will always be loyal and supportive of him. Mr. Tollinger is now in his advanced years and is suffering from dementia. His only son, Bernard is in charge of the enterprise, technically; however, Bernie is into alternative lifestyles and could care less about the company or its problems. This is especially true when the Lyric Opera and Chicago Symphony are in season. We moved the administration office to the Loop so junior would be closer to the Art Institute. Bernie isn't a bad person in my opinion, he just hears a different drummer. Adolph, like most doting fathers, is in denial of his only son's ineptitude. The senior Mr. Tollinger thinks the succession of management issue is totally resolved."

"You are describing a small, marginally profitable company with a severe leadership problem. Why do you stay there, Ann?"

"Aside from my loyalty to the founder, I hired over 75% of the current employees. I can attest that they are good people. Many are from Eastern Europe, which still trains most of the best metal workers. I know the people and their families. I feel an obligation to help them stay employed."

Adam, in the midst of his unemployment journey, understood Ann's motives without question. He was beginning to feel a tremendous respect for her loyalty, honesty, and creative bent.

"What is the biggest challenge facing you?'

"Good question, Adam! We have a lot of areas for you to investigate. The auto parts supply marketplace is the toughest bar fight going on in industry today. Because of the federal CAFE standards, we are being squeezed every year for lower costs, lower weight, tighter tolerances, and longer warranties. I don't believe we can continue to do this without the help of technology and good management. Because of poor performance in the past, our manufacturing people, particularly our plant supervisor Sam McDonnell, fights every high-tech initiative. Sam uses the terms 'computers' and 'automation' as substitutes for four letter words, he's thoroughly capable of using the traditional four letter words as well."

"Let me try to summarize, Ann. You are looking for someone to add technology to an extremely hostile audience. That audience of passionate skeptics is equipped with heavy, powerful tools. They reside within a company that could go belly-up at any moment due to regulation, market forces, and the lack of a solid management succession plan. Furthermore, you think I could pull this off with no experience in manufacturing. What were you drinking after you talked with Howard?"

"What's your next best alternative, Adam? Howard assured me that you enjoy a challenge!"

"This isn't a challenge. It sounds like suicide." Adam could now see why Ann met him by the lake. He wouldn't have given her an ounce of consideration in any other setting. Her honesty and earnest desire to protect the current employees impressed him. There was a straight, no nonsense, Midwest value in her approach that he found appealing. Her logic was impeccable, as he had no viable alternative, much less a better offer. This unorthodox, crazy idea is consistent with the short-term objective of the new plan, he reminded himself.

"When did you want me to start?" Adam asked, resigned to an uncertain fate.

"Today is Tuesday. I took the liberty of putting you on the payroll yesterday. You were underpaid at First Continental. I can't afford to pay you what you're worth, but I can increase what you were paid at the bank by 10%. I'm also sensitive to the fact that you might be hurting a little right now. We are a small firm and have never paid a signing bonus. We are making an exception in your case, as I want your clever mind devoted to solving our problems. Please stop worrying about paying the mortgage or fixing the garage door. I have a check made out to you for $5,000. I wish it could be more."

Adam was deeply touched by her kindness. He hadn't been treated with respect for years, much less with this level of sensitivity. Adam was also aware that Ann was one confident cookie. There was no telling how this would work out, but he was convinced a connection had been made. "How do I find your place?"

"Don't worry about that yet either. I want you to spend the rest of your week reading everything you can find on manufacturing, inventory control, and automotive suppliers. The Internet is full of stuff. You can't learn the whole industry in a few days, but you'll be surprised how much you can pick up. All I want is for you is to feel comfortable in your initial discussions with our plant personnel. These people aren't shy or reserved! Building up your confidence to handle them is an important first step."

She handed Adam the check, said good-bye to Scotty and left.

"Wait till Alice hears about this, Scotty!" Despite the desire to try the new corned beef, Adam knew he was taking the family out for dinner.

CHAPTER 14

Adam felt completely at ease on the 6:32 Monday morning train. He was reestablishing the routine that marked stability and purpose in his life. Being employed provided the entrée that affirmed he had earned the right to be in the midst of these familiar strangers. There would never be another complaint about the daily rut.

Ann had intuitively selected the correct strategy to build confidence. Adam was honor bound, due to her trust and faith, to exploit her strategy to the best of his ability. Trust begets trust, and as a result, he set aside "Project Freedom" to focus on the study of manufacturing. He reviewed Eli Goldratt's books: "*The Goal*" and "*The Race*" as part of the new education. A great deal of useful information was contained in the reports from the American Production and Inventory Control Society (APICS).

The most impressive reference was the "*Hawthorn Works Study*" conducted and published by Western Electric. Adam was convinced that if an effective college course on manufacturing efficiency were available, this would be the text of choice.

Adam was aware that all segments of industry utilized acronyms and "buzz words" to facilitate their activities. The effect was to create a foreign language that barred rookies from serious dialog and marked them as outsiders. Once an individual understood the terms and acronyms, it was possible to break the code. You could then maintain conversations with the old timers and gain acceptance. Adam wasn't at the "ready for bear" status yet, but he was no longer a complete novice. The APICS glossary of manufacturing terms provided a solid foundation.

"Project Freedom" would not be sidetracked indefinitely. Adam believed that in the long term, it was the only viable hope. Even now, with just a semi-formed concept, he felt enabled to make decisions with fewer concerns about personal safety. As a systems designer, he fervently believed in backups, but had never applied them to his personal life. The "Project Freedom" concept was his first attempt at creating a personal backup. Its existence emboldened him. It was embarrassing that the thought of applying business skills directly to his personal life had not occurred before now.

The position at Allied was consistent with Adam's short-term strategy. Once that was under control, a larger portion of his mental resources could be dedicated to "Project Freedom." Putting the "Project" on the back burner for a while seemed appropriate for another reason. He would need help to resolve two remaining major conceptual issues—the recruitment of helpers, and obtaining the funds to procure the items necessary to execute the plan. "It takes money to make money," was an axiom that applied to all endeavors whether legitimate or not. It would take time for the muse to appear and provide answers for those two issues.

The route from Union Station to Allied's office was the same as that to First Continental, but one block shorter. Adam arrived at Allied in quick order and immediately went in search of the coffeepot. He found it and a gentleman who was obviously enjoying his first cup.

"Hi. You must be Adam. I was told to expect you this morning. My name is Dave Stevens. I'm the bean counter that everyone loves to hate! Welcome Aboard!"

"Thanks, Dave. I must have a sign on my forehead. How did you know I hated bean counters?"

"That's easy! You look fairly intelligent. Just out of curiosity, where did Ann nail you?"

"While walking my dog." Adam thought Dave's question was somewhat unusual.

"She got me in my driveway just as I returned from the unemployment office in Elgin. She has an uncanny way of finding out about a person and getting her story across. She has managed to load this company with some talented people using her unorthodox skills and persuasive abilities."

"So, you were a customer of the State of Illinois unemployment office in Elgin. How did you end up there?"

"The CEO of my former employer wanted me to falsify some financial records. I told the jerk I'd rather die first. He took my comment as a personal challenge and almost made it happen. It was pure undiluted hell. Once you get a reputation for not being a 'team player,' finding new employment is most difficult. I was being blackballed within my industry. Ann was the only person who saw past the yellow snow.

"We have a boatload of problems at Allied, Adam. I know you will be able to help. The one thing we do not have is a phony empty suit or two. Therefore I really enjoy my job despite the frustration, risk and pace."

"That's very encouraging, Dave. In a 'snap shot,' what are the big issues facing Allied?" Adam reached for his second cup.

"Long term, the management succession issue inhibits our ability to get credit lines established with the major banks. A better balance sheet and income statement would help us gain access to credit in the short term. I know you want the latest, greatest software and hardware, but I don't have the bucks to fund any such expenditure. You should be totally aware of that up front. If I did have any capital equipment dollars, I would be tempted to buy new production machines for the plant. If we don't upgrade the plant capabilities soon, we could be out of business. Last but not least, I haven't been comfortable with the numbers being produced by my accounting system. I've tried, without success, to find a problem. Maybe my instinct is wrong. I know you are here principally to help manufacturing, but I would appreciate it if, in your free time, you would look at my system. I need to fix it immediately and do it without spending money."

"Thanks for the 'snap shot'. I'll be sure to get back when I need details!" Both men were laughing when Ann joined them.

"I knew you were our kind of people! You probably haven't been here 10 minutes and you're on a coffee break! Did you meet Dave?"

"Good afternoon, Ann, nice of you to join us today! Yes, I have met Mr. Stevens and received my first assignment." Adam had a strong feeling he was going to like these people. The connections were being formed effortlessly.

Both Ann and Dave were laughing at Adam's sarcasm. They respected people who gave as well as they got.

Ann escorted Adam through the office, introduced him to a staff of a dozen administration people and showed off the high points of the office. One of those high points included a mid-range computer of ancient vintage. Adam felt like he had taken a step back in time. Literally, everything in the office was five or more years old.

"The office isn't the Field Museum of Natural History, Adam. For that experience, wait until you get to the plant!" Ann, he now believed, could read minds.

"What happened?" He was now intrigued.

"Very perceptive!" Ann had been convinced that Adam was a winner. Everything he had said or done since their walk by the lake substantiated her belief.

"About five years ago, Bernie took a run at earning his salary. Junior brought in consultants, a new office manager, and controller. They were his personal friends. Those were the only major hires in 15 years that I had no say in. They purchased and installed new systems and shoved their methods down everyone's throat. It was an unmitigated disaster. We are still suffering from the hangover. Bernie finally recognized he had made a big mistake, and we made a deal. Bernie would stay away from operations, and I would attempt to clean up the mess. Hiring Dave was a big step. We finally feel we have a handle on the administration side, but there are still questions. Nature abhors a vacuum and so do companies. Dave and I have been so busy cleaning up the office and retiring debt, that we have been forced to ignore the plant."

"I can't wait to see the plant after that introduction."

"Not today, Adam. Your insurance doesn't kick in until tomorrow!"

"I'm sorry, Ann. What the hell does insurance coverage have to do with me visiting the plant?"

"Those guys down there have vivid memories of the last time the office tried to help them. They call us 'sea gulls'."

"That's a phrase that doesn't appear in the APICS glossary of manufacturing terms. What does it mean?"

"There are a lot of manufacturing terms in use at Allied that won't appear in any glossary. Most of them I won't repeat, but I know they are frequently used at the plant. 'Sea gulls' are managers known to fly in, create a loud racket, eat everything in sight, shit all over the place, and then fly away. We had an auditor, in a suit and carrying a clipboard, go down there two years ago. He claimed that the plant people threw hot metal at his feet and tried to run him over with a forklift truck. The good news is that the auditors won't go near the place anymore."

"Who runs the plant?'

"Sam McDonnell is officially the plant manager. In reality, he is God to every person in the plant. Sam is a good man, technically competent, totally honest, and physically very imposing. You can't run a plant like ours with feminine cunning and guile. Sam is perceived as being capable of beating the crap out of anyone. He was an amateur boxing champ in his younger years. He loves tools and has a personal machine shop at home that could probably out-produce the plant."

"How did you locate and hire Sam?" Adam was looking for a pattern.

"In the parking lot of a major competitor. I caught a break. Sam had just punched out a VP who wanted him to approve some faulty parts for shipment. To Sam, quality isn't a concept—it's a religion!"

"Tomorrow promises to be an interesting day. One last question: assuming I survive the plant visit, how will I be able to illustrate to you that I'm doing a decent job?" Adam believed this question was of supreme importance and a way to thank Ann for her trust.

"Good question. The standard answer applies, in part. There are many objective criteria that measure all of us: sales, income and profit increases—scrap, costs, and turnover decreases. They are all important, but at this stage, it would be irrelevant to put specific targets in place. I have one personal objective. I've had to do extensive research on and virtually tackle all new hires. Just once, I would like to review someone who voluntarily requested a position at Allied. If I could examine four qualified candidates that came looking for work for one position, I'd be in heaven."

"That may be difficult to accomplish under the circumstances. I understand your request and why it's important. It's quite a noble challenge. I'll do my best."

"Adam, I know you will. One last thing, do whatever you think is best at the time it needs to be done. I will back your play. I have absolute trust in your judgment and instincts. My only word of advice will sound crazy and seem to be a contradiction. Make haste, slowly! We are in a race to save the company, but we are in a culture that aggressively fights change. You will have to lead, not push!"

"At the risk of sounding stupid, I fully understand the oxymoron. There must be something in the coffee you serve here! I'd better get at the task. I'll obtain the required bulletproof vest during my lunch break. Thanks for your support, Ann. It means a lot!"

"Yes, Adam, I'd love to continue our discussion, but I've got a million quotes to get out. If we could only get faster input from the plant, we might sell something." Ann turned and started reviewing a colossal stack of paper.

Adam found his colossal stack of paper mostly in the form of computer-generated reports. They were virtually stacked to the ceiling. He grabbed one from the top of the pile. It was a daily job cost report that tracked every employee's time on a job down to a tenth of an hour. It was designed to account for every minute of the day for every worker. The criteria measured included production, training, breaks, rework, and downtime.

Adam gathered up the four-inch thick report and headed to the accounting office. "Excuse me, Dave. What is this report and what should I be doing with it?"

"That report is the most important effort we in the office put forth in the support of manufacturing. It's the centerpiece of the system recommended by Bernie's consultants. It represents 75% of the costs associated with your department. In addition, I have two people on my staff feeding it data full time. We courier multiple copies to the plant daily."

"How do you use it, Dave?"

"I don't even look at it. The thing has so many lies and half-truths in it that I won't touch it. I assume it is of great value to the plant. I've never had time to ask them how they use it. Since I answered your question, can you look at my stuff?"

Adam knew he was trapped. Reluctantly, he sat down and started reviewing Dave's system. It was a standard accounting package that Bernie's consultant had recommended and installed. Adam wasn't specifically familiar with this system, but had reviewed many similar packages in the past.

Unfortunately, small companies that relied on consultants for major projects were seldom taught the "Why" and "How" of the systems they bought. Allied was no different. When the consultants got something to work reasonably well, they quit. "Don't fix what ain't broke" was the prevailing sentiment. Adam was all too familiar with the expression and its inapplicability to software. This particular accounting system relied heavily on pre-loaded tables that had been installed hastily and never revisited. Adam and Dave reviewed the original installation and made numerous changes to the table values.

Then Adam spotted 10 new releases, or "fixes," provided by the software vendor neatly stacked on a bookshelf. None had been opened, much less installed. To Adam's horror, he found that the very first release contained a "fix" that corrected a major glitch in the sub-totaling routine. It took all afternoon to apply the releases in sequence and re-run the reports.

Dave was ecstatic with the results. The numbers finally felt right. That was the good news. The bad news was that between the incorrect tables, and failure to install the "fixes," Allied had understated their assets by 23% and overstated their liabilities by 10%.

"We're rich," Adam exclaimed! "Now I can build my glass enclosed high technology palace."

"Not so fast, Adam! This fix doesn't put cash in our pockets, but it may help with establishing lines of credit. Great job, I'll sleep better tonight!" Dave had the look of a man who had just taken a large, sharp stone from his shoe.

Ann joined the festivities. "Well, Adam. I had hoped the profitability of Allied would improve with your arrival, but I didn't think you would make great strides on the first day. Congratulations!"

Adam ended up catching the 7:48 to Bartlett. He was utterly exhausted. For the first time in months, he felt a sense of accomplishment. The realization that it was mostly luck did not dim the feeling. Being appreciated for your effort and talent by your colleagues negated much of the rest of the fatigue.

Although satisfied with the events of the day, Adam was anxious about his first meeting with Sam. It was scheduled for tomorrow morning and he hadn't found time to prepare. It wasn't a case of trying to impress Sam. Adam simply didn't want to come off as an idiot in this new environment. Doing so would severely impair his ability to affect the changes that Allied needed to survive. It would probably have a negative impact on his employment with Allied as well. Creating the "Project Freedom" backup plan was something he should have done years earlier. It would be his "rod and staff" as he "walked through the valley" of the plant.

CHAPTER 15

The traffic on the Eisenhower expressway this morning was brutal. It had been years since Adam had commuted by car to work, and he had forgotten how congested it could be. It appeared as though every vehicle produced in the Western world and Japan was sharing the highway with him. Adam had planned to take the Ike to Cicero Avenue and proceed south from there. There was now no question that he would be late arriving at the plant. What a great way to create a good first impression with Sam, he thought. The need for constant attention to traffic negated the deep thinking that had become a familiar routine on the train. I'll have to find a better way to get to the plant from home. It was late enough in the morning that he saw a *Sears*' store that was open for business. On an impulse, Adam drove in and went directly to the tool department.

Finding the plant's physical location once he left *Sears* was no problem. Even though he had never been in this particular section of the city before, it was possible to drive right to it. Chicago is laid out in such a logical grid that rank rookies can achieve excellent navigation results. Adam couldn't help but notice the potholes and cracks in the plant's parking lot as he found a space to park. Weeds protruded from every pothole and surrounded the lot in dense clusters. A large four-story abandoned facility immediately south of Allied dominated the skyline. The boarded up windows in the ancient structure seemed to stare at him with a vacant look. Litter of every imaginable type lined the curbs. The entire neighborhood surrounding Allied's plant looked depressed and rundown.

It was now 9:30 AM. Ann had set the appointment with Sam for 7:30. Seeing no other way into the facility, Adam entered the plant through an open truck dock. It was very dim inside, which created the impression that he was entering a cave. The noise from the production machines within the cave was an ear-shattering roar. Individual mechanical sounds of grinding and pounding were discernible within the background of the roar. Even in the dim light, Adam could perceive a cloud of light gray smoke from cutting oil, which hung in a haze layer 12 feet above the floor. The ceiling of the plant was high above and contained a large overhead crane. The windows near the top of the high walls were caked in grime, which permitted very little light into the facility. The ironwork of the trusses holding up the plant ceiling had a vague "Art Deco" design. That would date the original construction of the plant back to the 1920's.

Adam saw everything, but people who could assist him. He began to wonder if he would ever locate Sam. "Thank God, I didn't wear a suit to this meeting. It would be ruined in 10 minutes or less in this environment."

"Sea Gull Alert! Sea Gull Alert!" A great, loud voice came booming out of the dark factory abyss and could be heard clearly above the noise of the equipment. Adam figured correctly that Sam had found him.

A tall, lanky, physically fit man with a face of granite and just a wisp of a Scottish burr in his voice emerged from the darkness of the shipping dock. "You can't be sneaking up on us from the back door even though it's almost quitting time. We start here at 7:00 AM sharp, Mister Sea Gull. Is that too early for you wussies from the office?"

"No, that's universally recognized as the perfect start time for wussies. If I had arrived at that time or earlier, it would have shown you up, or worse, it would have denied you something to bitch about! My name's Adam, you must be Sam. It's a pleasure to meet you. Where the hell do you hide the damn coffee?"

"Glory be, we got ourselves a smart-ass 'sea gull.' We'll see how long that lasts. Come on, I'll show you where we keep the good stuff." Sam, despite his deep fears, enjoyed the banter. Ann had said Adam was a good man. Sam knew from experience that she was rarely wrong.

The two men got their coffee and strode into Sam's office, which was littered with the same thick reports that were piled up in Adam's office. "Just out of curiosity and before we get started, are those reports of any use to you?"

"Yes indeed they are! I use them to keep my door propped open when 'sea gulls' flap their wings and create a big draft."

"No, I'm serious, Sam! What value do you receive from them?"

"I'm serious, too. We don't use them. They are totally void of any practical data. Give me a bloody break! The costs illustrated are extended to four places to the right of the decimal, but nobody checks the value of the number to the left of the decimal. Bloody bean counters should all be shot or preferably drawn and quartered! I assume somebody downtown uses them, but we sure as hell don't."

"Well, Sam, I looked at a couple of the reports at some depth yesterday. It looks like machine center 43 consistently produces a lot of bad parts."

Sam instantly went to high alert status. He knew intuitively that this new "sea gull" was going to blame his people for poor performance. They always did, and Sam protected his troops like a "she" bear with an attitude. "We didn't need any bloody report to tell us that news! We were on the center 43 problem from day one."

"It's obviously not a people problem, Sam. The problem persists over all shifts and multiple operators. Could it be that the drive shaft is slightly out of round?"

"That's the first bloody thing we checked. We aren't stupid, you know! The shaft passed inspection, and it's a dog to pull it out and perform the inspection." Sam was peeved, but somewhat mystified. He didn't think a "sea gull" existed in the universe who knew a drive shaft from a Volvo.

"Why don't you replace it with a new shaft Sam, on a hunch that it's out of round to such an insignificant degree that it could be overlooked during the quality check."

"And where the hell am I to get the money for a new drive shaft, Mr. Smart-ass 'Sea Gull'? I'm way over budget on repair parts as it is."

"Call Dave. Order the new shaft and charge my budget."

"How come you got the bloody money? Damn, it's all I can do to hold this place together with spit and duct tape. Now you tell me there is extra money in the administration budget! The world is bloody crazy!"

"Hold on, Sam! I didn't say I had the money, but I'm going to generate some significant savings in the near future."

"Where the hell do you expect to achieve sufficient savings to pay for a drive shaft? They aren't cheap, you know!"

"I'm going to generate a shit load of savings because I have just decided to stop running that stupid ass job costing report. Not having to pay the courier fees alone could be enough to buy you two shafts, which I believe is a better use of the company's money."

Sam sat dumbfounded. He literally didn't believe what he heard. "I thought the dumb report was the Holy Grail for 'sea gulls.' Bernie's consultants were sure it would solve all of the plant's problems and cure AIDS worldwide as a bonus. Are you authorized to do this, Mr. Sea Gull?"

Adam pretended to frantically search his pockets. "I'm sure I've got the lousy authorization here somewhere. Give me a minute to find it. What does a dammed authorization ticket look like anyway?"

Sam was the kind of guy that didn't do anything halfway. He howled a large booming laugh that echoed down the halls! The plant grapevine, which was intently monitoring the meeting, was titillated and confused. Sam had never laughed when a sea gull was present, at least not in recent memory. He would curse aplenty, sometimes produce cynical cackles, but never provide deep, genuine laughter.

"You got yourself a deal, Adam! I would issue sleeping rights with my wife to get rid of that useless report and the effort we go through to prepare it. To get a new drive shaft to boot is one hell of a bargain. I may have to put out the word to be careful driving forklift trucks in your vicinity."

"Sam, I don't want you to think we don't want to support you. If you ever need a special, one time analysis to find a solution to a quality problem, I would be overjoyed to lend a hand."

"Well, that's mighty decent of you, Laddie. Let me clue you into something since you are green as grass. My guys, with their own dollars, have purchased more computing capacity than the rest of the entire Allied organization. They have the skills and desire to run multi-variable, statistical analysis on anything you can name. Please stop the patronizing, arrogant assumption that all the 'smarts' exist at headquarters. Also, that the 'dummies' at the plant can't get dressed in the morning without your assistance or approval. It's bad enough that I have to put up with that patronizing crap from the government. I refuse to accept that arrogant bullshit from my own company! We're not shy. Ask us what we want and we'll tell you. You won't have to guess."

"O.K., Sam. Your last point was well taken and it hurt. I never want to be confused with the Feds again. What can I do to help the plant?"

"Bloody good, Adam! I thought you'd never ask! I have stated this request to headquarters before, but not specifically to you. We need NEW PRODUCTION MACHINES. I don't want or need computer generated reports, newly designed letterhead, consultants or a new phone system. I want and need NEW PRODUCTION MACHINES!

Adam knew better than to question or interrupt Sam, who was now on an emotional tear. Sam's frustration was more than evident. "We couldn't bid on 10% of the automobile parts last year because we couldn't physically make the bloody things at any price. Our machines were designed to work with standard carbon steel. The new parts are more and more specified as stainless, or alloys, tougher than carbon steel. The only way I can produce a part that meets specifications is to run my machines at 50% to 75% of their rated speed. Even at the lower speeds, we go through tooling like shit through a goose. Headquarters response is: 'Why are you shipping late?' Hell, it's a miracle we get anything out at all, much less on time. If we can't compete on another 10% of the parts next model year you might as well close the doors. Every man down here knows that too. They look at the absence of investments in new equipment as evidence of a 'don't care' attitude by management. Even if I didn't have objective, business related reasons for the new machines, I would be pushing for them because of the bloody morale issue alone!"

"Sam, if I had a magic wand, which unfortunately I don't, what would be your choice for new equipment?"

"That's easy! The National 9300, it's a Computer Numerical Control (CNC), multi head, vertical mill. Its capabilities are best suited to our current workload and it would allow us to bid on some parts that we had to 'No Bid' in the past. We at the plant have researched this carefully. I have heard through some of my contacts that National is having some start-up problems, but that's common for new machines in general and National in particular. They will get the problems on the 9300 solved."

"Do you have the room and facilities to feed the 9300?" Adam had installed capital equipment in the past and knew this was a frequently over-looked question.

"I'll have to make some room. I have a National model 50 and one model 60 that we could scrap to free up floor space. Those two are really ancient machines with magnetic tape controls. I figure they're probably 45-50 years old. They would be impossible to sell, as they have no value left. It's unbelievable that we are still running them. It's like trying to play a Mozart symphony on a ukulele without the use of your hands."

At that moment, a whistle went off and Adam thought that cattle were stampeding inside the plant. "Lunch break," Sam remarked laconically. "Same thing happens at coffee breaks except if you get in somebody's way, they will flat knock you down."

"Sam, I don't want you to get all choked up and emotional on me. I picked up something this morning as a little get acquainted present. It's not the 9300, but it's the best I could do at the time." With that comment, Adam retrieved the package purchased at *Sears* from his briefcase.

Sam gave Adam a worried look. "Beware of 'sea gulls' bearing gifts, I say!" Sam opened the package with extreme caution.

"Why it's a set of Torx screwdrivers. I needed to get these!" Sam was sincerely impressed. He was smiling warmly and then suddenly froze. "What are you trying to do—buy me off?"

"No, Sam. I don't think that could be done based on what I have observed and from what Ann has told me. If it could, it would take a lot more than some screwdrivers. I knew you loved tools and assumed you hadn't had time to pick up the new Torx drivers yet. The real reason for the gift is that we are all facing some stiff challenges. If we pull this off, we can take turns with your gift, screwing all the people who said it couldn't be done!"

For the second time that morning Sam's laugh rolled out of his office and thundered down the halls. The plant grapevine took note and recorded history being made. Whoever this new "sea gull" was, he could make the boss laugh. This new "Sea Gull" was a guy you had to treat with respect.

"Adam, I'll treasure your gift, but not as much as you stopping the report and getting me a new drive shaft. As much as I enjoyed all of this, I'd swap everything in a heartbeat for a 9300!"

"Who calls on you from National?" Adam was totally unfamiliar with Allied's vendors.

"Bill Stokes has been calling on us for years. I don't know why. We never can buy anything. He's a good man, very sharp technically. Bill normally works out of their big fancy showroom in the burbs. Would you like his card?"

"Yes, Sam and thank you for your insights."

"Thank you, Adam. You may prove to be the only 'sea gull' in the bloody flock worth a damn. That assumption will not be proved until I get my 9300." Adam left, hoping to catch Bill Stokes at the show room.

*   *   *   *

On the command signal, police cars roared in from all directions with their sirens wailing. Squads of heavily armed officers stormed through the side, front, and back doors of the old warehouse on the West Side simultaneously. It was a well-choreographed assault that was perfectly executed. The officers' Kevlar armor glistened in the floodlights as they secured the facility.

The old warehouse turned out to be completely clean. There was a total absence of people, equipment, or inventory. Two drug-sniffing dogs were acting agitated, but unable to find anything.

The two detectives that orchestrated the raid viewed the scene with disbelief and growing anger.

"I know our information was solid. The way the dogs are acting proves there was plenty of stuff here, but its been moved."

The uniformed officers involved in the assault looked at the detectives with growing scorn. They appreciated the fact that they had not been met with a hail of bullets, but they hated dry runs almost as much as the real deal. The two detectives had just lost a great deal of their most valuable asset. Their credibility with the uniformed men had been significantly reduced.

"I told you Ron, the opposition aren't fools. They may be lucky to boot!"

"Perhaps they are just well informed, Luke."

CHAPTER 16

The old, rusty car could barely climb in and out of the weed-choked potholes that scarred Allied's parking lot. On one hand, Adam was thankful he was driving his second car that was normally used to drive to the train station. It was way beyond being damaged by the parking lot or by vandals in the neighborhood. On the other hand, the air conditioning was not functioning on the old beast. He would pay dearly for that choice today. The day was going to be a hot, humid late July scorcher. For the second time today, he was thankful he had not worn a suit.

He headed west to an expensive new office park near the affluent suburb of Oak Brook to find National's showroom. Adam decided not to call Bill Stokes first to establish an appointment. If Bill was there, fine. If not, Adam could still get much of the information on the 9300 from somebody. He wasn't totally sure of what approach to take or what kind of information to obtain. Adam sincerely believed Dave Stevens when the bean counter said there were no capital equipment funds to spare. Adam also believed Sam McDonnell when the head of manufacturing forcibly stated the need to have a 9300 now. Adam hoped the "muse" that had visited Stan earlier in the year at FIRST CON would visit him now.

National had provided ample guest parking in their well paved, beautifully landscaped lot. It was a short walk from the car to a magnificent entryway, which was flanked by masses of multi-hued Impatiens in full bloom. Entering the building was comparable to arriving at a "five star" hotel instead of a business office. There were so many potted palms in the lobby that the office could be mistaken for the Garfield Park Conservatory. Soft, classical music was playing in the background—Brahms, he thought. Adam could visualize the showroom being praised in a feature article by *Vogue* magazine. Despite the hot temperature and the banks of flowers in full bloom, Adam was convinced he was surrounded by "yellow snow."

It would be impossible to describe the difference between Allied's production facilities and the National showroom to Alice or any neutral observer. The differences went beyond what you could observe. The feel, sounds, and smells were totally at odds. He felt overdressed this morning at the plant and significantly underdressed this afternoon at the showroom. The enormity of the difference between the two locations jump-started the thinking process.

An attractive, well-attired receptionist warily eyed Adam as he approached her desk. The desk was constructed of sweeping curves of chrome and glass and was approximately the size of a 1962 Cadillac El Dorado. "Can I help you, sir?"

"Yes. My name is Jones. I work for Allied Manufacturing. Could you ascertain if Mr. Bill Stokes is available? I'm afraid my visit is a surprise, as Bill is not expecting me."

She responded with a stern look coupled with a hint of a sneer and said: "This is highly irregular. I'll see what I can do."

Adam took a moment to view the gargantuan showroom. It was stuffed with shiny, new equipment of all sizes. The room had to be over three stories tall. It was obvious that the entire building was designed and built to feature the showroom. There wasn't a solitary soul in the place. That could be significant, Adam thought. The muse was starting to work. He was beginning to formulate an approach.

Bill Stokes approached Adam with a confused look. The salesman was fairly young and wore a sport coat and slacks. Adam figured Stokes was trying to split the difference between a headquarters dress code requirement and his clients' standards, which probably made both unhappy. "I'm sorry, Mr. Jones. I don't believe we've met. My name is Bill Stokes. How can I help you?"

"We have not met, Bill. I just joined Allied yesterday. In fact, I don't have a card yet. I had an interesting meeting with Sam McDonnell this morning, and as a result, I was hoping to get some information from you. I apologize for not calling in advance."

"No problem, Mr. Jones! I know Mr. McDonnell fairly well and can fully understand your sense of urgency. Sam is a legend in our industry for his expertise and, shall we say, colorful personality. Sam can frequently be 'hell on wheels!' I just wish Allied would provide him with some funds to buy equipment. My hope is that the equipment would be purchased from National."

"Actually that is one reason I'm here. Sam seems smitten with your Model 9300. Could you possibly demonstrate the machine's capabilities to me?"

"I'd be delighted to. Follow me, please." As Bill led Adam to the center stage of the showroom, the salesman thought: "Maybe old Allied isn't dead yet. They've got a new executive looking at equipment. This could be my lucky day."

They approached the monster machine with five heads on the center stage of the showroom. It literally glistened under the spotlights from several coats of wax. "Is this an actual machine or just a mock up?" Adam asked.

"This is the real deal, Adam. It is a complete machine in every respect."

"O.K. Bill. Fire it up! I definitely want to see how the 9300 performs."

Bill Stokes was horrified at the suggestion. "I can't actually start the machine in the showroom. It's not even hooked up to electrical power. We can't feed the machine with raw material, nor are we set up to recover finished parts."

"I'm supposed to imagine parts coming out here and raw material feeding from over there?" Adam had pointed to where he thought the input and output were accommodated.

"That's exactly right." Bill replied.

"Does the machine shake a lot while producing parts?"

"We couldn't hold the tight tolerances our customers demand on the finished part if it moved a great deal. One of the strongest and most desirable features of the 9300 is its enhanced stability."

Adam reached out and touched the machine, holding his hand steady on the drill heads for a full minute. "Bill, I can see you are dead right about that feature. I don't feel a damn thing. You must have a patent on that enhanced stability feature." There was no smile on Adam's face while complimenting Stokes for his honesty. Bill was starting to feel a bit uncomfortable. He wasn't sure if Adam was making fun of his comment or if Adam was completely stupid. Stokes had given countless demos in his career, but none had proceeded exactly like this.

"How does the machine smell when running production, Mr. Stokes?

"I'm sorry Mr. Jones, I don't fully understand." Bill, with a wealth of experience as a senior salesman, had no idea where this was going. The ambiguity in Adam's responses and questions were starting to rattle his confidence.

Adam was starting to push harder: "I mean, how much aroma of burnt cutting oil do I get with the 9300 if it were running production? This unit obviously isn't running parts, so it's hard as hell to imagine how it would smell."

"Our vapor recovery system on the 9300 is state of the art. We capture over 95% of the fumes. The machine has virtually no smell at all. We at National are very proud of that achievement. We have been issued a patent on that sub-system."

Adam stepped back and studied the machine in complete silence for a full five minutes while looking at the large duct, which he assumed was part of the vapor recovery sub-system. "I really want to believe you, Mr. Stokes; however, in my imagination, the hypothetical job which is theoretically running in this palatial setting is actually generating an immense aroma. In my imagination, the 9300 is only achieving an 80% recovery rate. Should the hypothetical operator make an actual or imaginary adjustment to achieve compliance with specifications?"

"O.K., Mr. Jones. If you are trying to get me to agree that selling and demonstrating from the showroom is no substitute for a customer visit, you can stop. I agree. You win!"

"Then why didn't you offer me that opportunity at the onset of our discussion and presentation?"

Bill Stokes didn't respond. He was staring at his feet in complete silence.

"Is it because you are having troubles with the first few installations?" Bill silently nodded affirmatively.

"Look, Bill, I'm not trying to give you a hard time. I came here because I am a rookie. I wouldn't recognize a 9300 from a Tulip Tree. I know you will want between $500,000 to $700,000 for one unit. How can I, or any other prospect, justify that expenditure based on looking at a dead machine sitting in this luxurious setting? I had hoped to see, feel, and smell real production. I wanted to see metal chips flying. You are in sales. You know that it's the 'Persuaded that Persuade!' You are undoubtedly an honest man representing a reputable firm. Beyond relying exclusively on your reputation, how can I risk that amount of capital if I can't personally verify the features you are so proud of?"

"Adam, I couldn't agree more. That's why sales on a new model start so slowly. Many of my prospects know more about the machines than you do, but they still play the 'Man From Missouri' routine—Show Me!"

"Your prospects have no alternative. What I really wanted to do during this visit was check the dimensions of a finished part with a micrometer. They have to be perfect. We have to check, not because we don't trust you or your firm, but because that's what our customers do when they receive the parts from us."

"I'm very familiar with my customers' needs, Adam. My fellow salesmen think this showroom is as practical and efficient as a liberal congressman's prescription for the economy. Right now, I have to use it because there are only two installations at present and neither seems to be working well. My lack of sales and commission dollars of late directly reflect the situation."

"Do you think Sam McDonnell could make the 9300 sing?" Adam asked, calmly.

"More so than anyone I know. But even if Sam could, I would be very uncomfortable bringing any prospect to Allied's premises. The plant looks like hell! The parking lot alone looks like it has a severe case of acne." Bill sounded totally convinced.

"Would I be correct in assuming that the next biggest objection to buying your equipment is: "My people are too stupid to run this sophisticated equipment?"

Bill was shocked: "How did you know that?"

"Because some things are constant across industry lines. Now Bill, I'm going to ask you to use your imagination. How many prospects could voice that objection after visiting Allied? How many of your prospects think it's a step down when they leave here and go home? When they leave Allied and go home, they will think they have returned to paradise. Perhaps one of the reasons I couldn't imagine production on this dead machine in this showroom is that I keep expecting a butler in a tuxedo to approach with white wine and Brie. That confusion will never happen to any prospect who visits Allied!"

Bill Stokes' imagination was considerably better than Adam's. He could see customer visits coming off just as Adam had forecast. Seeing actual production being performed by real people had inexhaustible appeal. It would persuade people to invest. Persuaded people do buy equipment, which is the undeniable prerequisite for commission. Commission is the "alpha and omega" for all salesmen. Adam had fired Stokes' desire. "How could we make this happen?" Bill asked.

"I'm suggesting, in light of our companies' long relationship, that you ship this very 9300 from this glittering mansion to its rightful home at Allied. I want it considered as a 'no charge' demonstration machine for a year. We will want an option to buy at the end of the year with a significant discount, because by then it's a used machine. You pick up the cost for freight. We pick up utilities, insurance, and tooling. We will provide any prospect of National access to our shop floor to witness actual production being run at any time you request. We will make it perform perfectly. Bill, for the first time, you will have an adequate way to demonstrate the 9300's features while running in a realistic, non-intimidating environment. The 9300 should not sit in this velvet-lined emporium gathering dust. It should be at Allied, where it could be making actual finished parts for me and commission dollars for you!"

"Adam, what you are suggesting may not be that far-fetched. We are having problems gaining momentum with the 9300. I truly believe it's a good machine, but this phony showroom doesn't help us sell the unit. In addition, there is a rumor circulating that marketing wants the space in the showroom that the 9300 is now occupying. If we were to do this, would Sam be available for my prospects to interview? He is held in high regard within the industry."

"I don't think we could keep Sam away if we wanted to. One additional thought. We have a little United Nations on our payroll at Allied. We will try to train as many operators as possible on the 9300. I believe your prospects would have similar personnel within their ranks who are multi-lingual. It may be possible that we could provide answers to your prospects' questions in their native tongue, which could give you a big edge over your competition."

Bill Stokes could easily visualize the demonstrations and knew Adam made sense. Throughout his career, Stokes had never sold a machine without a customer visit. Moreover, he didn't know of any other National salesman that had either. To a man, they hated the showroom and its feminine ambiance. They used it only when they were without satisfactory customer installations. The entire initial sales effort was described as: "Getting the first olive out of the bottle."

"One possible problem, Adam. I'm sure my bean counters will require some type of down payment even for a demonstration machine. How do we answer that request?"

"I'm prepared to offer you a National Model 50 and a Model 60 in lieu of a down payment."

"That's little more than a pile of junk! Those machines have to be 45-50 years old. Why do you expect credit for machines that most firms would pay big bucks just to have carted away?"

"Bill, in my mind, I see them cleaned up and flanking the entrance to your showroom. What are you really selling? National has a track record for reliability and endurance. How is that illustrated in this showroom? How many of your competitors can claim that they have had machines running production for 50 years? We will be able to attest that we ran production on those units through this current week."

"Adam, I'm not sure at this point whether you're the smartest, dumbest, or luckiest man in the world. We have a new director of advertising who said much the same thing last week. There may be a perceived value for those old machines after all is said and done. I still think this concept is totally crazy, but I pledge my best efforts to get this approved. I would love to see Sam's face when the old man fires up the 9300! It would be the high point of my career."

"Please make it happen, Bill. I also apologize for any theatrics in our conversation."

"No problem. I think I learned something about sales today. I'll get back to you as soon as possible."

It was after 5:00 before Adam left the National showroom. He spent extra time gathering everything written about the 9300's software. The problems the other installations were having could be software-related. If so, perhaps he could play a direct role in making Sam happy.

CHAPTER 17

The first two days at Allied had been anything but dull. Adam reflected on the recent activities while settling into the familiar routine from Franklin Park to Union Station. As a break from the challenges posed by Allied's many problems, he allocated some time to think about "Project Freedom."

Perhaps his initial thoughts on how to approach a halted Brinks truck were in error. It was fruitless to ponder how to "crack into" the truck. Phil made the right assessment. You would need a nuclear powered can opener, and it was unlikely to be found for sale on the Internet. How could you create a situation where the guards wanted to get "out"? That could prove to be a more rewarding concept to explore. The Internet did have many web sites listing new and used armored cars for sale. The specifications of size and capabilities were illustrated in great detail. It gave Adam a framework and the basic data to work the problem.

Adam couldn't force his mind to work the armored car problem. Allied's issues kept screaming for attention. He was now convinced there was no one "silver bullet" that could turn the company around. That wasn't hard to believe. Every apparent problem had multiple causes and multiple effects. Even if he were successful in getting National's agreement to provide a 9300, it would only postpone the inevitable negative slide to bankruptcy. The turn to a solid positive direction would require far more than one new machine. There were additional problems with morale, sales, productivity, recruiting, housekeeping, and management succession. The on-going war to fix these many issues would have to be waged on a wide front, over a long time, and was bound to feature a multitude of battles.

Dave met Adam at the coffeepot. "Are you serious about canceling the job cost report?"

"As serious as a heart attack, Dave. It has no value to you—it simply drains your resources. Sam doesn't use it. He has first hand knowledge of the data the report is intended to provide. It's a complete waste."

"I agree, Adam. What should I do with the two people on my staff that input data to the dumb thing all day?" Adam could see that Dave was showing signs of anxiety, anticipating the "off with their head" answer that modern business practice dictated.

"Find other productive work for them, Dave. Perhaps Ann needs help with the generation of quotations. I don't care what the two do as long as it's productive. I will not establish a precedent of firing people as a result of cost saving ideas. If such an impression were created, we would never get co-operation from our employees. Additionally, I think it is our responsibility to invest Allied's human capital with the same care we use to invest our few dollars.

Dave looked relieved. "I was hoping that you shared my belief. You are correct in assuming that Ann needs help and I need somebody to assist me with shagging receivables. I'll make sure that both people recognize this as a promotion. I also understand I'm to purchase a new drive shaft from your budget?"

"Sam moves quickly, I see. Yes, Dave. I made that commitment to Sam. I hope I have enough savings in reduced courier costs and paper supplies to cover the cost of the drive shaft. If not, I'll give you an IOU."

"You're covered. For all it's worth, I think your decisions are long overdue." With that, Dave left to tell his people about their promotions and new responsibilities."

Adam grabbed some coffee and ran to his cubicle to answer the phone. He was pleasantly shocked to hear Bill Stokes on the line.

"Adam, you won't believe this. I'm not sure I believe it either, but Mr. Williams, our President, just gave the official approval to your idea. It's totally unprecedented! I have been asked to notify you that we are packing the 9300 for shipment to Allied. That work is progressing even as we speak. There are a number of options and accessories available on the 9300. I've taken the liberty of configuring the unit exactly as the quotation I prepared for Sam three months ago. The unit will have everything you need to manufacture your parts. We expect to deliver by company truck at 9:00 AM Thursday. Good Lord, that's tomorrow! In the excitement, I almost forgot. Can you have the Model 50 and 60 ready by then?"

"We'll have the two units ready if I have to pack them myself. Thanks, Bill. In my opinion, Mr. Williams' decision will be good for both of us." Adam couldn't restrain himself as he hung up the phone, shouting: "YES!" That brought Ann into his cubicle on the dead run. Adam motioned for her sit down while making a call to the plant.

"Sam, this is Adam Sea Gull. Stop wasting your time counting the silverware in an attempt to see what I stole during my visit yesterday. I need your help urgently!"

"I'm not counting the bloody silverware. We don't have any to count! Besides, we watched you like a hawk during your entire visit. Have you decided to go back on your word and reinstate that bloody report?"

"No, Sam! My decision remains intact. In fact, we're in the process of reassigning the people who generated it at this very moment."

"You mean you didn't fire them?"

"Sam, it's not in the company's best interest to fire good people, but we don't have time for management philosophy right now. Can you pack the Model 50 and the Model 60 for shipment by tomorrow morning?"

"I could. Why would I want to pack up my two oldest, dearest friends?"

"To make room for the 9300 that will arrive in the morning!" There was a long pause before Sam's reply.

"Don't play with an old man's heart, Laddie!"

"I'm not, Sam! The truck with the 9300 from National is supposed to be there at 9:00 AM. I want your two 'old friends' to be shipped out of Allied on that same truck."

"Mr. Sea Gull, if you are serious, how did you configure the bloody thing?"

"The unit is configured exactly as Stokes quoted you three months ago. Have you changed your mind or gotten cold feet?"

"No! That's exactly what we need, no more, no less. My God, this is a bloody miracle! If you are playing with my mind, I will personally show you several exciting new ways to use your Torx screwdrivers."

"Put the screwdrivers away unless you need them to pack the 50 and 60. Make it happen, Sam. I want to see the 9300 making parts." As Adam concluded the call, he thought he could hear a sob in Sam's voice. "That couldn't possibly be—not Sam," he told himself.

Ann was waiting for Adam to finish the call. "I apologize for listening to your conversation, but I couldn't wait for the good news. If I overheard you correctly, you've killed the job cost report, got me some help, bought a new drive shaft, and got Sam a new 9300. What happened to my advice of: 'Make haste slowly!' Did it go in one ear and out the other?" Ann had a huge smile on her face as she said this.

Adam related the story of his visit to National and discussion with Stokes. "You mean you got the machine for free?" Ann was incredulous.

"Not free, Ann! We have an option to buy in one year. It's a demo machine until then. We are a long way from making this a successful transaction. National still can't get the 9300 to run correctly at two installations. It may be a software 'glitch.' I'll look for that today. If we can't get the 9300 to work effectively, we will have lost two good, but old machines. Hold the smiles for a moment and keep your fingers crossed."

"I still think it's a great idea. Let me know how I can help." Ann returned to her office with a spring in her step.

Adam turned to the stack of documentation illustrating the 9300's software. He had everything needed, including the detailed listings that were used universally to "de-bug" software. It had been years since Adam had done this type of work. He wasn't familiar with CNC code specifically, but knew the language it was written in. This lack of experience, in a perverse way, could help. It was a "forest and tree" situation. Experienced people tended to overlook the subtle little errors that lead to intermittent failures. As a rookie, he would be forced to go through the listings line for line.

Five hours of concentrated review later, nothing had been found. Frustrated and exhausted, Adam got up from the desk for some coffee and a chance to rest his eyes. Dave was at the pot.

"Adam, I saw you were hard at work and didn't want to interrupt you. Is it true that you are going to install a 9300 tomorrow at 'no charge' to Allied?"

"Good Lord willing, we are, Dave. I thought that's what you wanted to do, along with Sam."

"I do, Adam, but from an accounting standpoint it gives me real grief. I can't list the new machine as an asset because we don't own it. I don't know how to account for the loss of two of our existing assets that we didn't sell or scrap. They will just disappear. I have no idea what the auditors will do or say."

"Dave, I understand your concerns. Take some solace from the fact that the auditors won't go near the plant. Take additional justification that without new machines we will soon close the doors. If I get the 9300 Thursday as promised, I will never give it up. My neighbor Frank quotes from *Star Trek* movies: If you can't win playing by the rules—change the rules! We need that machine and several more like it if we are ever going to win. Do whatever you have to do to make it happen."

"Aye, Aye, Captain Kirk!"

Adam returned to the listings muttering to himself, "damn bean-counters. They can always find a way to make the author of a good idea wish he'd never had it." Adam knew Dave was exposing himself to some personal risk by agreeing to juggle the books. Unlike the FIRST CON bean counters, Dave was at least trying to meet him halfway. The artificiality in all accountants' thinking was still annoying and the frustration made him spill coffee on the listings.

Suppressing a desire to shout vulgarities, he started wiping coffee from a section of the listing that he was just about to review. There it was! Beneath the coffee stain, he detected a simple, subtle mistake in the code. Adam left the office, walked in circles for two minutes, and returned. It was still there. He had not imagined it! The phenomenon was familiar to anyone who spent hours trying to find where a piece went in a jigsaw puzzle. You take a break to answer the phone, come back and suddenly you see exactly where the piece goes. Adam couldn't believe his luck. It was equivalent to finding that he qualified for a major deduction in income taxes. It was difficult, when successful, not to assign "divine intervention" to these phenomena. Adam did not, because it felt heretical. Not that God wasn't technically qualified; it was more of a belief that God was too busy with issues that are more important. Finding the problem was a big deal, but with his lack of experience, he wasn't sure of the best way to "fix" it.

"Sam, this is Adam again. Who is the best CNC programmer in your group?"

"That would be Vladamir Kursk. He just arrived in the States a few months ago from Russia. The lad speaks little English, but he's a bloody genius when speaking CNC. Why do you ask?"

"I may have found a problem with National's software, but I'm not sure how to fix it correctly. Can you free Mr. Kursk up so that I can work with him a little?"

"No problem. He's just about to finish packing up the Model 50. I was going to send him home."

"Sam, if he's your best man, why is he working on your oldest machine?"

"I'd tried to tell you yesterday that I've had to put my best guys on the old stuff. It takes a bloody genius to occasionally nudge good quality parts from that junk."

"You are right, Sam. I keep forgetting that the world is back assward! Don't let Vladamir go home. I'll meet him in the cafeteria as soon as I can get there."

Sam agreed and Adam hastily gathered the documentation, waved good-bye to Ann, and caught a cab to the plant.

Vladamir was an intense, nervous young man who eyed the "sea gull" with great suspicion. Other than saying "Hello," Adam was convinced he spoke no English. Adam opened the listing and pointed to the area that was highlighted. There was an immediate transformation in Vladamir. His eyes sparkled and communicated that he understood Adam's concern. The two men started communicating with math and the computer language "C." They didn't need conventional language to be productive.

Adam had been correct in determining where the error was. Vladamir confirmed it and produced a "fix." The "fix" had to be compiled and tested on the software simulator provided by National. The first solution brought to light another problem, which had resided in the shadow of the first discovery. That required another fix, recompile, and test. Finally, a third problem became visible that no one could see until the first two were eliminated. It's never easy, thought Adam. It was no surprise that National had not found the answer yet. While Vlad was contemplating his third "fix," Adam called Alice to announce that he might be late coming home for dinner.

"Thanks for remembering, Adam. It's 10:30 PM! I hope that sweet young thing you are seeing can cook!" Although it was a hot July night in Chicago, Adam could feel the cold wind of January coming through the phone. He mumbled an apology and told her not to worry.

Vlad's third fix had to be recompiled and tested. Then Vlad suggested several areas where the Russian thought the system could be improved. These were not "errors" in the strictest definition, but rather improvements in efficiency. Adam readily agreed. They finished their work in time to see the sun come up and Sam walking across the parking lot. Adam shook Vlad's hand and told him through gestures to get some sleep. The men had unconsciously formed a deep bond during the night.

"It looks like you're finally earning your keep, Laddie. Did you do any good?" Sam snarled.

"Good morning to you as well, Sam. I think we did good. We won't know for sure until we run the software on the actual machine. You were right about Vladamir. The lad has a real gift. May I borrow your car?"

"Sure. I'm not going anywhere. There is a lot of bloody work to finish before we can install the 9300. We have to hook up power, raw material feed and figure out how to take off the finished parts. There's enough balancing and adjusting to eat up most of the day. I'd forecast that we would be an hour into the second shift before we can actually run something, maybe later. Come back then, but after you gas up my car. We'll soon see if you did something good for a change or screwed off all night." With that, Sam tossed Adam the keys to a Ford pick-up truck and entered the plant.

Adam drove the heavily customized beast home. Scotty greeted him as though he had been absent for a week. Adam felt in many respects like he had. After a quick walk with his dog, some food, and a shower, he collapsed in bed for a five-hour nap.

He returned to the plant after leaving a note for Alice stating that he would return, but wasn't sure when. The plant was abuzz with activity. People were swarming around the 9300 doing a myriad of last minute checks and tests. Very few members of the first shift had elected to go home. They gathered in a circle, out of people's way, in anticipation of seeing something significant. It looked like a tailgate party before a Bears/Packers game without the beer. Adam recalled Sam's statement of how morale was impacted by new equipment. This installation was a testament that management "cared." It was proof that Allied's management wanted to compete in the marketplace without tying one hand behind their collective backs. The 9300's impact on morale was profound beyond measure.

Sam prowled around the unit, double and triple checking everything. He finally turned to Adam and asked for the new software. Vladamir had returned in time to be chosen as the first lead operator. Vlad fired some test shots and shut down the machine for some additional minor adjustments.

A hush fell over the crowded factory as Vlad approached the machine after completing the adjustments. Many people from the second shift joined those from the first, as they watched silently. Vlad looked at Sam, who gave the "thumbs up" sign.

The big unit quickly fired up and came alive. Vladamir checked all the gauges, status lights, and display screens and punched the start button. The unit roared like a mechanical lion as raw material shot in. All five heads were spinning at an incredible rate. The first five finished parts came off in what seemed like seconds. Sam grabbed them, and with his ever-present micrometer began checking tolerances. Nobody in the crowd would say anything until Sam spoke. After what seemed an eternity, the silence was broken as Sam yelled: "They are bloody PERFECT!" The crowd of men from both shifts cheered. A new day had arrived at Allied.

Adam silently observed all of this from the sidelines. He was now hooked and realized intuitively that he would always stay in manufacturing from this point on. The biggest thrill thus far in his business career was getting a big, dumb computer to do what it was told. He used to think that was a great achievement. Now with the 9300, he had the same dumb computer plus the sight, smell, and sound of actual production. The sound alone was seductive. At full bore, the 9300 literally made music. It was remarkably similar to Glen Miller playing Pennsylvania 6-5000. Adam watched, totally mesmerized, while the music played and metal chips flew. The burnt cutting oil was like perfume. Adam had never felt such a complete sense of accomplishment.

Sam rudely interrupted the state of euphoria. "It looks like Vladamir did a good job last night. Is my truck gassed and still in one piece?"

Adam was too beat and happy to take offense. "You are interrupting the beautiful music Sam. Just go away!"

"Not so fast, Laddie. This is a good start, but I need three more 9300's to really make a difference. When are you going to produce them?"

Adam knew that Sam was right, but at this moment, he didn't want to hear it. "I just want to listen to the music!" He delighted in seeing the parts flying off their new machine. "Sam, are you sure you don't work for the IRS? Both of you want more, more, more!" Before Sam could respond, Adam observed two men approaching, one being Bill Stokes.

"Sam, Adam, allow me to introduce Mr. Williams, the President of National," Bill stated proudly. "I convinced Mr. Williams into cold calling on you guys under the assumption you would have the 9300 in operation and as a payback for Adam's cold call on me earlier this week."

"I am profoundly grateful that you convinced me, Bill!" Mr. Williams interjected. "The sight of the 9300 firing up and the men cheering brought a tear to my eye. That's what we are in business to do!" Mr. Williams continued, "Adam, if I had any doubts about my decision to allocate the 9300 to Allied, they are long gone. How in the world did you get your unit to sing so well?"

"I found some software errors, and with some great help from the gentleman now operating the 9300, we fixed them."

"Adam, those 'fixes' are worth a great deal of money to my company and our existing customers. How much do you want for them?" Williams asked apprehensively.

"Mr. Williams, I came from an industry that's pretty accomplished at playing hardball and extortion. That's in the past. Maybe I'm old school, but I believe that 'one good turn deserves another.' You didn't have to agree with my proposal for the 9300, but you did. I'm very grateful. Here is a CD with all the software changes. I'll get whatever documentation you need shortly. Take this to your existing accounts, and I hope you sell dozens more!" Adam handed Williams the CD.

Williams stood perplexed and stunned. The President of National was prepared to offer six figures for what he had just been provided at no charge. "Adam, I also believe in 'one good turn deserves another.' An idea just popped in my head. Maybe we can both help each other."

Mr. Williams went on to explain that one reason they were so anxious to move the 9300 from the showroom was because they wanted to put the new 9500 on display. The 9500 was twice the size of the 9300 and could out-produce it by 300%. The 9500 just finished engineering development. According to National tradition, the machine would sit in the showroom until somebody bought the unit. Then they would finish the machine's development cycle in concert with the first customer's staff.

"What I have seen today tells me our policy is inefficient. We need to test the 9500 in the field. That's where the improvements are made. That's where the bugs get caught and fixed. From what Bill tells me, that's where they get sold as well. I want to move the 9500 to Allied on Monday instead of our showroom. We'll pay you to test it. Does that sound satisfactory to you?"

Out of the corner of one eye, Adam could see that Sam was about to whiz in his pants. "Not quite, Mr. Williams. Once it has been de-bugged, if you will allow me to keep the unit for one year to run production, we'll waive any rental charges. Secondly, I don't want any arguments between your development engineers and my people. If my people recommend a change when the unit arrives, just do it. They are reasonable and practical men."

"I agree, Adam. It won't hurt my engineers to get out of their ivory tower and learn from real people doing real work. It's a deal! Can you accept the 9500 on Monday? We can use more of your antiques for our showroom now that there's a huge hole from the missing 9300 and 9500."

Adam glanced at Sam who was nodding yes, vigorously. "We'll be ready! Thank you. Mr. Stokes, don't forget to bring your prospects by."

"Don't worry about that, Adam. Thank you for yet another interesting meeting." Both National men retired after one more look at the 9300 eating through the backlog.

"Adam, you SOB, you did it! Now we can start to kick butt!" Sam was delirious.

"I used to be a 'sea gull', now I'm an SOB?"

"That's an unbelievable promotion, Laddie!"

"Sam, I'll take your word for it. Is there any way you could give me a lift home?" Adam was suddenly tired.

"Indeed, I'd be honored to. You have done the plant a great service. On the way home, we may have to celebrate your loss of sea gull status. This is a very rare and sacred ceremony. It must be accompanied with the best of libations. Not too many, though, I have to be back here tomorrow to pack up four more machines."

Adam could recall nothing else from that point until he awoke at home late Saturday morning.

Chapter 18

Six weeks had elapsed since the installation of the 9300 and the memorable loss of "sea gull" status ceremony. The installation of the new 9500 had not proceeded as quickly or as smoothly as had the 9300. It was a large, complicated machine whose design incorporated numerous innovations. The skilled men of Allied inspected and crawled all over the 9500 when it first arrived. They attacked the machine as though it were a beetle trapped in their anthill.

The "emergency cut-off switch is mounted wrong," an Allied foreman proclaimed. It was moved. "The hydraulic pump on the raw material side was undersized," a lead operator complained. It was upgraded. Those and many other issues were resolved without question or delay by the National development engineers. The procedure dragged on for four days. Finally, they were ready to run.

Adam could not wait for them to finish. It would be more appropriate to miss a Bear's opening game than the initial production run for the 9500. The 9500 finally fired up and started making parts at the start of the first shift on a Friday. The world of Allied was filled with more glorious music! If the 9300 sounded like the Glen Miller Orchestra, the 9500 was the Chicago Symphony Orchestra with all members present and in good health. It was awesome. Sam thought the 9500 was playing Wagner with passion and precision. Between the two new machines, high quality parts began flying out of Allied in unprecedented numbers.

The men in the plant were starting to have the first inklings of concern about producing themselves out of the backlog when a fortunate phenomenon began showing itself, which was unprecedented in Allied's history. The automotive companies are generally triple sourced on all the parts they purchase. If one of the three vendors misses the schedule by shipping late or shipping poor quality parts, that vendor is penalized. The penalties, on each part, are reflected in lower quantities on the next month's release. The decrease penalty had been an all too common occurrence for Allied in the past. It worked the opposite way as well. Allied was now producing high quality parts and shipping on time. Allied's customers, the auto manufactures, reflected the performance improvement by awarding increases in release quantities every month. Individual parts that were once released to Allied in quantities of 5,000 were now up to 15,000. The seemingly overnight increases in quantities were ideal for the new machines. Longer runs meant lower unit costs. Income and profits at Allied grew dramatically!

Sam complained initially that there were more operators on the payroll than were needed. The two new machines effectively replaced six men. "Keep them on the staff," Adam pleaded. Adam suggested that Sam initially have his extra people remove everything from the "tool crib" associated with the old machines. All the tooling and spare parts for those machines were now obsolete. "Bring in all the suppliers and tell them that the vendor who offers us the largest "trade in" credit for the obsolete stuff will be rewarded with our total 9300 and 9500 tooling business for the next two years." Sam loved the idea and immediately adopted it as his own. The "extra" men recovered enough surplus tooling and parts to receive a $575,000 credit from the winning vendor. Dave Stevens almost had a heart attack from the size of the credit. The big benefit in Adam's estimation wasn't the dollar size of the credit. It was now possible to walk into the tool crib without the fear of things falling on your head. Fifty plus years of obsolete and surplus tooling could create one hell of an avalanche. For the first time in years, operators could find what they needed when they needed it, eliminating another excuse for late performance.

Bill Stokes brought dozens of prospects to Allied. The rest of the National sales staff brought dozens more. Since the 9500 was the one and only example in the world actually running, Allied even entertained some overseas visitors. Plant personnel were thrilled and proud at the attention paid to them by the visitors. The only visitors to Allied that they had seen in the past were from the County Health Department.

Bill Stokes started to use a sales "close" line with prospects that said: "If you are concerned with your people accepting and learning how to use this equipment, I can arrange for Allied personnel to assist with your installation and conduct your training sessions. The Allied men can frequently perform the training using the native language of your people!"

The number of prospects who took Bill up on this offer was amazing. Allied charged National's customers the actual costs for the men plus 10%. The client paid room and board for up to one week. The surplus of machine operators that once was a big concern soon evaporated. At any given time, Allied had three to four operators temporarily assigned to other companies to conduct training. Adam was pushing Sam to cross-train as many people as possible on the new units. Mostly it was for morale, but also to help staff the traveling road shows. The overall effort had become a profit center overnight. Vladamir worked almost full time writing custom code for National's customers for substantial fees. This was work Vladamir loved to do, and in the process, it enhanced his technical skills and command of English.

Ann was concerned at first about the reaction of the customers to the Allied men who were sent out to conduct training. There was no need for concern. The customers were delighted with the expertise of the Allied employees. As an added bonus, the first man who returned after a training stint regaled his fellow workers with how he was wined and dined like royalty. This was a totally new experience for any worker at Allied! Soon everybody wanted to qualify to go on the training trips.

It became obvious, that they couldn't send their trainers into the field looking like ragamuffins. Ann designed and had a local company procure a beautiful red, white, and blue coverall with Allied Mfg./Chicago on the back and the front shirt pocket. They were an instant hit. Everybody wanted one, including those who weren't planning to go on trips. That's when Ann, David, Sam, and Adam realized that "Pride" was back on the payroll. To further this sentiment, each operator that completed three successful training sessions received a "Master Trainer" patch to wear on his uniform. They were highly coveted, as the patch was accompanied by a $1,000 bonus check.

Each Allied operator that trained at a new customer site came back with something totally unexpected. They observed techniques, homemade tools, procedures, and insights that were practical and productive. They picked up these tidbits of "know how" like a magnet picked up metal filings. Most, but not all, were applicable to and adopted by Allied. One of the leading examples was the observation of a homemade tool, which when used with a forklift truck, quickly pulled drive shafts from milling machines. The Allied "Trainer" who observed the tool sketched it on the back of a napkin. The trainer then reviewed the drawing with Sam. Sam improved the design and built the new tool in his home workshop. Instead of taking two hours to pull a drive shaft, it could now be done in 15 minutes. Perhaps more importantly, employees' hands, arms, and backs were significantly less threatened. The trainers started an unofficial contest to determine who found the best idea.

None of these tidbits of time-tested "know how" were acquired illegally or in secret. At each plant visited, the ideas were voluntarily shown to an Allied trainer. Nobody at the customer sites thought their ideas were of any value because they had never been rewarded, acknowledged, or praised by their management for their innovations. The men being trained thought, "why not share these ideas with someone like the visitors from Allied who expressed interest in them? Obviously, the techniques were not worth anything."

These small acorns of expertise flooded back to Allied. There were new ways to organize the tool crib, as well as enhanced preventive maintenance routines and instrument calibration efficiencies. Each newly acquired technique was of some value. The cumulative effect was explosive. These ideas did not come from a consultant who never dirtied his hands. Allied's employees readily adopted these ideas because the improvements came from men just like them.

Adam's pig-headed refusal to dismiss extra personnel was rooted in an emotional response to unemployment. He had unwittingly unleashed a renaissance in innovation that transformed the old plant on the southwest side. The tiny acorns gathered by the trainers grew to oak trees of profitability, pride, and productivity.

Allied actually closed the plant over Labor Day. In the past, they had to work overtime during most holidays because they were so far behind in shipments. Pride and hope for the future were present once again. Virtually absent were scrap, rework, absenteeism, tardiness, and late shipments. The Bears looked good in this pre-season and so did the future at Allied.

Just after Labor Day, Dave had amassed enough money to buy the original 9300. The head of Finance felt infinitely better when he could list the unit under company assets. Dave also came up with enough funds for a down payment on an additional 9300. The second 9300 was scheduled to arrive at the plant in the first week of October. Even the plant cynics were aware that the tide had turned.

Everybody was enthusiastic now, but it wasn't always a smooth road. Adam had his biggest fight with Dave shortly after the 9300 and before the 9500 installations. Adam insisted that Dave tap bank credit lines for funds to clean up, paint, and repair the rest rooms and cafeteria at the plant. Dave agreed that it was a job that had to be done, but objected to using bank credit lines for "housekeeping" expenditures.

The banks demanded collateral and would prefer that Allied used credit lines for the acquisition of assets. It really got ugly before Ann stepped in on the side of Adam. The money was finally obtained and the work was accomplished. Adam had correctly sensed that without the remodeling, it would be difficult to maintain pride and emphasize quality. "How could we insist on quality production with credibility when our employees were working in a pigsty," Adam shouted at Dave. National probably would not have brought in half as many prospects without the cleanup either. Dave and Adam soon reconciled. Both men realized it was a dispute on principal and not based on personality.

Things had not always progressed smoothly between Adam and Sam despite Adam's loss of sea gull status. Adam had become increasingly concerned with the stampede by plant personnel during their scheduled breaks. The breaks were set at fixed times and the operators reacted to the whistle like "Pavlov's Dog." If a job was about to finish with just another two minutes of run time, they would shut the machine down and go on break.

Adam finally convinced Sam to start a new procedure. The individual operators would select their own times to go to break. "Treat these people like the skilled adults they are!" Adam insisted. Sam agreed, but was concerned that some people would take advantage of the new relaxed rules. "I'm sure they will until they determine that they can't get a rise out of the foreman, or until their fellow workers tell them to "cool it." Adam's winning argument with Sam was that the artificiality of the break times was originally established to make it easier to input the times to the "job costing report." "Do you want me to reinstate the report, Sam?" Adam proved to be correct with his assessment and Allied became a far more productive and happier place to work.

Throughout this six-week period, the action at Allied was hot and heavy. It was taxing, fulfilling, and rewarding all at the same time. There was scant time to invest in "Project Freedom," but there was some. Adam's mind functioned somewhat like a computer with both "Foreground" and "Background" modes engaged. Allied consumed all of his "Foreground," processing while the "Project" continued to play in "Background." It was ironic that problem solving in one activity complemented and enhanced problem solving in the other arena.

A common denominator across both areas of activity was the similarity of events to military history. Adam had maintained an active interest in such history and it served him well. Military history dictated that you had to know your enemy. At Allied, it was dozens of competitors and a stodgy internal culture. Within the "project," it was law enforcement. You had to establish "command and control" resources in both. You had to know when and how to enlist allies like National. You had to plan, use diversions, take advantage of the element of surprise, and exploit new technology.

One new technology Adam continued to exploit was the Internet. He had used it extensively to gather basic data for the "project." Now he wanted to use it to perform the "command and control" function. If Adam could create a web site with members of the team having ready access, the actual operational situation before the heist would be available for all on the team to see. The use of this technique would minimize confusion, eliminate communications mistakes, and permit flexibility. It might be possible for the entire team to interact without having to know the actual identity of each member. That would greatly reduce risk and cost. Adam had started working on the creation of the web page and master control program. The work proceeded slowly, as he still had to secure funding for the project and recruit the people required.

The pace would now have to be quickened. Stan sent Adam an interesting e-mail message last night from Europe. It confirmed that Stan was working at Swiss National. He was busy developing a competitive system to First Continental's "Trade Master." That fact didn't surprise Adam. What did surprise and shock him was that Stan had negotiated one hell of a signing bonus from Swiss National. Being an honorable man, Stan wanted to share that bonus with Adam. After all, Adam had provided great insights and support to Stan in the past. Adam retrieved the printout from his brief case and reviewed the actual words from the message.

"Please accept this $25,000 for many contributions to my own success. I hope you use the moneys to start a new enterprise. You have too big creativity to work for big outfit! I have put the money in account Renee set up for you. It will make interest until you need it. Thanks again and the best of the luck!"

Adam's initial reaction was that he really couldn't accept Stan's generous offer. After considerable reflection, and knowing Stan, Adam knew that Stan would be highly offended if he didn't accept the gift. Adam realized that he now had the seed money for "Project Freedom."

Adam became aware of someone tugging his pant leg from the first floor of the train. It was the conductor advising him to wake up and depart his second floor seat before the train left Union Station. Adam was in such deep thought that he hadn't realized the train had pulled into Union Station over ten minutes ago. Deeply embarrassed, Adam gathered his things and departed.

Entering Allied's office, Adam observed Ann leaving the ladies' rest room. It appeared that she had been crying. Adam was immediately concerned and went directly to her office.

"Good morning, Ann. How are you this fine Friday morning?"

"Oh, Adam!" The tears started flowing and Adam gently closed her office door. He sat quietly for several minutes until she regained some composure.

"Mr. Adolph Tollinger died last night." With that announcement, the tears continued for another few minutes.

"I'm truly sorry, Ann. I know you were close to Mr. Tollinger. I feel somewhat ashamed because I never met him."

"That's O.K., Adam. He wasn't himself for the last five years. It wouldn't have meant anything if you had met him." Ann was starting to gain control of her emotions. "It was probably a blessing. He went in his sleep. Yes, I was close to him. Adolph was a good man and he would have been proud of what you have accomplished." That statement initiated another bout of sobbing.

"I haven't done that much, but I have been pretty lucky." Adam thought he was helping soften the blow, but now Ann was crying harder.

"What did I say, Ann?"

"You really don't see it, do you? At times I love that you are such a Boy Scout and then there are times I want to slap you on the side of the head with a two by four!"

"Please explain." Adam asked gently.

Ann gathered herself before she started her explanation. "First of all, when a friend departs this world, it makes you aware of your own mortality. Mr. Tollinger's departure certainly made me aware of mine. He was like a father to me. Financially, he made sure I had what I needed at a very bad time in my life. For the past five years, I have dedicated myself to keeping the company afloat and the employees intact. I didn't plan for his departure and never considered how I would sustain myself when he was gone. Adam, I have no retirement benefits and I'm not that far away from needing them."

"You have been so concerned with the people at Allied and their welfare that you forgot about your own. Don't lecture me about being a Boy Scout!" That was a little harsher than Adam had intended, but it seemed to stop the tears.

"Yes, that's true, Adam. I kept thinking before your arrival that we would be closing the doors any minute. You don't worry about the future if you are convinced that you don't have one. Now you come along and suddenly the company actually has a future. It could be argued that it has a bright future. I just received my first four resumes for jobs at the plant that came in over the transom, totally unsolicited. You achieved the one goal I had hoped for and considered impossible." Now the tears came back in a torrent.

"Are you're crying because we may save the company? I thought that was the objective."

"It was, but you've done it too fast and too well. Now I have to think about my personal future because Allied has one. My big concern is that Bernie or one of his 'friends' will want to take over the company. We can't stop or influence that course of events. None of the current people that are actually running Allied are officers or board members. Nobody has or controls one share of stock. Allied is a private company that is now totally subject to Bernie's legal control. Adolph can't protect, reward, or punish anybody any more. Neither Bernie nor his friends would have touched this place six months ago. We were closer to bankruptcy than you will ever know. Now, thanks in large measure to you, everybody and their dog will want to control the enterprise and its people."

"Salesmen refer to this situation as a commission-dectomy."

"I'm all too familiar with the term, but never thought it would be applicable to me. It's absolutely perverted that you can be punished for doing a great job!" Ann resumed her crying, which if anything, was more intense.

"Ann, do you have any kind of a personal backup plan if your worst fears materialize?"

"Hell no, Adam! Why do you think I'm so upset? Nobody thought we could turn this dump around so fast. I hadn't planned to be successful. It's true; I'm a bigger Boy Scout than you are. The thought of losing all that we have accomplished with nothing to show for it makes me sick. I feel like robbing a bank and running off to a Pacific island. Let Bernie and his friends manage the plant and wrestle with all the problems."

Adam thought very carefully before asking: "Do you have any evidence that there is an outside interest pushing for a management position at Allied?" Ann shook her head no. "O.K. I agree with your concerns, but let's not overreact. I'm a systems guy and we love 'backups.' Spend some time over the weekend and try to come up with a backup plan just for yourself. I wouldn't fret about someone taking over just yet; however, I am afraid that your fears are valid."

"Thanks, Adam. You have calmed me down a little and I will consider options for a backup over the weekend."

Adam returned to his cubicle and did some busy work. His heart wasn't in it. Ann was dead on right. The Bernie threat was real. It was time to go home for a relaxed weekend and to walk with Scotty. It was obvious that he had to pick up the pace on "Project Freedom."

CHAPTER 19

Adam did not intend to drive to the plant this Monday morning, but changed his plans after receiving a cryptic e-mail at home from the President of National. Mr. Williams was urgently requesting a meeting at the plant by 9:30 AM. It must have something to do with a hot prospect, Adam thought. National had gone against industry tradition to assist Allied by providing the demo 9300. Adam was happy to do anything he could to return the favor. He desperately wanted to have a chat with Ann; however, she would be at Mr. Tollinger's funeral and would be unavailable until this afternoon at the earliest.

It had been a spectacular early fall weekend in Chicago. Adam let his mind reflect on the weekend activities while sitting in traffic. The numerous traffic delays provided ample opportunity for reflection. At this time of year, the blue flowered Chicory and the white Queen Ann's lace were giving way to Chrysanthemums. The first of many colored leaves began appearing on the Sugar Maples. The evenings were cool and the days warm and bright. The Bears won their season opener against the New York Giants on Sunday. Beating a New York team was almost, but not quite, as good as beating Green Bay. Scotty rejoiced in the cooler temperatures. It was a delight to walk with the Golden Retriever and scatter the geese, whose numbers now included migrants from further north. During one of these walks, they encountered Frank once again. Frank informed Adam that it looked as though he would not be adequately compensated for the recent "commission-dectomy." He was showing the early signs of financial distress and Adam pledged his personal support. As Adam considered the spectacular fall weekend, Franks bad news provided the only down note.

Reviewing Frank's predicament reminded Adam that he might be the next in line for a similar fate. Ann's assessment of Bernie's total legal control of Allied placed the entire management team in jeopardy. Why hadn't Bernie noticed or reacted to their success to date? The turnaround at Allied was partially reflected in its financial statements for at least a month. The real turnaround had been signaled in the eyes of the employees over two months ago. Perhaps that was the answer. You had to be on-site to feel and see the real changes. Substantive changes were never reflected accurately in the accounting numbers until well after the fact. Bernie never went near the factory. It's possible that he wasn't aware of the improvements. If this was true, the challenge now became how to keep him in the dark. It was vital to keep Bernie ignorant until the successful implementation of "Project Freedom." At that point, the legal heir could do whatever he wanted.

The only impediment remaining in the implementation of "Project Freedom" was acquiring personnel. Frank nailed it last February with the statement: "with the right people, you can do anything." Everything that Adam had experienced at First Continental and Allied underscored that essential truth. Ann was a proven talent in evaluating and recruiting personnel. She had a "gift" that Adam could not rationally explain, but willingly acknowledged. She could be the key asset in solving this last formidable obstacle. She probably had a database in her head, or on her computer, of the people with the right skills to do the job. Informing Ann of the plans for "Project Freedom" would require great trust on his part. "How serious was she when she said she was ready to rob a bank?" Odds were it was just an expression issued in an emotional outburst. Misplaced trust in Ann could lead to the loss of short-term security as well as jeopardizing the long-term plan. Of course, it was Ann who expressed confidence in him while walking beside this very lake. At that time, she had far less information to base her trust in him than he now had to trust her. Doing nothing at this time was a large risk as well. Bernie wouldn't stay in the dark forever, no matter what they did.

Adam pulled into the parking lot of the plant and immediately curtailed his ruminations on "Project Freedom." He was shocked to find a party in progress. A "Dixieland" band was pumping out favorites while caterers served delicious breakfast entrees to the entire first shift. Mr. Williams was personally serving coffee in a large chef's hat and having his picture taken with every worker. Williams stopped momentarily to greet Adam. "I'm sorry Adam, I'm going to cost you a little production this morning, but we'll make it up to you. We had to say thanks to your entire family. Their original suggestions for improvements on the 9500 and their training assistance have made the 9500 the most successful product launch in National's history. We are two years ahead of our development cycle and four years ahead of our projected sales. We just sold our 50th 9500! Later today, we will come back to treat the entire second shift."

"Thank you, Mr. Williams, but this wasn't necessary. We at Allied have benefited greatly as well."

"Not as well as we have. My God, Adam, our stock is up 25%! Today, we're attempting to close the gap and retire our debt to you just a little. Come with me, please."

Mr. Williams led Adam to the front of the 9500 where Sam, the foremen, Vladamir, and all of the operators had been gathered. Adam was asked to pose with the Allied group in front of the machine. Mr. Williams called for a drum roll. The entire facility fell silent. Mr. Williams then pronounced: "In appreciation for a job well done, I would like to present the "Title of ownership" for serial number 950000001 to Allied Manufacturing."

Adam knelt dumbfounded in front of the 9500 jointly holding the "Title" with Sam. They were surrounded by the entire first shift. Flashbulbs went off and men cheered while the band played "South Rampart Street Parade." The resulting picture was the only one in recent history that showed Sam actually smiling. Everybody in the picture was grinning and everyone would get a personal copy. It was with great reluctance that Adam left the plant to go to the downtown office.

"Adam, I was hoping to see you today. We have to have a meeting. There are some unusual and significant problems that we should discuss." It was odd to see Dave grin when talking about problems. Adam asked if Ann had returned. "She just did." Both men ventured to Ann's office. Neither was sure how well she had handled the emotions of the funeral.

Ann was remarkably well composed considering what she had been through this morning. "Gentlemen. What can I do for you?"

"I wanted to have a meeting," Dave started the conversation. "We are piling up some serious amounts of extra money. We either spend some of it, or give most of it to Uncle Sam. I need direction on a situation that I thought would never occur while I was at Allied." Dave was almost delirious with joy. Ann looked like she was going to start crying upon hearing Dave's revelations.

"Before we address your problem, Dave, indulge me while I ask some questions," Adam interjected. "Does Bernie ever ask to review your financial reports when he visits?"

"No, never. I think he's convinced that they are terrible. The consultants advised Junior years ago that they would never get better. Bernie thinks he avoids pain by not looking at them."

"Ann? Does Bernie ever ask you 'how things are going' or words to that effect?"

"No. He simply comes in once a month for the salary check. He's pleasant, but rarely spends more than ten minutes in the office. I don't believe he's been to the plant for years. I just visited with Bernie at the funeral and he expressed zero interest in anything related to the company. Why do you ask, Adam?"

Adam explained to Dave their concerns regarding Bernie's possible interest in becoming active again in the control of the company. That potential interest might be ignited if the sole heir found out that there was some initial success in turning Allied around. There was an instant recognition of the threat by Dave. The bean counter was so busy doing his job and performing substantive work that he hadn't thought of the political implications of success. The demise of the senior Mr. Tollinger had made the threat immediate. "My God! I feel stupid! I never saw that coming. What do we do?"

"One possible reason for Bernie's inactivity is that he simply doesn't know how much has been done. I believe it would be wise to continue along in exactly the same vein. We need to concentrate our resources in the plant where we get maximum return and minimum visibility." Both Dave and Ann nodded in complete agreement. "I had hoped to find some extra funds for a new mainframe computer and software for the office. I had also hoped, Ann, to replace your duct tape repaired chair with something more appropriate for a lady. Both efforts, I now believe, should be put on hold. The office must remain exactly as it is. Where would you like to spend money in the plant, Dave?"

"We have a backup for the 9300 coming in October. I think we should start reducing the debt on the 9500 so I can put it on the balance sheet." Dave would never be comfortable with demonstration machines and the inability to correctly reflect them on the balance sheet.

Adam smiled and said: "You will have to redirect your thinking. Allied now owns the 9500 free and clear." Adam slid the title to the 9500 across the desk to Dave. "Put the dumb thing on your balance sheet under assets and in indelible ink."

Adam let Ann and Dave shout for joy and giggle for a few minutes and then resumed the meeting. "As much as I would like to solely direct our extra funds to equipment, I think now is the time to reward our workers with some tangible evidence of their good work. I recommend a 10% salary increase across the board at the plant."

"People will enjoy better job security if we continue to reinvest our profits into the plant," Dave retorted. That started the familiar debate that has raged in manufacturing companies throughout time. Dave was absolutely correct in his financial reasoning. Adam was closer to the reality of worker resentment. The workers saw "The Company" benefiting with nothing going to them. Ann broke the deadlock with the observation that for the first time in decades, Allied workers were being solicited and pirated by competitors. They needed to increase salaries to remain competitive.

"I still want to address our needs within the plant." Dave declared adamantly.

They agreed as a team to use the equity in the 9300 and 9500 to serve as a down payment on a new 9500 for delivery in January. Some of the extra funds would be used to enhance the lighting at the plant and improve the heating and air conditioning systems. The new machines had greatly reduced the gray cloud of smoke that had hung in the plant for generations. New air conditioning would remove the remainder. Dave left the meeting to call Bill Stokes and place the order for the new 9500.

"Adam, we better get some new accounts before the second 9500 arrives. We have substantially reduced our backlog. The new machine could be gathering dust instead of making parts."

"I agree, Ann. In fact, would you give this gentleman a call and do your Human Resources bit?" Adam furnished Ann with Frank's telephone number.

"I'd be happy to, Adam. We really need new accounts, not just increases in sales from existing customers."

"Did you find any time over the weekend to formulate a personal backup plan, Ann?"

"I had the time to think, but there is no evident solution. I'm slightly too old to be attractive to a new employer. Additionally, my experience base is too general, too entrepreneurial for most big firms. How do you describe the activity of general management on a resume?"

"I concur. I was advised to lie about my achievements by a head-hunter on the basis that everybody does it."

Ann just sighed. "The Bernie threat is as real as cancer. All my life I was told that his lifestyle selection was wrong. Now I'm told in countless publications to be more 'tolerant' and 'accepting.' Perhaps I could be. The plant personnel that I'm familiar with will not be tolerant. Does that make them wrong and Bernie right? I don't know any more what's 'right' and what's 'wrong'. I do know that the plant people will quit in droves if Junior assumes operational control. So what do we do, hide behind our duct taped chairs hoping that we can fool Bernie, and try to keep 225 people gainfully employed? It's all crazy. Adam, how do you manage to remain relatively cool and confident under the circumstances?"

"I take direct, self-administered Novocain shots to the heart. It was a technique I learned over the years while watching the Bears.

"I'm serious, Adam. Any other company that had made the progress we have made would be engaging in an advertising and public relations blitz. Their management would be entertaining the thought of going public during a meeting in the executive dining room. We sit here, doling out paper clips instead of bonuses. How on earth can you stand it?" Ann was clearly angry.

"I have constructed, at least in my own mind, a backup plan. It serves as a very effective 'rod and staff' to protect me from the ironies of this crazy world."

"Would you mind sharing your invention with someone who needs a 'rod and staff' of her own? At least it sounds better than direct shots of Novocain to the heart."

"Be careful of what you wish for, Ann."

"Adam, you aren't listening. I have no alternatives. I have no retirement options. The more I think of it, I have no economic freedom. I'm not sure how I got into this mess, either. I have always played by the rules, and where did it get me? In the meantime, people who lie and cheat are fawned over by the press. I am willing to entertain virtually anything, including your backup plan."

Dave, beaming with great excitement, rejoined them to announce that Bill Stokes was overjoyed at receiving an order for a new 9500. He would ensure the unit's delivery by the first of the year. Sam is selecting several old machines for retirement to make room for the new 9500. Sam also agreed on the lighting and air conditioning upgrades. Sam had previously interviewed and selected good candidates from a host of competitors. He now had two vendors ready to go. Dave authorized the spending, and actually whistled as he left Ann's office.

"Hold your thoughts, Ann. I'll get back to you. In the meantime, please call Frank. It's possible that he may be the solution for obtaining new accounts."

CHAPTER 20

Adam arrived home early this evening and immediately took Scotty for a walk to take advantage of the remaining light. The decreasing daylight of autumn was incontrovertible proof of the onset of winter.

He was overjoyed that Dave had interrupted his discussion with Ann at a key moment. Adam concluded that it was impossible to advance "Project Freedom" in a timely fashion if he did not confide in Ann. It was the only way to accomplish the recruiting phase. The project appeared necessary for both of them because of the Bernie threat. He was impressed and somewhat frightened with the degree in which Ann's independent thinking had matched his. She actually used the same language and phrases that he had. How could he, in all honesty, confide in her without one more serious examination of the plan? Were all the bases covered, he wondered?

The Brinks truck was the only viable target that contained the minimum amount of money required for a "one time" shot. The truck ran a religiously strict route through the Loop, where it stopped at all the major banks. It then proceeded south to stop at two banks on the near south side before turning east on Balbo to Lake Shore Drive. It continued north and exited at Illinois Street to service three banks on the near north side. Its final stop was at the Federal Reserve Bank and then to the barn.

After watching hundreds of hours of video traffic coverage, Adam was convinced that the key move was the turn the truck executed from Balbo to the Drive. If there were a way to raise the Lake Shore Drive Bridge at that point, the truck would come to rest beside the lake. There was a long stretch of shoreline that ran due north and south, creating an enormous amount of room to work with. A variance of plus or minus two minutes on the bridge raising would cause no major concerns. He would not have to be as precise as the 6:32 METRA coming into the Bartlett station. The optimum point to approach the truck would be on the concrete apron due east of Buckingham fountain. That would place the truck south of Du Sable harbor and the famous "S" curve, and north of Meigs and the Alder Planetarium.

The Chicago police boat also had a predictable routine. It patrolled the river at the time the Brinks truck rounded the turn from Balbo. The river patrol was necessitated in part by the requirement for a crew change at lunch. The crew change took place at the Michigan Avenue landing. If notified of the robbery instantly, it couldn't be near the action on the lake for 20 minutes or more. It would have to traverse the lock between the river and lake to be a threat.

The Coast Guard had moved its helicopter and cutter last year to the State of Michigan in an attempt at economy. The Chicago police helicopter was stationed at Midway. It was theoretically too far away to interfere. The Chicago TV station helicopters were similarly stationed at Midway or Palwaukee airports and shouldn't be a problem if he could think of a way to delay their departure.

Adam was still working on diversions, which were the key in disabling police patrol cars and interference by average citizens. The problem of how to actually open the truck had yet to be resolved.

The escape by boat would be easy if the weather cooperated, and would provide a way of hiding the proceeds until the Federal Statute of Limitations expired in five years. The loot could easily withstand five years under fresh water sealed in specially designed waterproof trunks. Thanks to the Global Positioning System (GPS), relocating them five years later in the vast lake would be an easy task to accomplish.

The optimum time to execute the liberation was becoming more certain. It would have to occur in the summer to minimize adverse weather influences and to gain the protective shield of other pleasure boats on the lake. It had to be done on a weekday for the Brinks truck and police boat schedules to apply. Probably a Thursday would be ideal. July, with the "Taste of Chicago," Fourth of July fireworks, Venetian Night, and the Mackinaw race was unacceptable. The vast crowds attending those events could interfere with the operation. An ideal time would be the first week of August just before the Air and Water Show. The question was could he, with Ann's assistance, recruit three additional people with the right stuff and complete the construction and testing of the props required in time?

As Adam continued to review the general concept, he became more convinced of its feasibility. It was also apparent what was really bothering him. The Air Force developed a phrase during new weapons development projects called "UNK-UNK'S," short for unknown unknowns. Computer technicians running models used the phrase "Exogenous variables" to excuse why a model did not predict accurately. Programmers talked about "bugs" or "glitches." Politicians described the "Great Law of Unintended Consequences." All disciplines referred to essentially the same phenomena. They had all failed to account for a factor in their great plan. Like the programmer who forgot to account for Leap Year Day every four years, they were acutely embarrassed when those gifted with 20/20 hindsight brought it to their attention.

Adam, like all planners, was determined to eliminate "UNK-UNK'S" before presenting his ideas to Ann. It simply couldn't be done. Adam was only mortal and to think he had God-like powers of infallibility was heretical. He had left some details intentionally vague with the hope of assistance from some of the new team members. All he could do at this time was broadly sketch the approach and get out of the way of talented people who would bring their own skills and experience to the fore. The similarities of managing "Project Freedom" and "Trade Master" were frightening. The skills required for both endeavors were virtually identical.

Scotty began his little dance as Frank approached from behind. "Hi, Adam, and you too, Scotty. I guess I owe you one, Adam. I just talked with one of the most persuasive individuals I have ever encountered. I now represent Allied Manufacturing. Scotty, that dumb guy holding your leash is largely responsible."

"Don't thank me, Frank. If you didn't have the right stuff, Ms. Persuasive would have dealt with you like a used Kleenex! Besides, I don't want you to build any false hopes. The house of cards called Allied could fold at any minute."

"Adam, dear boy, I have stopped building up positive hopes, false hopes, and hope in general years ago. Every one of my past employers was arguably a house of cards. Ann was explicit in telling me of your concerns. I found that remarkably refreshing. Imagine, someone talking about problems in the present tense. Being a representative is similar to surfing. You pick a company instead of a wave, and ride it until it peters out. Then you must venture forth and find a new wave. Allied has simply become the latest wave in a long series. If Allied diminishes over time, it would be nothing new.

"Ann is very impressed with you, Adam. She would follow you anywhere."

Very interesting, thought Adam. I wonder if that sweeping endorsement would include an invitation to commit a crime. He had an overpowering urge to ask Frank, but could not. "You will be an independent representative for Allied I assume, and not listed prominently on the payroll?"

"Yes. That fits my style and Ann's as well, as she was not anxious to add me to the payroll. Just pay me my commissions, Adam. I'll take care of my expenses, and don't ever send me any phony 1099's!"

"You've got a deal. Can you explore obtaining some new customers that aren't exactly automotive, but have similar needs? We need to expand our base of operations. We have far too many eggs in one basket."

"That's my objective, Adam. I have some good contacts at *Caterpillar*, *J. I. Case*, and *Navistar*. Your new capabilities should help them with some of their requirements. I'm anxious to find out. I still feel I owe you, and I'll guarantee my best effort. Well, I believe it's time for dinner. Thanks again."

"Thank you, Frank! Your best is all anyone could ask for. Enjoy your dinner."

Adam continued the walk with Scotty, although it was getting dark. Where were the "UNK-UNK'S" in the plan hiding? It would be necessary to find a helper who owned a boat. There were insufficient funds to acquire a new one. Additionally, the acquisition of a boat just for this mission could be traced. The boat would undoubtedly be observed leaving the crime scene. How does one camouflage a boat? He would have to come back to that issue later because there was no apparent solution.

It would be necessary to create many diversions to divert the police. The research on the Internet provided sources for commercially available "smoke bombs" used in testing for leaks in underground pipes. They burned for ten minutes and gave off fulsome amounts of smoke. Adam felt that it was possible to ignite them remotely using cell phone receivers called by a master computer program. They would have to be set in place at least a week ahead of "D" day. How do you hide such devices in plain sight?

He would need a van to ride on the shoulder of the Drive to approach the stopped Brinks truck. That's why it didn't matter too much on the exact timing of the bridge raising. The van had to appear innocent and non-threatening. It would have to be equipped with a cherry picker as the most vulnerable part of the Brinks truck, according to his research, was its roof. The cherry picker would allow for a speedy deployment to the roof. Raising the bridge on time without a physical confrontation with the bridge tender was another nagging detail.

This had to be the most audacious plan in recent history. Adam was not a violent person, and assumed that none of the unknown helpers would be either. It suddenly dawned on him that they were planning to steal $10-12 million without firearms and with no intent to harm a soul. All of this was to occur in broad daylight in the middle of the city. Furthermore, the work had to be accomplished by personnel with perfect records and no previous experience. The line used in a hundred "B" movies reverberated in his mind: "This is just crazy enough to work!" Adam hoped that was true. He was sure that nothing like this had ever been tried before. Good luck to the cops who relied exclusively on the technique of "*Modus Operandi.*" If apprehended during the event, perhaps they couldn't be charged with armed robbery. Or could they? That might take yet more research to determine the correct answer.

The "key" however, was to be audacious, creative and unusual. That's what allowed the element of surprise to work. With the right technology, it would appear that an army pulled this off, versus five kindred souls looking for financial independence. Frank's comment from last winter still rang true. Consider this planning exercise as a business formation problem. Adam was forming in his imagination a high-tech, low overhead, single objective and short-lived enterprise.

It should be relatively easy for Ann, if he could enlist her capabilities, to locate associates with the right equipment and skills. There was no way to know for sure without seeking her help. How difficult would it be to locate people with no previous records who were financially independent enough to wait for the Statute of Limitations to expire? Additionally, he was asking for living oxymora—"honest crooks!" Moreover, they had to completely trust each member of the team without the benefit of actually knowing each other. Could there be honor among thieves? The real question is could there be "honor among honest crooks?" Maybe that was too much to ask for. These subtle, non-objective attributes could prove to be the Achilles heel of the entire plan. Only an experienced expert like Ann would have a chance of finding the "oxymora." He wasn't even sure she could do it. Perhaps nobody could. There was only one way to find out, and he could risk the whole ball game with that question. Well, nothing ventured, nothing gained. He would ask her first thing in the morning.

"Scotty, let's go home so the self-condemned man can have a last meal with his family."

* * * *

The senior bank executive viewed the sun as it slipped below the horizon from his 40th floor office window. The early departure of the sun angered him because it foreshadowed the arrival of winter. He had never enjoyed the prospect or reality of winter in Chicago. Now that the banker had actually acquired a second home in Belize, it bothered him more, as Belize was an undeniably better alternative. Be patient, he cautioned himself. Next year he would be able to vacation at the new home, and in the not too distant future could move permanently to the new house.

The joint operation that he forged with the syndicate was running smoothly and had grown beyond his wildest dreams. It was now so large that he had to include an associate to help handle the volume of transactions. Fortunately, he was able to locate the right man on his current staff at the bank. The new recruit was ambitious, totally loyal, and dumb. He wasn't so dumb as to make a mistake, but not smart enough to figure out a way to influence the executive's relationship with La Morte. The bank executive made sure of the new associate's loyalty by promising him control over the entire operation when he happily retired to Belize. Based on the tremendous income being generated, that day would not be far off.

The banker couldn't help but smile and feel proud. His fellow executives thought he stayed late to constantly work on bank security issues. Actually, he was awaiting a large deposit of funds to be laundered into bonds. He had devised the perfect plan and cover. He casually observed average citizens walking the busy streets far beneath the window. He loved the view from the top floor because it made him feel like God.

Chapter 21

Detective Ron McHugh slid into his favorite booth in the "White Castle Grill" at Canal and Roosevelt and waited for his partner to join him for breakfast. The all—night diner was a favorite meeting place for the two officers as well as an eclectic group of taxi drivers, cops and people who worked the night shift at establishments throughout the Loop. The two men had worked together for a total of eight years. They started as rookies in vice, completed a quick stint in robbery, and were currently assigned to drug enforcement. They achieved good results in their first two areas of responsibility, but only managed a few small busts in drug enforcement, which greatly frustrated both men.

"How many bad guys are we going to put away today, partner?" Luke Sawyer asked as the physically imposing detective slid into the booth and searched for a cup of coffee.

"That's a hell of a question, Luke. Have you ever thought about how close we've come to nailing some big fish, only to come up with nothing? Do you think we're dumb, inept or unlucky?"

"Given only those choices, I would select unlucky. Why do you ask?"

"I'm getting a strong hunch that it is none of the above. I don't believe in luck, and I know we aren't dumb or inept."

Luke eyed his partner warily. He wasn't sure he liked where this was leading. "Spell it out, Ron. What's bugging you? I recognize the look in your eyes."

"I know according to departmental guidelines I'm not supposed to even think, much less state this, but I believe we got a major leak topside. Someone has flipped on us and is providing crucial info to the "mob" whenever we get close to any big time bad guy. It's the only logical way to explain our lack of success."

"I was afraid that was what you were thinking. Forget about it! The department will have your badge and your head for just muttering that sentiment out loud. However, just for you, dear partner, I'll admit that the thought has crossed my mind on more than one occasion. Out of a deep concern for my family's well-being, I quickly dismiss the thought and advise you to do the same. Why is this such an issue with you today?"

"I received a call from a 'snitch' last night who claimed that the mob is rolling in dough. Apparently, they have developed an extremely efficient way to launder drug money. They are actually bragging about it. Purportedly they are getting assistance from a high-flying executive at one of the big banks downtown. I'd love to investigate that lead, but I'm afraid to mention the possibility of the scheme to the watch commander. If my hunch is correct, it will leak. If the word gets topside, the lead is gone forever if there is an informant within our ranks."

"Ron, drop the idea of chasing this lead. I have followed you into blind gangways at night in pursuit of armed gang-bangers. That was risky, but not entirely stupid. I'm not going after some politically connected executive at a big bank based on a tip from a 'snitch'. Going after a 'suit' is unhealthy for your career. That's a polite way of saying it's stupid. You have done enough carpentry work over the years to know that it's the nail that sticks out that gets hammered. Just go with the flow like everybody else in the department does nowadays."

"Sometimes you have to fight for what you think is right, Luke. My late father had a porcelain turtle on his desk for years. There was a sign on it that read: '*Behold the turtle; he only makes progress when he sticks his neck out!*' The money-laundering portion of drug dealing is probably more important to the mob's profits than the physical production and distribution of the crap. I feel obligated to pursue this lead because of its importance and out of respect for my dad."

"Maybe you're right for once, partner, but please don't act on it now. You don't have anything that will hold up in court and you don't know for sure who is on your side. It's not easy to distinguish the good guys from the bad guys today."

"O.K. Luke, I'll sit on it for a while and try to develop it a little further, but not for long."

* * * *

The phone in his cubicle was ringing incessantly as Adam entered Allied's dingy outer office. He didn't take time to get coffee, but did observe that Ann was preoccupied with two other members of the office staff who had arrived early. His greatly debated meeting with Ann would have to be deferred. Plans never seemed to quite work out. He picked up the phone with the primary objective of stopping the noise. Finding out who initiated the call was of secondary importance.

"Well, you finally got in! I hope that someday I can work in an office environment and be able to sleep in every bloody morning. I wouldn't call it work. I'd call it early retirement."

"Good morning, Sam. I see that you didn't take your usual medication with your morning coffee."

"Aye, that's true, Laddie, and perhaps I should have to counteract the news of this bloody raise." Adam could feel the muscles in his stomach tighten in anticipation. "What was this all about?"

"Hell, I haven't earned the bloody raise! This place is running itself without me! I haven't yelled at anybody in three weeks nor broke up any fights. It's bad enough that I feel useless. Now you go and increase my salary for doing nothing. I feel more and more like a bloody sea gull."

"That's a damn serious affliction, Sam. Heaven forbid that word leaked out that you were becoming a sea gull. I promise you—our lips at the office are sealed. Your secret lifestyle change is safe with us."

"Don't try to intimidate me, Laddie. If there is any bloody intimidation going to take place, I'll do it. Let me clue you in to a fact that you in office-land may have missed. If you increased wages to stop our people from being 'pirated', you could have saved your money. It isn't going to happen."

"That's an interesting piece of news. Why are you so certain of your observation, Sam?"

"We lost one of our best men a month ago to my least favorite local competitor. The dude came back after two weeks, hat in hand, pleading for his old job. I accommodated the request because he is a good man, and I wanted him to spread the word within the ranks. It seems the former turncoat disliked being told when to go on break. In addition, the restrooms and cafeteria at the new employer were pigsties. The word is out like it had been broadcast on the bloody public address system. I don't expect any additional defections. The damn grass on the other side of the fence doesn't look so bloody green anymore. I have to admit the raise helps as well. Those changes in our procedures and the improvements in housekeeping were a good call on your part. It proves the old adage that even a blind squirrel can find an acorn or two."

"Your kind words and expansive compliment will live forever in my heart, Sam."

"It wasn't a bloody compliment. It was just a casual comment. The question remains. How am I supposed to earn my keep?"

"It's funny you should bring that up, Sam. Actually, there are a number of items that I believe will keep you challenged. First, you will likely get a call today from an official at the Chicago Board of Education. It looks like they have figured out that kids might learn better from experienced people who do real work. We may provide them with two of your best men who know how to 'do' and 'teach' to train their students. One will be for Lane Tech and one for Chicago Vocational. It can't start before January, which is ideal timing, because that's when we have the second 9500 coming in. I want this to be a reward for the men selected. Allied will have most, but not all of the cost covered by the Board. I'm really interested in spotting good young talent. The best of the high school students should be ideal candidates for hiring during summer vacation as apprentices. There is no substitute for being on the job doing real work to help an individual determine his life's vocation. Additionally, it would help us man our production machines during the summer vacation schedule."

"You want us to start a farm team like the White Sox? That is something I've wanted to do for years! It helps us build for the future."

"Exactly, Sam. Nobody, especially me, knows what the future will bring, but why not take a positive view? Most importantly, we help kids learn to perform correctly in high paying jobs. Incidentally, the raise was not intended to head off 'pirating', per se, although it was discussed. It was time to reward your guys for a job well done."

"O.K. I accept that sentiment, and I think the establishment of a farm team is a damned good call. What am I to do with the rest of my extra time?"

"We have just retained a new sales representative whose name is Frank. He may provide us the opportunity to obtain new types of customers like a *Caterpillar* or *J. I. Case.* Frank doesn't know our manufacturing capabilities yet. If we can bring in new work that is optimally suited for our plant production capabilities, and bid the work correctly the first time, it will enhance our profitability. I want you to accompany and help Frank on his initial sales calls. Only you, Sam, have the experience to recognize the opportunities. Getting into these shops as an untested vendor is difficult. That will be Frank's job and he is good at it. The first thing these new accounts will throw at us will be 'problem' parts—those parts that their existing suppliers are falling down on. There may be a reason or two why their current suppliers can't make the part. You can spot the reason and present a solution. To quote scripture, we have been hiding your light under a bushel. My only reluctance in letting your light shine before this was the concern about what happens to the plant during your absence. Your announcement that the plant is 'running itself' is music to my ears. Congratulations Sam, you'll love sales!"

"Hoisted on my own petard! You're the sneakiest 'ex-sea-gull' in the world. I have a challenge for you. How about some new equipment? We do more than machine parts at this plant. We stamp out a fair number of parts as well. Consolidated Equipment makes a model A111 that would suit our needs for stamped parts perfectly."

"I talked to the Consolidated salesman Friday. He's upset that we are favoring National. He wants to bring in the A111 as a demo machine in two weeks. Do you have room?"

"Hell, yes! That's great news. Allied is becoming quite a sophisticated manufacturing powerhouse with the new equipment. In summary, I'm to make room for, install, and train on the new A111. I'm also supposed to support sales calls and train a new peddler. In my spare time, I'm to establish and staff a farm team. Adam, upon review, I don't think my raise was enough."

"No more raises yet, Sam. I have an additional assignment to prevent your decline to sea gull status. Run the new A111 in concert with the old stamping machine. That gives us a backup. The new 9300 and 9500 provide backup for our first two machines. I never want to be in a late shipment mode again. That still leaves us with extra floor space. I have a hunch that we could extend our service to customers and increase our profit margins if we did some secondary treatment to the finished parts. Maybe we should do some painting, heat-treating, or plating. We need to start slowly and gain experience. When you and Frank start visiting our prospective new accounts, keep your eyes open for such an opportunity. Locate that opportunity and make it happen. Then, and only then, would I consider an additional raise as a reasonable request.

"You are the devil incarnate, Adam! It's funny, though. I always felt that secondary processing was an area we could exploit. I even recommended that we do it years ago, but of course, nobody in office-land listened. I'll keep my eyes open for the opportunity. Thanks. I now have a couple of things to accomplish and you must be exhausted from thinking about how to load me up with assignments and will need to take a nap. I'll catch you later." Sam, as usual, terminated the call abruptly and with the last verbal barb. Adam smiled and thought he could rob the Brinks truck with just two Sams, instead of five normal souls.

Ann was standing by the front of Adam's cubicle. "I don't believe you were totally honest with Sam. The Chicago Board of Education didn't think of anything. I don't think they ever have, and probably never will. I believe someone named Adam called them and initiated the idea for student training. Why don't you take credit for an outstanding contribution for the kids and potentially to Allied?"

"Because, Ann, implementing the idea is the objective. Good ideas are a dime a dozen. What separates the men from the boys, if I may use that chauvinistic phrase, is the ability to get it done. If foregoing credit enhances the implementation results, then so be it. I'm worried about saving the company, not building a personal legacy."

"I also heard you mention the key phrase backup in your conversation with Sam. I recall that we were having a conversation on that very subject yesterday before Dave interrupted us. Come on, I'll buy you a cup and let you stare at my attractive, 'Early American' duct-taped furniture while we continue that conversation." They secured the coffee, which Adam desperately needed, and retired to Ann's office.

"Dave is out selecting a final vendor for the new lights in the plant. Yesterday I confirmed to you that I did not have a personal backup plan and inquired as to why you stayed cool and confident. You were not able, or chose not to respond to that question. Now would be a great time for an answer." Typical Ann, Adam thought. A good, complete summary, and a call for action.

"It's a long story."

"I love long stories, Adam."

How does one summarize years of activities, experiences, and observations? As succinctly as he could, Adam reviewed everything with Ann. Starting from the pastor's sermon, he continued with Frank's views, First Continental, unemployment and the IRS audit. Ann was an excellent listener interrupting only with questions for clarification. Adam concluded with: "I am determined to win my economic freedom by securing about two million dollars. That would allow me to pay for my sons' college expenses as well as protect me from the Lewis's, Park's, Palmer's and perhaps the Bernie's that one meets along life's path."

"Two million ought to do it, Adam. That's almost the same number I came up with. How on earth can one secure that kind of money in this economy?"

"I've explored a number of options, Ann, and there is only one viable way to reach that goal. I plan to steal it."

Ann gasped. "That is almost exactly what I said!"

"I know. Scary isn't it?"

"Adam, I could never seriously entertain that. I despise violence. I couldn't live with myself if I hurt anybody or anything."

"What if there was a way to accomplish the goal without hurting anybody, but perhaps an insurance company?"

"That sounds impossible; however, you have a proven track record in achieving the impossible. Can you elaborate on your thinking?"

Once again, Adam took a deep breath and described the entire general scope of the project; why he selected a Brinks truck, the location on Lake Shore Drive, and the diversions. Adam concluded with: "I believe I have a fundamentally sound plan and the funding. What I don't have are the people that the project requires or the skills to obtain and evaluate them. You could be the key to solving that portion of the problem. Perhaps what I'm asking for isn't feasible. In addition, you must answer the profound questions first exposed to me at church. Do you want to be sick? Do you want to live with the constant fear of loss? Do you want economic freedom?"

"I can answer those questions most definitively. Yes, I want my freedom and I'm tired of being pushed around. Furthermore, I don't see anything wrong with the viability of your plan at this point."

"How about the unambiguous Commandment: *Thou shall not steal?"*

"Oh, Adam, that's hitting below the belt."

"No it isn't, Ann. When you first told me about Allied, you gave me the whole story, warts and all. I have the same obligation to tell you the whole story. I've wrestled with the moral dilemma for some time. I've elected to go for freedom, not because I ignored the moral imperative or attempted to rationalize it away. I have a little voice in my head that sounds just like Mel Gibson in *Braveheart* shouting 'Freedom.' I may be risking eternal damnation, but I have chosen to heed that voice. Let there be no doubt about the decision, however. It is morally 'wrong.' I can't make the choice for you. I have an obligation to make you aware beforehand of all the parameters. I also respect your total confidence on this entire subject."

"That is why you said—'be careful of what you wish for'."

"Exactly. Once again, dreaming about a solution versus 'picking up your bed and walking' are two different agendas. Keep in mind that if you elect to take the same path as I have, we incur the obligation to present the same information to others. We need to recruit 'honest crooks.' I don't need angry young, or for that matter angry old men. I don't want people seeking revenge, or who just lust for material wealth. I want technically skilled, dedicated, honorable people with a longing for economic freedom. That's a very tall order to fill and may be the ultimate stumbling block in this whole plan."

"Adam, you have given me a great deal to think about. I'm honored that you trust my confidence and respect my talent for evaluating and recruiting people. I'm not sure how this will work out. I think your fears about finding enough 'honest crooks' may be misplaced. I have heard the essence of your yearning in hundreds of interviews. None were as articulately stated as your arguments, but they were subtly present nonetheless. The amount of frustration with the 'system' is at a record high in my opinion. I know I can find the people you need, and perhaps in quick order. Give me a little time to see if Mel Gibson will speak to me."

"Take as long as you need, Ann. It's crucial that you do. I respect the fact that you must reflect on all of the parameters!"

The meeting concluded with both participants emotionally drained. Asking someone to take an active role in a felony isn't like asking whether an individual preferred thin or deep-dish pizza. Time will tell, Adam thought.

CHAPTER 22

It had been over a week since Adam asked Ann to consider her need for a personal backup plan. "How strongly did she feel the need for financial independence and economic freedom?" Adam was starting to feel anxious about the time that was lost in starting the implementation while she deliberated. It was early fall, and in one sense, next summer felt like an eternity away. On the other hand, the number of action items that had to be accomplished and coordinated would make the time fly. Additionally, Bernie could strike at any minute.

Yet Adam was impressed with the time Ann was spending reviewing her options. He didn't trust a knee-jerk response to a very significant decision. There was little time to spend wondering about Ann's decision. Sam was driving Adam nuts with a slew of details on the A111.

Sam and Frank made their first call on *Caterpillar* at the Mossville production facility. As surmised, "Cat" wanted them to look at a new part that was perfect for the A111. The problem was, it had to be painted in "Cat's" famous yellow paint and then cured after stamping. They were experimenting with a new process that utilized a special epoxy paint cured in a chemical oven. The goal was to make the finish on the part rock hard. The part was designed by Cat to be exposed to the weather. Durability under the harshest of environments was the crucial specification. None of Cat's current suppliers had produced it correctly to date, and Cat was in big trouble with production delays. The part was deemed a potential "line stopper," which was the most despised designation possible for any part.

After reviewing the part's specification and the process used to manufacture it, Sam decided he knew a better way to produce the finished part. Characteristically for Sam, he boldly bid the part while standing on the floor of Cat's plant. The Cat people in attendance, impressed with his courage and acumen, granted an immediate verbal purchase order. Frank then asked if they could also have a relatively easy part to produce, to help offset the costs of developing the new process. That seemed reasonable to the client, and Sam and Frank emerged with not one, but two new part orders. Better yet, they now had a customer from within an industry segment that had never purchased from Allied in the past.

Sam immediately began to design, build and install a paint booth and curing oven. Within a remarkably short time, the distinctive yellow parts were seen throughout Allied's shop floor. Sam thought the new parts were indestructible and would outlast the Great Pyramid at Cheops. More importantly, the customer believed the same. New orders for the high profit margin parts began flooding into Allied.

Adam had almost completed the review of new orders from *Caterpillar* when he decided to grab some coffee. He was joined briefly by Ann who simply said: "I keep hearing Mel Gibson shouting in my ear. What's my first assignment?"

It was the perfect way to carry out a privileged conversation—in plain sight. Adam had grown to recognize how any organization's grapevine achieved efficiency. When he was training Scotty, Adam was told that the pet watches his master 10 times more than the master watched the pet. The office worked the same way. Eyes were watching constantly for any change in routine or mood. A closed-door meeting would instantly raise suspicions. Casual conversation at the coffeepot was more likely to be perceived as discussions about the Bear's latest win. No one would imagine that the two managers were actually talking about a plot to seize a Brinks truck.

They casually carried their coffee back to Ann's office. Adam elected not to rehash Ann's thinking on the subject. He knew her thinking was thorough and exhaustive. She also never took time to second-guess herself. Adam now had a partner with unique and highly relevant skills.

"Let me start with some ground rules to protect everyone's security. All direct communication within the group will be through you. Indirect communications will be via a web page that I have established. These security measures are important to minimize the risk of exposure. I don't want to know the actual identities of any of the helpers, nor do I want them to know our actual identities. From this point forward, we will all use assumed names. You will represent to all prospective candidates that your role is that of a 'go-between,' and you are not scheduled for active participation in the actual event. All risks must be explained in full. I believe you know what intangible, character-related attributes we are looking for."

"Yes, Adam. I believe at the risk of sounding crazy, I know how to spot 'honest crooks.' What is the web page called?"

"It is established as the Johnson family reunion page, www.Johnson.com. The reunion will be in Chicago and is tentatively scheduled for August 9, next year. I will be *Zack* and you will be *Wilma*. The web page will not be encrypted. If it were, it could produce unwarranted attention by various federal agencies. Therefore, using it will require discretion. Your first assignment is to recruit *Victor*, who in addition to the previously discussed character attributes, needs to own a boat. Furthermore, Victor will require a shed to house the boat and conceal the work that he will have to perform on it."

"What kind of boat is required?"

"It has to traverse Lake Michigan with speed. I would guess 32-38 feet in length and draw less than four feet. Victor must own the boat outright and have no outstanding tickets or violations. Our candidate must also possess a valid Coast Guard certificate to operate the craft."

"May I ask why this recruit should be first? The others may be easier to find."

"I agree Ann, but this is the long lead-time item and without this element in place, we don't have a plan."

"Should we be thinking about an alternate method of communication for anything bulky, like video tapes or drawings? I could set up a mailbox under an assumed name."

"I've thought about that, Wilma. It won't work. It could be traced before or after the event. More importantly, we have to inspire trust in these recruits without me actually dealing with them. A coworker of mine once said, 'when trust fails, all else is gone.' Your role is so vitally important. You have to locate, evaluate, recruit, and inspire. Only human contact and direct eye contact can achieve that. This must be a high-tech, high-touch operation. You'll also have to carefully monitor if any of the team's initial enthusiasm for the project wanes over time."

"This is a lot of work, Adam. No one person recruited will know the whole plan, or the identities of others involved. Nonetheless, I have to sell this like they have worked together for years."

"I couldn't agree more. This may end up being more work than we are doing at Allied. I'll drop the whole idea in a second if you can prove to me that Bernie isn't coming around the corner anytime soon. The thought of another trip to the State's unemployment office bolsters my personal enthusiasm for the project."

"Well stated, Zack. Let me begin to review my vast collection of personnel information to find out where Victor resides. I may have to pay him a visit."

"That's another of your many strengths, Ann. The grapevine won't start buzzing if you are out during a recruiting session. That's your normal office routine."

"That may be true, Adam, but this is not a normal recruiting effort. I'm thinking we may need some type of down payment to secure commitment from our recruits. It may be helpful to impress on all concerned the need for absolute security. I may ask them for a signed blank confession and power of attorney to hold in escrow until the event is accomplished."

"That could be a good idea, but I'll leave it entirely in your hands. You can also advise the selected recruits to start thinking of ways to explain to friends and family how they came into so much money when we finally collect. It's a real problem, and indicating that you are concerned about that now is a very positive statement. Personally, I plan to win the Lotto, but I'm going to have to start buying some tickets to make the reasoning credible with my wife."

"O.K. Zack. Let me go to work. This will be difficult, but it beats constantly groaning about Bernie!"

"That's the spirit Wilma." They both laughed and Adam hurried back to the cubicle to pick up the phone.

"Well, I see we are graced by your presence today. I thought you had gone home for a Boy Scout wiener roast."

"Nothing that important, Sam. Based on EPA rules, I'm now out of that business. I was reviewing some new orders from *Caterpillar*. It looks like you and Frank finally did some good. Wait a second, that proves two blind squirrels can find acorns at the same time!"

"I'm bloody impressed that you listen to me occasionally, but I wish you'd impart the wisdom I disperse and not just the words. I need you to come down here so I can present my case for an additional raise."

"O.K. Sam. You've earned it, I'm sure. Give me a few minutes."

Allied had made one improvement in their operations that greatly pleased Adam. They secured a reserved parking space at the downtown office building and a company van. It was now infinitely easier and more convenient to commute from the office to the plant. Adam arrived at the plant within 30 minutes.

Sam met Adam with a huge smile and obvious pride. The plant manager led Adam behind the new A111, which now had a "Rube Goldberg"—like attachment to the output. Parts were being funneled automatically to a spray booth. After painting, they headed to the curing oven, which had an unbelievably large number of tubes and vents protruding from it.

"I designed and constructed most of the equipment myself in my home workshop! By adjusting heat and chemical concentrations, we learned how to cure parts in 30 minutes. None of our competitors can do it in less than 90 minutes. This gives us a significant competitive edge on a high profit margin part. Frank, who by the way is a good man for a bloody peddler, is taking maximum advantage. We're getting all kinds of new orders!"

Adam picked up one of the gleaming yellow finished parts. The finish looked more durable than baked enamel and he could easily envision that they could withstand the elements and endure forever. "How does the curing oven work?"

"That's the real key, Adam. We run methyl mercaptan, a strong oxidizer, into the oven. It rapidly cures the special epoxy paint to a rock hard finish."

"What the hell is mercaptan?"

"It's the same stuff the gas company adds to your natural gas in small amounts to warn you of bloody leaks. It's one of the more active ingredients in a skunk's spray and many other extremely disagreeable smells in nature. Come over here for a second." Sam led Adam to a test port and opened it for less than a tenth of a second.

Adam thought he had been hit on the side of the head by a two by four. He instantly wanted to throw up. "My God, Sam, that's awful!"

"Aye Laddie, that it is. That's why we have spent a great deal of time constructing airtight seals, vapor recovery sub-systems, and an incineration oven. If this crap leaked to the environment, our bloody plant would shut down and the neighbors would be over here in a heartbeat with their shotguns. Other than stinking worse than a political scandal at City Hall, it won't hurt you in low concentrations. In high concentrations, it is flammable, but otherwise not too dangerous. I think I've earned a bloody raise for just working with the crap. The fact that we are producing a shit load of profits is beside the point."

"I totally agree, Sam, great job! Let me go to work." Adam started back to the office clearly recognizing the need for Sam's new raise. Adam also clearly recognized that Sam had inadvertently provided the answer of how to get the guards out of the Brinks truck. Nobody on the planet could withstand the smell of mercaptan. Adam also realized that it might be possible for him to borrow a small amount from the plant in such a way that it couldn't be traced.

Dave met Adam upon his return to the office. The bean counter was pacing up and down and clearly agitated. "Adam, I don't think you realize how much of a problem I have. We're making money like Walter Payton racked up yardage. The new machines don't require as much tooling as the old ones. We have produced scads of parts and have hardly touched the credit balance we established earlier with our tooling supplier. Now that the order volume is up, we are buying our raw material at a much greater discount. Our unit costs are down to a level that would be hard to measure even if we still ran the stupid job cost report. What am I going to do with the unanticipated profits? I sure as hell don't want to send them to Washington."

"I want Sam to receive a significant and meaningful raise in salary. I'll leave it to you to determine the correct amount, but don't be cheap. The office staff needs one too. We got skipped on the last go around. Call Consolidated. Tell them "Thank you," and send them a check for the A111. See what you can get for the old stamping machine on the used market and use those funds for the down payment on an additional A111. That should keep you busy for a while. If you need more places to spend the loot, see me. Don't forget yourself in this, Dave. You're doing a hell of a job!"

Just as Dave left, beaming from ear to ear, Ann stuck her head into the cubicle.

"My initial research has located two potential Victors. Both own boats and have the additional required qualifications. The only significant difference between the two that I can see at this point is that one is heavily into the hobby of flying radio controlled model airplanes."

Adam leaned back in his chair and thought for a minute. "Go for the one who's into remote controlled model airplanes."

"The gleam in your eye tells me you just thought of something, but I don't want to know what it is."

"No, Ann, you really don't. Since you're making progress and time is running out, let me acknowledge two additional needs. We need to find *Tad* and *Steve* as well. One of them must have extensive automobile repair skills and possess a shop and tools. The other must know electronics, particularly telephones. All three have to be 'handy' and reasonably fit."

Ann just rolled her eyes. "I haven't got one candidate pinned down yet! You have obviously spent too much time with Sam. You are absorbing his personality. However, it does help to know about the other two needs in case I run into them while looking for Victor. If the reasonably fit attribute applies to you, I would suggest that you begin working out."

"Indeed it does Ann. I start the workouts this weekend. You seem to have been influenced by Sam's personality as well, with a crack like that!"

Adam started packing up his things for the walk to Union Station. It was evident they were entering into the action phase of "Project Freedom" which was a relief and yet frightening at the same time. The project was alive and moving forward. Major questions remained to be answered. Would Ann be able to locate and recruit the talent required? Where were the "UNK-UNK'S?" Would they have enough time before Bernie emerged from his self imposed blindness?

CHAPTER 23

It was a beautiful Monday in October. The sky was a sunny bright blue, which emphasized the reds, oranges, and magentas of the turning leaves. As the train lurched toward downtown, Adam was thinking that autumn had to be the best season in Chicago. The Bears won their fifth straight and they were tied with the Packers for the lead in the division. All too soon, winter would arrive, but at the moment everything is wonderful. Scotty was enjoying the fact that Adam was starting to jog during their walking sessions. Scotty's companion had already lost five pounds.

Dave managed to locate the funds that allowed the company to give raises to everyone in the office, including Adam. For the first time since he and Alice had been married, they were close to being debt free. The opportunity to join Allied had been a Godsend to the Jones family. Adam enjoyed the people within Allied and the feelings of accomplishment. He fervently prayed that somehow they could keep the company intact.

Sam concluded his discussions with the Board of Education. Allied would provide an experienced operator for both high schools at the start of the second semester in January. Men at the plant were competing for the opportunity to teach the kids. The employees were actually preparing for the future with a sense of optimism. The question was—would there be a future if Bernie arrived?

Ann was particularly efficient in preparing for the future in her own way. She performed her difficult task at a rate faster than Adam's highest expectations. All three helpers had been located and recruited. The tentative date established for the heist could now be achieved. It was by the grace of God that Adam had secured a used Internet server for cash at a computer show. He installed the

"Johnson" family web page just days before enlisting Ann's help. The server used a dial-up DSL to an Internet Service Provider from Adam's home. There was no "hard link" to the server and virtually no way for authorities to trace activity on the page. All three recruits had logged on and said hello to Zack.

Adam instructed Victor via e-mail to read about a ship named the "Atlantis," the German commerce raider of World War II. The "Atlantis" was a disguised merchant ship that could change its identity by changing its shape. Adam wanted Victor to do the same with his boat, a 32-foot, Egg Harbor Yachts Pacemaker. An outer skin would need to be designed that would change the apparent length, color, and lines. That skin should be painted in an unusual, but not too gaudy color like deep purple. The skin would have to be readily discarded on command with little effort, like a butterfly emerging from a cocoon.

It took two days for Victor to respond via e-mail. "I thought you were completely nuts until I finished your recommended reading. I now understand what needs to be done, and I will be back with additional details."

Tad was instructed to find and acquire a used Ford or Chevy van equipped with a cherry picker. Adam wanted it acquired discreetly, hopefully in a cash transaction. Tad quickly acknowledged the assignment.

Steve, the electronics expert, was instructed to install a phone tap on the bridge tender's office on Lake Shore Drive. Once installed, it would collect and forward all messages in and out of the office in batch mode. Steve simply responded with "no problem." Adam, with his understanding of Internet security, had hacked into the City's computer files and learned the names and schedules of all the bridge tenders. He also determined to whom the bridge tenders reported. The team didn't know what they said to each other in daily communication or how they sounded. Steve's mission was designed to fill that void.

Adam realized, as the train arrived at Union Station, that events were unfolding at a rapid rate. He could only hope they had foreseen the majority of the "UNK-UNK'S."

Ann greeted Adam at the coffeepot. "How about dem Bears! Does the rest of the family enjoy them as much as we do?"

"I haven't heard much from the family. They all seem to be busy with assignments." A secretary who had been getting her coffee smiled and left them alone.

"How did you get these guys so fast, Ann?"

"I tried to tell you. There are thousands of souls like these guys out there. Finding the specific technical skills was more difficult than the subjective character concerns. They all have varied stories to account for their motives at a detailed level. At a general level, all the stories are about the same. None of the individuals on the team is particularly angry or resentful. I would characterize them as disappointed in the system and desirous of freedom. They remind me of you in that respect and Sam in their technical abilities. Steve doesn't quite fit the mold. He's the youngest, and he married late in life. His new wife is pregnant with their first child. Thus, his motivation is far more pragmatic than the others."

"This is a surefire bet if they are all like Sam!" Adam chose not to respond to Steve's marital situation. It troubled him to think of the risk.

"It better be a surefire bet, Adam! I'm counting on this."

"We all are. How do we pay the family members for their expenses?"

"I told each of them that we would provide some help if required, but that we wanted financial support from them as well. It has been my experience that most people will work with greater diligence if they invest some of their own funds. I told them to record actual expenses incurred. I promised we would pay those first before splitting the balance of the proceeds."

"Great call, Ann! In the Navy we referred to your philosophy as 'Plank-Holders.' They were the crew who first served aboard a ship when newly commissioned. In effect, they secured an investment in the future of the ship as a result of being the first to serve. There is great pride in being a 'Plank-Holder.' It also helps greatly with the budget."

"It applies to me as well. What can I do?"

"O.K., Wilma. We need a dozen cell phones—nothing fancy. They just have to work and be obtained as discreetly as possible."

"Consider it done, Zack." Both of them headed for their respective offices as additional people wandered in.

Adam retired to the office and fired off an e-mail message to Victor. "Are you familiar with a radio controlled aircraft called the Cessna Skymaster 337 from Global Industries?"

Dave entered Adam's office shortly after sending the message. "Adam, we may have an unusual opportunity that I want to review with you. The old, abandoned building just to the south of the plant could be obtained for back taxes. It's virtually free. Should we go for it? What would we do with it if we got it?"

"If we can afford it, as well as the cost of tearing it down, I would recommend we proceed full speed ahead."

"Why tear it down, Adam?"

"Dave, the building is truly dilapidated and a terrible eyesore. We can use some of the land that comes with the place to expand our parking lot. Let's donate the remaining land to the city for a park."

"The City would love it. There is no park within blocks of our location. We could use the tax write off as well."

"If the City agrees, make sure they install a ball diamond next to our parking lot. The guys would enjoy a game of 16-inch softball during lunch. They might end up in a league, and they could use the field after work."

"Adam, you are something else. Where did you learn the 'secret' of managing? I must admit that I was concerned when you first arrived because you didn't know anything about manufacturing. How do you do it? Are you just brilliant?"

"Hell no Dave! I'm just an average guy, but I can read. With the state of education being what it is today, maybe that is unusual. When Ann first hired me, she wanted me to read everything I could about manufacturing. Some of the most interesting stuff came out of Chicago. Specifically the old Western Electric plant called the Hawthorn Works. There are no secrets left in the world. The information is available for anybody to read. Obviously you have to invest the effort to read the stuff."

"Can you give me an example?"

"The study proved, among a host of things, that almost anything you do within a plant would enhance productivity—change the lighting, clean the place, whatever. The increase in productivity will wane over time. You have to keep things moving. You have to stay personally invested. It tells the employees that management 'cares' or is 'trying.' That's why the ball diamond fits the strategy. It's just another chapter in the book that contains many new chapters. One consistent pattern emerges: there are multiple causes and effects to everything you do.

"I fought you on some of those very items, initially. I couldn't see any direct connection."

"The connection is almost always indirect, Dave. The 'Hawthorn Works' study isn't the only text to reference. The Good Book contains great advice, particularly the concept of 'do unto others.' I don't want to be told when to drink coffee. Why should we dictate the time for workers in the plant? It doesn't take a genius to figure out that Ann has hired some great people. Support them and get out of their way." Adam wished he could add that having a personal backup plan helped as well. It allowed you to play to win, instead of playing not to lose. He could not confide this to Dave. It was important not to implicate Dave in any way with the proposed heist. If "Project Freedom" and the team were busted, Dave and Sam would be free to run Allied. Adam owed that to the 225 employees now on the payroll.

"You have made some interesting points for me to consider. By the way, Consolidated is happy with their check. They will ship a new A111 in concert with our moving the old stamping machine out. We found a buyer for the old one yesterday. The whole transaction should be completed in two weeks. Thanks, Adam."

"Thank you, Dave!"

Adam received an answer from Victor. "Am I familiar with the Cessna 337? I own one! It's one of my favorite planes to fly. Why do you ask?"

Adam replied. "We may need it for the reunion. Can you fit it with a couple of video cameras, batteries and a microwave transmitter?"

It was time for another cup. As Adam strode to the coffeepot, he became aware of the intensity of sound throughout the office. The place buzzed, phones rang, and printers spit out paper. A visitor didn't need a financial report to know what was happening. The atmosphere reeked of people happily hustling and achieving progress. If Bernie came in now they were dead. Even a deaf-mute who was oblivious to the world would notice the difference in Allied. Adam had to talk to Ann about this threat.

"Ann, when does Bernie come in for his check?"

Ann smiled warmly and coyly stated: "I don't think Bernie will be coming in. I suggested to him that with the opera and symphony season starting, he would be less inconvenienced if I courier the check to his apartment. Junior was overjoyed and immediately accepted the offer. Now, Adam, would it be possible to have my duct-taped chair replaced?"

"It shall be done, insightful one." Adam was still discovering talents in Ann.

Victor's return e-mail reflected his general knowledge of world events. "It looks like you want a toy for the reunion that would look and act like the Department of Defense's Predator." The DOD's Predator was a high-flying, unmanned, remote controlled reconnaissance aircraft utilized extensively in Afghanistan and Iraq.

"You are exactly correct, Vic. It will be a big hit at the reunion with the kids and an opportunity to teach current events." Adam didn't have to wait long for a reply.

"Understood—consider it done. I'll assume the output will reside on the home page via a hand held hub at ground level. I can launch the plane from the boat with the assistance of a jury-rigged catapult. If that is in concert with your educational requirements, there is no need to reply."

Beautiful, thought Adam.

Now it was Steve's turn. "Mission completed. I have output in the form of magnetic tape for Wilma" to pick up.

Within seconds, Tad joined the fray. "I just obtained the perfect vehicle for the reunion. It was virtually donated by a contractor who used it to replace stree-tlights for a suburb. The contractor is going out of business. I completed the transaction for $5,000 in cash. I could use a little help with that cost if you will need this truck 'really clean' and perhaps repainted for the reunion. Were you thinking of any particular color?"

Adam believed that the request for financial support was fair. The "really clean" reference had to be in accordance to Wilma's instructions on removing all VIN numbers or Vehicle Identification Numbers from numerous locations on the van.

"Yes Tad, it must be very clean. I've always liked the color of the State of Illinois forestry trucks. Wilma will provide help and details. Love, Zack!"

Adam reached into his briefcase and produced four photographs of a large State of Illinois truck that he snapped while taking Alice and the kids to Starved Rock State Park. It was the detail of the State Seal and markings he wanted duplicated. He placed the photos and a web address for the state, which showed additional information, into a plain envelope and marked it Tad. Next, he electronically transferred $5,000 from the Swiss account to Ann's personal account.

"Wilma, excuse me, but you need to schedule a visit with some family members. Nobody was within earshot, but it was fun to play the game. I've transferred funds to your account. Draw a $5,000 money order for Tad and give him this package. Also, Steve has a package for you."

"No problem, Zack."

Adam returned to the small cubicle and reflected on the progress. It seemed to be flowing very well. He had spent less than 30 minutes receiving and sending e-mails to the team. To anyone walking past Adam's open cubicle, it would appear that he was de-bugging more CNC code. Nobody would have guessed that he was helping to plan a felony. There were thousands of cubicles just like his in Chicago alone. If Ann was correct about the number of kindred souls "out there," there might be competition for the same Brinks truck. The thought of that "UNK-UNK" staggered him.

CHAPTER 24

By Chicago standards, the current winter was a "nothing-burger." There had been little snow and scant below zero weather. Alice was starting to embrace the "global warming" propaganda. Adam knew better. "Every once in a while we earn a reprieve," he told her.

"We've done nothing to earn a reprieve," she answered. Adam could not offer a reason to refute her argument, and like all husbands over the ages, retreated into silence.

The late March weather continued its mild streak, and now signs of spring began to appear. As he turned the car onto Interstate 290, Adam caught a glimpse of a robin along the roadside. The first sighting of the year always provided a thrill. It bode well for the future.

The future looked good at Allied as well. Ann received her new chair and a new desk to go with it. The entire office had been upgraded to the point of respectability. The two plant men at the high schools were greatly enjoying their teaching assignments. Six promising students were scheduled for apprenticeship training at Allied this summer.

Sam and Frank were becoming known to Allied's competitors as the deadly duo. It wasn't clear if Frank was learning the business or Sam was learning about selling, but together they were bringing in truckloads of new orders—not just run of the mill orders, either. Large orders from new accounts were their specialty. The second 9300, 9500 and the new A111 had been in operation for weeks.

The big news was from National. They were developing the 9700, a truly gigantic machine with 20 heads. In theory, it could out-produce the 9500 by 300%. Sam was uncharacteristically cool to the concept of the 9700.

"It's too bloody big, Adam! We don't run enough really large jobs to justify that kind of output. It's like trying to kill a fly with a sledge hammer." Adam relayed Sam's concerns to Mr. Williams, who readily understood Sam's reluctance.

"Our market research has illustrated the same concern. We are looking at the 9700 as having a small impact on the overall market unless we come up with a unique idea to increase its versatility."

Adam discussed the 9700's lack of flexibility with Vladamir over coffee one day. In actuality, it was less of a discussion than an exchange of formulas. Vlad came up with a concept of having National add an additional controller and raw material feed to the 9700. He was convinced he could write software to permit two different jobs to run simultaneously on the 9700. That would allow an operator to put the full potential of the 9700 to bear on the occasional big job. In the absence of a big job, the machine would be versatile enough to run two smaller jobs concurrently.

Mr. Williams thought it was the best idea he had ever heard. Sam started drooling and Vlad started writing code. The prototype dual job 9700 was expected at Allied in February of next year. If the installation worked as planned, Allied would become a first tier supplier overnight. The future for Allied, if there was one, looked very bright. New people, new accounts, and new capabilities were a great combo.

One never knew what the future would bring, Adam thought, as he exited south on Illinois Route 83. After the initial flurry of activity with "Project Freedom" assignments last fall, progress slowed to a steady, sustainable pace. The list of items that had to be obtained seemed endless. Adam acquired three gas masks from a variety of Army surplus stores throughout the city, then two laptop computers from computer shows. It took awhile, but he finally secured over three-dozen "smoke candles" from assorted plumbing supply houses. All of the transactions were for cash. There was now precious little of Stan's gracious gift left.

Adam wasn't alone in his spending. Ann acquired 12 cell phones on a "pre-paid" basis with 50 minutes each pre-loaded. Nobody in the various locations where she purchased them could care less about her identity. If she had cash, she got the equipment.

The other members of the team had acquired pipe strapping, 12 electronic igniters, M-80 firecrackers, toy multistage rockets, metal tubing, construction material, door lock and keys, a voice synthesizer, two handheld Global Positioning System (GPS) receivers, two water-tight trunks, coveralls, hard hats and gloves. Ann, in exasperation, once said she thought the object of the plan was to gain economic freedom and wondered if they would be in debtor's prison before they reached the objective.

Despite the rising costs, progress was being made until the first part of January. Ann was becoming more and more concerned with what she felt was a flagging of enthusiasm. "Adam, I'm not sure what it is, but I feel it. I believe it's too much to ask these guys to lay everything on the line without knowing more about the plan, the other members of the team, or Zack. There is no substitute for the human touch to build such trust. I'm asking you to reconsider your concerns for security. We need to have a meeting."

Adam thought about Ann's comments for some time before agreeing with her assessment. He called for a meeting where everybody would use his or her assumed names. Their first meeting was held at the Portillo's restaurant in Elmhurst over Italian beef sandwiches. Elmhurst was a good central location within the Chicago metro area and was large enough for them to achieve relative privacy. The "golden oldie" rock and roll music in the background provided additional cover. The first meeting had occurred at the end of January.

Each man came in, obtained a meal, and found Wilma. It was an extremely productive and profitable meeting. Tad did not realize that two men would have to stand in the "cherry picker," and it would have to allow fast exit to the top of the Brink's truck. One man had to inject gas to the driver's compartment while the second man injected gas to the rear compartment with the guards and the money. Research showed that an airtight seal separated the two compartments; however, both sides had independent air vents. Adam had forgotten to tell Tad, who responded: "No problem, I can fix it."

Vic showed the group Polaroid pictures of his new boat. He had fabricated an entire shell around the actual craft that made it seem 6 feet longer and 3 feet higher. More importantly, the hull was covered in what looked like mahogany planks. The new boat looked exactly like something a jerk would have produced in his garage while drinking a great deal of beer. It was gaudy, but not unseemly. The boat's "new" name was displayed on the stern in huge gold leaf script—"The Klutz" out of Green Bay, Wisconsin. It was far more than Adam could have hoped for.

Tad provided pictures of his new "State of Illinois" van. Steve brought additional recordings of the bridge tender and his boss. The sharing of these items showed the group's determination and the level of planning for the event. A real team formed that evening, and the enthusiasm went off the scale. Security had been compromised, but not severely threatened. New assignments were given out and readily accepted. A second meeting was scheduled during the January encounter for March at the same time and location.

* * * *

The two depressed partners sat quietly at their booth in the "White Castle."

"What the hell happened, Ron? I've been reassigned to robbery starting tomorrow and told to find a new partner!"

"Don't feel bad, Luke. I've been reassigned to traffic court to catch citizens who haven't paid their parking tickets. It's obvious to me that somehow the word got out that we were sniffing around looking for a connection to a big bank executive. I don't think the forces that control us believe we found anything, but the best way to stop the investigation was to bust us apart."

"If what you are saying is true, we are being punished for doing a good job. Damn, we missed our calling, Ron. We should work in the private sector where they reward you with big raises, promotions, and maybe a bonus when you do good work. I think some in private companies get ticker tape parades down LaSalle Street."

"Very true, Luke, but we made the choice 'to serve and protect' years ago and we can't go back. I think you personally are relatively safe, but I'm in deep yogurt. It was my 'snitch' that started the ball rolling."

"What else can they do to you, Ron?"

"I suspect that if I'm not more forthcoming to our superiors in the next several months I'll be placed on unpaid administrative leave to loosen my tongue."

"They can't do that! You must be the hardest working, honest cop on the force."

"They make the rules, Luke. They can always find something wrong technically to justify their actions. Put this in perspective. If the drug-laundering scheme were busted, it would severely affect the syndicate. If it turned out there were a big bank connection to a politically connected hot shot, there would be hell to pay. There is even something more sinister. We've both had a hunch that someone was tipping the mob to our plans in the past. That, theoretically, could have been a data-entry clerk, secretary, or anyone with access to the information flow. What just happened to us illustrates that the syndicate has access to someone high in our organization. That 'someone' has the clout to reassign officers. That limits the field of potential informants to about six high ranking individuals."

"My God, Ron, I think you nailed it! This isn't a border skirmish with the bad guys—this is thermo-nuclear war. If the media ever got hold of this, they would sell an enormous number of papers. Some columnist like Jason Gompers would beat it like a drum. The City's image would be deep-sixed."

"Keep a sharp eye on your back as you go about your robbery duties, partner. We are dealing with some powerful forces here."

"Why don't you just tell them what they want to know Ron? Protect your career, family and perhaps your life like everyone else does."

"That would be the smart play, Luke. You have always commented on my lack of smarts during the years we worked together. It shouldn't surprise you that it's not in my nature to be intimidated. If I am ever forced to spend time on unpaid leave, I may change my tune. A loss of income even for a short time would be devastating."

* * * *

Adam pulled into the large parking lot of the Elmhurst Portillo's to conduct the group's second meeting. It was time to forget about spring and robins and get to work. God willing, only one more meeting should do it. This situation was just like Allied. It took constant personal attention to motivate people. His doubts about the wisdom of meeting as a group were long gone. He would remain eternally grateful for Ann's insights and leadership.

Adam entered the restaurant, ordered a "jumbo dog" and chocolate malt, and found Wilma in a remote booth in the far corner. The rest of the team soon joined them.

Vic, who Adam was recognizing as the most analytical of the group, began the session. "Zack, I have continued to review your plan in detail and I'm convinced it will work. My only concern is whether that bridge will go up when we want it to. It's critical that it does. Do we have a backup?

In the last meeting, Adam explained what he and Steve had accomplished. The bridge tender that they predicted would be on duty lived in constant fear of his boss, a ward committeeman. The boss was aggressive and blunt with a distinct, raspy, Chicago accented voice. By splicing together actual words used by the ward committeeman and those from a voice synthesizer, Steve came up with two phone messages. The first one said: "Now listen up. I don't have time for questions. I may have to call you later today to raise the bridge. We have some kind of federal security drill going on. When I call and tell you to raise the bridge—DO IT!' The second message was: "Raise that God damn bridge

NOW!" Everybody on the team agreed after listening to the messages on a Walkman with headphones that it would work.

"You are absolutely correct, Vic! That bridge must go up when we want it to. When Steve set the phone taps, he checked the lock on the door to the bridge tender's control room. It's a secure lock that can't be readily picked, even assuming you could do so with a flood of traffic going by. Therefore, I have duplicated a City of Chicago work order to replace the lock. We now have a new message: "I'm sending over someone to change the lock—let da guy in!" Steve will come by with the new lock and a set of keys for distribution to the other bridge tenders. We will keep one of the keys so we can get in. Wilma will stand by with fake FBI credentials to go in and instruct the bridge tender to raise the bridge. It's not a perfect backup, but it helps. "Can anyone come up with a better solution?"

Tad asked: "When will you replace the lock?"

"About a week before 'D' day. If nothing else, we get to test our bridge tender's reaction to his master's voice." Everybody smiled at that. It was well thought out and practical like every other aspect of the plan.

Vic showed video on his laptop of the Cessna radio controlled aircraft flying with a video camera providing continuous video output. "What's the purpose of the eye in the sky, Zack?" Wilma asked.

"We have to monitor exactly where the Brinks truck is as it approaches the lake. We need to time the bridge raising to the truck's line of travel down Balbo. Since the truck can be plus or minus five to ten minutes on its route, it's critical that we don't initiate the bridge raising until the correct moment. The plane's camera will allow us to monitor the truck from Michigan Avenue, and it is much safer than having a spotter. Vic's testing proves it can work. He'll launch it from the boat and then the plane will be programmed to cruise in a circle over Grant Park. The timing will all be controlled from a master program that I have written."

The team was more than satisfied by the answer and the degree of thinking it represented.

"I wish I could show you this next thing in person, but the risk was too great to assemble the team in a forest preserve for an actual demonstration. We need a lot of diversions to pull off this plan. Steve has devised a great remote controlled trigger to ignite smoke bombs. Let me show you." Adam activated a file on the laptop of Steve's test on some farm in the middle of nowhere Indiana. Great billows of smoke issued forth from a canister with no one near by. "We will chain these together to give us twenty minutes of smoke from key locations around the city. They will be activated by cell phones that will be called by the master program." The entire team was in awe of the amount of smoke. It did not take an overactive imagination to sense the confusion that would result.

Adam continued. "These devices will have to be placed and phone reception verified by Steve and Tad about a week before 'D' day. If you drive around while placing the devices in a State truck, it's unlikely City or County authorities will challenge you. They hate to get involved in inter-jurisdictional fights. If they do, tell them that you are searching for evidence of the 'Longhorn Asian Beetle.' There has been enough publicity about that particular insect to provide cover. That's one reason why you are in a state forestry truck. Wear your coveralls and Tad's newly painted 'State of Illinois' hard-hats."

"How much money will there be in the truck, Zack," the ever-analytical Victor asked?

"Based on hearsay, about 10-12 million. I could try to confirm that amount, but it would draw a lot of attention. There is no reason to incur the risk. It's more than enough money for our needs. Actually, I hope it's not more than what we anticipate."

"What?" Steve asked incredulously. "Wouldn't more be better?"

"Not necessarily. Ten million is a lot of money to everyone present tonight, but it's not too much for most insurance companies. The banks will be quickly reimbursed, and the heat will be off. After a few weeks, the media will give up on it and we'll be relatively safe. The more money we liberate, the greater the effort by police officials and the media to solve the crime."

"Speaking of the media, don't believe anything you read or see after we complete the effort. The police frequently plant false stories to confuse the perpetrators. I pledge to always provide the truth to you. I'll keep the web site up between 7 and 11 PM after 'D' day to allow for communication. Our cover will be that we are planning for another family reunion in five years. That will be accurate, because that's the time we go fishing in Lake Michigan."

The full dimension of the planning was now becoming evident to all members. Adam now knew this couldn't be effectively conveyed over the Internet. Steve, who was a likable guy and related well with the entire group, said: "Zack, you are one hell of a planner and I'm growing more confident by the second. I hate to bring this up, but I do see one area of concern."

"Fire away, Steve. That's why we're here."

"I'm convinced that the mercaptan will flush out the guards, but are we applying enough pressure to get the stuff into the truck?"

"Good point! Do you have a recommendation?"

"Why don't we combine the flow of mercaptan with a carbon dioxide extinguisher. That will give us a pressure boost plus a roaring sound. It will scare the hell out of anybody, plus smell to high heaven."

Tad jumped in. "That's a great idea Steve. It also lowers the temperature dramatically, which eliminates any concern about ignition of the mercaptan. I can slave two canisters together with a common trigger.

"I agree gentlemen. Tad, you have earned a new assignment. Don't forget that you need to construct two devices. Any additional questions or comments?"

"We haven't talked about the need for alibi's," Wilma interjected.

"Another good point! Actually, there are two levels to consider. Each of you will be responsible for developing your own story for family or friends to cover your absence during our 'D' day activities. I can't help you with that.

"The second level involves the creation of an alibi for the authorities. The strategy inherent in the plan is that the best alibi available is to eliminate the need to have one. Remember, the authorities need 'probable cause' to initiate a search or conduct an interrogation. We have taken elaborate steps to eliminate any clues that could lead to the establishment of probable cause. Once we deposit the monetary proceeds and the paraphernalia associated with our activity into Lake Michigan, we won't need an alibi. If we get busted during, or shortly after the heist, no alibi would suffice anyway.

"Once again, any questions?"

"O.K. Let's wrap this up before we draw undo attention to ourselves. We have about four months to complete all of the remaining assignments and think of additional questions. I know there will be more. If possible, let's try to resolve these through the web page. We invite risk with every physical meeting; however, I think they have been helpful. Anyone on the team can call for one at any time. Remember to get in shape and start preparing a cover story for the acquired wealth you'll have at 'D' day plus five years."

"The timing is perfect. My wife is due this fall." Steve had the glow of an expectant father. The group started to disband one at a time. Wilma was the last to remain.

"You did a fantastic job of recruiting, Ann. They are great guys as well as creative and resourceful."

"It is starting to look good, Adam. I just wish that we would be able to beat the Bernie threat. Junior could re-appear at any time. I wake up in the middle of the night worrying about it. Four months is a long time away; but the good news is that I don't see the flagging of enthusiasm in the team that I saw earlier this year."

"The Bears looked good at the start of last season, Ann. Then they fell on their face in the play-offs. Thank God, they beat the Pack twice or it would have been a disappointing season. I agree, we look good now, but I want to finish good as well. We have to win the 'Super Bowl' on our first and only attempt, and we will need every minute of the next four months to refine details and perfect the plan.

"I still wake up in the middle of the night worrying about 'UNK-UNK'S.' That's another reason for the meetings. Holes in the plan have been spotted and filled with team suggestions. Having the meetings was an outstanding idea, Ann. Many people saw us eating here tonight, but were oblivious to what we were talking about."

"Well Adam, don't push that thought too far. We don't know what they were talking about at the other tables either. Who knows how many competitors were in here tonight with their eyes on the same Brinks truck. Everyone on the team has instructions on how to prepare for the future. Based on what I've seen and heard in this meeting, someone at Brinks should start worrying about 'UNK-UNK'S' and their future." That brought a smile to Adam's face as they left the restaurant.

CHAPTER 25

Standing and waiting impatiently in the parking lot of the Franklin Park train station was a new experience for Adam. It was the first time he had departed the 6:32 short of Union Station. This unorthodox event was simply another step in their many security procedures. He planned to join fellow members of the team and proceed to Grant Park in the van this morning. Joining the team at the Franklin Park station should negate being seen by a neighbor in Bartlet, which would be difficult to explain.

He told Alice that National was hosting a day of fishing on Lake Michigan for their favorite customers. It was a perfect, clear, warm August day for such activity. She strongly supported the idea. Alice often expressed the opinion that Adam had been working too hard and needed a break. It was the perfect alibi in that it accounted for his absence and could explain any sunburn acquired during the days activities.

Adam detested the fact that he had to lie to Alice, but he didn't want her implicated in any way with what he was about to do. Their trusting relationship was severely endangered after the team's third and final face-to-face meeting. She couldn't understand or accept the frequent late-night meetings. She wondered why her husband was losing so much weight. It was bad enough to commit to a crime, now he was dangerously close to being accused of having an affair. Adam knew that his wife used a different burden of proof than that of the courts. This was yet another example of an "UNK-UNK." Neither he nor the other team members had fully evaluated the amount of time required for planning a criminal activity. Instead of no meetings, they ended up having three, which took a toll on his marriage.

The third meeting took place in May, and like the first two was extremely productive. The team nearly forgot to include a change of clothes for storage on Vic's boat. They had to wear something after ditching their coveralls. That exchange was handled during the meeting. Tad received two five pound bottles of mercaptan from Zack to combine with the carbon dioxide canisters. The mercaptan bottles had to be handed off in person. There was no way to ship them on common carriers under the law. Even if it had been possible to ship the gas, it would have left a paper trail. Thus far, they had avoided all temptations to leave an audit trail from any of their many activities.

Everyone was instructed to bring two combination locks of their choosing to the last meeting. When Vic illustrated the two Alumilite reinforced, watertight and weighted trunks he had constructed, they understood why. Each man would put his own lock on each of the two strong boxes. This illustrated to the entire team in a tangible way that they were all equal partners. Vic tested both trunks to make sure they were watertight and not buoyant. Nobody on the team wanted them to float away after the deposit on the bottom of the lake.

The most poignant moment of the third meeting was when Vic mentioned that the project's success would be greatly aided by the dastardly terrorist attack on New York.

"People will panic when they see the clouds of smoke. They will jump to the conclusion that it's an attack!"

That comment stunned and bothered the entire team. "You're right Vic, but I can't change history. If it really bothers you or anyone else, we can cancel right now, no hard feelings." Zack responded. After much silent gnashing of teeth, everybody voted to continue. As loyal Americans, they wanted no help from the terrorists, even the unintentional variety.

The official countdown for "D" day started in the second week of July with the physical placement and testing of strategic diversionary devices. Steve had successfully changed the lock on the bridge tender's office during the last week of July and provided a key to Wilma. Scripts and assignments were reviewed and rehearsed on the web page numerous times. It was of immense comfort to the group that the bridge tender had accepted the phone call and the prerecorded message from his boss to change the locks as authentic. The van, airplane, and boat were double-checked, fueled, and ready. With everything in place and the weather holding, Adam gave the "Go" signal yesterday afternoon. If everything was working correctly, he should be picked up any second.

"What the hell are you doing," the voice inside of Adam's head shouted? The full enormity of the planned activities finally dawned on him while he waited to be picked up. All projects, including "Project Freedom," took on a life that grew so large you could lose sight of reality. It's easy to become so immersed in the details that you tend to forget the objective. "It isn't too late. You could pull the plug right now and no harm would be done" the little voice in his mind declared.

There was a sign near the railroad tracks at the Franklin Park Station indicating the direction to Elgin, the last western stop on this line. Seeing the town's name brought back the unpleasant memory of unemployment and the potential threat posed by Bernie.

At that moment, Zack saw a "State of Illinois" van pull into the station's parking lot. Steve and Tad were onboard.

* * * *

Things were not running smoothly at the Second Republic Bank this beautiful morning. Mr. Alister Lewis was vacationing overseas. Mr. Lewis left Nelson Powers, his assistant, in charge of operations. Lewis provided specific instructions not to be disturbed under any circumstances during his vacation. The instructions were somewhat redundant, as Powers was determined to illustrate that there was nothing he couldn't handle on his own. It wouldn't help his image to whine or ask for guidance from a vacationing senior. Powers was also anxious to prove to Lewis that he was totally capable of handling the senior's secret, special project.

On the other hand, the problem Powers faced this morning was without precedent. The bank would have a large work crew, consisting mostly of outside contractors, in their vaults replacing the fire protection system.

For years, Second Republic had used Halon as a fire suppressant within their vaults, but the EPA had recently banned the use of Halon. The bank would have to switch to carbon dioxide or be out of compliance with environmental regulations. This reconfiguration of fire suppressants involved a considerable amount of re-piping.

The head of security was scared to death that something of value could "walk away" with the construction crews working inside the vault. Almost everything of value could be secured except for Mr. Lewis's top-secret file. Powers knew what was in the file and he was also frightened.

"Look, it's only for one day. Why don't you transfer the Lewis stuff to the Federal Reserve Bank for safe keeping?" Second Republic's security chief asked Powers.

"That may be a good recommendation. Mr. Lewis has always stressed that if you're going to err, err on the side of security. I have a good friend in security over at the Federal Reserve. I'll ask him for a favor."

Powers' friend at the Federal Reserve agreed to watch over one locked bag for one night. "Send it over on the regular Brinks run. We'll keep it overnight and send it back to you in the morning." Powers felt secure in the thought that he had done the right thing, and that Lewis would be proud of his decision-making capabilities under pressure. Powers stuffed the contents of the secret lock box to a standard cash transfer bag and put three small locks on it for additional security. Mr. Lewis's proud assistant then scheduled the bag for shipment by armored car on the normal afternoon run to the Federal Reserve Bank.

* * * *

Zack nodded "good morning" to his comrades and put on latex gloves before entering the vehicle. He could feel the tension within the van and took note that his companions also wore gloves. Adam retired to the back of the van and changed into coveralls. There was nothing more to do until they reached the lakefront but worry.

Vic re-checked the Fathometer, fuel levels; GPS system and the radio-controlled airplane nicknamed "Big Eye." Everything was in order and he gently guided his now ugly boat, the "Klutz," out of the channel and onto Lake Michigan. The big engines groaned under the additional weight of the camouflage. "Be patient, my dear. I'll have you back to your slim, beautiful self in short order." As Vic set sail for the Chicago lakefront, he logged on to the Johnson family web site. Everybody had checked in. The boys on the pick-up team were in the van and headed downtown. Weather was holding beautifully. It looked like a go. Vic keyed in his status and ETA to the web site.

Wilma was trying to keep down a cup of coffee in a Michigan Avenue *Starbucks*. She had never been so apprehensive in her entire life. She felt sick. She told herself repeatedly to get over it. There were too many people counting on her. It was almost 11:00AM. It's time to get in position, she thought. She checked her pocket for the tenth time. The key to the bridge tender's office was still there. "Good God, I hope I don't have to use it," she said under her breath. She checked again for her phony FBI badge, gathered her laptop, and started the long, slow walk to her assigned position.

The team's van, sporting its "State of Illinois" markings, was now headed east down the Eisenhower expressway. Adam could see that they were approaching the old post office, which sat astride the expressway like a huge mother hen. Officially, the road changed its name at that point from the "Ike" to the "Congress." The south branch of the Chicago River was just yards east of the building. If everything works well, that's where we'll delay the police boat, Adam thought. He didn't envy what the drivers on this section of road would endure in the immediate future. The van crossed the river, went through the Loop, crossed Michigan Avenue, and entered Grant Park. This was the same route the Brinks truck will take, he thought. He scanned for any unscheduled construction activity or accidents that could impede the plan as they turned south on Columbus for a block and then east on Balbo. They then ran the two blocks of Balbo and turned left onto Lake Shore Drive. After continuing north on the drive about a hundred yards, they pulled onto a concrete apron due east of Buckingham fountain.

The men put on their "State of Illinois" hard-hats and dark sunglasses. They placed several rubber cones around the rear of the vehicle and readied the cherry picker.

Adam went to the east or lakefront side of the van out of the view of passing motorists and logged on to the web page. Steve and Tad busily wiped down the entire interior of the truck and readied the fuse for the van's destruction. Adam entered the arrival time of the van at the lakefront to the master program. The web page showed "The Klutz's" actual position, compass heading, and speed on the lake. Wilma was in position on the upper level of Wacker Drive with a good view of the river. All diversionary devices were on-line and standing by to receive the phone calls. All members of the team knew everything about the situation without the need for radio transmissions, which could be intercepted. Adam quickly went to the weather—channel web page to check radar. There were no storms for 300 miles to the north, south, and west. Adam gave the preliminary "Green Go" signal without conscious thought.

Vic received the message almost simultaneously. That was his cue to pick up speed and start the launch sequence. Vic had previously calculated that "Big Eye" couldn't get airborne unless the "Klutz" was doing at least twenty knots into the wind.

Wilma spotted the police boat entering the lock into the river at 12:20. It was a bit late from its normal schedule. She reported to the web page that the boat was through the locks and heading west down the Chicago River.

That was Adam's cue to initiate the first of the two previously recorded calls to the bridge tender. All Adam had to do was hit a control key to have the computer dial the call and play the first message. The same keystroke told Vic to launch the aircraft. Before the airplane actually took flight, the bridge tender was given the pre-recorded "heads-up" call to raise the bridge at some point later in the day.

The plane was launched due north into a slight breeze at twenty-two knots. It began a pre-programmed lazy circle over the boat once it gained its altitude of 1000 feet. Vic slowed down and started to make his way into the Chicago harbor.

Adam took control of the "Big Eye" from his laptop and directed the plane to circle over Grant Park to the immediate south and west of the van. Adam could hardly pick it out with his naked eye, but the continuous live video feed from the bird was perfect. The traffic flow could be clearly seen in amazing detail. He shouted to Steve and Tad, "Bird's in position."

Zack's shouted instruction was the cue for the two men to raise the cherry picker just high enough for the tree immediately north of the concrete apron to obscure their upper bodies. They had their gas masks and bottles of mercaptan and carbon dioxide at the ready. Motorists going north could see nothing but coveralls on legs sticking into a tree.

Adam could not believe how nervous he was. There was no way a person could realistically prepare for this, he thought. Adam had not practiced using the laptop with latex gloves and he found the task difficult. He cursed himself for not thinking about training with the gloves actually on. The months of training and preparation did have one advantage—it allowed you to perform most of the actions required "on automatic."

The front grille of the Brinks truck came into view on the video feed. It was facing due east ready to cross Michigan Avenue when the light changed. Without thinking, he hit another control key, which initiated Phase I of the diversionary events. The computer automatically placed six calls in rapid sequence to six cell phones. The ring circuit gave the signal to the electronic igniters, which in turn created pandemonium on an unprecedented scale.

A large column of white smoke poured out of the upper right field bleachers of Comisky Park, home of the White Sox. Immediately to the east of the ballpark was the Dan Ryan expressway, which was always packed with north/south traffic. A "gapers block" of historic dimensions ensued while the smoke obscured much of the major highway.

A similar column of smoke soon emerged from the new parking lot at Midway airport. The ugly plume was immediately spotted by the control tower. A senior FAA official grounded all outgoing flights instantaneously. That ruling included helicopters. The decision by the FAA to ground all flights prompted a huge inter-agency squabble between Federal, State, and City officials. The chaotic debate was resolved and the police copters were eventually given permission to fly. The team gained 15 minutes of valuable time. The exact same scenario was replayed at O'Hare and Palwaukee airports. Those squabbles effectively grounded the TV station copters.

The last two diversionary devices were planted on the Eisenhower in the cave-like tunnels under the old post office. One was for the eastbound tunnel while the second obscured the west bound traffic. It looked certain to motorists and police officials that the enormous old structure was burning down. All east-west traffic on the major highway ground to a halt. Fire and police sirens started resonating throughout the Loop. A multitude of eerie wails reverberated through the concrete canyons of the central business district.

Adam watched the video feed as the Brinks truck crossed Michigan Avenue and started east down Balbo. Adam's hands were shaking uncontrollably. As the truck crossed Michigan, he hit the control key to send the second recorded message to the bridge tender by mistake. "Damn these gloves!" Adam knew it was too soon, but perhaps it was still within tolerances. All of a sudden, a car pulled in front of the Brinks truck from a parking spot along the curb of Balbo. It looked like it had "out of state" tags. The Brinks truck almost stood on its front end from the braking pressure applied by the driver. "Damned tourists! I hope the truck didn't hit him!" Adam swore to himself. The Brinks driver reacted very quickly. He avoided hitting the tourist from Wisconsin by a fraction of an inch. Everybody stopped and looked for a minute for damage before they started moving again. The intricate timing dictated by the plan was ruined by a near miss from some hayseed tourist operating with a bratwurst for a brain.

Wilma watched the action on her laptop. She knew that Zack had given the command to raise the bridge, but wasn't sure why he did it so early. According to the plan, Zack should have waited an additional two minutes. She was standing below the tower under the office of the bridge tender with the key in her hand. I'd better adjust my timing and go in now, she thought. Suddenly, lights started flashing and gates descended over all lanes of the Drive. The great bridge started to rise with a mechanical groan. "Thank you, God!" Wilma was totally relieved and vowed that she would never do anything like this again. She crossed the drive to secure a direct line of sight to the south so she could gain control of "Big Eye" from her laptop.

Adam could see the traffic backing up and filling the northbound lanes of the Drive. The Brinks truck was just getting to the left lane to turn north onto the Drive. He had initiated the command for the second call too early and the near accident cost them more time, but paradoxically it seemed to help. Adam shouted "Stand-by." Steve and Tad put on their gas masks. Adam slipped into the driver's seat and started the van. He made sure the plastic pipe strapping handcuffs were in the front seat with his hard-hat. As soon as the Brinks truck turned north Adam fired the second set of diversions and logged off. Wilma assumed control of "Big Eye" from the confines of Millennium Park. Vic maneuvered into the inner harbor and was ready to tie up by the concrete walkway. Vic could clearly see both the truck and van from his position on the bridge of "The Klutz."

Four large, three stage toy rockets with M-80 firecrackers as payloads roared into the clear sky of Grant Park. They were fired remotely from cleverly designed metal tubing constructed to look like the "Don't dig here—underground pipe" signs that everybody sees, but ignores. They made ideal launch tubes. At 300 feet, the M-80s ignited with a tremendous roar. The sound ricocheted from the walls of the buildings on the west side of Michigan Avenue in a way that magnified its effect. Smoke started billowing out of the Pertillo band shell near Columbus Drive, shutting down that major highway. One more smoke bomb ignited at Michigan and Wacker drives adjacent to the Michigan Avenue Bridge. The bridge tender was so spooked that he raised his bridge. He felt it was a sound decision because the Lake Shore Drive Bridge to the east was up and he had smoke to boot. Traffic throughout the metro area of Chicago had not been this discombobulated since the blizzard of 1967. People were evacuating buildings in large numbers along Michigan Avenue and the East Side of the Loop in response to the explosions, sirens, and smoke.

Zack couldn't believe his good fortune. The Brinks truck rolled slowly past them and stopped just 20 feet to the north of their position. It turned out perfectly despite the misfire and delay. Perhaps his initial calculations were in error. The Brinks driver saw the "State of Illinois" truck on the shoulder and never thought twice about it or the fact that the bridge was going up. The veteran Brinks driver had witnessed this disruption many times before over the years. Additionally, he was still recovering from the emotional travail of a close encounter with a tourist.

Adam lowered the cherry picker and advanced the 20 feet to the side of the Brinks truck. Steve and Tad jumped to the top of the Brinks truck and shot the gas mixture into the air vents of both the truck and cab. The gas rushed into the Brinks truck with a tremendous roar. Zack had already placed the gas mask on. He grabbed the set of "hand-cuffs" and the last smoke bomb. He ignited the "bomb" and threw it under the truck while running to the rear doors of the vehicle. Tad jumped down beside him. It took less than 30 seconds for the door to open and two gasping guards to emerge. The identical situation occurred with the driver with Steve beside the cab. All of the Brinks men were in extreme distress. They were gasping, coughing, choking and their eyes were running. The guard nearest to Zack had thrown up. Zack asked if the guard was O.K. while strapping the guard's hands together behind his back. The guard simply nodded yes. The three guards were disarmed and their guns thrown down a manhole in less than one minute. All three Brink's men were secured and carefully placed on the grass shoulder beside Lake Shore Drive.

At first, the people trapped in cars behind and adjacent to the Brinks truck didn't know what to do. The stopped traffic appeared normal, but the smoke and obnoxious smell sure weren't part of the daily routine. The smarter drivers immediately heeded the "First Rule of Urban Survival" which is to "go the opposite direction from any action with great haste." Many of the remaining drivers left at the first whiff of mercaptan that the breeze pushed in their direction. Even highly diluted, it was enough to make you run without locking your car or turning the engine off. The same was true for a handful of pedestrians and bike riders on the concrete path by the lake. The only soul in view was Vic.

Adam swung the rear door of the Brinks truck open and saw stacks of moneybags. He motioned for Steve and Tad to start loading their "Illinois" van as he checked the first bag. It contained stacks of newly printed bills from the treasury. No good, he thought! These bills are in serial number sequence and can be traced. That bag seemed to be the only one with freshly printed bills. Impulsively he broke the paper strap from several stacks of bills, ran to the median, and heaved them as high as he could into the breeze. It wasn't part of the plan, but it was an excellent opportunity to create more confusion. He repeated the procedure three more times before helping Steve and Tad load the balance of the bags into their van.

Each stack of bills stayed together for much of the journey into the air. At the apex of the toss, the breeze broke them apart and the individual bills began to separate, twist and float down the Drive. It was like a daylight fireworks display in the unique shade of green that was universally recognized as newly minted bills. The new bills traveled swiftly in the brisk breeze and soon passed Balbo heading south. That's when the hundreds of people trapped in their vehicles recognized what was going on and responded as though they had one mind and purpose.

The crowd didn't really see money. They saw tax-free income for new appliances, sump pumps, and tuition. They saw "Manna from Heaven." Nothing or no one would interfere with their gathering of that "Manna!" Adam and the team had zero interference as they finished loading their van and backed it to the lake for the final transfer to "The Klutz." Adam did one last screen of the Brinks truck. Most of the remaining bags contained coins, in which they had no interest. One had three locks and was relatively light in weight. Not entirely sure what it contained, he grabbed it and ran to the boat. They quickly loaded the boat and set the fuse to the "State of Illinois" van before shoving off. The entire sequence lasted six and a half minutes, a full two minutes less than they had anticipated.

Vic guided the boat south along the sea wall until he could turn east through the breakwater and onto the lake proper. The team members collapsed below and were completely out of sight. Vic was shielded from view behind smoked glass windows, sunglasses, and a baseball hat. They were in open water in two minutes and Vic opened up the two big engines to reach twenty knots. At least four different individuals on boats within the harbor, out of the hundreds at anchor, took note of their departure. Two called the Coast Guard and two called the Chicago Police.

Adam looked aft from an interior cabin in time to see an enormous cloud of black smoke and flames engulf their van. It was a positively ugly sight against the beauty of Buckingham fountain. The thought struck Adam that one off-duty police officer in the hundreds of cars stranded along the Drive could have stopped them cold with a BB gun. That possibility had been overlooked. Another reality overwhelmed him. There were no backup plans for the family if he had been caught by an off-duty cop. He had thought about the executives who would run Allied, but not who would head his family! He didn't deserve the title of father and husband even though he was conducting this exercise for Alice and the kids. Instead of feeling a rush in accomplishing the first part of the mission, he felt sick. "Maybe it was better to be lucky than good," was his lame conclusion.

Wilma, having passed control of "Big Eye" to Vic, secured her laptop and casually walked west into the panicked city. There was no need to hurry. She wouldn't be able to depart to the rendezvous location for hours because of stalled traffic.

The men started quickly transferring money from the bags to the watertight trunks. They didn't take time to count it. It was obviously more than they had planned for; it was going to be difficult to physically fit it into the two trunks. It was all previously circulated cash, which was perfect for their needs. Vic yelled down to the cabin that he saw no one trailing them on radar or from "Big Eye."

Adam located a bolt cutter and broke the three locks on the light sack he had thrown in at the last minute. It contained hundreds of "Bearer Bonds" issued by a foreign country. He had no immediate recognition of what they were or why they were there. Adam took out one bond for $5,000 and placed it in his duffel bag for later research. That action broke one of his cardinal rules for security, but the foreign bonds intrigued him. The remainder of the bonds just managed to fit into the trunks.

The skyline of Chicago was barely visible as Vic shouted to the team, "we better execute the change now. I'm worried about those damned helicopters." Vic slowed the boat to a crawl and then detached the false stern, which swung aft like a gate on a fence. Zack unlatched the false bow while Steve and Tad untied two center straps from just before and after the bridge. Vic slowly backed aft and the beautiful sleek lines of "Sweetness" emerged from the phony covering of "The Klutz." The false covering on the flying bridge was removed. The smoked glass plastic wrap came off the windows. Bright chrome railings replaced the dingy gray fake ones. New flags were hoisted. The metamorphosis was now complete. It looked like a completely different boat to the naked eye.

The heavily weighted false covering of "The Klutz" quickly sank in the 500 feet of cold water under the keel. Over the side went the empty moneybags, coveralls, hard-hats, gas bottles, gas masks, laptops, and tools. With great reluctance, they crashed "Big Eye" into the lake. It served them well, but was almost out of gas.

When the transformation was completed, Vic gunned the twin 270 horsepower Crusaders to maximum speed. "Sweetness" raced at 25 knots for the Michigan shoreline. The boat seemed happy to be free of its ugly duckling false coat and virtually flew across the sparkling blue water.

The City's emergency communication systems were overwhelmed. Everybody on all networks wanted to call somebody. Radio discipline within all the police agencies had suffered as well. Confusion was rampant and the traffic hopeless. It didn't stay that way for long. Professionalism was regained as the smoke cleared. The Chief of Police sensed that much of the action reported was diversionary; there were no reports of injuries, death, or damage. The report of a strange boat leaving the harbor intrigued him. On nothing but a hunch based on experience, he concluded that the boat was the real enemy.

The Chief, after several attempts, got through to the Police Helicopter. It was finally airborne and just departing Midway Airport. He directed the copter to search for a boat going east at high speed from the Chicago harbor. The pilot laconically asked for a description since there were hundreds of boats on the lake at this time of year. The Chief provided a complete and accurate description of the boat. He was completely confident of the description provided to the pilot, since it came from two different sources and both sources concurred on many of the details. Each description included the name of the vessel in question, its color, and size. The Chief was amazed at the degree of agreement in the two eyewitness accounts. That had never occurred before in his many years on the force.

Vic slowed the boat and mounted two large fishing poles aft, one to starboard and one to port, then turned north. They were on the new course for approximately five minutes when a police helicopter flew over them from the west at high speed. It didn't even slow down as it passed overhead. "Sweetness" continued northeast looking and acting like hundreds of other pleasure craft fishing for salmon.

They eventually arrived at a point just north of Warren Dunes State Park and south of St. Joseph, Michigan. Both trunks were stuffed and Zack had each man place his individual locks on each case. Each case had handles on the sides and weighed about 150 pounds. The Fathometer indicated a shoal at 40 feet. Adam confirmed Vic's latitude and longitude reading with the two portable GPS receivers. All three were in agreement. They took a compass reading from the power station stack at Bridgman for the final check. Both cases were deposited in the "Lake Michigan Bank and Trust" without ceremony, but with great relief. All forms of direct physical evidence that could tie them to the robbery were now discarded. The threat of an arrest had been significantly reduced, but not completely eliminated.

They turned the boat south and for the first time relaxed. After cruising south for 30 minutes, they realized they needed to take a quick dip in the lake to rid themselves of any last traces of mercaptan. Finally, at about 8:00 PM, Vic glided into the public pier in Michigan City, Indiana. Three tired, but happy "fishermen" were met by Wilma and given a ride to Chicago and access to public transportation.

* * * *

Detective Ronald McHugh watched the local "live" TV coverage of the activities along the lakefront from his couch at home. Ron had been placed on indefinite, unpaid leave of absence almost a month ago. He wondered if the day's activities at Grant Park would affect his life and current status. The Detective didn't have long to wait. His Commander called at 8:00 PM and told him that he was now restored to active duty. Ron was to report to the main conference room at the Conrad Hilton at 7:30 AM and coordinate with the FBI as official liaison from the City to solve the Grant Park robbery. "I'll be there," was all Ron said.

CHAPTER 26

Detective Ronald McHugh walked through the main lobby of the Conrad Hilton taking note that virtually everyone in the hotel lobby was reading one of the two major Chicago papers. Big point "War" headlines were featured on both papers. The *Tribune* went with: **"MAJOR HEIST STOPS CITY."** The *Sun-Times* announced: **"WE WAS ROBBED."** Most of the major networks were carrying the story "wall to wall" and the cable channels were in a full feeding frenzy mode. CNN claimed a major coup during an exclusive interview with a former Clinton War Room official who stated he had "proof" that the heist was directly attributable to Republican economic policy and tax cuts.

McHugh believed he knew why he had been selected for this assignment. The Mayor, always known to local citizens as "Da Mare," hated crime in his city. He especially hated crime in the First Ward, where tourists and conventioneers hung out. The heist occurred in the middle of the First Ward. This was extremely bad for the City's image. The economic vitality of the City was endangered unless the perpetrators of this foul deed were quickly nailed. The big money at City Hall knew this crime would inevitably fall under the jurisdiction of the FBI. If the Feds solved the heist, fine. If they didn't, Ron would be the perfect "fall guy" for the city to offer as a sacrifice to the media. It was all part of his punishment for being too aggressive and resourceful in pursuing a drug lead. Ron understood the hidden motivation behind the grand plan, but took the assignment anyway. He needed the money; his wife had just informed Ron that their kid needed braces.

Finding the correct conference room of the many available was no problem—it was the largest one at the Hilton. Ron walked into face a sea of uniformed and plain clothed individuals that must have numbered in the hundreds. The Secret

Service, FBI, Coast Guard, U. S. Marshals, ATF, FEMA and of all people, the U. S. Forest Service, were present. Ron couldn't believe that the two-armed "Smoky Bears" from the Forest Service had a reason to be present. My God, he thought! I hope they don't burn down any of the trees in Grant Park as they have in any number of western states lately. Over the years, I've become quite fond of our trees and my dog adores them. Ron knew that all the agencies were present to show their relevance to the country. Congressional debate on funding was just around the corner. The States of Illinois, Wisconsin, Michigan and Indiana had sent high-ranking representatives from their police forces to the meeting as well. County sheriffs from a variety of districts were also in attendance.

It was total pandemonium inside the conference room. Heated arguments raged throughout the room on jurisdiction issues and who was in charge of press releases. At least a dozen people were debating whether the newly formed "task force" should adopt a unique name and perhaps a "logo" for the latest "crime of the century." Another group in a different corner of the room, having already decided that a special name was in order, was deeply divided over the color choices of the prospective logo.

Standing quietly in one corner was Agent Alex Evans. Alex had spent his entire career with the FBI in Chicago. Alex turned down many opportunities for a career-advancing move to another location because he loved the city and wanted to stay here with his family. His career suffered because of the refusal to accept transfer despite his knowledge of the city. Alex also developed an extensive stable of "snitches" over the years. Ron had worked with Alex on a case three years earlier and formed a reasonably good working relationship with him. Their relationship was a rare exception to the general pattern of extreme distrust between the Chicago Police and all federal agencies, particularly the FBI.

"Good morning, Alex. If it's not politically incorrect, may I ask some police-related, crime solving type questions of you?"

"Be my guest, Ron. It would be a nice break from the babble going on at present. Have you been assigned by the City to coordinate with us?"

"Yes I have. I was hoping that would mean working directly with you, as I don't have a partner anymore. You are certainly the most qualified individual in my opinion. Will you be the 'Agent in Charge' on this case?"

"No Ron, I won't be. They are bringing in a hot shot from Atlanta to head the case, but I will actually be doing the work. It's the same old political routine. Headquarters is grooming this southerner as a possible future Director of the FBI. You can't be promoted to Director without 'notches in the gun handle.' The greater the publicity surrounding a given crime, the bigger the notch becomes.

This crime has more publicity than most, and it is perceived initially by headquarters as an easy case to solve. Bring on the politicians and the potential new Director, say the powers on high. That's not me, Ron. I just work here and look forward to working with you."

"I know the game all too well, Alex. Why is this particular crime perceived as easy to solve by the big shots at the FBI?"

"This was a well thought out, perfectly executed and planned robbery. We figure it had to have a cast of 15 to 20 people involved and cost over $100,000 in front money to execute. Very few criminal enterprises in the world are organized well enough to pull a stunt like this. They undoubtedly had help from the inside. At least that is the pattern and MO on all previous armored car robberies. The leading candidate at this juncture would be the Chicago mob or some of its allies from other cities. It could be Russian gangsters or a Chinese Tong, but that's unlikely."

"Is there any chance this could be connected with international terrorists?"

"No way! Their objective is to kill and maim as many Americans as possible. The only people who were injured yesterday were hurt fighting over greenbacks floating down the Drive. In addition, we didn't receive any early intelligence indicating any kind of a threat, nor has anyone claimed credit for the deed. Officially, the international terrorists connection has been ruled out."

"How much in total did they take?"

"Very interesting question, Ron. The short answer is, we don't know. Normally, at this stage, we would know down to the penny. Apparently, Second Republic had something of great value on that particular Brinks truck. We're still trying to get answers on that. The rest of the contents, as far as we can tell, totals 15 million in cash."

"Alex, there hasn't been an attempt, much less a successful one, on a Brinks truck in the Loop for 30 or more years. Are you telling me that on the first successful attempt, Second Republic, by coincidence, placed something of great value on that particular truck? Give me a break! There has to be a connection!"

"That's exactly what I thought about nine hours ago. When Nelson Powers of Second Republic was first told of the theft, he went absolutely ballistic. We were tempted to sedate him so we could begin to have a conversation. Powers wanted to join the Witness Protection Program and we hadn't even alleged, much less charged him with squat. That is strange behavior for your average victim or witness. We are attempting to reach his boss for comment. The big boss is on vacation at his second home in Belize. Something stinks about this whole deal, but I'm not convinced it's related to the heist. The heist itself bothers me as well.

There is something odd about it that I can't quite identify. It certainly doesn't fit any MO that I ever heard of. I think our hot shot from Atlanta will have some unforeseen problems." Ron thought he saw a flicker of a smile cross Alex's face.

"A second home in Belize sounds strange to me, Alex. Banks generally award titles instead of money. It's your case, but I'd push both of the gents from Second Republic real hard." Ron respected Alex, but still didn't feel comfortable confiding to him about a lead he and Luke had once been following up. Perhaps he had just found the missing mob bank connection, but he couldn't prove it. That situation might change if he remained patient.

Alex continued, "the irony of the entire episode is driving me crazy! I had a van with nine fully armed agents in Chicago yesterday for training. They were in school at Quantico and we brought them up here for some urban experience. They crossed the Lake Shore Drive Bridge going north just moments before it was raised. It's a game of inches I guess."

"That reminds me, why did the bridge go up when it did?"

"That's another tantalizing mystery, Ron. The bridge tender swears his boss called and told him to raise it. So of course the idiot did, even in the complete absence of a ship."

"Now that makes a great deal of sense, at least to me. The bridge tender job is highly coveted by City workers. If the guy thought his gig was remotely in jeopardy, he would do whatever was requested by the boss without question."

"That is an excellent point that I failed to consider. In this case, his boss was taken from the main office about an hour before the bridge was raised suffering from a kidney stone attack. The big boss was not in position, or in shape to make the call. The bridge tender passed a lie detector test though. He remains adamant that he received not one, but two calls. I'm not sure what to think at this stage."

"Anything from forensics, Alex?"

"It's still early for those guys, but preliminary results don't look good. The vehicle left at the scene had every single VIN number expertly removed. The truck is burned beyond recognition. We know it's a Ford, but we're not sure what year or model. Initial results have identified mercaptan as the active ingredient used to force the guards out of the truck."

"What the hell is mercaptan?"

"Same stuff the gas company adds to its product to warn you of a leak. Skunks have used it for eons. It was the perfect choice for the criminals. It would force anybody out of the truck, including me. It stinks worse than you can imagine, but is unlikely to hurt anyone seriously at relatively low concentrations. Don't bother to ask, Ron. It is widely available commercially and virtually untraceable."

"I'm starting to see what you mean about this heist being difficult to solve. It looks like the perpetrators took extraordinary pains not to harm anybody."

"Ron, you won't believe this, and it's confidential at this point, but we have no hard evidence that these guys were even armed!"

"What? A major heist in the middle of the First Ward during daylight with no guns, that's almost un-American! Alex, you've sold me. This is no run-of-the-mill heist. It would be easier for me to believe that we are going to elect a Republican as mayor than accept the concept of unarmed felons. I wonder what it all means?"

Both men took their seats as the meeting was called to order. A tall, handsome, well-dressed southerner introduced himself as Special Agent in Charge. The meeting would reaffirm that the FBI would head the investigation. Only the FBI would notify the press and public of news. There was the normal rejoinder about "no leaks."

The high-level police representatives from the neighboring states related to the assembled officers that they had found no one in any of their many harbors along Lake Michigan, who had seen or heard of "The Klutz." Nobody had seen a boat with a large group of men disembark Thursday afternoon either. The Wisconsin representative stated forcefully that "The Klutz" was not registered out of Green Bay, nor had anyone ever seen such a boat based on the detailed description provided. He summarized by saying that no self-respecting citizen from the Great State of Wisconsin would name his boat "The Klutz." Ron asked from the floor if there were any self-respecting "Cheese-heads" with or without a boat. Guns were almost drawn before order was restored.

Alex addressed the group with much the same data as he had provided to Ron earlier. There were a few additional details. It took major funding to run this kind of theft. The FBI was asking all offshore banks for assistance in reviewing American owned and managed accounts for suspicious activity. The FBI concluded that at least $100,000 and probably $200,000 was required in up front costs. Traditionally, overseas banks, particularly the Swiss, politely ignored police requests for help. In this instance, a series of banks had been robbed, and banks always stuck together. Officially, the European banks would ignore the request. Unofficially they expected a considerable amount of support.

Alex concluded with a plea that local authorities closely monitor their "snitches." "There had to be 15-20 people involved with this heist. Sooner or later, one of them will get drunk and brag. It's a part of their nature. They will boast to a friend, neighbor, or mistress. Act immediately if you hear such gossip and we will, undoubtedly, break this case."

Ron was asked to summarize any findings from the interviews Chicago uniformed police conducted with the hundreds of drivers and passengers surrounding the Brinks truck. "That's easy," said Ron. "We got nothing. Nobody saw, heard, or thought about anything." Ron concluded that he was sure some people claimed to have witnessed nothing so they could keep the cash they had scooped up. For others, it could be the absolute truth due to the amount of smoke and the speed of the transaction. Then again, many citizens had viewed a remarkable parade of Washington officials on TV claim: "They couldn't remember," and get away with all kinds of illegal activity. The Chicago motorists caught behind and adjacent to the Brinks truck apparently learned their lesson well. Regardless of the rationale—"nobody saw nothing!"

Calvert, the newly appointed Agent in Charge, was visibly upset. He advised the assemblage that the initial interviews with the guards had provided no information of value. All the guards saw were men of average size with coveralls and gas masks. They could have been green aliens from outer space from what they witnessed. Forensics had nothing. The rockets used as a diversion could be obtained at *Wal-Mart.* The "smoke bombs" were readily available in hundreds of commercial establishments. Calvert reemphasized Alex's point about the "snitches." The meeting concluded with the realization that they had damned little to work with. This is frequently the situation with many major cases at the onset. It generally took long hours of diligent police work to break a case. This one was no different, thought Ron…Or is it?

Ron renewed acquaintances with some of the attendees before departing the conference room. Alex's concerns about the case were starting to chew on him. Ron left the hotel and started walking south down Michigan Avenue. His intent was to physically walk the route of the Brinks truck. Sometimes it helped to review the lay of the land or spot a clue that had been overlooked.

A large black Cadillac pulled next to Ron on Michigan Avenue and interrupted the walk. A burly man emerged from the right front door, opened the back door, and motioned for him to enter. It was an invitation he could not readily refuse.

An elderly, impeccably attired gentleman smoking a Cuban cigar shared the back seat. "Mr. La Morte, I assume." Ron recognized the man from his many pictures in the papers. Mr. La Morte was the reputed head of the Chicago syndicate.

"You assume correctly, Detective. Please excuse this extraordinary introduction and meeting room, but I believe neither of our careers would benefit if we were seen talking together. I believe you are coordinating with the Feds on the recent excitement in Grant Park."

"You are well informed Mr. La Morte."

"It's healthier for a man in my position to stay well informed. That's one reason I wanted to chat. It's possible we can help each other in solving a crime that detracts from the carefully crafted image of our beloved city."

"I was unaware of your feelings of civic duty, Mr. La Morte. I am deeply touched."

"It has nothing to do with civic pride, Detective. It's all about business. We never conduct or condone activity of this type in the First Ward. It would bring on a ton of heat, and heat I don't need. We didn't do the job and we don't know who did. I want to offer my services to catch the punks who did this. Such action would help both of our careers!"

"To the Feds, you are the number one suspect. How do you want me to convince them that they are wrong? I need facts. The civic pride thing makes some sense to me, but I grew up in Chicago. The Feds will never buy it. They never buy anything that doesn't fit their predetermined template."

"That's a fair observation, Detective. Look, my people know our family didn't do it. If they think I allowed some other family from another city in on their turf, it would upset them greatly. If they think someone came into Chicago without my approval, then I'm weak and undeserving of respect. Either way, I'm in considerable trouble. Additionally, some of the loot belonged to legitimate firms in which we have an interest. Why would I steal from myself and hurt my leadership standing at the same time? It's crazy to think that we were involved."

Ron thought carefully for a minute. La Morte made a great argument and his logic helped explain Nelson Powers' reaction to the news of the heist. Ron's informant from months ago had been correct. There was a connection between the mob and a big Chicago bank. The bank appeared to be Second Republic, and in all probability centered on the Powers guy and his boss in Belize. Whoever did the Grant Park job was getting more than they bargained for if they stole mob money. "Are you telling me that some of your assets were in storage at a major Chicago bank?"

"Where else are you going to park big money? There is an unbelievable amount of crime in the world these days. The bank is supposed to be safe. Who the hell can you trust anymore? The moral climate in this country has gone to hell. There is more than safety involved. We were trying to reduce our tax burden. I'm in good company, Detective. If you read the paper much, you should be aware that CEO's over the entire country are doing the same thing. The government accuses me of exorbitant interest rates on 'juice' loans. Hell, compared to the Feds, I'm nothing but small time. They are killing me with taxes. It's not easy, as an independent businessman, to make or keep a buck today. Believe me, the first rule of extortion is never 'kill the goose that lays the golden egg.' The stupid Feds are oblivious to the rule. They keep wanting more and more."

Ron found himself almost feeling sorry for the old man. At least Ron understood La Morte's logic. It was totally surreal. They were natural enemies, law-breaker versus law-enforcer, attempting to work together. The only thing they had in common was a total distaste of the tax code. Ron realized that La Morte was speaking the truth. If you wanted to be the "Alpha" male in a pack of wolves, you could never appear weak. The major heist in the heart of Chicago reflected badly on Mr. La Morte as leader of the pack. In addition, the apparent fact that mob proceeds had been taken provided great incentive for the mob to help solve the crime. This was "Real Politick" in action. Ron, as a veteran cop, knew that despite appearances La Morte wielded enormous power. He's capable, totally ruthless, and would kill in an instant to keep his position and power. Ron also knew that La Morte had at least one high-ranking informant within the police department. Ron would need to exercise extreme caution before replying. Should the Detective accept the help of his sworn adversary?

"Let's say for a minute that I believe you Mr. La Morte. There is no evidence that foreign interests engineered the job. If it wasn't you, then who could have pulled off a job of this magnitude?"

La Morte's face turned red and he turned angrily in the seat. "Damn it, aren't you listening, Detective? Why am I forced to turn to you for God's sake? We don't have a clue."

"Could it be the Russians?" It was the only question Ron could think of after being startled by the intensity of La Morte's reaction.

"No! There are a few groups of Russian thugs running around the city. One group on the southwest side seems to be growing, but it's all strong-arm stuff. They extort their fellow countrymen who have jobs. You know the con—the old fashioned threaten the folk's back home gambit. It's been done for over a hundred years with different nationalities. It's all muscle and no brains." La Morte paused for a moment and reflected.

"Perhaps I spoke too quickly, Detective. It's not wise in my business to underestimate a foe. It could be that the Russians recruited some commando types from the motherland. If they added some people with an IQ greater than a zucchini, they could be formidable. We will check it out. You may have a point. I would request that you keep me informed and let me know how we could be of additional help." La Morte slipped Ron a card with a telephone number; he assumed Ron's compliance. Nobody in the past had ever refused his request. The car, which had been slowly circling the Loop, let Ron out at State and Randolph.

* * * *

It was now early morning in Europe. Stan reviewed the instructions from the CEO of Swiss National that had been provided via Renee. Stan was to search "all" American owned accounts for withdrawals over $25,000 within the last year. He was instructed to secretly forward any information uncovered to the FBI.

Stan kept in touch with Chicago through satellite TV. He viewed the mayhem in Grant Park on WGN. Stan was also aware that Adam had been withdrawing amounts from his account. There was something about the audacious nature of the theft that appealed to Stan and reminded him of his old friend and former boss.

It couldn't be, Stan thought. This was not Adam's style. Perhaps Adam took my advice literally and started a new enterprise. Uncertain of what might have happened or would happen in Chicago, he reread the bank's instructions. Review "all" accounts was clearly stated. "I guess it all depends on your definition of 'all.' Surely, 'all' would not mean, 'all' accounts. It must mean 'all' accounts that weren't friends of the bank. Friends of the bank had courtesy accounts. Thus, 'all' accounts should be defined as 'all' accounts other than courtesy accounts." Satisfied with the new definition and his ability to defend it, Stan completed the review and provided the FBI with information on six accounts. That information proved useful over time in the prosecution of four drug cases, but provided nothing of value for the solving of the Chicago robbery.

* * * *

The weekend had started in Chicago and normal work ceased. The fight against crime never took time off. Two FBI agents found Mr. Lewis in Belize. Lewis was most uncooperative and quickly dismissed the agents. When they returned for a second interview, they were dismayed to find that Lewis had committed suicide.

Powers was notified of Lewis's suicide on Sunday afternoon and started singing like a robin in the spring. Powers confirmed that he had placed $85 million in bearer bonds on the Brinks truck. Lewis had been pumping up Second Republic's earnings and laundering money for the mob while concurrently reducing their tax liability. It was a perfect plan and had been running smoothly for years. The entire investigation team that unearthed the plot was sworn to secrecy. The huge amount of money in the form of "bearer bonds" could be a significant wedge that could be utilized to crack the Grant Park heist.

CHAPTER 27

There was no doubt about the desirability of buying a paper for the train trip on this Monday morning. The big bold point headline in the *Trib* shouted: **"$100 MILLION TAKEN AT GRANT PARK!"** Adam thought it had to be a planted story until he read the details. The news account described the addition of bearer bonds from Second Republic to the cash previously reported stolen for a grand total of $100 million. That, according to the *Trib*, was a world record. It was interesting to note that the article failed to identify the government entity that issued the bonds. It's a trap, Adam thought. The article also noted that an individual was providing valuable information to the FBI from Second Republic. That made sense to Adam, because it would have taken an experienced bank official to even find where to buy these bonds. The physical security of bearer bonds is paramount. What better place to store them than the vault of a big downtown bank? Who at Second Republic was providing information?

Over the weekend, Adam used the Internet to research the sample bond he had taken during the event. The bonds were issued by the Bank of Sierra Leone and were currently paying a 20% interest rate. Adam hadn't seen a bearer bond in years, much less one from Sierra Leone. The US Government stopped issuing bearer bonds in 1982, opting instead for easily tracked registered securities. As the name of the bond implies, banks paid cash to the "Bearer" or physical holder of the bond. In the past they were referred to as "death bonds." It was a great way to pass wealth between generations of a family without paying estate taxes. They were the same as cash except the bonds could be of any denomination.

There was no way to physically stuff $85 million in actual cash into their two watertight trunks. Without the "bearer" bonds, there would have been no world record. The record-breaking amount insured active participation by every law enforcement agency in the country and perhaps many from overseas. The good news was the team was potentially filthy rich. The bad news was, all the heat in the world would be targeted on them.

Adam's banking experience told him that someone at Second Republic was laundering drug money. Large amounts of unregistered securities issued from a foreign country residing in a domestic bank screamed that fact. It had to be drug money behind the bonds. Money laundering on this scale equaled the "mob." If the mob was looking for the bonds as well as every police officer in the Western Hemisphere, the team had a real problem. This was extremely bad news.

Adam felt sick to his stomach. The old adage: "never play pool for money with a guy who has a table in the basement" kept repeating in his mind. The quest for economic freedom yielded both a new world record and cause for great concern. Adam was now in an environment that he was totally unprepared to address. His initial lack of experience in manufacturing could be offset with the study of literature on the Internet. There were no study guides on how to deal with unusual loot in record-breaking amounts on the web. Adam could only hope that he and the team had done a good job in covering their tracks!

In a small side story, he noticed that Alister Lewis, his old nemesis, had committed suicide in Belize. That story cinched his hunch. Lewis was behind the laundering and he probably shielded his clients from income taxes at the same time. If Lewis wasn't the source for today's story in the *Trib*, it had to be Powers who was talking. The realization that the same guy who sent him a phony 1099 was talking with the FBI was very unnerving. If their discussions evolved to Internet security, Adam could be implicated. That one lousy attempt to gain $5,250 could unravel the potential gain of $100 million. The quest for Mark's braces was impulsive and unplanned. The preparation for the liberation of 100 million was thoughtful and meticulously planned; however, if God meted out punishment in direct relationship to the amount illegally acquired; he was in for a world of hurt.

For a moment, Adam reflected on the good old days of his youth when he loved to watch westerns. It was easy when he was younger. The good guys wore white hats; the bad guys wore black hats. You always knew whom to root for. Adam had no love lost for Lewis, but thought of him as an average, articulate bank executive who could be exceptionally persuasive. Adam never dreamed that Lewis was capable of wearing such a large black hat. Frank mentioned during one of their walks: "nothing is as it appears to be in business." Why was Frank always right? Well Adam, what color hat are you wearing nowadays? He asked himself.

He usually enjoyed the morning train trip, but not today. There was an unusual buzz among his fellow passengers prompted by the headlines. No one started with the sports page. The normally stoic strangers were comparing stories on where they were and how they reacted to Thursday's events. They were babbling like a bunch of teenage girls at a slumber party. It seemed like people were constantly eyeing him when they weren't talking. It was as though they could see through his thin veneer as a businessman and recognized him as a common crook. Adam was also certain they could see into his briefcase and view the sample bearer bond from Sierra Leone. He wasn't sure what to do with the damn thing. He certainly didn't want to get caught with it, but dared not leave it at home. The loss of freedom of movement in public and the constant fear of being watched were the first causalities of the attempt to gain economic freedom. Now when Scotty got nervous, Adam would wonder if it were a squirrel or an undercover cop. He had not planned for or anticipated any of these emotional consequences.

Another article in the paper caught his eye. This one was a gossip column by Jason Gompers, who speculated that average, hard working Americans thinking they were "Robin Hood's" perpetrated the "$100 million heist." It had to be nothing but the author's imagination, thought Adam, but it was too close to the truth. The net effect of all three articles on his mood was dismal beyond belief.

He saw Ann on the way into the office and immediately sensed she had read the same paper with identical results. Fortunately, they were alone.

"Well Adam, I guess we're famous. 'Make no little plans,' said Burnham. May a co-holder of a rather dubious World Record ask: What do we do now?"

"We have no alternative but to ride out the storm, Ann. I hope that the emphasis we placed on security plus making sure our acquisitions were untraceable will serve us well. We may need a diversion for the Feds if the heat increases dramatically."

"Oh my God, Adam! Not another job, I could never do that."

"It won't be another job, Ann. A deal is a deal. Our objective was to do one job without anyone getting hurt. We accomplished that goal. In actuality, we greatly exceeded the goal."

"I guess we did! O.K., let's ride it out. Sam called earlier. He needs to talk to you."

Sam convinced Adam during the call that his presence was required at the plant. Adam gathered his things and returned to Ann's office. "Sam needs me at the plant. Apparently, he has some concern about Vladamir that may need my involvement. Please notify the 'family' to disregard the headline in the *Trib*. It's a police plant. I warned them about that possibility at one of our earlier meetings." Ann nodded her agreement.

*   *   *   *

Detective McHugh finally reached his new partner Alex at the FBI Chicago regional headquarters. "Who the hell leaked the story about the bonds, Alex? We were all sworn to secrecy and within 12 hours I read about it in the morning paper!"

"As usual, Ron, we'll probably never know. If I were a betting man, I would guess our new Director apparent was intimately involved. The huge media coverage establishes this as a really 'big notch' on the gun belt." Alex was clearly upset. He felt betrayed by one of his own people.

"Has any of the loot shown up yet?"

"Hell, yes! If some economist ever wanted to track the movement of money in our society, we have ample data. Individual bills have shown up in numerous spots across six Midwest states, plus Tampa, Orlando and Phoenix. Mostly small amounts under $100 are showing up at gas stations, *Sears*, *Wal-Mart*, and fast food restaurants."

"That has to be the cash strewn down Lake Shore Drive that apparently nobody ever saw or collected. It looks like enough was picked up for some citizens to go on vacation or engage in a shopping spree."

"Exactly, Ron. We have no evidence that the actual 'perps' have spent a dime of the loot or made any large deposits at any bank domestically or off shore."

"That almost gives credence to the 'Robin Hood' theory by Gompers in today's paper."

"Robin Hood, my butt. The 'perps' knew exactly what they were doing. The bills in question came directly from the treasury and were in serial number sequence. That's why we can track them now. One of the bad guys was smart enough to recognize that they were useless to them. They scattered them on the road as an exceptionally effective diversion. We even know the amount that was in the truck for dispersal—$150,000."

"You mean they gave up $150 thou to avoid tracking."

"I'm trying to tell you, Ron. This is a different deal. These guys are smart. We have no clue as to what they are doing with the loot, but they aren't buying yachts. My 'snitches' have detected no parties or wild celebrations. There has been no boasting or claims of credit. If anything, the 'mob' seems as interested in finding the 'perps' as we are! That proves to me that the bonds are the result of laundering drug money. I'm also convinced that the 'mob' had nothing to do with the heist. My boss doesn't agree with my assessment, but that's nothing new."

"I'm picking up the same thing." Ron thought it was still wise not to confide in Alex about the meeting with La Morte, so he changed the subject. "Is Powers still cooperating?"

"No! Second Republic sent over one of its high priced attorneys and now Powers has clamed up. The lawyers are arranging to have Powers released later today."

"My God, Alex, don't let Powers go! It could be hazardous for his health."

"I know that Ron, but we have nothing we can charge him with. Lewis was the obvious mastermind and he's dead. Powers was a pawn at best and not a very smart one either. What are you planning to do today?"

"I want to talk to Jason Gompers to see if he has any facts to support his story. It's not likely Gompers will tell me, but I'm going to apply some pressure anyway." The phone call concluded with Alex realizing that Ron's efforts were a long shot. At this point, it was about all they had to work with.

* * * *

Sam met Adam in the parking lot of the plant. "Adam, let's talk out here for a minute. I have no idea what's bugging Vlad. Everything at the plant is running smoothly, but Vlad acts depressed and is very morose. It must be a personal problem and not work-related. His performance lately is terrible. I'm tempted to bloody fire the bloke. If Vlad were any less of an employee, I would. You seem to relate to the lad very well. Can you try to get to the bottom of this before it gets worse?"

"O.K. Sam, I'll see what I can do."

Adam found Vlad in the plant and invited him to go for a walk outside. Between Vlad's reluctance to talk and language differences, it was not an easy conversation to maintain. Adam finally ferreted out that a gang of his fellow countrymen was extorting Vlad. Adam was familiar with the age-old practice. Adam's grandfather had suffered the same plight years before. Vlad had been paying protection to a man for years in escalating amounts. The threat was to Vlad's parents who still resided in the old country. Like most recent immigrants, Vlad didn't trust the police in his new country and refused to seek their help.

Specifically, Vlad was concerned about a collection visit from the leader of the thugs this very afternoon. Vlad simply had no money left to give him. The brute was a big intimidator and totally ruthless. Vlad feared for his own safety as well as that of his parents. No wonder his performance at work had suffered. Vlad was in fear for his very life!

Adam could actually see the terror swelling in Vlad's eyes. This observation produced great empathy and concern for his gifted friend. Reluctantly, Adam concluded he was honor bound to do something to help. Adam told Vlad to wait outside while he returned to the plant to use Sam's vacant office. Adam quickly slipped on a pair of latex gloves that he now carried wherever he went. Adam located a blank sheet of paper and a plain envelope from Sam's desk. On the blank sheet of paper, Adam sketched a crude map of Grant Park and placed an "X" where the Brinks truck stopped. He carefully placed the map and the bearer bond from his briefcase into the plain envelope and rejoined Vlad outside.

"Try to listen closely and understand clearly, Vlad. You give this envelope to your Russian friend and tell the jerk it's his last payment. Don't open the envelope. I think this will help." Vlad looked tremendously relieved. He didn't care what was in the envelope. Vlad just wanted to offer something to the vicious animal when he showed up this afternoon. Vlad returned to the plant walking like a new man. Adam reported to Sam that maybe he had solved a personal problem for Vlad. Only time would tell. Adam then returned to Allied's downtown office.

Two hours later a tall, hulking Russian approached Vlad outside the plant during Vlad's lunch break. In excited tones, Vlad spoke to the thug in their native tongue. Vlad claimed that this was a larger payment than required and the last he would ever make. The big Russian just smiled. He had heard it all before and didn't have time to argue. He was on a major collecting mission and had to visit 25 more victims that afternoon.

The Russian completed the collection round and returned to his office to tally the receipts. He opened the envelope from Vlad and threw it and the crude map into the trash along with the dozens of other envelopes from victims. The bond had great appeal with the $5,000 face value appearing in bold print. "Bearer bonds" were far more common in Europe and he knew how to redeem the bond for actual currency.

The Russian chose to go to a branch of Second Republic Bank in southern suburban Palos Heights. The thug waited patiently in a long line. Once at the teller, he presented the bond and demanded: "Give me money, please!" The teller smiled sweetly and asked him to wait while she obtained the cash. Two guards, with guns drawn, appeared as if by magic and had the Russian handcuffed in less than one minute.

Alex called Ron on his cell phone. "We just got our first break! A Russian was arrested on the southwest side with a Sierra Leone 'Bearer Bond.' We are bringing the suspect downtown for questioning. Do you want to join in?"

"Not yet Alex, I'm just outside Gompers office. Let me finish with this task. You guys know how to question a suspect. I'll join you later. I was just about to give up hope for good news. Thanks."

Gompers, like most celebrities, hated the public at large. He especially disliked cops. When it became evident that Ron would not take "no" for an answer, he reluctantly agreed to a short discussion.

"I don't know why you are here and bothering me Detective. I have a 'First Amendment Right' not to discuss sources."

"I fully understand, Mr. Gompers. I'm just trying to solve a major crime. I was hoping to ascertain what facts you used to support your theory of a 'Robin Hood' event in today's column."

"My theory is just as good as anything you have, Detective. In all probability you have nothing to work on!" Gompers was very contemptuous of the civil servant.

"Off the record, Mr. Gompers, we have just arrested a suspect with a 'Bearer Bond.' Without identifying who the suspect is, I can assure you he's not Robin Hood material." Ron realized he possibly compromised security with that admission, but he wanted to put the arrogant SOB on the floor and count to ten.

Gompers was clearly upset at Ron's announcement. He had hoped to spin the "Robin Hood" theory for a week's worth of columns. The fact that this recent arrest would destroy his theory after only one day in print was disappointing, and a clear indication that he needed to work, or worse yet, think. "O.K. Detective. There are no facts underlining the theory. The theory simply came forth from my fertile imagination."

"Do you feel comfortable or justified in articulating an unsupported theory in a major paper?"

"My job is to sell newspapers, Detective. Reporting the facts doesn't always help me do that. If I have to lie to create interest, I'll lie. Hell, everybody does it!" Ron, having confirmed his worst fears about the media, started to walk out of Gompers office.

"I shouldn't have thought that there was any truth underlying your story, Mr. Gompers. My mother was very strict in teaching us as kids to avoid eating yellow snow." Ron realized that what Gompers and so many of his kind were doing today didn't even measure up to the historical standards of yellow journalism. Ron hurried to get to the FBI office.

Alex met Ron behind a one-way glass mirror in the FBI interrogation room. The Russian was seated with his arms crossed. Two agents were seated across from him trying to start a conversation.

"Get anything?" Ron asked anxiously.

"Yes! One complete sentence in perfect English, 'I won't talk without my lawyer.' It's amazing how fast they pick up the system. He must watch a lot of political coverage on TV. His lawyer is on the way."

"Just out of curiosity, Alex, how did this low life get permission to come to our country in the first place?'

"Some idiot at INS and perhaps another at the State Department thought he was an excellent candidate for a student visa."

"You've got to be kidding me! I don't think he can tie his own shoes without assistance. Can you extradite the Russian on a visa charge?"

"Probably not, Ron. His lawyer will undoubtedly produce evidence of a correspondence course or something. Technically, he will be in compliance. From the Federal viewpoint, that's all they care about. There is no 'wrong' or 'right', 'stupid' or 'smart' in the federal vocabulary. Either you are 'In compliance,' or 'Out of compliance' in our way of thinking."

Alex went on to describe how earlier in the day they "shopped" to get a judge the FBI wanted. That judge granted them the right to search the Russian's office and home. It took three hours, but they considered themselves lucky because they had reached the only judge available who thought "bad guys" actually did exist in the real world. That judge, unfortunately, had left for the day.

The Russian's lawyer arrived and immediately started screaming about police brutality, racial profiling, and ethnic prejudice. The attorney wanted to see a judge for a bail hearing immediately. His client obviously hadn't stolen anything. The client found the bond floating down the street. Ron watched in agony as their leading suspect made his case in front of a liberal federal judge. She was extremely sensitive to claims of intolerance by the police. She actually believed the suspect had been racially profiled when he went to the teller with what appeared to be a stolen security. Alex was called away for a message during the proceedings.

Alex returned to tell Ron the news from the FBI search team. "His apartment and office are clean as a whistle, Ron. Somebody beat us to both locations. They were torn apart and effectively searched. None of our Russian suspect's associates can be located for questioning either."

"I wish the 'mob' had to operate with our set of rules, Alex. It's not a fair fight. They consistently win because they play by their own rules."

"You know we can't change the rules, Ron. We would become just like them. It is tempting on occasions like this to want to play by their rules. Are you sure it's the mob that beat us to the punch in checking out our Russian friend?"

"Yes! They are very well informed. While you shopped for a judge, they were working away. I'm convinced they were tipped by someone." Ron still could not tell Alex of his suspicions of a high-level leak within his department. La Morte knew Ron was assigned to the task force and where to pick him up within hours after Ron's initial assignment. That internal informant had to tell La Morte of the Russian's arrest and his home and office address. It was yet another clue that the informant was highly placed. Ron continued: "I believe the organization wants their money back. If I were that Russian, I would accept some federally sponsored housing and hospitality right now. His lawyer is pushing all the right buttons with the judge. I am reminded of the movie *Dead Man Walking*! Have you checked the bond for prints?"

"Oh, indeed! Mostly they were from the Russian. He has a paw as big as a tennis racket. Some were from the bank teller; the remainder was from the bank guards. In other words, a dead end."

"Don't feel bad, Alex. Gompers was a dead end as well. Jason created the entire story from whole cloth. I think the only viable link to this crime is about to walk out of here. I don't think the Russian did it. He doesn't appear to have the savvy to design and execute such a crime. I would like to know how the thug came into the possession of the bond. That might tell us something."

The two lawmen watched their only suspect leave the FBI office with a big smile, arm in arm with his attorney. The federal judge felt she had defended the rights of the accused and helped stamp out ethnic discrimination. She would sleep better tonight in her gated community.

Ron went to a pay phone and called the number listed for La Morte on the business card. As expected, it was an answering machine. Ron identified himself and left the following message: "You don't need my assistance. You apparently are receiving adequate information without me!"

* * * *

Adam had difficulty concentrating on traffic while returning to the office. "What had he done?" Perhaps the Russian would accept the final payment from Vlad as a conclusion to the extortion. It's not likely, but possible, he thought. If the extortionist were arrested when attempting to cash the bond, which is more likely, Adam would receive information on how to deal with the remainder of the bonds. The police would have a valid suspect to review, which would reduce heat on the team. The government would undoubtedly extradite the brute and Vlad's problem would be deported on the first available flight. That was the most likely scenario as he thought about it.

Ann greeted Adam upon his return with news. "The family has checked in and have no problem with the story. They seemed more concerned with the Gompers column, which I had missed."

"It's just a gossip column, Ann. Gompers must have made up a theory to sell papers. Was there anything else from the Johnson family?"

"Yes! Tad apologizes for his comments on the boat that were critical of you for scattering the money on the drive. In looking at the media coverage of the melee on Michigan, he now thinks it was ingenious."

"It would be more accurate to describe it as pure dumb luck. We couldn't use that money anyway."

"Last, but not least, Steve is a new father. The proud parents of a two week premature boy are very happy."

"Thanks, Ann. That's really good news. I needed a break from the present, thinking about a baby forces you to think about the future. The plant is running well and we completed our mission. The future does indeed look a lot brighter."

CHAPTER 28

TGIF—Thank God It's Friday, Adam thought, as he boarded the familiar 6:32 METRA. Adjustment to normal life after the big event of last week was more difficult than he could have imagined. Alice noticed the change in her husband's deportment. She was constantly inquiring if he was feeling all right. There was always the hope that a sense of calm would return eventually. Perhaps after the newness of being a felon wore off, if it ever did. The plan required that Adam and the team remain normal and calm for five more years. Fall was approaching fast and there was no end to the number of chores that he would have to complete to prepare for a Chicago winter.

One of Adam's least favorite tasks at this time of the year was cleaning leaves from the gutters. How many prospective multi-millionaires clean their gutters, he wondered? The contradictions from what he had imagined his life would be after the heist compared to reality was driving him insane. Adam couldn't help but wonder how it was affecting other members of the team. Nobody on the team had considered the dimension of how to stay normal after successfully committing a felony.

His life had been irrefutably changed. The decision to buy a paper in the past was a consistent habit, but in theory an optional purchase. Now the paper was a mandatory element of the morning ritual. He no longer started with the sports section even though the Bears had entered into pre-season activity. Now he inevitably started reading the paper by exploring the Jason Gompers' column.

Gompers, on Tuesday of last week, had suddenly dropped the "Robin Hood" theory. His columns now read as if he had never floated the concept. On Tuesday, Gompers started with the "Russian Gangster" theory for reasons that were unknown to Adam. As a businessman, Adam was totally, blissfully unaware of the world of "snitches" and "leaks," and was still naive enough to believe in journalistic integrity. Adam was unaware that Gompers' new theory was created in part by a visit from a Chicago cop and other sources. Today's column claimed proof that this new theory was correct. Adam quickly turned to the front page and his heart stopped. An unknown Russian was found stuffed into the trunk of a car at O'Hare. The victim had multiple gunshots to the head. The reporter characterized the murder as "a classic gangland hit."

Could the very dead Russian at O'Hare be the same Russian that was strong-arming Vlad? Adam knew instinctively that it was the same man. That meant Adam was indirectly responsible for causing the death of a man he had never even met. Even though he understood the brute to be a total low-life that was stealing the American Dream from dozens of people, he was overcome with guilt.

* * * *

Ron couldn't help but notice the big black Caddy. It was parked directly in front of his apartment this morning. La Morte must know everything including my address Ron thought, while sliding into the back seat.

"Good Morning, Detective," La Morte appeared to be in an excellent mood. Ron politely returned the greeting.

"In your message I detected a tone of bitterness in your voice that suggested you were not happy. Please don't take it personally, Detective. I strongly believe in 'backups.' I have information coming from many sources that I find useful. Timely, solid information beats muscle every time. You should be overjoyed, certainly not bitter. We have solved your 'crime of the century' and saved the State of Illinois multiple millions of dollars in legal fees." La Morte was wearing gloves despite the heat. He casually reached into his suit pocket and handed Ron the map of Grant Park. Using a handkerchief to protect the document, Ron reviewed it and placed it in his jacket pocket.

"May I ask where you obtained this document?"

"It was located in the Russian's office. It proves to my people that he was involved with the heist. The Russian never talked about where the rest of the bonds were or who helped him, despite our most persuasive attempts to initiate dialog."

A chill went down Ron's spine as he imagined the torture endured by the Russian. Ron intensely disliked the thug at first sight, but nobody should be subjected to that treatment. Ron finally stated: "The map looks very incriminating, but I don't know if it will stand up in court."

"We have a different burden of proof than you use in your courts, Detective. My people are delighted to know that none of our friends or associates was involved at Grant Park. The Russian gang was a growing threat to our monopoly position within the city. Now the threat has been eliminated. Unity and discipline have been restored within the organization. It's interesting that we both employ the use of 'capital punishment' to achieve our goals of social harmony. The policy of capital punishment works efficiently for us because it's certain, quick and highly visible."

"You still don't know where the bonds are."

"That's correct, Detective, but even if I found them in the glove compartment of this very car, I couldn't use them. My associates would endure the same fate as the Russian if they tried to cash them in. The bonds are useless to all but the U.S. Treasury Department. Besides, it's only money. We can recreate the wealth in short order as long as our image is untarnished and our discipline is intact. I could care less what the Russian said or didn't say about the bonds. It's all about keeping the family happy. Which reminds me, the Russian had a number of associates. They were strongly influenced to leave town, if not the country. Don't bother looking for them!"

Ron recognized the last statement as a command and not a request. Probably all the associates were wearing concrete boots and resided at the bottom of Lake Michigan. It could be that they were provided with one-way tickets to Russia. Either way, they were out of Ron's jurisdiction. "It would appear that your objectives have been fully realized Mr. La Morte."

"Indeed they have, Detective. Your services are no longer required. You didn't actually help, but you were sympathetic and discreet, especially with the Feds. That means something in my book. Where can I drop you?"

"Anywhere downtown that's convenient for you, Mr. La Morte." Ron was dropped off adjacent to Union Station and started to walk across the Jackson Street Bridge to the FBI office. For a short distance, Ron walked directly behind a businessman with a briefcase and a worried look.

*   *   *   *

Ann greeted Adam once again for coffee. They had the place to themselves this morning, but not for long. "I received an emergency request from Steve last night for a meeting. Steve provided me with some video footage and still pictures of the new addition. He is absolutely adorable. Unfortunately, with the photos came bad news. The baby needs heart surgery in the next six weeks or he will die. The operation will cost over $150,000 and Steve has no insurance. He requested that amount from his share of the proceeds ahead of the schedule originally agreed upon."

Adam felt his knees buckle. "My God, Ann! We can't accommodate Steve's request. We have a veritable herd of cops that are looking for us and the deal we made with everyone on the team was to wait for five years."

"I know that, Adam! It's not as if Steve lost control of his sanity and spent money that he didn't have. Steve broke my heart with the story. He told me that he had always fantasized about having big money. The dreams included going to exotic locales, driving a big fancy car or living in a mansion. Steve now realizes that none of that is as important as his newborn son's life. He voluntarily gave me the combinations to both locks on the trunks. He then renounced all future claims for the proceeds. All Steve wants is enough to cover the cost of the operation for his son. Adam, we can't turn our backs on him. If we did, we would be no different that the cold, heartless organizations that helped promote our desire to do the heist from the beginning."

Ann's last comment cut to the quick. "Does the apparent acquisition of big money numb the heart? Does it justify the murder of a loathsome foreigner?" Only God knows the answer to these questions, he thought. It's a good thing there is a God for those answers. The world was considerably beyond a mortal's capability to comprehend or forecast. Their plan had considered every external threat to security. The threat of an internal breach of security had never crossed their minds.

Ann watched Adam's face intently. He was so transparent most of the time, but strangely opaque at others. It was obvious that he was wrestling with some weighty issues and was entering into an opaque zone.

"I am in no way showing any disrespect for Steve or his integrity. I may be the only person alive who believes there is honor among thieves. However, I can't justify jeopardizing the team's security without some evidence for verification. Do we know Steve's story is true?"

"You always said Chicago is a small town. My sister works at the hospital where Steve's baby, who they have named Ryan, is in intensive care. She and all the workers there know the baby's story. Even as an infant, Ryan has a captivating personality, as do Steve and his wife. They are good people."

"O.K. Ann. This is what you would call an 'UNK-UNK,' it's been a hell of a week for them. Please call Allied's bank and establish a not-for-profit account called the 'Save Ryan' fund. Let me think about this situation for awhile."

The phone was ringing at Adam's desk before he got there.

"Adam, this is Sam. I don't know what the bloody hell you did with Vlad, but he's a new man. He thinks you walk on water. Of course, I know better. Then again, maybe I'm wrong for the first time in my life. We employ a number of other Russians at the plant and they all seem happy. How the bloody hell did you do it?"

Adam wished he could actually tell Sam. He wanted to confide in someone, somewhere, but couldn't. "Sea Gull Magic, Sam—nothing more, nothing less."

What was "Sea Gull Magic?" Adam pondered the question and recalled the night he offered the "fixes" to Mr. Williams at no charge. That established a greater sense of obligation in Mr. Williams than if he physically threatened him. Steve, with no knowledge of the transaction with National, had done the same thing to Adam and the team. Steve didn't threaten or attempt to intimidate the group by saying—"help me or I'm going to the cops!" Steve provided the combinations, renounced his share, and simply asked for help from the team. Adam felt honor bound to find a solution to this dilemma. The irony was that there was more honor and integrity in his band of felons than in all the members Congress combined. The question of "why" that was true would have to be explored at a later date. He didn't have the time.

* * * *

Alex greeted Ron warmly as the Chicago cop entered the agent's office. "Good morning, Ron. How bad was the traffic on your ride in this morning?" Ron paused in his tracks as if he had been shot.

"You SOB, you had me tailed!"

"You think too highly of yourself Ron. We tail La Morte constantly. We were a little upset that you didn't confide with us about your first trip with him. Then I realized that if the situation were reversed, I wouldn't tell anybody either. Nobody would believe me."

"Bingo, Alex! I'm an old fashioned dumb, honest cop. Why would the head of the 'mob' want to talk to me unless I was on the take? If the truth sounds like a lie, you are better off saying nothing. Rather than say anything incriminating, let me give you something for analysis." Ron carefully handed the map that La

Morte provided to Alex. Ron knew that the FBI crime lab would check it carefully for prints or other forensic evidence.

"We've known for years there has been a high-level leak in your organization, Ron. We know it wasn't you. Actually, you helped us out. When La Morte requested your personal assistance, it proved to us that his organization was not involved. I don't for a minute think any Russian, much less the recently departed one, had anything to do with it either."

"I can't really feel sorry for a small time punk like that Russian. They put him through hell and didn't really care what the Russian said or didn't say. Then they advertised that fact by locating the body where it was sure to be found."

"They are animals, Ron. They mark their territory with dead bodies like wolves urinating on trees. They were sending a message with that killing: Stay out of our city!"

Ron wondered how Alex knew of La Morte's specific request for help, but decided not to go there. The FBI had just confirmed his worst fears about a leak. Ron knew better than to ask where they were in the investigation. Then it hit him that the unknown group that engineered the Grant Park heist accomplished what Ron and his partner failed to do. They inadvertently put a significant crimp into the syndicate's operations and eliminated a band of Russian hoods as a bonus. The guys in gray hats ended up scoring a touchdown on a broken play.

"That leaves us where, Alex? We now know who didn't do the Grant Park job, but who the hell did do it?"

"I don't know. Our famous profiling group has thrown in the towel. They've never seen anything like this. It wasn't one of the Chinese tongs either. It's simply not their style. What's your best guess at this point?"

"Disregard the source for a moment and think about Jason Gompers' 'Robin Hood' theory."

"That's hard to do, Ron. Gompers is an arrogant idiot."

"Yes, he most certainly is, but his initial theory won't leave my mind. What if we were wrong about the size of the group? With automation and high technology, we might be talking about five or six people in total to execute the job. What if they were squeaky clean? What if we are dealing with a group of amateurs with no previous records, photographs or prints on file?"

"Keep going, Ron."

"I know my idea sounds crazy, because I can't begin to imagine the motivation. Nor can I visualize the type of person who would do this. Whoever it is, it's obvious they have brains and are meticulous planners. This group eluded the attention of the high-level leak in the police department as well. La Morte had no advance warning for once. There appears to be a wild card in this game."

"Let me help you out, Ron. Everything we've collected so far at the crime scene continues to be off the shelf, commercially available, and untraceable. That includes standard pipe wrapping instead of handcuffs, cell phones that were pre-paid, toy rockets and fireworks. We have gone over the burned out van three times and haven't found a thing."

"You mean you're leaning the same way I am?"

"It's just you and I so far, Ron. My management believes it was the Russian. That allows my hotshot 'Director to be' to take unofficial credit for a 'notch.' In fact, he's now been reassigned. We'll leak that to the press. I want the real 'perps' to think the heat is off. Unofficially, I will continue to push the investigation. The U.S. Treasury wants those bonds located and returned to them. I want you to stay involved. I appreciate your honesty, intuition and brains."

"I just proposed that we may be combating 'honest crooks' and you think I have brains."

"Good brains and instincts! Let me announce something we just found out about that will bolster your theory. We interviewed the guards extensively, with no significant results. They passed several lie detector tests, as did all employees of Brinks in Chicago. They are an honest and reputable firm. This was not an inside job. As a last resort, we interviewed the guards under hypnosis. It was an attempt to see if there was something lurking in the sub-conscious mind. Only then did one of the guards recall that a 'perp' asked if 'he was O.K.,' as the guard was led to the shoulder of the Drive."

"He asked the guard if he was O.K.?" Ron was flabbergasted.

"It sure doesn't sound like your average terrorist or 'mob' hit man. The guard later admitted that he never felt particularly threatened during the actual robbery. The guard was more concerned about what his boss was going to do and say than anything else. One reason the guard didn't feel threatened was that he confirmed our earlier suspicion that the 'perps' used no firearms."

"Are you telling me that we have actual confirmation that a bunch of polite, unarmed, goodie goodie's lifted $100 million in broad daylight from Grant Park?"

"Can you think of a better way to square the few facts we know? No wonder our profiling group gave up. Furthermore, what will really blow your mind is that I believe the bonds were placed on the truck by pure accident. It was a total fluke. I've given up trying to sell the concept internally. I can hardly believe it myself.

You have independently come up with a similar conclusion without the benefit of some of the facts I have. One could conclude that both of us are certifiable."

"Can we get to Powers to confirm your theory about the bonds?"

"He's nowhere to be found. I don't think the 'mob' got to him the way they did the Russians. I think Second Republic smuggled Powers out of the country. Probably took him to some country with no extradition treaty. It's not in the best interest of the bank to tarnish their image. The image destruction could occur if Powers were talking. It's somewhat ironic that neither the bank nor the 'mob' wants witnesses who talk. Both are concerned with their image. The Securities and Exchange Commission investigators are swarming all over the bank as we speak. Their image is likely to suffer regardless of Powers' fate."

"Why can't we find out something about the boat, Alex?"

"The boat is the element that I first thought would break the case. We have four independent eyewitness descriptions of the boat. They are remarkably consistent and full of details. Since the robbery, we have been supplied with a poor quality home video of the boat actually leaving Du Sable harbor. The video confirms exactly the same details as the eyewitnesses' accounts. We can't find a boat that comes close to looking like the 'Klutz' that left Chicago. We have conducted searches throughout the Great Lakes region plus Canada. It's not likely they sank the dumb thing with themselves and the loot. It's more likely it was camouflaged which is difficult and time consuming to do. Indirectly, that's why I think it was a fluke that the bonds were aboard that truck. It might take over a year to develop a way to 'hide' the boat. Coordinating that activity with the timing of the reconstruction of a new fire extinguisher system at Second Republic is impossible. The question remains: Where did the boat go?"

"So a world record bank heist by a bunch of sensitive amateurs accidentally uncovers a major drug laundering operation and tax dodge haven. This gets more bizarre by the second. Where do we go from here?"

"I'm down to one last bullet. The mercaptan gas is the only somewhat unique thing they used. I have lists from the chemical manufacturers who produce the stuff showing where they shipped in the Chicago metro area within the last six months. There are scores of places that receive it. It's a dog, but they have to be checked out."

"Old fashioned, wear down the shoe leather police work. Why can't I ever find a high-tech, cushy assignment?"

"You and I both know that's how cases are really solved, Ron. Which half of the list do you want?"

* * * *

Ann entered Adam's office and found him deep in thought. He's struggling with a big issue, she thought. I don't believe he will give me an honest answer on what's bugging him if I ask. He will lie—not to deceive, but to protect. She wondered how Adam could cope with the stress. "I have the account set up, Adam. What's the next step?"

"Let's go to the plant, Ann." They drove swiftly to the plant and completely surprised Sam. Adam asked Sam to bring everybody into the cafeteria for a meeting. This was unheard of at Allied and created quite a buzz. Adam strode to the front and looked out at the assembled men.

"My name is Adam. I've met many of you, but perhaps not all. Most of you know Ann. She was involved in hiring many of you present here today. There are many items we could talk about that relate to Allied and its progress over the last several months. Let me just say that we are all proud of your accomplishments and hard work. However, my reason for coming here today is totally unrelated to business.

"Ann has a sister who works for a hospital on the South Side. In that hospital resides a newborn infant with a serious medical problem. That problem can be eliminated through expensive surgery, which the parents of the baby can't afford. Ann's sister has fallen in love with that child. We are in desperate need of your help. There are perhaps hundreds of children in Chicago in a similar situation. We know about this one. Chicago has always been known for its big heart. It is part of our Midwestern heritage to help our neighbors. We have established a 'Save Ryan' fund at the company's bank. We would appreciate your help and contributions."

Ann circulated several pictures of Ryan to the assembled men as Adam stepped down. Vlad leaped forward to make his contribution and others soon followed. Bill Stokes from National viewed the presentation, and after the meeting took some pictures with him. Adam wrote a check for $750.00 and gave it to Ann. It was the last of Stan's seed money.

* * * *

Ron checked out six users of mercaptan throughout the afternoon without success. He desperately needed a drink. In his desire to follow up on the leads, he almost forgot about an invitation to a cocktail party at his neighbor's apartment this evening. Normally, he avoided those parties as if they were Tupperware socials. As with most cops, he didn't blend well with some, perhaps most segments of society. This particular neighbor was a little too much into academia for Ron's tastes. At this time of day, the blend issue no longer mattered. Booze was booze and Ron urgently needed some.

Ron entered the neighbor's apartment and with great difficulty started some small talk with guests he had never met. Ron was introduced to a Professor of Business Management from the Kellogg Graduate School at Northwestern University. On a whim, Ron told the Professor about his current assignment. Then he asked a probing question to the business Professor.

"Just hypothetically Professor, if the Grant Park event had been planned by somebody within the business community, what kind of person would I be looking for?"

"That's an interesting, but somewhat unlikely hypothetical, Detective. For whatever reason, individuals who acquire the skills of management and planning don't seem to have the inclination to pursue violent crime. Assuming the removal of any moral constraints, there are any number of professions and specialties that would qualify from a technical skill perspective. System engineers, product managers, investment managers, actuaries, design engineers, architects, and programmers are just some of the possibilities. Actually, the list is virtually endless." The Professor paused for a moment pondering the question before continuing.

"The more I think about it, someone who is, or has, turned around a failing company would probably find the planning and execution of such a crime a relaxing activity or diversion by comparison. You should be delighted that these types don't frequently find the path of crime desirable. If they ever did, you would be busy around the clock trying to solve perfectly planned and executed crimes."

"Thank you very much Professor."

"One last thought, Detective. There is one exception to my generic hypothesis. In my opinion, moral values don't reside just beneath your skin for removal by surgery. They don't exist in an internal organ that can be turned off or mitigated by drugs. The only sure fired way to eliminate the source of moral values within an individual that I'm aware of, is years of Law school study. If you find anyone in the list of specialties I mentioned with a law degree, you probably have a potential crook. It's not likely you will find a 'turn-around' type of businessperson with a law degree. Turn around executives must be practical and likable to be successful."

"Professor, let me buy you a drink."

CHAPTER 29

Ron and Alex spent the last four days independently checking out the dozens of mercaptan users throughout Chicagoland. The list seemed endless, and they hadn't found a thing that was remotely of interest. Two full weeks had elapsed since the heist. The trail was getting colder and the media was starting to lose interest. Ron was becoming increasingly concerned that they were wasting their time as he pulled into the parking lot of Allied Manufacturing. It was difficult at first to find a place to park. A construction company had a large crew tearing down an old plant to the south of Allied. Their equipment took up most of the available space in the lot.

Ron asked to interview the plant manager after displaying the proper police identification. A foreman informed Ron that the plant manager was on a sales call and offered his assistance as a substitute. Ron indicated that he was only interested in how they used mercaptan. With great enthusiasm the foreman took Ron behind the A111 where they viewed the numerous "Cat" parts being stamped, painted, and cured.

"Do you have any idea, Detective, how much mercaptan the bad guys used at Grant Park?"

Everyone on the list had asked the same exact question. Ron had no idea how much was used or how it could be measured in the first place, and it made him feel stupid. Ron just shrugged his shoulders.

"The reason I ask is that mercaptan is nasty stuff. We monitor its usage closely during production, down to three parts per million. We would have caught even a slight decrease on the input side of our process. After parts are cured, we vent the excess mercaptan to an incinerator for destruction. We can't have the stuff wafting around the plant or outside to our neighbors. If someone siphoned off some mercaptan from the 'output side' before entering the incinerator, our records wouldn't reflect a thing. There isn't much mercaptan left on the 'output side', but it might be enough to get the guards out of the truck. The stuff really stinks like hell!"

Ron believed this was the most helpful, cooperative and informative individual he had meet in his travels. There was certainly nothing sinister to cover up at this plant. It also helped explain why the mercaptan chase would probably not lead to anything.

"Thank you, sir. You have been most helpful. I'll be on my way and let you get back to work."

"I'm sorry that I could not be of more assistance, Detective. Good luck—I hope you catch the creeps." The foreman escorted Ron to the door, silently smiling to himself. The Detective may have gotten a different reception from Sam if he were here. Sam hated all authorities, especially police. The foreman hated lawbreakers and wanted to provide any possible help.

"I'm sorry, I keep seeing posters for 'Save Ryan' on the walls. What's that all about?'

"We are trying to raise money for an infant without insurance who needs heart surgery," the foreman replied. "Our Vice President made the appeal earlier this week. Mr. Jones is a new and very popular executive. He has really helped turn things around here at Allied. At this time last year, I was sure we would all be laid off by now. Instead, we have more overtime than we can handle. All the guys in the plant think it's the least we can do to say thanks when Mr. Jones asked for help."

"That's a great story." With that, Ron slipped the foreman $20.00. "I can readily support any cause that helps a kid!"

"Well thank you, Detective! I'm sure Ryan and his family will be pleased at the support of the Chicago Police Department."

Ron returned to his car disappointed that he received no tangible help with the investigation; however, he was pleased to meet and work with good people. One of the problems with being a cop is that you see so many bad people that you lose sight of the fact that there are many like those within Allied that were good, hard working, law abiding types. The brief visit helped restore Ron's faith in humanity.

After checking three additional locations, Ron met Alex for lunch. Neither had seen nor found anything of interest in their travels. "Did the examination of the map that I received from La Morte produce any prints?"

"None, except for the Russian. It illustrates to me that the thug was set up. In all likelihood, it was La Morte behind the action. Remember that La Morte needed to prove to his organization that neither their family nor their associates were involved. La Morte was also becoming concerned about the growth of the Russian gang. I think he killed two birds with one stone."

"How did the Russian obtain the bond if he was set up by La Morte?"

"Ron, we don't have definitive proof that the bond the Russian had was part of the loot from the heist. Lewis and La Morte apparently were running this deal for years before the Grant Park episode shed light on it. The bond turned in could have been from a previous transaction or simply purchased by La Morte on the open market and slipped to the Russian. None of the bonds are registered securities. We simply don't know."

"Why would La Morte's people buy the story? There are many unanswered questions and holes big enough to drive a Mack truck through."

"Now you're thinking like a lawyer, Ron. La Morte's organization has a different 'burden of proof.' They bought the story because they wanted to buy the story. They needed to maintain the 'status quo.' Look at recent political history if you want examples of how people will reject facts and common sense to preserve the 'status quo.' The appearance of truth is frequently stronger than the truth itself."

"That makes sense Alex, but it doesn't leave us with much. The trail is getting colder by the day." Ron then enlightened his friend from the FBI with the information obtained at Allied. If the 'perps' were clever, they would have taken the mercaptan required in such a way as to leave no trace. Ron also relayed his conversation with the business professor.

"That could be very useful, Ron. Let me forward that insight to the profiling staff and let them run with it. It makes sense to me because this heist has a private sector aura and mentality to it. The diversions were set off remotely using cell phones. That significantly reduces the manpower required and implies expert technical acumen. We now know the bridge tender's phone was tapped. It took three searches to find it. That effectively eliminates the bridge tender as a suspect. Originally, I had a strong belief he had to be an accomplice. Raising the bridge with no ship present and at just the right time was too much of a coincidence. Whoever tapped the line was an expert. We don't know how the tap led to the phony phone calls. However, that maneuver also reduced manpower. Government types simply don't think that way. Their creed is: The more money and manpower, the better."

Alex was now in deep contemplative mode. Ron could almost see the wheels turning. Both men were patient, dedicated lawmen. Alex continued. "There is another tidbit that I should tell you about. On major cases like this, the FBI reconvenes some retired agents to pool their historical reservoir of knowledge and insights. They call themselves the 'Old Farts.' One of them was active in World War II and he entertained us with stories about the German commerce raider called the 'Atlantis.' None of the newer guys had ever heard of the vessel. That absence of historical knowledge is yet another clue to the effectiveness of our esteemed educational system."

"Didn't the 'Atlantis' change its shape and identity to confuse merchant ships? World War II history was extensively covered in my home schooling. My parents also stressed the teaching of 'how' to think and not 'what' to think."

"Congratulations, Ron. There may be a position available for you with the 'Old Farts.' We now believe 'The Klutz' was designed to be observed. The 'perps' knew it would be spotted and provided a wealth of details for the eyewitnesses to announce. We were set up just like La Morte set up the Russian. They must have reconfigured the boat in the middle of the lake out of sight of anyone on the shore. We have no idea what the 'real' boat looks like other than it wasn't a sail-boat. To use your favorite expression: 'We were served a big helping of yellow snow.' Let me add a factor to your input on the businessman profile. I think we're looking for someone with a good knowledge of military history."

"I would think it would take a lot of time and advance money to alter the color and size of the boat. Have you received any data from the bank searches?"

"As predicted, we have received more cooperation on this case than on ones in the recent past. Still nothing, no prior withdrawals or major deposits have been reported. We have received information that has led to breaking a number of other crimes, but nothing on this one. What really scares me is the 'perps' may be willing to wait out the 'Statute of Limitations' on this."

"I'm getting a bad feeling about this case, Alex!"

"Why is that?"

"Both of us have dedicated our lives to catching bad guys. As a kid, I grew up watching westerns. I always wanted to be the guy wearing the white hat and catch those in the black hats. As long as that process continues, an efficient society remains intact. People's property and lives are safe and they sleep better at night. Job security for me was assured because the percentage of people in black hats was fairly constant. Let's just assume that the inclination to commit crime is the result of bad DNA. What if the 'perps' in this case were people in white hats with good DNA who decided to commit a crime for whatever reason? If that were true, we could never keep up. The people with good DNA vastly outnumber those with bad. Moreover, they seem to possess more creativity. The 'thin blue line' that now protects society from itself would collapse and anarchy would rule."

"That's a chilling scenario, Ron. I wish like hell that I could shoot it down. If your theory is true, we must solve this case to provide a disincentive to anyone with good DNA from succumbing to the 'dark side of the force.' However, we've run out of leads and the bureau is pulling in their horns. My budget has been cut to nothing. I just found out that Calvert was convinced our bad guys would repeat their successful technique for stealing large sums of money. He firmly believed they wouldn't think they had 'enough' and would want 'more' loot. Incidentally, being a good bureaucrat, that's exactly the way he thinks. On that personal assumption, he placed numerous agents along the shores of cities from Milwaukee to Buffalo looking for the 'perps' to show themselves. The army of agents succeeded in scaring the hell out of hordes of innocent fishermen throughout the Great Lakes. In the process, they wasted all of my budget dollars and found nothing of substance. Since the performance hasn't been repeated, the FBI, like the 'mob,' wants to believe the Russians did it. It protects the 'status quo.' We are going to need a lucky break to solve this one, I'm afraid."

* * * *

Bill Stokes was impressed with Adam's appeal for funds to assist Ryan. The salesman made copies of Ryan's pictures and circulated them to each member of the National sales team. They in turn circulated the request with many of their customers and prospects. Mr. Williams was very moved and wrote a significant check. The Allied "Master Trainers" revisited all of their previous contacts with the same request. High school students at Lane and Chicago Vocational chipped in. Money was accumulating into the "Save Ryan" account at an amazing rate.

Jason Gompers' column this morning indicated that the FBI had all but officially concluded that the Russian gangsters were the perpetrators of the Grant Park heist. Gompers, of course, supported that finding because it was his theory to begin with. Adam didn't buy it for a minute, and would have sent e-mail to that effect to the Johnson family except for one additional item in the column. Jason concluded today's piece with a "feel good" story about a manufacturer in Chicago rallying to save an infant who needed surgery. It was well written and a real "heart tugger," but fortunately it did not mention Allied by name.

Sam interrupted Adam's busy morning routine. "Look Laddie, I know we are going into the Labor Day weekend and National said we couldn't get the 9700 until January. I am asking you to exert yourself and put some bloody heat on them. We might need that machine sooner than we anticipated. Frank and I just returned from Navistar, where we picked up more orders. One more big machine in this plant and we could really be competitive. I've always dreamed of this day. Make it happen!"

"I'll talk to Mr. Williams, Sam. I don't think he will be too receptive as they are pushing very hard as it is. Is Vlad ready with the software?"

"Indeed he is. Vlad ran a successful test yesterday on the prototype."

"I'm glad you and Frank can continue to find some acorns. It's amazing the plant doesn't self-destruct during your absence." Adam enjoyed teasing Sam with that detail.

"Don't joke about that, Adam. Just today, while I was out, some dumb flat foot prowled around the plant asking about mercaptan. What a waste of taxpayer dollars. There aren't any crooks here. I would have thrown the flat foot out on his ear if I had been here."

Adam thought very carefully before asking: "What the hell was the cop looking for?"

"Apparently the group that robbed the Brinks truck in Grant Park used mercaptan. The flat foot was trying to determine if we were the source for it. Hell, he didn't have a clue how much was used. My foreman must have answered the cop's questions satisfactorily because he actually gave $20.00 to the 'Save Ryan' fund."

"Well Sam, it's an ill wind that doesn't blow some good. It looks like it was handled appropriately despite your absence. Congratulations on the new customer."

Adam concluded the call and reflected for a moment. He vividly recalled his late-night visit to the A111 to fill two bottles of mercaptan. The original plan was to fill them from the "input" side, but he couldn't locate the appropriate valve. He couldn't ask anyone for assistance so he filled both bottles from the "output" side and prayed there was enough in the tanks to do the job. If the cops were chasing down every user of mercaptan, that must mean they didn't have much else to go on. Maybe not, since they have vast resources and armies of people to do things. They could be checking on a number of things including mercaptan. The guard must stay up regardless of the situation, he surmised.

* * * *

On the near North side, a producer for WGN-TV finished reading the Jason Gompers column. The "feel good" story was just the thing the producer was looking for. The attempt for balance in journalism today wasn't between liberal and conservative. Balance was defined as "feel good" versus "blood and gore." There were never enough "feel good" stories to achieve anything close to balance, so the producer immediately assigned crews to get "on-air" interviews for the "Save Ryan" story. If they hurried, they might make tonight's 9:00PM local news show.

* * * *

Ann reported to Adam that the "Save Ryan" fund was growing thanks to the help of many people. They weren't quite at the turning point, but gaining steam. Her greatest concern at the moment was that Tad had requested an "emergency" meeting with Wilma and Zack. Adam groaned inwardly. "What the hell could that mean?"

The WGN staff was very efficient. The evening show had interviews with Steve and his wife holding Ryan. You had to be made of sheet rock not to be influenced by their plight. Interviews with Sam, Vlad and the foreman at Allied were featured. While on the plant floor, you could clearly see the bright yellow "Cat" parts and new equipment when the camera panned to show the many posters. An outdoor shot of the plant was shown as a backdrop while the address of the "Save Ryan" fund was highlighted on TV monitors throughout the city.

Bernie Tollinger was in his luxury apartment at Harbor Point nursing a bad cold. Normally Bernie spent his few "free" evenings at the opera or with friends. Junior watched the local news incredulously. "There must be another Allied! This could not be the Allied that he gave up on years ago. It looked familiar in the video, yet somehow different. What the hell was going on," he asked himself.

Ron was feeling depressed. With every passing day, the trail was getting colder. He was convinced that solving this particular crime was perhaps more important than any other case he had ever been assigned. Ron turned on the local news just in time to see WGN's feature story. He instantly recognized Allied Manufacturing as one of the factories he visited looking for the source of mercaptan. "That's right! He had contributed to the "Save Ryan" fund." They were great people and very helpful. Ron hoped the added publicity would help them reach their goal. The foreman indicated during the visit that they had experienced quite a "turn around" in the last year. "Wait a minute! The plant was on the southwest side." The Russian claimed that same area as his territory. A VP had turned around the plant and they used mercaptan. In the back of Ron's mind, the vague beginnings of a "hunch" took shape. Despite access to the best crime labs and science available, most cops swore by intuitive "hunches."

Adam finished walking Scotty in time to catch the local news. He watched, dumbfounded, and concluded he had just viewed the biggest "UNK-UNK" of all time. The publicity from trying to do a good thing was going to hurt. Adam didn't know what the effect would be, but in his gut, he knew it would lead to problems. He may now have to actively consider a diversion. It was becoming imperative to concoct a way to get the authorities to chase something else. How could this be done without exposing the team or his family, he pondered?

CHAPTER 30

There was a switching problem near Western Avenue this morning, and the 6:32 was uncharacteristically late arriving into Union Station. Bernie was waiting with Ann and Dave in Ann's office when Adam belatedly entered Allied's recently refurbished offices. It was apparent that some level of communication had occurred before Adam's arrival. Ann looked pale, drawn and depressed. Dave appeared defiant and angry. Ann, without enthusiasm, made the formal introduction of Adam to Bernie. Adam had completely forgotten that the formality of an introduction had not occurred before this morning.

Bernie appeared uncomfortable and attempted to clear his throat before addressing the three executives. "Well, where to begin? I simply could not believe my eyes watching the news last night. I kept thinking WGN was reporting about another company called Allied or I had an affliction far worse than a common cold. When I came in today, all of my doubts and confusion were removed. WGN was, in fact, talking about my beloved Allied. My God, what a difference! What in the world have you people been up to?"

There was a long, nervous pause before Adam responded. "We have elected to try and improve a few things in an attempt to save the company from bankruptcy."

"Improve a few things! That may be a world record understatement. Dave just showed me the latest financial reports. You have pulled off a major miracle. I had assurances five years ago that this place couldn't be saved. I spent a small fortune on the best consultants in America, and they couldn't see a future for Allied. I was advised, in emphatic terms, to write off my inheritance and seek greener pastures."

"You received bad advice." Ann responded.

"Indeed I did." Bernie was gaining passion as he continued his remarks. Bernie was clearly angry and his face was getting redder. "I kept saying to myself with each monthly check that Allied provided, this will be the last. I can't find the words to express my shock over the turn around performance that you have achieved. This unbelievable progress will mandate some major changes for the firm and in my thinking."

The three Allied managers looked like they had just received a death sentence from a hanging judge. Adam thought Ann was going to cry. She was biting her lower lip in an attempt to hold it off. Her worse fears were coming true as anticipated. Dave started assembling his sacred financial reports before walking out the door. Adam started to wonder if there were any changes in the staff at the Elgin unemployment office. Bernie stood up and started pacing regally around the room.

"My recently departed father wanted more than anything to see his company grow and prosper forever. I was supposed to be the bridge to his vision of the future as the only heir. I just didn't have the right stuff to fulfill my father's desires. I thought by bringing in brigades of consultants I could compensate for my many shortcomings. I had the most noble of intentions, but I was wrong. My activities helped push the company closer to the grave, as Ann can readily attest. You people in this room, as well as Sam at the plant, did what I could not do with all the King's horses and all the Kings men. Bernie paused for a moment to catch his breath and looked out the window.

Adam sat bewildered during the pause, while a host of questions swirled in his mind. "Why hadn't he embarked on "Project Freedom" at an earlier date? Should he have expedited the schedule once the team was in place? How would Adam feed his family for four years until it was possible to recover the loot? Would it be necessary to violate security and break his pledge to the team by obtaining the loot before the plan dictated?"

Finally, Bernie turned from the window and addressed the three apprehensive managers. "I believe it's in the best interest of all parties that you continue your efforts in honor of my father's memory. You don't need me hanging around as a potential threat to your hard work. I am willing to sell the company outright to your entire management team if we can agree that the current team stays intact."

Bernie's proclamation was greeted with absolute, stunned silence. Everyone in the group was speechless. Other office members had arrived for work and were drifting into the general office. Dave quickly rose and closed Ann's door. The grapevine will be titillated beyond belief today, the bean counter thought. Dave was the first to recover from his shock. "Speaking just for myself at the moment Mr. Tollinger, I find your offer most generous. I doubt we would have any difficulty keeping the team intact; however, none of us is particularly rich. I don't know how we can come up with the necessary capital to buy you out despite our desire to continue with the company."

"I'm aware of that, Dave. Remember, I just reviewed the current financial reports. You're not taking extraordinary salaries and to date, not one bonus has been issued. Virtually all income has been plowed back into the firm. That's one reason why I'm impressed. All of you are hard working and honest, which are attributes in very short supply these days. I don't believe in punishing hard work. I would like to set the sales price for Allied at the level it was before your major efforts kicked in. The payment terms can be made flexible enough that you can pay me over time from cash flow. I really am committed to seeing the company continue as is."

Adam regained enough composure to respond: "Mr. Tollinger, we would be happy to continue running this company in a way that would make your father proud. I appreciate your understanding and your generous offer. What's the next step?"

"Adam, I'll have my lawyers prepare the necessary papers. It should not take more than two or three weeks. Dave, we will need your help in setting the value of the firm retroactively. I want the three of you and Sam to decide who will be the new officers and what your respective titles and duties will be."

The three current managers of Allied shook Bernie's hand as Junior left the office. Bernie was effusive in his praise of each of their accomplishments. After Bernie left, Dave excused himself. "It's way too early in the morning and I never do this, but I need a drink!"

Ann was as pale as new fallen snow. After Bernie's departure, she had not been able to mutter a word or move a muscle. She sat for a moment after Dave left trembling in her new chair. "Oh Adam, we didn't have to do it!"

"Don't start second guessing yourself, Ann. None of us knew what would happen with Bernie. All of the evidence available to us suggested that Bernie would react quite differently than he just did. If you want to drive yourself nuts, you could speculate that if we hadn't conducted 'Operation Freedom' our worst fears would have been realized. The past is the past. All I know is we can't give the money back and say we're sorry. I can assure you the police won't be as generous in their attitudes as Bernie apparently is. To use a football analogy, we were successful because we had nothing to lose. Now we are about to gain total legal control of a company that is doing fairly well and positioned to become very profitable. We definitely have something to lose now. If we start playing defensively, we could lose it all."

"You're right. I had not thought of it that way. We have to play the hand that's dealt. This must be national "UNK-UNK" week. I almost forgot we must meet with Tad early this evening. He would not indicate why he is so anxious to meet with us."

"Perhaps Tad wants to provide us with tickets to the Bears home opener."

"I don't think so Adam, but I appreciate your attempt to soften the day with humor. How will the Bears do this year?"

"I haven't had time to follow them during pre-season. Alice is convinced beyond a doubt that I'm seriously ill because of my lack of interest. Normally this is the time of year that I ask her if she has anything to say before the season starts."

* * * *

Ron tried once more to convince Alex. "I know it's just a hunch, a long shot at best. However, I don't believe in coincidences. Adam Jones is the Vice President at Allied Manufacturing who effectively led a turn around effort. Adam is a system designer by training. That is almost the exact profile established by my friendly Professor from Northwestern. Jones controls a plant that uses mercaptan extensively in production. That plant resides on the southwest side and employs a number of Russians. Certainly, you can free up a few bucks and a couple of men to do a surveillance based on that information."

"Ron, you're repeating yourself. I understand the apparent connections, but I would have to get approval from the very Judge who let the Russian thug walk. Do you think she would permit surveillance on an apparent honest citizen? You told me this guy has no priors and is living within his means. What are you going to offer to the Judge as evidence for 'probable cause?' 'I have a hunch.' Don't bother thinking about how the Judge will decide. Thanks to Mr. Calvert, I don't have the money or manpower to conduct surveillance if the Judge pleaded with us to perform the surveillance!"

"O.K., I see your point. I'll never get the resources from the City of Chicago either. To my superiors, it's an FBI case to win or lose."

"Then let it go, Ron. It wasn't meant to be. It's a real long shot under the best of definitions. The only reason we're remotely considering doing this is that we don't have anything else to go on."

"I don't give up that easily. I haven't forgotten the importance of solving this case. We can't let a bunch of amateurs gain a victory of this magnitude. We are indirectly encouraging honest citizens to adopt a life of crime. Wait a minute, I just remembered and old IOU! I have a friend who's a private eye. He owes me a big favor. I wonder if I could talk him into a freebie. If I can, do you have any objections?"

"How could I have any objections? I don't know a thing about it."

* * * *

Adam left Ann's office to call Mr. Williams at National. Williams was reluctant to commit to an earlier ship date on the 9700 than Christmas week. He promised to do his best. That was all Adam could ask for. New products happen when they want to. It was difficult to accurately predict beyond what was committed to by Williams.

Adam called Sam to inform him about the possibility of a slightly earlier date on the 9700. "Good afternoon, Mr. President!"

"What the hell are you talking about, Sam? Did you forget to take your medicine again?"

"Ann, Dave and I just concluded a conference call while you were gabbing with Mr. Williams. We had a vote and you are our new bloody President. As a relative newcomer to Allied, we didn't think your vote meant anything. So congratulations on becoming head 'sea gull.' The ceremony eliminating your status from 'sea gull' is automatically revoked when you gain a title like President."

"Don't count your chickens yet, Sam. Until the deal is signed, it isn't a deal."

"You may have a point, Laddie. I'll wait to make any announcements until it's a done deal."

"That would be wise. There have been many strange things going on of late. I would recommend you wait before you get on my case. National will try to get us the 9700 a week or two earlier than their original promise. I hope they make it. Be ready!"

Ann was standing by Adam's door. "It looks like Sam stole my thunder as he so frequently does. Congratulations, Mr. President. You've earned it."

"Thanks, Ann. I'm still trying to recover emotionally from Bernie's decision. I assume Dave will be Chief Financial Officer, Sam as Vice President of Manufacturing and you as Executive Vice President?"

"Great minds think alike. By the way, the publicity from WGN has been fabulous. We are now officially oversubscribed on the 'Save Ryan' fund. We have amassed enough to cover the operation and provide a substantial college fund for Ryan. I'm scheduled to present the check to Steve on Monday. Good grief, that's Labor Day."

* * * *

Ron was able to reach Paul Barr at his office. Mr. Barr was hesitant to acknowledge his debt to Detective McHugh. Barr had been exceptionally busy of late and had just concluded an assignment. The Private Detective was looking forward to a long weekend with his family and watching some football. Ron McHugh could be very persuasive, and Mr. Barr recognized the value of a friend in the Chicago Police department. With great reluctance, Barr accepted Adam's name and address and relented to a weekend of surveillance.

* * * *

Adam and Ann left the office independently and rejoined at a back table at Berghoff's. Tad joined them shortly thereafter.

"Please excuse the request for the emergency meeting. I'm aware of the need to maintain security, but my problem simply can't wait. Let me assure both of you that all physical evidence of our recent activity has been destroyed. That includes photos, records of purchases, and my disc drive. Here are the combinations to both of my locks."

Ann and Adam sat stupefied while Tad collected his thoughts. "I have just received a diagnosis of cancer. It appears to be in my pancreas and is spreading rapidly. It will be very quick. My Doctor gives me less than 6 months to get my affairs in order. Some preliminary treatment starts next week, which may adversely affect my mind and body. It was imperative that I talk to you while I still have full control of my mental faculties. You guys represent the only affair that I have to address. I've led a good, but extremely dull life, at least until Wilma showed up at my garage one day."

"My God Tad is there anything we can do?" Ann inquired.

"No, believe me, you've done plenty. The 'job' had to be the high point of my life. I enjoyed the planning and the execution more than you will ever know. It's funny in retrospect. The money never really meant anything to me. Being part of a team that respected each other and achieved its goal filled a real void. I've been pushed around all my life by one thing or another, and it felt good to push back, if just a little."

"I know the feeling, Tad. How is your family going to cope?" Zack asked.

"Thank you for asking. My wife is set up well financially. I have good insurance coverage and her family has some money. I don't see any problem, but I would appreciate if you would look in on her occasionally. It's possible she might need some of the proceeds down the road, but I'll leave that in your hands. I really trust you people, and whether you realize it or not, establishing that trust filled another major void in my life. As of now, I renounce all personal claims to the loot. It was an honor to work with you and all the members of the team."

Ann was starting to cry. She couldn't help it. It had been an extremely emotional day even before Tad's news.

"I guarantee we will keep an eye open for your wife Tad. I only wish we could do something about your predicament."

"There are many things in life that you can't control or plan for, Zack.

"I couldn't agree more, Tad."

CHAPTER 31

Adam celebrated this Saturday morning by sleeping late. It was one of life's little luxuries he had not been able to enjoy for months. There were many chores connected with the preparation for winter that had to be accomplished on the average fall Saturday; however, he had an extra day this holiday weekend to accomplish them. It was a risk to relax for one day by doing nothing. In Chicago, nature dealt harshly with the unprepared and lazy.

For the second year in a row, Allied would celebrate Labor Day by closing the plant. They were current with their shipments to customers, thanks in part to their decision to add a full third shift. The tension of running Allied concurrently with planning and executing "Project Freedom" had taken a toll. The extra sleep this morning helped a great deal. Adam now felt somewhat refreshed, but knew he would never achieve total relaxation.

As he urgently searched for that coveted first cup of coffee, Adam wondered if Bernie was fully cognizant of what he was walking away from. Allied was more than just profitable. The firm was well positioned to take advantage of a strong economy if one would ever return. Allied's production capability, enhanced with all of the new equipment, was nothing short of first rate. Their people were now the best trained in the industry and they had established a "beach head" for future talent at the high schools. The customer base was more diverse than it had ever been in the company's history. The plant was a cleaner, brighter, safer, and happier place to work. If the economy took off, Allied's sales and profits would fly high beside it.

There were still countless problems at Allied requiring attention. Adam was aware that he didn't have good intelligence on future trends within the industry.

This lack of insight would mandate more "face time" with Allied's customers to see what they were envisioning for the future. In particular, he needed more data on new materials under development that were stronger and lighter in weight. The newer materials might require a new class of machines and process techniques. Would they need to develop expertise in ceramics? Where would the capital for those expenditures come from? It was more than one man could do just keeping up with the trends, much less reacting positively to them.

In his amazement at the range of problems facing Allied, Adam couldn't help wondering how the Feds managed. "I can hardly cope with the activity of a small firm that has now grown to 300 souls. The government attempts to manage thousands of people in hundreds of different activities and locations."

Adam knew why the thought of the Feds jumped into his head. He was still trying to reconcile the death of the Russian. "Why did the Feds even let the idiot into the country? Why didn't they deport the thug when they caught him with the bond?" The thought that he had inadvertently caused the death of a human being troubled Adam greatly. It was easier to accept the Lewis situation. The arrogant hypocrite had been involved with the "mob" for years. Lewis took his own life rather than face the swift and certain brand of justice issued by the underworld. That outcome was ordained by fate.

He was greatly moved by Tad's dilemma, but there was nothing more the team could do. At least they found a way to save Steve's boy without apparently jeopardizing security. The irony that some of the money that would have gone to the Russian gang was redirected to saving an infant seemed poetic. The publicity surrounding the "Save Ryan" fund still troubled Adam. It was impossible to predict how it would play out.

Alice greeted Adam with a cup of hot coffee. "Decided to join the family this morning did you! We're so pleased. The kids have been asking who the strange man is who occasionally stops by and leaves us with dirty clothes and dishes."

"Are you trying to tell me something, my dear? In this small intimate gathering place that is our kitchen, there is no need to be subtle. Just come right out with it." Alice simply frowned and gave him "the look" universally recognized and feared by husbands since the Bronze Age. Although it was a warm, sunny day in early fall, Adam could feel the cold winds of January in his wife's relentless stare.

"Get yourself a cup of coffee and sit with me, Alice. I have an interesting announcement for you. You are joined this morning by the newly named President of Allied Manufacturing."

Alice squealed in delight. "Oh, Adam, that's great news! Does this mean more money?"

"I hope so. Time will tell." Adam went on to explain Bernie's deal and all that led up to it. Adam was convinced Bernie would follow through, because he had effectively written off the company years ago. Whatever Bernie received from Allied at this point was a bonus. As an added benefit, Bernie would be honoring his father's wishes.

"So you believe that Bernie will walk away from his birthright just because he has already written Allied off and wishes only to honor his late father's memory?"

"Those are the reasons that he announced at our meeting, but there's more. His attorney introduced himself to us the day after Bernie made his decision. The lawyer suggested that he would insist on a special clause in the sales contract. We would be penalized if we made extra payments or paid too soon. Then the attorney mentioned how much he was looking forward to working on the sales agreement as a break from doing all of Bernie's tax work."

"I don't know if I understand the importance of the lawyer's comments, Adam."

"The clues are quite subtle, Alice. Dave Stevens pointed out to me that the position taken by Bernie's attorney was one that would be taken if his client had tax concerns. It certainly isn't consistent with a client who desperately needed funds. After some investigation work by Ann, we found out that Bernie has become a financially successful independent producer of plays and concerts. It's keeping Bernie busy—producing a truckload of money and it's in the arena of life that he adores. The short story is that Bernie doesn't need Allied. That's great news because we don't need Bernie. The deal will be finalized and it's good for everybody."

"I still can't believe that Bernie would walk away from the company even if he does have tax problems."

"It happens every day across the country, Alice. Families sell farms and small businesses because they can't afford the inheritance taxes. In political parlance, it's referred to as 'income redistribution.' There are less polite terms for the process that many citizens use, but I'll leave that to your imagination."

"Why do you seem so ill at ease with the promotion, Adam?"

"I am concerned as hell about my qualifications to run the company. There is so much I don't know. The company is in a relatively strong position, but failure for the enterprise lurks just one bad decision away. I have been successful to date because I felt I had nothing to lose. Now I am forced to worry about the fate of over 300 employees in addition to you and the kids. It changes one's perception of the world. The good news is, when the position becomes official, we will alter the pay structure to reflect reality. We will also address the pension issue to be current with the times. Our family's money fears for the future have been eliminated. That is just an assumption based on the hope that the current economy improves greatly."

"I fail to see why you are not jumping up and down with joy like a kid on Christmas morning. Personally, I am ready to sing Hallelujah!"

"I am happy, Alice. This promotion is what everybody in business dreams about, but it comes with a price. Take Sam, for instance. We have usually agreed on things when we were equals. Now I am the official boss. Subconsciously, Sam reflected that yesterday when he reinstated my 'sea gull' status. I could now become the 'empty suit' that I so despised in the past. As President, you receive God-like power. I have never been comfortable with that notion. Like the good hymn says 'All Glory, Laud and Honor' belongs to the Lord, not some simple minded mortal with a title."

"It seems to me you are forecasting that your personality will change because of this promotion. You're not sure if you or I will like the new Adam. How can I be of assistance?"

"Very perceptive, my Dear. You can help by putting on the one pair of sharp, spiked, shoes that you own and plant them firmly in my posterior when the occasion demands. If I get too full of myself, slip a laxative in my coffee. I don't want to lose sight of you and the kids by worrying about Allied. My family is far too important to me for that to happen. Perhaps that realization occurred later in my life than it should have, but believe me, it's present today."

"I might come to enjoy this new assignment. Are you going to take Scotty out after you get cleaned up?"

"That's the plan. I knew I could count on your enthusiastic help for maintaining my discipline."

After a light breakfast and a shower, Adam slipped on Scotty's leash and started the all too familiar routine. Adam thought that whoever fashioned the phrase: "The more I work with people the more I love my dog" knew what he was talking about. There was undiluted joy in Scotty's eyes at the prospect of another walk.

As they started down the street, Scotty became far more agitated than usual. "What's the matter, big fella?" Then Adam spotted an innocuous van parked just down the street from the house. The van was unremarkable except for several antennas protruding from the roof. "I see it, Scotty." The faithful dog never took his eyes off the van as they slowly walked past it. "It's O.K. Scotty, I understand. Good boy."

As they continued their walk, Adam was totally mystified. Could it be that someone was checking to see if a neighbor was having an affair? That didn't seem plausible. It did look like a surveillance operation. How was he supposed to know? There was no training in his background to teach him to recognize if he was being followed or watched. "You are entertaining denial, Adam. Face reality," the little voice within his mind demanded. He was, in fact, being watched. It wasn't just run-of-the-mill paranoia on his part. "How could he have been selected for surveillance out of the millions of candidates living in Chicago? What were they looking for? Who was behind this?" The questions assaulted his mind.

The wave of questions completely eroded the comfortable emotions of just minutes ago. "It has to be the Feds," Adam concluded. They are the only ones with unlimited resources. Adam couldn't prove it conclusively, but he thought it had to be from the WGN publicity. One of Frank's favorite expressions was: "In this life, no good deed goes unpunished." Leave it to Frank to come up with a pithy story or comment. Maybe Frank augments his income by writing bumper stickers or greeting cards. The SOB was always right!

Paul Barr watched Adam and the dog walk by. The private eye was concerned that the dog "made" him and blew the cover. The suspect didn't seen to notice the dog's behavior, so maybe the cover was still intact. Barr was totally confused by the assignment. He wasn't sure why Ron McHugh wanted a "tail" on this dude, but there had to be a reason. Barr had known McHugh for years and didn't think of him as frivolous in any way. However, all of the information that he gathered prior to the "stake out" showed this potential suspect to be an outstanding citizen. It must be drugs, the former cop thought. If it were drugs, Ron was trying to establish "probable cause" to begin an interrogation. Ron was prohibited from working in Bartlett because he lacked jurisdiction. How could he help his friend, terminate the surveillance so he could go home, and enjoy the weekend? Maybe the suspect received drugs from an associate while walking the dog. That would be a clever technique. Barr decided to leave the van and discretely follow the suspect and his dog.

Adam continued the worried walk and saw Scotty start his anxious routine again. "Now what?" Frank approached the pair and Scotty's tail started wagging in anticipation of walking with the familiar neighbor.

"Adam and Scotty, I'm glad to find you." Frank was carrying a shopping bag that appeared to be quite heavy.

"Hey Frank, good to see you. I was just thinking about you."

Barr was standing behind a tree about a quarter mile back. Just as I thought, he mused. Barr began dictating into a small tape recorder: "the suspect was joined by an unknown white male of average height at 1:53 PM. The unknown subject is holding a shopping bag that appears heavy. I estimate the weight at 2-3 kilos. Conversation between the two continues as they walk northeast."

"I just returned from making sales calls in Detroit, Adam. Allied really keeps me running, I must start a new trip early Monday morning so I'm happy to run into you today. I have something to give you."

"I'm truly sorry that we keep you so busy, Frank."

"No apology required. I love being busy. I'm making good money for both of us. Working for Allied is the best thing that ever happened to me. It's a pleasure working with honest, competent people. Sam is a piece of work. It's an honor to consider him a friend."

"What happened to the bitter cynic who recommended 'crime' as a solution to all of our problems not so long ago at this very location?"

"Well Adam, I may have given you a bum steer on that point. I had hoped you had forgotten my passionately expressed observation. I was wrong!" Adam felt a wave of nausea developing within his body as Frank continued.

"You have to remember that I never represented a good 'house' before. Representing bad companies affects your worldview in a profoundly negative way. Working with people who respect your talent, treat you as an adult, and do what they say they will do greatly changes your perception. If only Uncle Sam would let me keep some of my hard earned money, I'd be completely and blissfully happy."

"I'm afraid that even with my new title I can't help you with that issue, Frank! I wish to God I could. Every decision I make at Allied is colored, doctored or governed by tax implications, with the possible exception of deciding when to use the rest room. We never seem to make a decision based exclusively on what's best for the employees, vendors, customers or stock-holders."

"I know better than to ask you for help on the tax code, Adam. What can anybody do? Our representatives turn a deaf ear to any complaints. What can one man do? Even a man as talented and resourceful as you can't assault the impregnable fortress of stupidity called Congress."

"This is a special day, Frank. We are in total agreement. It's truly sad that we have joined the growing ranks of frustrated, apathetic and resigned citizens who feel government won't work for their interests."

Barr continued the dictation: "suspects have stopped walking and are continuing their conversation at 2:02PM. I suspect the drug transfer is about to take place. I will close in and attempt a citizen's arrest upon transfer. There are no additional people in sight. Neither suspect appears armed and the dog looks friendly." Barr stopped his dictation and started to rapidly close the gap to the suspects. The former police officer had been involved in numerous drug busts over the years. The transfer would be taking place any minute. Barr could "smell" it.

"Adam, let's get back to something more positive. It's not just me who feels strongly about Allied's performance. The customers do as well. Their opinions and judgments are always far more important than mine are. Let me show you." Frank reached into the bag and pulled out an enormous plaque of walnut and brass.

Scotty, for the first time in Adam's memory, started growling as the plaque came out of the bag. That confused Adam, until he spotted a stranger approaching from the north on a dead run.

Frank, who had his back to the stranger announced: "The Ford Motor Company has presented Allied with its Supplier of the Year Award! I just picked this up late yesterday."

The stranger stopped dead in his tracks, a mere four feet away. Scotty barked continuously and was very aroused. Adam tried to comfort his normally calm pet. The stranger politely asked: "Excuse me, that looks interesting. May I see it?"

Frank, who had no idea who the guy was said: "Of course, we just won the Supplier of the Year award from the Ford Motor Company. It's a highly coveted award throughout our industry and I, for one, am anxious to show this to everyone in the world, including you."

The stranger just smiled and said "Congratulations." As Barr departed, Adam thought he saw the bulge of a handgun beneath the jacket on the stranger's right hip.

"This is fabulous, Frank! I'll take it to the plant on Tuesday. We'll hang it in the cafeteria. It will mean a great deal to everybody."

"Thanks, Adam. I'd like to be there, but I have other calls to make. Tell Sam thanks for me as well."

"Will do, Frank. Enjoy your abbreviated holiday."

Frank departed and Scotty began to settle down. Adam could not. Who was that stranger? He certainly wasn't a new neighbor, park ranger, or dog walker. He had to be a cop and connected with the van. Did the cop think there was money or maybe bonds in Frank's shopping bag? The stranger only stopped running when he saw the plaque. He was obviously looking for something else.

Get hold of yourself Adam, he thought. If the cop knew or suspected your role in the heist, you would be on your way to an interview. My God, I don't have an alibi! The thought of an alibi seemed redundant during the initial planning, but not now. However, he wasn't asked to come in for a little chat. The surveillance had to be an exercise in general research. Sam said the cops were checking out people with access to mercaptan. That had to be the link—the plant and the mercaptan. What if they interviewed an Allied employee who confirmed that both Ann and I were absent from work on the day of the heist? "Shit!"

"Stay calm, think clearly," that damned little voice in his mind commanded. "That's easy for you to say, Mr. 'Know it all,' my stomach is in my throat!" Adam said aloud.

Scotty froze at the outburst from the boss. He didn't recognize a key word or command like "sit" and was confused. Then the dog realized his master was retreating to some far off place without leaving his side. It always frightened him when Adam did this because his master was likely to walk in front of on-coming cars during this transformation. Scotty's breeding now dictated that his job was to watch for traffic.

Adam realized he could not rewind and replay the past to correct mistakes in planning. He had to find a way to reduce the attention being paid to him. It was time to run a diversion. There had to be a way to get the authorities busy chasing somebody else or some other crime. What a great concept, but how the hell does one implement it? Where is the damned muse when you need it?

* * * *

Barr was livid when he returned to the van. He was totally embarrassed when the 2-3 kilos of cocaine turned, as if by magic, into a walnut and brass plaque. The private eye quickly started the van and left the neighborhood. After several tries, he contacted Ron from his cell phone.

"This surveillance is officially over, Ron. I don't know why you wanted it done, but you fingered the wrong guy. He's the official last remaining American Boy Scout. Jones doesn't even have a frigging parking ticket on his record. He has an Honorable Discharge from the Navy, is happily married, has two kids, and is a church member who I can personally guarantee just received a plaque as Ford's Supplier of the Year. I talked yesterday with a Mr. Palmer at First Continental, his former employer, who rues the day Adam left. They even tried to hire him back, which is officially against bank policy. Your hot suspect has virtually no debt, lives modestly, doesn't gamble, doesn't chase women, and has a credit rating 'to die for.' He loves his dog and his dog loves him. This guy is spotless; gilt edged, flawless, perfect, and even well liked by his neighbors. My God, Ron, I have neighbors who don't like me. Who else do you have on your hit list that you want me to check out for free—The Pope?"

"O.K. Paul, you've made your point. It was a long shot on my part. I appreciate your efforts." Ron knew that Barr, like himself, was a devout Roman Catholic. Paul Barr had met a fair share of "bad guys" over the years and knew exactly what to look for. If Barr favorably compared the suspect to the Pope, it wasn't hype and Adam Jones wasn't a crook.

"Alex, this is Ron, my suspect is clean. I was caught looking in the wrong place. I give up!"

"Not totally, Ron. The profiling group thinks you are correct about the business mentality. That's the good news. The bad news is, if we continue with that assumption, they were smart enough to leave us no clues. Furthermore, the business mind would have researched Title 18 of the Federal Criminal Code and determined the Statute of Limitations as being five years. The 'old farts' think that one reason we haven't seen any of the loot is the bad guys are sitting on the proceeds. They will wait patiently for the five years to elapse before they move. It's a entirely new concept and quite clever."

"That theory would explain a lot of inconsistencies. Where would they physically hide the loot?"

"That's where it gets interesting, Ron. The profilers think it's on the bottom of Lake Michigan along with many other clues. With access to GPS, the 'Perps' could easily retrieve the loot from the lake when the time is right. The advice from Washington is to cool our jets until the five year anniversary date."

"What happens then? The clock will have run out and we can't legally touch them."

"We own the best attorneys available, Ron. We'll figure out a way to extend the Statute or bend the law. First of all, we have to catch them. We have set in place a plan for the fifth anniversary date and the week thereafter. We will bring to Lake Michigan over half of the Navy's reconnaissance aircraft plus the assets of the Coast Guard for training. The U. S. Treasury wants those bonds back and they have authorized the funds to get them. You want the case solved as a disincentive to any who would break the law. I want to nail them because they piss me off! Fear not, Ron, we'll get them."

* * * *

Adam and Scotty remained by the lake long after Frank and the stranger had taken their leave. The need for a diversion was obvious. The surveillance, lack of an alibi and the encounter with the armed individual were deeply troubling. Staring at the large plaque from Ford provided no solace.

To be effective, a diversion would have to occupy federal law enforcement agents for quite some time. They, by definition, were only concerned with the activities involving crime. Logically, Adam had to commit a crime to get their attention. However, he pledged to Ann and the team that they would only do one job. A deal is a deal. Adam could not involve the team. Mentally, it was a perfect stalemate. Whatever he was going to do, it would have to be done alone. Adam would be denied the feedback and recognition of "UNK-UNK'S" the team provided during "Operation Freedom."

There were actual armies of federal law enforcers. As far as Adam knew, the FBI, ATBF, Secret Service, Postal Police, DEA, Federal Marshall's, Custom Agents, Border Guards, and Forest Rangers were all in hot pursuit. How could one individual catch the undivided attention of such a multitude? The Minutemen of old had a relatively easy time by comparison. They only had to contend with the British Redcoats and a handful of hired Hessians. It was like an ant declaring war on a bloated whale. Even if he could think of an appropriate harpoon, he wasn't big or strong enough to throw it into a vital organ. Hell, he didn't know if this particular whale had a vital organ.

The fruitless search for an answer was depressing. Why could he come up with creative answers for FIRST CON and Allied, yet find nothing for himself? The muse must be on vacation. It was difficult to concentrate on the problem at hand. Other questions forced their way into his thoughts with a vengeance. "Will I be sent to a minimum or maximum-security prison? What will the food be like? Will they allow visitation by Alice or Scotty? Who will I draw as a cell mate?"

"O.K. Scotty, let's go. Alice will think we've both drowned in the lake. I'm getting absolutely nowhere."

Chapter 32

Winter returned with a vengeance and historical vitality this year. The onslaught appeared unusually early, which intruded rudely into autumn's splendor. The first indication of brutality appeared shortly after Labor Day in the form of an early frost. Adam wondered if the encounter with the armed stranger and the advent of winter were somehow related. The first significant snow was in early November. Cold winds and heavy rain preceded the snow. The citizens of Chicago had received a welcome reprieve the previous winter, and now they were paying for it.

Each day during this miserable weather Adam and Scotty ventured forth in search of an answer to the diversion question. It was a fantastic time for Scotty. The snow was great fun and 'Goldens' seem impervious to the cold.

Unfortunately, Adam's creativity was as cold as the winter weather. Not a single plausible idea came forth during the walks. Over time, Adam gained some recognition of the possibility that a vital organ existed within the whale of Federal Law Enforcement. That vital organ was money. With the enactment of recent budget constraints, every government agency complained of insufficient funding. The same complaint was raised each year regardless of administration or economic conditions, so funding must be of vital importance. Any action that threatened the Fed's money supply would surely get the attention of law enforcement. Additionally, whatever the eventual diversion activity turned out to be it would have to garner tremendous publicity to be effective. The media would have to be intimately involved to get the armies to take heed. The whale's vital organ seemed to be one part money and one part media attention. Beyond these stray concepts, which appeared as remote from each other as any two things could be, Adam had nothing brewing. Time was not on his side and his inability to think of a solution was depressing.

Big, heavy flakes of snow rode the 40-mph winds from the northwest as Scotty and Adam stumbled around the ice bound, snow covered lake. This wasn't the "Winter Wonderland" so often featured in Hollywood movies. The flakes weren't daintily floating down producing a magical scene with beautiful background music. This crap was coming in on a horizontal plane with a plaintive roar.

Fortunately, it wasn't likely that surveillance would take place today due to poor visibility. It was also unlikely that Adam would run into Frank today. Frank enjoyed walking with Scotty a great deal, but he was too smart to come out in this blizzard. Adam actually looked forward to running into Frank. The good neighbor and excellent sales representative for Allied always had something pithy to say. He was also full of good advice like the night he advised me on how to…obtain…an amended…1099!

"Adam, you idiot! Scotty, you have been accompanied on your walks by the dumbest SOB this side of Washington DC!" Adam shouted the phrase against the cold wind. Scotty wasn't sure what to make of his master's abrupt tone, but was relieved to see a smile on Adam's snow covered face, which was barely visible beneath the fur-lined hood.

In retrospect, the final solution for the diversion was simple. Good solutions are always simple and can actually be implemented. A thorough review of his life's experiences was all that was necessary to determine the correct course of action. Reflecting on his experiences had been the key to creative thinking in the past while at Home Depot and with the batting cage analogy. The answer was staring him right in the face. "How could he have been so dense?"

Adam rushed home, fired up the computer, and grabbed a cup of coffee in an attempt to warm up. Weeks of cold walks had produced nothing. Now he couldn't stop the flood of ideas that were competing for attention!

Adam vividly recalled the torture at the hands of the IRS when he received the bogus 1099. Allied's payroll software program generated 1099's as a standard feature. He would send bogus 1099's to the creators of the monster tax code. That approach would target individual members of each of the US Legislative bodies. The overall concept had an aura of justice that appealed to his devious side. Such an action would be perceived as a threat to the cash flow of the government. If handled correctly, it might generate sufficient media attention.

The diversion plan pivoted on the premise that no member of Congress actually prepared his or her own taxes. Adam thought if the politicians actually prepared their own returns, the agony suffered by all taxpayers would have been simplified years ago. The legislators undoubtedly had staff members assigned to plow through the forms and numbers. Would a staff member interrupt a busy Congressperson for a small amount of income reflected on a 1099? They probably wouldn't dare to do so! They would simply add it to the total gross income, calculate the tax, and have the politician sign the return. The physical 1099's would never be attached to the completed return. There is no requirement to add them as there is for the W-2. The dummies had no idea what they were signing.

It really didn't matter if the staff did the work as theorized or if the staff person consulted with the congressperson before signing. Adam would insure that the numbers submitted to the targets wouldn't match the amount stated in the electronic version of the 1099 that he would independently send to the IRS. The IRS computer, sensing the miss-match, would force a non-negotiable audit. Members of Congress would get to experience first hand the tender mercies of a Ms. Meyers or her counterpart, as Adam had. The IRS auditors might eventually accept the concept that the 1099 was bogus, but they would still search past returns looking for mistakes. The additional review of past returns could get very interesting. It was also possible that the media might pick up on it.

It was an elegant solution that Adam could easily and inexpensively accomplish by himself. The diversion embodied the essence of "judo," the ancient Japanese defense of turning your opponent's strength to a weakness. All Adam needed was individual social security numbers of the targets and EIN's (Employer Identification Number). To an experienced computer security expert, these numeric codes were relatively easy to obtain. They were recorded in any number of federal databases. It just took time. If he started immediately, the deadline for tax filings could be met.

There was a new campaign in the media calling for a non-partisan approach in Washington. Well, I can enthusiastically heed that call, Adam thought. All 435 House members and 100 Senators would receive the bogus 1099's. To members of the Senate Finance Committee, and the House Ways and Means Committee, he would send multiple 1099's. Since members of those committees had the principle responsibility of writing the tax code, Adam felt he was being fair. Since being fair was so important, he would also send bogus 1099's to major members of the Executive Branch such as Cabinet heads. Diversity was an important ideal in Washington as well. Why not send the bogus 1099's to members of the US Supreme Court? Remembering the earlier thoughts about generating publicity, he would target major media news anchors, newspaper editors, cable TV "stars," and carefully selected Hollywood celebrities. In total, he quickly determined that

3250 individuals and 60 carefully selected employers would be the beneficiaries of the educational exercise and diversion.

Perhaps publicity could not be achieved by target selection alone. Upon reflection, there appeared to be need for an additional angle. Adam had to make it hard for the recipient of a bogus 1099 to receive an amended copy from the issuer. "Was there a way to employ the Image God to work on his behalf?"

Adam tried to envision a hypothetical example to test the theory. If I sent a 1099 to the CEO of *General Motors* from the *Ford Motor Co.*, what would happen? The CEO from GM would be embarrassed to admit to the back wall of his closet, much less to the GM Board, that he received funds from an arch competitor. The CEO's carefully crafted image would be destroyed. Likewise, *Ford* would be embarrassed to tears and would not admit to sending money to a competitor. Of course, they wouldn't admit it. They didn't do it! Why would any company amend a 1099 they hadn't sent in the first place, thought Adam. The assault on both the recipient and issuer's image would provide conflict, controversy, and carnage sufficient to sell newspapers. Adam would tailor the mailings to Congress to magnify the effect of this insight.

Allied had recently upgraded its mail handling equipment. They routinely sent out mass mailings of 5000 to 6000 pieces. It was ridiculously simple to fold and stuff 3250 pieces during a weekend trip to the office. The fact that the postage expense would be written off against Allied's taxes seemed entirely appropriate. The hard part of the entire diversion effort was affixing stamps to the pile of mail—the postage machine could be traced.

By law, 1099's had to be submitted by no later than the end of January. Adam began stuffing small amounts of letters into various mailboxes by mid-December. Congress was in holiday recess, so it didn't hurt to be too early. Adam filed the electronic 1099's to the IRS shortly thereafter. By Christmas, everything had been mailed and the phony 1099's rode the mail stream with cards offering hope for a "Happy New Year." This diversion, at best, was a long shot, but Adam surmised it was worth the effort.

Adam actually forgot about the diversion once the forms were mailed. The fabled 9700 arrived from National shortly after Christmas day and its installation took every available minute of time.

Adam was now officially the Chief Executive of Allied. The negotiations with Bernie proceeded smoothly. They received very generous terms and all parties were happy with the final outcome.

* * * *

Captain Cox, of the US Army Rangers, had just returned to the U.S. from duty in Afghanistan. It was an extremely dangerous tour. The Captain had acquitted himself with great distinction. His superb physical shape allowed him to survive the heat, sandstorms, and combat. He crawled into caves and was shot at on numerous occasions. The reassignment to Pentagon duty was done to enhance his career and provide a reprieve from hazardous duty. The Captain was enjoying a Christmas leave with his family.

* * * *

A Senator from a western state called a press conference in the first week of January. Adam watched a tape of the conference on the local news. The news account gave the first tangible evidence of the result of the bogus mailings. The Senator was incensed that she had received a 1099 indicating payment of $750.00 from the National Rifle Association for a speaking engagement. She vehemently denied ever speaking to the group, or receiving a payment. She was beet red and because of her anger, little orbs of saliva went flying through the air, illuminated by the TV floodlights throughout her spirited denial. Adam thought that if Scotty's vet were present he would have automatically given her a shot for rabies. Perhaps the harpoon hit home after all. Obviously, a staff person caught the issuer's name and brought it to the Senator's attention.

The news channel then cut to a press conference conducted by the NRA. Their spokesperson was in total agreement that the NRA never paid anything to the Senator. He was adamant that they would never support her, send money, or listen to anything she said. The spokesperson went on to say that no self-respecting member of the NRA wanted to be in the same zip code with the aforementioned Senator. He too was red and shaking and wanted to assure the good, hard-working, dues paying members of the NRA that the Senator got absolutely nothing from them. Hell would freeze over before they would agree to provide the Senator with an amended 1099.

The media, as with most issues, was totally confused and didn't know what to make of the exchange. It was amazing to the reporters how few Congressmen seemed to know what a 1099 was. The fact that not one of the media types knew what one looked like was of little importance to them.

Other exchanges of the same type started occurring almost daily. Congress people were angrily denying reports and spokespersons from special interest groups diametrically opposed to the policies of the congressperson involved were angrily AGREEING. It was hard to determine which side or group was the most upset. The media started ranking the performances of all participants exclusively on emotional content. It went from "utter contempt," to "totally physically ill." The public loved the emotional fireworks. It was fascinating to watch individuals and groups in "agreement" becoming so agitated. It was far more comedic than anything on prime time TV, including the commercials. The nation was enjoying a good laugh.

* * * *

Mr. Twilliger had completed an outstanding year. The inspector was selected as OSHA's "Employee of the year." The major justification for this award was the unprecedented number of citations that he issued. Unknown to his supervisors, Twilliger decided to augment his self-defined paltry government salary by soliciting bribes as well as citations. Twilliger was very careful to receive payment from targets only in cash. Thus, when he received a 1099 in December he discarded it. Actually, the inspector had never seen a 1099 and was unaware that a separate copy went to the IRS. Twilliger filed his 1040EZ early, reveling in all of the tax-free income he had received and failed to report.

Twilliger was surprised at the IRS summons to appear for an audit. Upon arriving for the audit, he instantly recognized the office décor as being the same as the OSHA office. He was quickly ushered into see Ms. Meyers.

"Look, Ms. Meyers, I don't know what this meeting is about, but as a fellow federal employee, I insist on some professional courtesy!"

"You can insist all you want, Mr. Twilliger. We don't play favorites in our agency. I'm trying to overlook the fact that your agency received more funding last fiscal year than we did. Additionally, you didn't claim income from a group entitled 'Citizens for a Flat Tax' in the amount of $50,000. I don't appreciate tax cheats regardless of their employer. I especially don't like the group you worked for, as it's a threat to my job. Are you represented by counsel?"

"No, I am not! There is absolutely no need for an attorney. I didn't do anything wrong! Twilliger was very upset. He didn't like being pushed around. There was no way on Earth the IRS could know about the bribes he had received and failed to report. Twilliger's firm belief that the IRS couldn't possibly know anything about the undeclared income could not prevent the small drops of perspiration from forming on his forehead.

He's hiding something, thought Ms. Meyers. She had seen it before in countless audits. If the two of them had to sit there all week, she would find out what the inspector was evading. "Mr. Twilliger, just out of curiosity, do you have a Swiss bank account?"

* * * *

A well known movie star and singer from Hollywood who championed liberal causes for years was notified by her staff that she had received a 1099 from the Ku Klux Klan. They had to call the paramedics to administer oxygen as a direct result of the notification. It was a front-page story for days.

* * * *

Captain Cox reported for duty to the Secretary of Defense after completing Christmas leave. Cox was resplendent in his dress uniform. "Welcome home, Captain! I'm afraid we're not quite ready with your new assignment. As a personal favor to me could you check out this 1099 I received while we get your assignment ready?"

The good Captain had no idea what a 1099 was, but he was a "message to Garcia" type and quickly acknowledged the request with a "No problem, Sir." The Captain then took the 1099, which was for $1,000.00. The employer on the 1099 was identified as the IRS. Other staff people informed Captain Cox that the 1099 had to be a simple error. The IRS doesn't pay people for anything. They take money from everyone. All Captain Cox would have to do is simply call the IRS and obtain an amended 1099. Then the Secretary of Defense could file his tax return.

* * * *

The media was starting to notice the growing buzz. Other reports started surfacing through leaks. A Senator from the Northeast was upset about a purported 1099 from Alcoholics Anonymous. A Senator from a state with legalized gambling was livid about apparent monetary support from Gamblers Anonymous. A conservative representative denied any speaking chores or income from the Sierra

Club. A conservative Senator was adamant in his denial of support from the ACLU. This was some of the buzz, but certainly not all of it. Other representatives and senators merely filed their returns and paid tax for income not actually received. Their staffs had not notified them of who sent the 1099's because it didn't seem to be worth the effort. By signing the return, the politicians endorsed and verified the bogus 1099's.

Adam watched the news daily, as did most Americans. It was hilarious to see the bloated egos squirm from all sides of the political spectrum; however, Adam knew what awaited all of the targets. Off camera, in some federal office, they would be asked serious questions. Adam could easily visualize the singing diva hitting many high "C" notes when asked to prove she hadn't received money from the Klan. "The fact that you don't like them doesn't prove you wouldn't take money from them." All the posturing, panting and braying at news conferences was for naught. The real action was forthcoming. Adam relished the thought of the anchors of the Sunday shows, who prided themselves on asking hard questions, being confronted by the real experts at the IRS. "Don't tell me you didn't know about the 1099 from 'The Liars Club'—isn't that your signature?"

* * * *

Captain Cox spent four difficult days in an attempt to get answers from the IRS before reporting back to the Secretary of Defense. "I must apologize, Mr. Secretary. I have logged 293 calls and four personal visits to the IRS and have failed to talk to anybody. Despite using your name and that of the department, I have been unable to find a person within the IRS who will accept responsibility for sending out 1099's. It was far easier to negotiate with Al Qeada terrorists, despite the language barrier. I absolutely hate to admit failure, but if this is supposed to be a 'rest and relaxation tour,' I would humbly request a transfer back to combat in Afghanistan."

The Secretary restrained himself from laughing aloud and asked: "Captain, are you suggesting there are Taliban types residing within the IRS?"

"There appear to be many similarities, Sir!"

"I agree, Captain, and for that reason I do not hold you in any disrespect for not getting an answer. It was my fault for assigning you to this in the first place. You are a man of courage, honor, and integrity. I have a better assignment for a man of your caliber. I should have assigned this 1099 fiasco to a staff lawyer. They are better equipped, character-wise, to deal with this type of enemy."

The Secretary was greatly amused by the incident and told the story to an assistant. The assistant in turn was amused, and told the story to a group of staff members over coffee. A maintenance worker who received extra income by serving as a source for the *New York Times* overheard that rendition of the tale. The maintenance worker was always referred to as a "high-level" source from within the Pentagon by the New York paper. The editorial board of the *Times* initially had trouble with the "high-level" designation until it was pointed out that the maintenance man frequently climbed ladders to replace light bulbs. It all depended on your definition of "high-level."

The headline of the *New York Times* screamed: **DOD LINKS AL QEADA CELL TO IRS**. All hell broke loose as the nation's many media outlets slavishly followed the *Times* lead. The facts be damned, this story sold papers. Subsequent on-the-street polls and interviews found great support for the story from everyone who had ever been subjected to an audit by the IRS. Poll results equaled the truth to the media and the laughter in the country quickly turned to concern.

*   *   *   *

A spokesperson for the ACLU announced that the many reports circulating within the media of 1099's originating from her organization were categorically false. The ACLU had never sent 1099's during their many years of existence. The IRS found that statement to be of great interest. "Surely, the not-for-profit organization paid people in the past for services rendered. They were obligated under the law to file 1099's. Could it be that members of Congress avoided paying millions in taxes because special interest groups were not sending 1099's?" All financial records of the ACLU and six other groups were subpoenaed as a far ranging investigation began.

Somehow, the *Wall Street Journal* found out about the subpoenas issued by the IRS and began an investigation of its own. Their editorial headline ran several days later: **NO WONDER THEY WON'T CUT TAXES—THEY DON'T PAY ANY!** The *Journal* had ascertained that it was a common practice to pay honoraria or speaking fees to politicians and then "forget" to file a 1099. They further asserted that was the reason why some members had paid taxes on the phony 1099's. They had so much money coming in that was tax-free they simply didn't care.

The *Journal* article and the subsequent coverage hit a raw nerve with hundreds of thousands of average Americans. The public mood now changed from concern to white-hot anger. It was inconceivable to hard working citizens who searched diligently through mountains of regulations and receipts to find a single deduction, that representatives would voluntarily pay taxes on income they hadn't received or receive substantial income with no tax liability.

In Boston, an "ad hoc" group formed spontaneously in reaction to the news coverage and threw several boxes of tea into the harbor. It was shortly duplicated in every major city in the country, even those in the desert.

A live interview with the President of the Michigan Militia was aired on CNN. The Militia Chief was a huge man with a flowing red beard and wore a baseball cap featuring the logo: "Live Free or Die!" Supporters carrying shotguns and deer rifles surrounded him during the conference. "If the Federal government refuses to do anything about the God-damned nest of terrorists at the IRS—we'll take care of it ourselves!" A large raucous cheer arose from the men and several shots rang out. Later reports, which proved erroneous, stated that the Ohio State Police intercepted a large caravan of pick-ups and SUV's heading for Washington, DC. Even though the reports were proved false, 40% of the IRS staff applied for emergency family leave.

Waiters and waitresses across the country got into the act. For years, the IRS had routinely abused them over their "Tip" income. Within days, web sites providing support to reformers became active. The "silent majority" was slowly finding its voice. The little people were learning to stand tall. Shortly thereafter, it was impossible to be served coffee or a meal without a request to sign a petition to change the tax code. Restaurant owners were initially reluctant to condone the activity until patrons insisted on signing the petitions before ordering food. Soon bartenders and taxi cab drivers joined in. You couldn't get a beer or a taxi ride without signing a petition. Mountains of petitions started flowing into congressional offices in every district across the land.

Sales professionals who had been routinely audited for years over their "mileage" claims went berserk at the thought of legislators receiving tax-free income. They assigned themselves new quotas for petitions signed. Many started petitions of their own. The voice was getting louder.

* * * *

Ron received an urgent phone call from Alex. "Ron, I can't order you to do this, but I would appreciate it if you could join our special task force to determine who was responsible for the false 1099 mailings. All federal law enforcement officers have been ordered by the Attorney General to drop everything else and concentrate on this issue."

"I can't help you, Alex. I have regained a partner and we are making real progress. We just closed two major drug cases based in part on information you provided from offshore banks solicited during the Grant Park investigation. It's about time you Feds got your act together. We were about to give up hope. What's the big deal about the 1099's? I've rather enjoyed the coverage."

"You don't understand, Ron. Washington is tied up in knots over this. Many in Congress would rather receive mail with Anthrax than a 1099. It is almost impossible to get a phone line. Circuits are jammed and web servers are overwhelmed. Serious people have been embarrassed. Every two-bit politician in both houses is screaming for an immediate investigation. I go out of my way not to view the bastards on TV. Now they are physically parading with placards in our lobby. This isn't about some small farmer in Omaha or a machinist in Toledo."

"To me, Alex, those are the really important people. The politicians, celebrities and media can all go to hell!"

"Ron, listen to me. The President of the United States, the Commander in Chief, got a 1099 from the IRS, and he can't get a real person on the phone to talk to him about what to do! He's livid. He's not sure whether to send the Army or the FBI over there to kick butt. We would do it, but we don't want to give credence to the *Times* story. By the way, do you know why you have your partner back?"

"I'm tempted to say it was the result of my clean living; however, I know that one of the major honchos in the exalted ranks of the Chicago Police Department resigned suddenly for health reasons, and everything in my life improved dramatically with his departure."

"I'm glad to hear your rendition, Ron, because that's the cover story. Actually, your former nemesis is in federal custody. This must remain confidential for about two weeks until we bring charges. Suffice it to say the leak to the syndicate has been plugged. I wish you well on your future progress. You now have the animals back on their heels. Remember that fact before you make any snide remarks about us Feds getting our act together!"

"Alex, I appreciate that information more than I can say. I'm tired of constantly looking over my shoulder, and I humbly take back my ill-advised comment. It looks like the Grant Park mob of amateurs scored again. Which makes me wonder, do you think there is any connection with the 1099's and the Grant Park heist?"

"Hell no! Ron, you are seeing connections that aren't there. Get on a new drug case before you go nuts, if you haven't already."

"Thanks, Alex. I appreciate your consideration. Good Luck."

* * * *

A wily old congressman from Kentucky called for a press conference. He was renowned among his fellow representatives for the uncanny ability to gauge public sentiment. The Representative always believed that leadership was finding a parade and getting out in front of it. He announced to the press that in reviewing previous personal tax returns, some might have been in error. The Congressman was re-submitting all of his previous returns for the last eight years and voluntarily paying back taxes and fines. The Congressman from Kentucky thought that by coming clean, he would be viewed by the press as the essence of virtue.

It backfired! Citizens realized that all the previously reported stories were true about tax-free income for members of Congress. Now they had proof! Other members in the House were in favor of lynching the Kentucky Representative on the spot. The press conference had put them all in a box. Reporters were now asking all members of Congress "when," not "if," they would resubmit their returns. They turned on the politicians and circled each and every one they found like a herd of jackals.

A state representative from Illinois announced that he was going to resubmit tax returns. The *Journal* headline shouted: **"TAX FRAUD AT ALL LEVELS."** The number of petitions doubled overnight. The post office was scrambling to find trucks to carry the letters of protest and petitions to Congress. They also announced they might break even this year, because of the heavy mail.

The entire government was slowly grinding to a halt. Citizens with legitimate 1099's were now claiming fraud. It would take armies of clerks at the IRS to sort all of it out. Most of the clerks that hadn't taken emergency leave were calling in sick rather than face hostile crowds that now gathered daily at every IRS office in the country. The Congressmen that used to elbow their way into TV stations for interviews could not be found.

Editors and Hollywood celebrities having received 1099's were suddenly sounding like Rush Limbaugh. It was similar to the story about the liberal who had been mugged. The same ardent supporter of victims' rights then became an overnight supporter of "concealed carry." A mugging had occurred on the tax code in the form of bogus 1099's and the transformation of core beliefs of many in Congress was something to behold. Rush, in turn, was acting like a hungry dog in a meat shop. Tens of millions tuned in daily for the latest factual updates.

To Congressmen there was one element in the confusion that engendered real fear. That element was the calls from the local party chiefs back home. Every member of the House and one third of the Senators were being assured of a tough primary fight in the next election. The party elders guaranteed financial support to all of the challengers if the incumbents didn't do something—now! Incumbency was no longer a virtue; it was an albatross around their necks. The loss of their cushy jobs perhaps more than anything gave the members some backbone.

The special interest groups were no longer busy lobbying. They were tied up in IRS hearings or in front of Grand Juries trying to explain why they never bothered to comply with the tax law. Closed-door emergency meetings came into vogue on the hill. No newspaper reporter or cable TV host could find a Congressperson to speak to on the Thursday and Friday of the last week in March.

In a rare session, the House met on Saturday morning and without dissent or amendment passed a 15% flat tax retroactive to the first of the year. The old progressive tax system was gone as well as the estate and capital gains tax. The Senate passed the exact same version Saturday afternoon. The President signed it Sunday afternoon. The 6000-page tax code now consisted of 25 pages of readable English. The hours of preparation time spent by average citizens were vaporized. The need for enormous files of receipts and records was eliminated. Tax schemes and the practice of transferring company headquarters offshore were made obsolete. The vast army of tax preparation professionals was facing unemployment.

The following Monday the stock market jumped 603 points, setting a new record for a one-day gain. The volume of shares traded also established a new record. The markets continued to gain over the weeks and months ahead. New business formations in the country tripled.

Adam arrived at the plant for an "all hands" meeting shortly after the tax bill had been passed. His intent was to describe the long overdue pension plan to the work force. The men were very pleased with the presentation. Adam wasn't sure if they were happy with the new pension plan or their new paychecks. By coincidence, the timing of Adam's announcement occurred with the men's first paycheck under the new tax bill. Each and every one of the employees thought he had received a significant raise. All of the company's attempts to illustrate the difference between "gross" pay and "net" pay over the years were for naught. They all instantly credited Adam for the increase.

When workers across the country received their "raise," many thought it was time for a new car. Allied supplied the auto manufactures and business took off dramatically. The new machines, particularly the 9700, allowed maximum participation in the revived economy.

Adam should have been pleased. He would have liked to acknowledge the credit from the men for their raise, but could not. Adam could not tell a soul. He hated the tax code and didn't care much for Congress or the media, but he was troubled. Adam told Alice that he wasn't comfortable with the godlike power that went with the title of President. The godlike power, it turned out, didn't reside with the title, but with his computer and imagination.

One man helped push the country to its "tip" point. The "tip" point in a jug or caldron of steel was the point where you could not stop the flow—the liquid just flowed on its own. The energy of a nation of people "tipped" because of his attempt at a diversion. Was the country ready to "tip," taking its cue from any source? "Did he exclusively provide the incentive?" Adam would never know, but it scared the hell out of him. Maybe even Frank would now be happy. Hell, every working, producing American was overjoyed.

CHAPTER 33

When the broad outlines of "Project Freedom" first coalesced in Adam's mind, he was concerned that one of the most difficult dimensions of the plan was the requirement to wait for the Statute of Limitations to expire. Ann had specific instructions to look for team members who could financially afford to sit quietly for five years. It was the critical element for reducing the security risk of the operation. It was ironic that the group's original thinking emphasized exclusively the financial concerns connected with the long wait.

The unique situations of Steve and Tad were not, and perhaps could not have been foreseen. Tad beat his doctor's prediction on the duration of his life, but not by much. Cancer took him seven months after his poignant announcement. His wife seemed to be coping financially in the intervening years, and Ann continued to discretely monitor her status as they promised Tad they would do.

Initially, Adam speculated that the five-year wait would produce the same apprehension he experienced as a child waiting for Christmas morning. Surprisingly, that emotion rarely materialized. What did materialize was frustration, and it was inevitably connected to routine household chores. Every time he cleaned gutters, shoveled snow, or did yard work, Adam fantasized about the $100 million on the bottom of the lake. That was an enormous amount of money that would shortly be split three ways. He would hire a "yard" man if he did nothing else. Then he would recall that the car was overdue for an oil change, the front tire had a slow leak, or the brake pedal seemed soft. That's when fantasies of hiring a chauffeur would appear.

The fantasies didn't appear often, but the anxiety of being watched became Adam's constant companion. The encounter with the armed stranger four years earlier was indelibly etched in Adam's mind. Even though he had not witnessed a comparable event since, he couldn't shake the feeling of being relentlessly hunted. Logic told him the 1099 diversion worked and the heat for "Project Freedom" was greatly reduced. Nonetheless, he was constantly looking, always worrying that someone had figured out what he had done.

Alice noted that Adam began purchasing lottery tickets weekly. "Adam, I thought you wouldn't touch the Lottery because the odds of winning were so ridiculously low!"

"Yes Alice, they are, but I find buying a ticket now and then is a nice diversion from the daily grind." A flimsy excuse to be sure, but he could hardly tell Alice that he needed a cover for his share of the $100 million he took from Grant Park!

The effort of running Allied was all consuming. Adam was so wrapped up in the daily activity that he frequently forgot about the proceeds of "Project Freedom." When Congress enacted the Flat Tax three and a half years ago, Allied was barely able to keep up with the influx of new sales orders. The installation of the first 9700 was difficult and required much more time than the previous machines. Learning how to run it efficiently after it was debugged devoured several more weeks. The second and third 9700 installations proceeded like clock work. The experienced crew at Allied developed procedures that made the 9700 out-perform even National's wildest expectations.

Two years after the first 9700 installations, Dave Stevens approached Adam looking enormously pleased. "Adam, we have finally achieved my personal goal to mark a successful turnaround. Ann told you what her personal criteria was early on, but I never confided to you what mine was."

"Pray tell, Dave, what was your personal criteria?"

"When I first started with Allied, many banks, especially the big downtown banks—would never take a phone call from me. It was as if I had 'AIDS' or something. Now my phone is ringing constantly with offers of help, lunch or golf from all of the big, marble encrusted movers and shakers. First Continental just invited me to lunch in their executive dining room. Everybody loves a winner, and I believe we have finally been recognized and accepted as a winner by the big banks."

"It's your call Dave, but if it were up to me, I would recommend we dance with the small banks that got us here."

"That's exactly what I plan to do. I anticipate showing the big banks the same courtesy they have shown me in the past."

"Maybe the banks are telling us something, Dave. If we are being noticed as a winner in the business community, perhaps now is the time we should consider taking Allied public."

The analysis needed to make the initial public offering proved a daunting task requiring countless hours of dedicated effort. The financial experts viewed it as an enormous risk. Many didn't think it was feasible for the small firm. Adam knew he still had to remain aggressive. This was not a time to play prevent defense. In Adam's view, there was never a time to become defensive or behave in a timid fashion. Besides, certain key executives at Allied would soon have access to a huge pot of money that could be used to back the play.

Allied successfully launched their stock two and a half years after gaining control from Bernie. In the booming economy caused by the adoption of the flat tax, it turned out to be a "can't miss" deal. The stock was over-subscribed at its introduction and climbed continuously from the date of initial offering. Allied gained needed capital for a plant expansion and yet more equipment. The executive team and employee pension plan made out very well as a by-product.

It was now only four months until the fifth anniversary of the Grant Park liberation effort. The Statute of Limitations would expire and the long wait would finally end. The last vestiges of winter were being replaced with signs of spring. Adam recalled the words from the first line of *Shakespeare's Richard III*: "Now is the winter of our discontent..." Soon summer would return, and with it the opportunity to go fishing in Lake Michigan. Adam and the team could finally fulfill their fantasies.

Ann received an e-mail message from Victor requesting a meeting concerning the Johnson family reunion in August. That makes a world of sense, thought Adam. Vic owned the boat and was probably wondering how to prepare it for the retrieval operation. Adam wondered if he and Vic could lift the merchandise without additional help. They might have to install a crane of some type and obtain scuba gear. He instructed Ann to set up a planning session at Simon's, a Greek restaurant in Villa Park.

* * * *

Ron was finally able to track down Alex on his new cell phone.

"Alex, are you still in hot pursuit of the 1099 desperados?"

"Actually Ron, we have backed off on that a little. The performance of the U.S. economy since the tax change has given the Bureau second thoughts about pursuing the culprits. It's possible that there would be public pressures to give whoever did the mailing the Congressional Medal of Honor instead of jail time. It's just as well. We have zip to work with. In that regard, it does remind me a little of the Grant Park case. Are you still working on that?"

"Only part time, Alex. We don't have anything new on that case either. I hope you haven't forgotten your promise to me from five years ago?"

"I hope your memory is better than the 'perps.' You are exactly right. We've gone to ground hoping that the 'perps' will let their guard down. The skies over Lake Michigan will be black with aircraft on the anniversary date. I will keep you in the loop, Ron. Thanks for the reminder."

"No problem, Alex. Not solving that crime is like a stone in my shoe. It's the only stone left in my shoe since you helped rid us of an empty suit." Both men were in full agreement. They would remain unfulfilled and unhappy until justice was served. It was an intrinsic part of their nature to never give up.

* * * *

Victor joined Ann and Adam at a back table in the busy family restaurant. They almost didn't recognize Vic. It had been more than four years since they last met. Vic appeared to be in outstanding health and fashionably attired.

"It's good to see you guys again. Before I forget, I wanted to thank you for your efforts with Steve. It was pretty amazing to see the way people contributed. I hope the little guy will be O.K. I'm also really sorry about Tad."

"You seem to be coping very well, Vic. What are you doing that makes you look and act so young?" Wilma inquired.

"Funny you should ask, Wilma. I took Zack's advice to heart when he suggested that I prepare a cover story for my newfound wealth. Shortly after completing our project, I decided to start playing the stock market. Your former boat driver didn't know a thing about it at first. I literally couldn't tell you the difference between a dividend and a divot. Selling 'short' was a totally alien concept. I learned a great deal about the market very quickly. It seems that I have a natural talent for picking stocks. My broker now calls it a gift from God. Initially, he called me stupid and reckless because I bought a wide range of penny stocks in what he thought was a completely random fashion. When Congress passed the Flat Tax, my portfolio took off like a rocket powered by high octane fuel."

"Is that why your broker changed his description of you?" Zack was intrigued.

"Not completely, Zack. The tune my broker was singing changed dramatically when I purchased the brokerage firm he was working for last year." Neither Zack nor Wilma could control their laughter or hide their admiration.

"I'm not being fair to my broker. He didn't know I would soon have access to a big hoard of cash. From his perspective, I was reckless buying into a bunch of small cap stocks. I felt I had nothing to lose. I was just trying to prepare a cover story and I couldn't help it if I kept picking big winners. This dumb rookie became a very rich 'guru' overnight. My biggest claim to fame was when I went very heavy into an Initial Public Offering on a small company that nobody had heard of. You guys probably never heard of it either, but Allied Manufacturing has made me rich."

Wilma started to choke on her diet Coke, which gave Adam the time to recover his composure. Adam looked closely at his analytical boat captain. Vic apparently was playing it straight. The new stock market guru appeared to have no idea of how all of this related. Then again, maybe Vic knew everything. It would be impossible to prove the truth either way. The entire situation was so surreal, Adam wasn't sure if he knew what was related to whom or the "why" of anything.

"Are you O.K., Wilma? Try not to drink too fast. At any rate, I'm glad you gave me the chance to tell my story. It's not just the fact that I have a gift for picking good stocks. With the elimination of capital gains taxes and the reduced income tax, I can finally keep a good portion of what I earn. To make a long story short, I don't need the Lake Michigan bundle. I have achieved my economic independence and don't want to jeopardize that freedom by potentially getting caught recovering the money. Here are my personal combinations to the two lockers. I formally renounce all claims."

"Hold on, Vic! Are you aware of what you just said?" Zack was incredulous.

"Indeed I am, Zack. I have analyzed this very closely despite my newfound desire not to. That might sound crazy. Let me try to explain. My obsession to over analyze situations in the past has always been a deterrent to my success. Throughout my life, I have been presented with multiple opportunities to succeed. I analyzed each opportunity until I found some reason why the idea wouldn't work. You could have awarded me a trophy for the world champion 'can't do' idiot. It made me so depressed that when Wilma approached me about the 'project', I simply said 'why not' and went with the flow for the first time in my life. I remained skeptical of the idea until I saw the depth of thought surrounding the exercise. Our eventual accomplishment made me proud. It worked exactly as planned, but I couldn't tell a soul about it." Adam and Ann sat transfixed as Vic bared his deepest thoughts.

"Shortly after our well planned activity, I was taking out the garbage and thought to myself "a prospective multi-millionaire shouldn't have to do this mundane chore." It was then that I realized I didn't have to worry about the future. My economic future was assured. I started playing the market with that attitude. It was as though I had been using a mental crutch all my life, and I simply threw it away. Discarding the crutch made me feel alive. The constant feeling of 'Analysis Paralysis' disappeared. As a result, I have prospered. Now I have earned economic freedom on my own. I can brag to everyone on earth and on the high seas about my achievements. Just the thought of what laid beneath the waves of Lake Michigan and not the loot itself, freed me to discover the talents I always possessed, but was afraid to use due to mental constipation."

Upon hearing Vic's words, Adam's mind raced back almost seven years to his pastor's sermon. The pastor was correct. Vic discovered talents within himself that allowed him to "pick up his bed and walk." He intentionally chose not to be "sick."

Adam wondered if Vic had analyzed the possibility that the water seals broke on their lockers, or that someone had observed the deposit activity from the Michigan shore and retrieved the loot the next day. Those were extremely unlikely scenarios, but they were possible. There was no "proof" that the money would be there when they went for it. Just the thought that it would be there allowed Vic to throw the crutch away. For perhaps 38 years, Vic allowed the "fear of failure" to trump his hope for the future. It couldn't be that easy, Adam thought. Or could it?

Ann watched Adam intently during Vic's comments. She saw the recognition and understanding in his eyes. She knew that Adam had been transformed in much the same way as Vic. She had been as well.

"Very well, Vic. I can't disagree with your logic, although I hesitate to call it logic. It may be what theologians refer to as faith. We both wish you continued success without your crutch." Vic departed after a round of handshakes and hugs.

"It's late Friday afternoon, Ann. Could you bring Dot by for a walk tomorrow morning about 10:00? Scotty hasn't seen her for awhile." Ann quickly nodded her consent.

* * * *

It was a gorgeous, early spring Saturday morning when Ann and Adam started walking their respective Goldens around the lake. Both dogs were older and mellower, but they still enjoyed the ritual greeting and the chance for a walk together. Every home that surrounded the lake seemed to have Tulips and Daffodils in full bloom in their yards.

"This is were it all started, Adam—my decision to offer you employment and your decision to accept it. That interview profoundly influenced both of our lives."

"All of the decisions we make affect our lives, Ann. Most of the time we aren't aware of how profoundly our lives or the lives of others are altered by our choices. Think about it. Our initial meeting wasn't the first step in this chain of events. We would never have met if you hadn't talked with Howard. In turn, Howard wouldn't have interviewed with you if I hadn't fired him. I wouldn't have fired him on my own; I was forced to because a secretary, in an attempt to secure revenge against FIRST CON, filed a complaint with OSHA. The precursors to our meeting go on and on.

"Before this sequence started, it was as though you and Allied existed on a different planet or in a parallel universe. We had absolutely no knowledge of each other. Then a series of events took place that made a connection between our two worlds. Physicists or sci-fi aficionados call this a 'warp' in the space/time continuum. I can't bring myself to get that fancy. It seems that when connections between unknown worlds occur, the equilibrium in both is lost, and all hell breaks loose. Chaos reigns supreme and the fact that we live in a non-linear environment is emphasized. Events become even more unpredictable.

"When we made the decision to launch 'Project Freedom', we set off a series of connections that are still reverberating around us. The worlds of Steve, Victor, and Tad became connected with the worlds of Wilma and Zack. The unique connection of these worlds has affected the equilibrium of countless other worlds. Some of the changes were good—some were bad. Many we just don't know about, and I refer to those as UNK-UNK'S. They may remain mysteries for months, years, or perhaps eternity. We just have to adapt our lives to live with the reality of the changes in the world as we know it."

"Adam, are you saying that the universe is filled with UNK-UNK'S which result from the chaos of newly connected worlds?"

"Yes, and I think it's a growing phenomenon. Within the last generation, we have gone from not moving more than twenty miles from our birth homes to routine international travel. Modern technology and communication have allowed us to make more connections with more people, faster than ever. A diverse number of worlds are becoming connected more frequently. The growth of chaos and non-linearity is extensive. It's enough to give planners extreme heartburn. Nobody will be able to control, forecast, or predict anything. Mysteries will multiply exponentially."

"Do you mean there are problems that you can't solve through a diligent search of the Internet and informed deductive reasoning?" Ann couldn't help but smile to herself. She knew how much reliance Adam placed on logic and high-tech tools.

"Yes, Ann, that's exactly what I'm saying, and it's a difficult concept for me to accept. For some answers, you have to search your heart and soul as diligently as you search the web. I have come to believe that there are mysteries that we as mere mortals will never solve. I am slowly becoming reconciled to that realization. Sometimes I flatter myself into thinking it's a sign of maturity."

"You don't have to sell me on the growth of "UNK-UNK'S," Adam. We saw plenty of them with 'Project Freedom.' I fear we haven't encountered the last of them yet. I'm not sure I understand your comment about non-linearity. Can you give me an example?"

"You know how highly I think of Sam. His talents, skill and leadership were of paramount importance to our results at Allied. As good as Sam is, he failed to recognize that the world of Allied perfectly mirrored the chaotic, non-linear world we now live in. Sam's singular solution to the company's problems, expressed in the strongest of terms, was NEW PRODUCTION MACHINES! His intentions were noble and his analysis was accurate in part, but not in total. Other factors such as morale and sales flew beneath Sam's radar. If we had not worked concurrently to resolve the multitude of causes adversely affecting Allied, the patient would have died."

"I never used or understood your term, Adam; however, I am totally familiar with the situation you describe. Trying to run Allied before your arrival was like running on a treadmill without spilling a handful of Jell-O. Every time I thought I had a handle on a problem, I would discover another cause and/or effect. There never seemed to be a single silver bullet to kill any one problem."

"Just looking at the results we've achieved at Allied, it could be argued that we have enjoyed some success, Ann. Maybe we got here by dumb luck rather than by plan, but we got here nonetheless. That positive feeling is offset by the realization that along the way we committed a crime. We certainly did not enhance the moral climate in the country with that action!"

"Well Adam, I wouldn't worry too much about the country's moral climate. It seems to have improved remarkably since Congress changed the tax code. How in the world did politicians in the past defend the marriage tax penalty? Now the marriage rate is up and the divorce rate is down. I guess that's another example of non-linearity. I never thought about the connection of morality and taxes or read anything that illustrated the linkage."

"The linkage between morality and taxes makes perfect sense to me, Ann. At least it made sense once I gathered data on Europe while working on 'Trade Master.' My project team, at that time, derided foreign countries for the bribes it took to get one of their bureaucrats to take action on a simple request. The project team, like all Americans, thought we were exempt from the 'shake downs' by bureaucrats because we had a superior moral foundation. Perhaps we do have better morals, but we also have far less regulation. The team was astounded at the amount of regulation we chronicled in foreign countries. Every new regulation is another opportunity for extortion. In that regard, we are rapidly catching up to the rest of the world. Changing the tax code greatly reduced the regulation imposed by the old system. Less regulation equals more freedom and leads to better morality in my book.

"You are correct, Ann about not seeing the connection examined in the media. The multiple causes and effects of regulation and taxation on morality and other cultural items were never rationally analyzed or portrayed."

"I hadn't thought about the foreign country example before. Knowing how you diligently gather data, I'll accept your findings. I wonder why the total effects of the old tax system were never discussed or debated in the media? The examples and evidence were staring us in the face. Thank God for the 1099 fiasco! That reminds me, Adam. Didn't you receive a 1099 when you worked at First Continental?"

A large flock of Sandhill Cranes interrupted the bucolic scene by flying directly overhead. The strange, guttural calling between members of the flock was clearly audible from the high altitude and drove the dogs to a frenzy. Both dogs barked uncontrollably and raced to a small rise to get a better look at the high-flying birds. Adam took the interruption as an opportunity to recall Frank's sage advice that "if the truth sounds like a lie, you are better off saying nothing." He reluctantly decided to ignore Ann's question.

Ann silently observed Adam during the interruption and quickly connected the dots. Adam once surmised that it might be necessary to create a diversion. The diversion for "Project Freedom" had to be the bogus 1099 mailings of four years ago. Adam must be the author of that activity and could not, or would not, admit to it without implicating her. How noble of Adam and somehow totally within character. The new CEO of Allied was above the average citizen only in his abundant naiveté. He was the quintessential average guy, yet he achieved a goal that great statesmen could only dream about. She instinctively knew to drop the whole subject once the dogs regained control.

"Adam, that leaves us with one final question. We are now the sole recipients of a $100 million-dollar fortune and we don't have access to a boat. I also realize we can't give it back. In the eyes of the law, we are, and will always remain felons. What do you suggest we do now?"

"It's a definite problem, Ann. I don't think the authorities have given up, despite the lack of media attention. We might have to obtain additional help to physically raise the money in addition to finding a suitable boat, which greatly expands our risk profile. What do you want to do?" Adam breathed a sigh of relief that Ann had not pursued her earlier inquiry on the 1099.

"Do either of us really need the money at this moment in our lives?"

"Excellent question. The answer is probably no. We have played catch-up with Allied's pension plan and with our stock options we have probably eliminated our future financial concerns. It's important to remember that our original objective was to gain economic freedom. However, we haven't completely eliminated the risk to ourselves or Allied's welfare. We sneaked up on many of our competitors in the past because they had written Allied off. New orders and accounts will be bitterly contested in the future when the economy cools. Problems and risk never really go away. They just change names or descriptions."

"I don't fear the competitors, Adam. I'm actually thankful for them. They force us to keep our costs under control and our quality standards high. Pursuit of the money on the bottom of the lake could be characterized as greed at this juncture. That's one of the seven deadly sins if I remember correctly. Perhaps we've sinned enough. Let's leave it in the lake. We can continue to think about it as the 'ace' up our sleeve."

"Thank you, Ann. I was hoping you would agree. We couldn't have done the job without your able assistance and talent. If you required the money for any reason, I would feel an obligation to go out and retrieve it. A deal is a deal."

"Let it be, Adam."

The two continued to walk in silence along the lake. It was a joy to watch the dogs romp through the grass. The simple act of walking Scotty always brought peace to Adam.

Ann interrupted the silence with a question: "I know you too well, Adam. You won't be entirely at ease without a backup plan. What will your backup plan be now?"

"I really don't know, Ann. Maybe I'll write a book!"

0-595-27992-9

Printed in the United States
1540000004B/123